The ELOPEMENT

Tracy Rees was the first winner of the Richard & Judy Search for a Bestseller competition. She has also won the Love Stories Best Historical Read award and been shortlisted for the RNA Epic Romantic Novel of the Year. A Cambridge graduate, Tracy had a successful career in non-fiction publishing before retraining for a second career practising and teaching humanistic counselling. She has also been a waitress, bartender, shop assistant, estate agent, classroom assistant and workshop leader. Tracy lives on the Gower Peninsula of South Wales.

T0205010

Praise for Tracy Rees

'A warm, original and upbeat novel. Tracy Rees is a natural storyteller and I couldn't stop turning the pages. I loved the setting of Victorian Hampstead and its vivid range of characters. What a treat it is!'
Rachel Hore

'Tracy Rees has a rare gift for creating characters you are rooting for from the first page. The writing is fresh and engaging, with a gentle humour . . . The research is meticulous, and the women's stories are told with immense compassion. This is a novel that immerses you in its world as if by magic, and keeps you enthralled till the very end'
Gill Paul

'Beautifully written and vividly imagined, *The Rose Garden* strikes the perfect balance between period drama to savour and compelling escapism to devour. Tracy Rees has such a talent for writing engaging characters who stay with you. I loved it!'
Hazel Gaynor

'A rich, compelling and intricate tapestry of women's lives . . . Their wants, needs and dreams through the characters' diverse lives. I couldn't put it down'
Liz Fenwick

'A rich historical drama that is both a subtle study of the treatment of women and an entertaining escape. Pure joy'
Jo Spain

'Such a treat . . . I loved Tracy's elegant writing and the vivid and relatable characters, and historically rich story . . . wonderful and uplifting'
Nicola Cornick

'A truly captivating tale of female friendship, courage and empowerment, all wrapped up in the wonderful escapism of an exquisite period drama'
Samantha King

'*The Rose Garden* is an absolute delight to read and holds you spellbound from cover to cover. Full of wonderful characters woven into a story that tugs at your heartstrings, this is a truly beautiful novel that confirms Tracy Rees is at the height of her game'
Rebecca Griffiths

'Gorgeously written, deeply atmospheric, tense and vivid and a total page-turner'
Jenny Ashcroft

'In this engrossing novel Tracy Rees takes the reader directly into the drama and action, her writing bringing every scene to sparkling vivid life . . . Totally unputdownable'
Dinah Jefferies

The
ELOPEMENT

TRACY REES

PAN BOOKS

First published 2022 by Macmillan

This paperback edition first published 2023 by Pan Books
an imprint of Pan Macmillan
The Smithson, 6 Briset Street, London EC1M 5NR
EU representative: Macmillan Publishers Ireland Ltd, 1st Floor,
The Liffey Trust Centre, 117–126 Sheriff Street Upper, Dublin 1, D01 YC43
Associated companies throughout the world
www.panmacmillan.com

ISBN 978-1-5290-9863-1

1 3 5 7 9 8 6 4 2

A CIP catalogue record for this book is available from the British Library.

Typeset by Palimpsest Book Production Ltd, Falkirk, Stirlingshire
Printed and bound by CPI Group (UK) Ltd, Croydon, CR0 4YY

Visit **www.panmacmillan.com** to read more about all our books
and to buy them. You will also find features, author interviews and
news of any author events, and you can sign up for e-newsletters
so that you're always first to hear about our new releases.

For Kat, Patsy and Becky

One

Pansy

Thursday, the middle of February. It was cold and dark, the wind and rain battering the attic roof. A most begrudging sort of a day. But Thursdays were sacred to Pansy. Even during the cold snap in January, she'd struggled out through deep, crisp snow on her day off, because every Thursday, Pansy went home.

She checked her reflection by candlelight in the small, chipped mirror that Maisie, one of the other maids, had brought upstairs. The glass was dark and stained, the light wavering, but she could just about see that her new blue hat sat well upon the chestnut waves that she usually wore coiled beneath a servant's cap, and that her green eyes looked hopeful for once. She glanced away from the bitter lines that were starting to pinch at the sides of her mouth and hurried down the stairs: two, three, four flights, then another to the basement. In a moment she would let herself out through the kitchen door into the waiting morning and her heart gave a little skip. Lashing wet and dark it might be, but it would take a force greater than nature to keep Pansy from Elstree on a Thursday. At Garrowgate Hall, however, there *was* a force greater than nature: the will of her mistress, Maude Blythe.

Mrs Clarendon, the housekeeper who enforced that will,

was lurking in the shadows of the flagged and draughty basement corridor. 'Charlotte's sick. You're needed,' she said when she saw Pansy.

And with those four words, Pansy saw her wonderful Thursday – her mother's smile, her sister's hugs, home cooking and all the other joys of a day in Elstree – vanish like a genie.

'It's my day off!' Pansy exclaimed in anguish. 'Mrs Clarendon, ma'am,' she added.

'I'm well aware. But do you suppose the mistress cares about that?'

'Not for one minute,' said Pansy with some rancour, briefly forgetting her manners.

'Enough of that tone. Back upstairs with you and change into your uniform. There's not a moment to lose, the house won't run itself.'

Didn't Pansy know it. The round of daily tasks was endless, their monotony relentless. It was inevitable that she would obey. Still, she couldn't move for a moment, disappointment rooting her to the floor. 'But my mother expects me. She'll be worried. I can't let her down like that.'

'You should be concerned not to let *Mrs Blythe* down, the woman who pays your wage, to whom you owe your loyalty.'

Pansy couldn't care less about letting Mrs Blythe down but she only said, 'Yes, Mrs Clarendon. Only, when can I go instead? Will I swap with one of the other girls over the weekend?'

The housekeeper huffed and rolled her eyes. 'How on earth would that work? You can go next Thursday, for heaven's sake, girl, it's only a week.'

'But it's in my terms, Mrs Clarendon! Excuse me, but it is. A day off every week! It's a condition of my employment, ma'am!' Pansy was aware that she was talking in exclamation marks, but she was boiling with outrage.

'So is stepping up when needed. I won't debate this, Tilney. Get changed or find another position.' Clarendon turned on her heel and the kitchen swallowed her up.

Pansy was still having trouble moving. *Only a week.* Clarendon said it as though a week was a mere seven-day snippet, when for Pansy it was a desert a thousand miles wide. But it wasn't just that. Her Thursdays contributed more to her survival than food and water, she firmly believed it. They allowed her to get through the next week. Her days at home were the most treasured part of her existence; the only time she truly felt like herself. The rest of the time, she wasn't really sure who Pansy Tilney had become.

She'd been working as a maid for the wealthy Blythe family for seven years now and during that time her personality had been dulled, her sense of hope eroded and all her better traits methodically replaced, one at a time, by less admirable ones. She was simply Tilney, a functional being. It was only on a Thursday that she could recapture something of the girl she used to be, before she left home at sixteen on what was to have been her great adventure.

Eventually she turned and dragged herself back upstairs, chancing the main staircase as it was nearer; she'd already loitered long enough and Mrs Clarendon would be champing at the bit. It wasn't as though any of the family would be up and about at this time. But, as if her day needed to get any worse, she ran smack bang into none other than the mistress on the second-floor landing.

'Beg pardon, ma'am,' she muttered, keeping her head down and dodging to one side. Servants were supposed to be silent and invisible, like good fairies who did all the work and made everything run like clockwork, so the family could enjoy its genteel hours under the illusion that life just happened like that.

Nowhere was this the case more than in the Blythe house. Some employers looked for diligence, honesty and a willingness to work hard when they hired their domestic staff. The Blythes looked for all that and more: a pleasing appearance, a genteel voice, considerable height, a graceful build, a light tread, the ability to stay out of sight, to stay spotlessly clean even when cleaning out coal fires or emptying slop buckets and to know intuitively when they were about to cross paths with a Blythe and melt away. Pansy excelled in all of these requirements but she wasn't *supposed* to be at work today. Her senses had briefly deserted her. And when was Maude Blythe ever out of bed and fully dressed at seven in the morning?

She crept past, hoping that if she didn't look at the mistress, the mistress somehow wouldn't notice her. No such luck.

'Wait!'

The voice was imperious. It could crack glass. Pansy stopped. 'Turn!'

Pansy turned round and reluctantly raised her eyes. Maude Blythe wore purple and her pale blue eyes were appalled. 'Who are you and what are you doing in my house?'

'It's Tilney, ma'am, housemaid. It was to be my day off but one of the other girls is sick. Mrs Clarendon caught me on my way out and sent me to change. I'm stepping in.'

There was a little pause, as who knew what thoughts went through Mrs Blythe's mind. Then she said, 'Ah,' and walked away.

Pansy watched her disappear, feeling her face screw itself into a caricature of disbelief. The mistress hadn't said one word of commiseration or thanks. She couldn't even recognise her own staff when she saw them out of uniform. Well, of course not; she never *looked* at them. The last time Mrs Blythe had looked Pansy in the eye was when they were introduced, seven years ago, when Pansy had been given the job. She'd been happy and proud then, if you could believe that.

She climbed the last stairs to the attic and sank onto her bed. She shared her room with two other girls, Lou and Maisie, but they'd been hard at work for two hours already. Removing her coat and bodice felt more difficult than carrying water buckets or firewood. She couldn't quite believe that her Thursday, her lovely Thursday, had been taken from her.

'You've been an age,' said Mrs Clarendon when Pansy finally appeared in the kitchen, wearing her morning uniform of pale blue print with white apron and cap. In the afternoons they changed into black dress, white apron and white cap with streamers. It felt odd being her work self and dressed to fit, when twenty minutes ago she'd been in her own hat and coat, ready to be Pansy. 'Prepare the drawing room. Fresh flowers, lay the fire, oh, and Thursday's rug day. Take them out and beat them. Miss Blythe's expecting Miss Crawford – oh, I should call her the young Mrs Blythe now! I keep forgetting. Quick sharp, now.'

'Bad luck, Pansy, love,' muttered Lou, hurrying past with a slop bucket.

Pansy did the fire first, then the India rugs, one at a time. There were six in the drawing room, all in shades of turquoise, powder blue and gold. They were huge and heavy. She carried the first into the yard and struggled to hoist it over the line. Then she beat that rug as if her life depended on it.

It was still raining, though not as hard. With each stroke, she pictured Rowena Blythe's perfect face and imagined hitting the hell out of it, knocking her pearly teeth down her swan-like throat and bruising her satin skin purple as a grape. Then, for variety, she pictured Rowena's mother, Maude Blythe. Then her father. When she came to beating the second rug, she imagined she was whacking old Clarendon and then the young Mrs Blythe, Verity Crawford as was, who had married the eldest Blythe son at Christmas. When she was satisfied that she had sufficiently vented her feelings towards Verity Blythe, she imagined Rowena all over again. She hated Rowena most of all.

When did I become this person? she wondered, as she carried the final rug back to the drawing room and spread it in place before the gold damask divan. *When did so much hate creep inside and fill me up?*

As she left the room to search for flowers to fill the vases and jugs of lustre and crystal, she bumped into John Hobbs, senior footman, and the love of Pansy's life.

'Good morning, Pansy!' he exclaimed, beaming that good-natured smile of his. 'Whatever are you doing here on a Thursday?'

'Morning, John. Charlotte only went and got sick. Old Clarendon collared me on the way out. I can't go.'

'That's terrible.' John more than anyone knew what Thursdays meant to Pansy. They were friends, the two of them; they talked and laughed and confided in each other. They'd been working together for seven years now, living in the same house and, among the large staff, the two of them had formed an immediate rapport. John often said Pansy was like a sister to him – which drove her mad. And that was as far as it went because, as helplessly in love as Pansy was with John, so was John with someone else. It was doomed, and he knew it was doomed, and Pansy waited achingly in the wings for him to decide to allow himself a chance at happiness. She wouldn't mind being second choice if it meant she could be with John Hobbs, the kindest and best man she had ever met.

But he was steadfast in his love – though the object of his affections, in turn, probably didn't even know his name. She would *never* conceive what a good, noble heart he had, simply because he wasn't a duke or a lord, or a bloody *king*. And so they were both trapped here; Pansy doomed for ever to follow John around, and John to trail worshipfully in the wake of Rowena Blythe.

Two

Rowena

'I *loathe* February. Such a misery of a month. One feels that nothing enjoyable will ever happen again.'

So says Verity Crawford, my best friend, or Verity Blythe as I must learn to think of her, for she has recently married my elder brother Felix. I suppose we are sisters now.

'Rowena! Did you hear me? You're miles away, dear.'

'Yes, February. Dire, absolutely.' I sigh and reach up to ring for a servant to come and poke the fire.

I shift about on the green silk divan, finding it hard to get comfortable. I ate too much at breakfast and then there's the *ennui* . . . I don't know what's the matter with me lately. I must have heard Verity say something along these lines every February for the past decade and usually I agree. But this year, bored and dissatisfied though I am, I do not think the commencement of a season of spring balls will improve things. In fact, I feel quite weary at the prospect. That is worrying; if the thought of a ball cannot set me right, what will?

'A plethora of parties over Christmas and New Year, and then . . . nothing,' Verity persists, stretching her neck to the left and then the right. 'A social desert.' She makes a little moue of dissatisfaction. I'm expected to chime in, I know. We've been friends since the age of five so our conversations are a script I know by heart. But the truth is, I don't think I can put my complaints into words. I don't think they have to do with the listlessness of February or the empty pages in my diary. What then? I cannot put my finger on it. It hovers in the margins like a ghost, flickers across my heart like the shadow of a passing bird.

'Of course, as a *married* lady I at least have the comforts of matrimony to entertain me,' says Verity, her eyes suddenly sparkling. '*You* have no such distraction, dear. I must say that your brother is a most . . . *attentive* husband. You know, just between us, the physical side of marriage has proved—'

But there is a knock at the door and a maid comes in to poke the fire, so I must wait, thank heavens, to hear Verity's thoughts about the physical side of marriage; we never speak in front of the servants. I glance idly at the maid. She is quite pretty, with chestnut hair and big green eyes, but she has the most insolent look on her face. She stabs the poker into the subsiding flames as if the fire is the heart of her worst enemy. I wonder who it is she's thinking of as she thrusts away. I look away, uncomfortable. It feels as though her exaggerated movements are making a point. 'Can't you poke your own fire?' they seem to demand. 'It's four feet from where you're sitting.'

Suddenly I wonder what they think of us – the servants, I mean – and what it is they *do* all day when they're not in front of us, serving us soup or curling our hair. There! That is it, the change in me. I never wondered such things before. I don't know anyone who does. But lately, life has felt full of question marks.

Was it the turning of the year that prompted them? Later this year, in June, there will be a diamond jubilee – celebrations aplenty to delight Verity then! – since the queen will have been on the throne a full sixty years. I suppose that is a cause for reflection. Or was it the surprise – dare I say the shock? – of my best friend marrying my brother, with very little warning? I rather suspect it dates back even further.

Last August, there was a great charity ball, held to launch the Westallen Foundation, a worthy cause intended to help the unfortunate and blah, blah, blah. Olive Westallen, whose brainchild the foundation was, is someone I see rarely, yet when our paths do cross, she has an unsettling effect. Like me, she is fabulously rich. Like me, she is privileged, pampered and pleases herself. Except the way Olive lives makes *my* life seem . . . small. Colourless. Even . . . pointless? In what world would *I* ever establish a charitable foundation, for heaven's sake?

The maid rams the poker back into the holder and stalks from the room. She has a lovely figure, I notice as she goes.

'Goodness!' says Verity when she's gone. 'What was the matter with *her*? Have you ever *seen* such a face? She's lucky Mother wasn't here or she'd be out of a job by now.'

Verity has adopted the unsettling habit, since her marriage, of calling my parents Mother and Father. She calls her own Mama and Papa, but still, I get confused sometimes. She's right that Mother (mine, not hers) has dismissed a servant for less in the past.

'Rowena!' she prompts, exasperated. 'Did you hear me?'

'Yes, yes. How would *I* know what was wrong with her? Trouble with a sweetheart most likely.'

'Or perhaps an especially painful monthly. I hope so. It would serve her right coming in here like that when we're trying to have a pleasant morning.'

I look at Verity. Sometimes she can be surprisingly vicious. And she can say some quite unladylike things. Talking about monthlies, indeed, and before eleven o'clock! I wonder if servants *do* have monthlies. I suppose they must. Now she has me at it, for goodness' sake! *I* should not like to be on my feet all day at those times, but perhaps the pains are not so bad for that class of person. I'm sure they are far more robust than I. I go to the window to divert my thoughts but the view without is nothing salutary. The weather is an absolute beast.

The door opens again and this time it is Father. He is not the tallest of men, but he has tremendous presence, with his thick moustache, piercing eyes and air of authority. 'Ah, Rowena, there you are. I need to speak to you. Good morning, Verity. With us again?'

'Good morning, Father,' says Verity. 'Yes, I came for a heart-to-heart with Rowena.'

'Setting the world to rights?' Father chuckles. 'All the important issues, parties and balls.'

'Precisely!' cries Verity. 'And servants' standards slipping. You know, this morning—'

'What did you want with me, Father?' I interrupt. Verity wouldn't hesitate to get that girl into trouble and it's true she was shockingly bold, but I'm not convinced that poking a fire too hard is worth all that fuss.

'We've decided to have your portrait painted.'

'*Again?*'

'The last time was nearly five years ago. Your mother wants something really up to date. Standing on the grand staircase in evening gown or some such. She can tell you. I'm just here to let you know that you'll be needed from Monday. Set the week aside, if you please. I've booked Lethbridge.'

My heart sinks. Verity squeals with excitement.

'Yes,' continues my father. 'He's quite the artist of the moment, second only to Joshua Reynolds, but these days *everyone* has a Reynolds. We want something more distinctive.

Lethbridge painted you, Verity, didn't he? It's taken some time
to secure a commitment from him, but Maude *will* have the
best.'

'Yes indeed,' observes Verity. 'Splendid, that will pass the
time for a week. You know, Father, we were just saying . . .'

But Father is already gone; he has little tolerance for female
conversation in the main. I groan.

'What's the matter *now*?' Verity demands. 'You're the
most appalling misery today, Ro. You should be delighted;
Lethbridge's reputation grows by the month. He paints royalty,
you know. He really is terribly talented. And rather a devil. Did
I tell you? When he painted me, he adjusted my hair ornaments
and in so doing his hand brushed my bosom. Well, he found
it necessary to adjust them several times after that, you may
deduce, and each time the same. I didn't know whether to
be scandalised or diverted.' She bursts into peals of laughter,
pink-faced at the memory.

Yes, I did know. Yes, Verity did tell me. And thus the basis
of my reluctance. I don't know how Verity can find something
like that funny. I would hate to have some old goat of fifty
with long straggly hair stroking my breast in the name of art.
I should be sick all over his shoes. But this is not the kind of
thing I can talk to Mother or Father about. Once their mind
is made up, the thing is carved in stone. I stay quiet and Verity
sighs.

'I'm bored,' she says, standing and walking to the fireplace.
To my astonishment she grasps the poker and flicks a coal onto
the rug. It rolls a short way, leaving smuts of black.

'What did you do that for?' I ask, aghast.

Verity rings the bell. 'I'll tell that maid *she* did it, and repri-
mand her for sloppy work. Then I'll tell her to clean it up.
That'll teach her.'

I don't know what to say. Verity is my closest companion. There isn't an occasion I can remember when she wasn't at my side; the bonds of familiarity and affection run deep. But sometimes, lately, I find myself questioning how much I actually *like* her.

Three

Pansy

On Sunday mornings, the entire Blythe household, family and staff alike, attended St Michael's Church on Highgate Hill. It was compulsory. The church was a ten-minute walk uphill from Garrowgate Hall. Of course, the family didn't walk, they rode in the carriage.

The servants left the house at a quarter to ten and walked three abreast up Highgate West Hill. They formed an impressive crocodile since there were twenty-three of them in total: the butler, Mr Benham; the housekeeper, Mrs Clarendon; an under butler and an under housekeeper; the cook; three footmen; four kitchen maids; four housemaids; two upper housemaids; three parlour maids; a scullery maid and an 'odd man'. They always walked in the same configuration.

Pansy's position was halfway down the procession on the left-hand side, nearest the walls and railings, with Lou beside her and one of the Sarahs – there were three – on Lou's other side, next to the street. Pansy could see John's tall figure a few rows ahead. All the footmen were tall but John stood out anywhere for Pansy, even just the back of his head. Mrs Clarendon led the way and Mr Benham brought up the rear.

'You look full of the joys of spring,' observed Lou in a mutter, since they weren't supposed to talk.

'Shh,' said Sarah, who was the self-righteous sort – unlike the other Sarahs who were both fun-loving and flirtatious given half the chance. Lou rolled her eyes.

'What spring?' fumed Pansy, glaring at the iron-grey sky. At least it wasn't raining. There was only one thing worse than sitting for an hour through one of Reverend Astley's dull-as-ditchwater sermons and that was doing it wet.

'It ain't pretty,' Lou agreed. She was the only servant at Garrowgate Hall who spoke with a cockney accent, though hers had softened in the three years since she'd arrived and she could erase it altogether when she needed to. How she'd persuaded Clarendon to give her the job, Pansy couldn't imagine, since the Blythes insisted that their staff be pleasing to the eye and ear, but then Lou didn't take no for an answer. Thick-skinned, she was, in a way that Pansy would never be; the slights and indignities of domestic life at Garrowgate Hall were water off a duck's back to Lou. When Pansy told Lou how she admired her, Lou just shrugged. 'Better than what I had before, ain't it?'

Perhaps that was it, thought Pansy. Perhaps, all told, life working for the Blythes wasn't the worst thing in the world, but compared with her life before, it was dreadful. Her childhood had been so happy. Did that make her lucky? Or the opposite? Pansy could never work it out. Surrounding themselves with a genteel class of servant might have felt harmonious to the Blythes, but it felt cruel to Pansy; all those people who were only there because they were down on their luck. The Blythes were like carrion crows, swooping in and snatching up the vulnerable. And spitting them out when they no longer served the purpose. Before Lou and Pansy shared their room with Maisie, they'd shared it with Patricia, a curvaceous girl who was let go when she'd put on a little too much weight.

'You've been like a bear with a sore 'ead ever since Thursday,' continued Lou. 'It's a cryin' shame, I reckon. That lovely ma of yours, that lovely cottage she got. You needed that day at 'ome.'

Pansy nodded. The day had gone from bad to worse, with Rowena and Verity summoning her back to upbraid her for dropping a coal on the rug – which she certainly hadn't done. Which of them had cooked up that idea? Either of them was capable of it. What on earth had Felix Blythe ever seen in vile Verity? She was pretty enough and her brown ringlets were impressively shiny but that was really all that could be said for her. 'I don't mean to be a baby about it, but I *need* to get away from all this once a week. The boring work and the senseless rules and the horrible people and these *stupid* bonnets!' She tugged at hers in frustration. It was the most uncomfortable bloody thing she'd ever worn. If her mother could see her now, would she laugh or cry?

The servants weren't permitted to wear hats to church, lest anyone might think they were ordinary people. Instead, they were issued flimsy bonnets of no identifiable shape or fashion that looked ridiculous and itched like hell. Oh, and which they had to pay for out of their own wages. The men went bare-headed. For Pansy, who had never been vain but always dressed nicely and appropriately, the bonnets were the final stripping away of dignity.

'I asked Clarendon if I could send a note to my mother, to explain. I thought I could run down to the shop and Mr Ollander could take it for me. But she wouldn't give me the ten minutes off to do it. I could've been dead in a ditch for all Mum knew, but Clarendon doesn't care. It's like the bloody Blythes are the only people in the whole wide world who matter.'

'What I'll never understand,' murmured Lou, 'is why you

don't find something else. This ain't exactly anyone's idea of the high life, but you hate it more than most. You're a smart girl, got a bit of book learning. There must be somewhere else you could go, surely?'

'Shhh!' hissed Sarah loudly.

'No talking!' Mr Benham's authoritative tones floated over their heads.

Lou subsided and Pansy was spared from answering her question. If Lou only knew that the reason, all six foot two of him, was walking a little way ahead. Lou was right, of course, and not a week passed when Pansy didn't think about resigning. Her mother, too, often pressed her to make a change.

'You're twenty-three, love,' she would sigh. 'You should be enjoying a *nice* life, meeting nice young men, not slaving away in that house. How will you ever meet anyone when you only have one free day a week and you always spend it visiting me? I want you to get married, Pansy, have a family.'

Pansy would have liked all that too, but only with John. Every time she thought seriously about leaving the Blythes, she would imagine how it would be to wake up each morning with no prospect of seeing John and it caused an ache like a cavern in the depths of her stomach. As much as it infuriated her that he was smitten with Rowena Blythe of *all* people, if he felt about her half the way that Pansy felt about him, she truly sympathised. And so they were stuck, the two of them, in this theatre of heartache. For now.

Because it would surely all come to an end when Rowena married. It was common knowledge that whilst the Blythes didn't want their daughter to throw herself away, she had turned down so many proposals now that they were getting impatient. Rowena was nearly twenty-three after all; in a miserable little flourish, fate had arranged for Rowena and Pansy to be the same age, as if to draw attention to the disparity in their lives. The Blythes were putting some pressure on her to make a choice. It wasn't as if she didn't have dukes and lords and whatnot paraded under her perfect nose every week. When she married, she would be beyond the reach of John's hopes in a whole new way. And she would leave Garrowgate Hall.

John would be broken-hearted and Pansy didn't want that for him. On the other hand . . . then he could start to look for another position with kinder employers. And so could Pansy. They could both move on to sweeter pastures. They would stay in touch and one day, his heart would heal. Then he might turn to his dear friend Pansy . . .

Part of Pansy knew that this was not a sensible way to live. She was conducting her entire life according to a daydream that may very well not come true. Part of her clamoured to make the break now, pursue her own happiness, and let the cards fall where they may with regards to John. But she simply wasn't strong enough to pull herself away.

They reached St Michael's and filed in silently. The church was tall as a mountain and thin as a needle, so pinched and bony that Pansy couldn't help thinking it gave its succour grudgingly. Pansy used to love Sunday service in Elstree. The family church wasn't as fine as St Michael's but neither was it as narrow and austere. Now, church was yet another hour of Pansy's week that was hard to endure, during which the faults and failings of humanity were listed and condemned in exacting detail.

The Garrowgate Hall staff always had to sit in the same places. From Pansy's seat, in the centre of her pew, she could see John if she looked to her left, and Rowena near the front, slightly to the right. Often, when Pansy looked at John, he would be gazing spellbound at Rowena. Then Pansy would look at Rowena too, and wish more than anything to be in her shoes, not for her wealth or beauty, but because hers was the face that held John in thrall, hers was the heart to which his was bound.

Pansy could only see a little of Rowena's face beneath her stylish hat and the luxurious coils of her corn-gold hair, but it was enough to discern her peach-satin skin, the tip of her flawless nose. Pansy sighed, earning a poke in the spine from old Clarendon, who sat behind her. Everything Pansy had suffered, everything she hoped for, all depended on this one thing to happen to make it right: Rowena Blythe must choose a husband and do it soon.

'Tell me, John, what is it?' asked Pansy later that afternoon. She was polishing silver in the scullery and John, who often had spare time on Sundays, had come to give her a hand. Pansy was grateful; it was an enormous job, since there were three hundred and sixty pieces in each cutlery set and the Blythes had ten different sets. Then there were the candlesticks, the ornaments, the salt and pepper shakers in the shape of hunting dogs and the mustard pots in the shape of bears.

'What's what?' asked John, grinning as he buffed a bear's behind.

'What is it about her? You know who I mean. I know she's beautiful, I've never seen *anyone* more beautiful. But why do you . . . ? What makes you . . . ?'

He looked so sad that Pansy regretted asking. 'I'm sorry, I shouldn't have asked,' she said, getting up to open the scullery window. It was still cold out but the scullery was small and the smell of silver polish was choking her.

'No, it's all right,' he said slowly. 'Only I don't know if I have an answer, Pansy. Yes, she's beautiful, I'd have to be blind not to notice, but it's more than that.'

'What, though?' Pansy persisted. Her superficial personality? Her howling indifference to others? Her extensive knowledge of Paris fashions? Pansy honestly couldn't see the appeal of Rowena Blythe to a sensible man like John.

'I think it's because she's sad.'

'Because she's *sad*? John! *I'm* sad! If sad was the reason, you could fall for me! And you wouldn't do that, would you?'

'Of course not. You're like a sister to me. It's not that sadness is appealing in itself. But she's sad and she doesn't even know it. Nobody knows it. They all just dress her up, admire her, dance with her and cover her with diamonds . . .'

'Poor woman.' Pansy's tone was somewhat scathing.

'. . . And no one ever asks her what *she* wants. There's more to Rowena Blythe than meets the eye and it intrigues me.'

'But what makes you think it?' Pansy had often been told that she was dogged. But she liked to understand things. It wasn't every man you could have a conversation like this with, but John was gentle and thoughtful. The staff were all endlessly fascinated by the family, and Rowena in particular, but Pansy was the only one who knew how John felt.

John set aside the newly gleaming bear and reached for a bon-bon basket. Pansy was glad of that; they were fiddly little sods. 'Just a feeling, I suppose. I see a look on her face sometimes, and I think to myself, *This life looks as if it should be right for her. But it's not.*'

Pansy was by no means convinced that Rowena had hidden depths but she wasn't going to argue the point with a man in love. 'But, John, suppose you're right. Suppose she yearns for some other life. *What* life? With you? Don't get me wrong, any girl would be lucky to have you. But *her*? It's too big a leap. Even if she did stretch herself that far, they wouldn't let her. You'd be out of this house and your name blackened all over London so fast you wouldn't be able to breathe! You'd have nothing to offer *anyone*, let alone her majesty.'

'I do know that, Pansy. I know it'll never happen. I'm not fooling myself that there's something between us and it's only a matter of time.'

'Then, John, you should move on, give yourself the chance to forget her. You'll *never* get over her when she's under your nose every day. You deserve a good life, John.'

'Bless you, Pansy. Hetty says exactly the same.'

'Your sister's a smart girl.'

'But I can't, Pansy. You know how it is with male domestics these days. And I don't know how to do anything else.'

Pansy did know. Service as a profession for men was in decline. Fewer and fewer households were employing footmen and parlour maids were taking over the duties traditionally carried out by men. The role of footman, essentially decorative now, was seen as unmanly these days. John had been employed at Garrowgate Hall sixteen years ago, aged twelve, as an errand boy. He'd been promoted to page boy at fifteen, then became footman, then senior footman . . . He was a career servant through and through.

Apart from anything else, Pansy worried about John. Although he was dearest to her heart, he wasn't the only man to catch her eye in seven years. She had often thought that Felix, the eldest Blythe son, was as fine-looking a man as his sister was beautiful. He was courteous too, in a way that the others weren't. It wouldn't be hard to fall for a man like that. But Pansy had never allowed herself to indulge these thoughts for all the reasons she had just said to John; he was too far above her and she had an innate sense of self-preservation. She only hoped John had one too.

Four

Rowena

Dreaded Monday has come at last. Because the afternoon is the time for social calls, Mother has persuaded Lethbridge to come in the morning. However, he possesses a reputation for always being late, so Mother has vanished to see to other things, and I am left alone in the drawing room, shivering in a champagne-coloured silk-satin evening gown and diamonds, at the ungodly hour of ten o'clock.

I sit as close to the fire as I dare. The dress leaves my shoulders and décolletage completely bare except for a delicate gauze. I begged Mama to let me wait in a shawl but she insisted that, when the great artist arrives, he be greeted by 'the full effect'. I think of Verity's tales of the lecherous genius and feel utterly miserable. Normally at this hour I would be luxuriating in bed, giggling over *Punch*, thinking about ringing for breakfast.

I hear the front door. Surely he is not prompt? I cannot receive him alone! One of the maids enters, the one Mother hesitated to employ because her hair is quite red, and announces, 'The gentleman from the artist.' It seems an odd way to phrase it and a little hope flickers in my goosebumpy breast.

'You mean Mr Lethbridge?'

'No, Miss Blythe, not him. A gentleman on his behalf.'

Mother's not going to be happy about this. Well then, she should not have abandoned me. 'His *name*?' I demand. Honestly, these *people*!

The maid's face floods with colour. 'I . . . I can't say, Miss Blythe. I did ask, I promise. Only I can't pronounce it.'

I sigh and roll my eyes. 'Oh, for heaven's sake! What is the world coming to when a parlour maid can't pronounce plain English? Very well, show him in, I suppose.'

'Very good, miss.' She bobs a curtsey and flees.

I stand to greet this unpronounceable stand-in for Mr Lethbridge. I don't know much about artists but I assume they're all pretty much the same. Imagine my astonishment therefore when, instead of a fifty-year-old with long, unkempt hair and a reek of cologne to cover the smell of spirits, I am confronted with a young man so beautiful, so radiant, he could be Adonis. I feel my eyebrows arch sky-high.

He steps into the room, at once confident and deferent, and sweeps me a low and courtly bow. 'Miss Rowena Blythe, I presume,' he says, in an accent I cannot identify. Well, of course I can't. Garrowgate Hall, in fact my entire social world, is a sphere entirely free of accents. Mama doesn't even allow cockney speech in the house which is why all our domestics are from more or less respectable backgrounds.

He straightens up and gazes at me with an expression of delight. Heavens! I can't take my eyes off him! I meet men all the time. *All* the time. My parents have been wanting to marry me off for years now. I have been courted by dukes and earls and wealthy men of every stripe. Verity often asks what on earth I'm waiting for and I've never quite been able to tell her, but . . .

'Miss Blythe?' he says again and I shake myself.

'Yes!' I exclaim, flustered for the first time ever, I think.

'Indeed. Pardon me, sir. You are not . . . Lethbridge. You are not . . . what I was expecting.'

He inclines his head with a little smile. 'Allow me please to explain. Miss Blythe, I am . . .'

He says his name, but it sounds like a sneeze. I make a mental apology to the red-haired maid. I wrinkle my brow, then realise I am doing it and stop. Mama hates me to frown in case it ages me. 'I beg your pardon?'

He grins, showing white, even teeth in a golden-brown face. His skin looks as if the sun, even now in February, still lingers on its surface. 'I am Bartolej Stanislawski Woźniak, Miss Blythe, but please, call me Bartek. I am not sufficient important for to be formal with me. And many English people, they find Woźniak too difficult for to say.'

I smile, relieved to feel less stupid. 'Thank you. And where are you from, Mr . . . Bartek?'

'I am from Poland, Miss Blythe. I *should* say Russia for officially no Poland now. Poland only to be found *here*.' He places his palm over his heart then smiles. 'Like Bohemia.' I nod vaguely. I assume that Bohemia is the region from which he hails. 'Now, I am proud London-dweller,' he concludes. 'Here one year, but still with strong accent and still with difficult-to-say name.'

'Your accent is . . . charming. And you are here instead of Mr Lethbridge because . . . ?'

'Ah, yes, I must explain at once. I am assistant of Mr Lethbridge. He is sick, but he is busy man. He has set aside two weeks for to come to Garrowgate Hall for to paint famous beauty, Rowena Blythe. Likely he is sick most of week but he has not time for to miss so many days, so I come to do preliminary work, sketches, assessments, et cetera. That way, when better, he can . . . dive straight in – is that right?'

'Yes. I see. Well, thank you, Mr Bartek, for stepping in. Ah, my mother will wish to meet you but she is elsewhere at the moment. I believe she thought Mr Lethbridge might not be so prompt . . .'

'Lethbridge, yes, he is always late!' He laughs. 'Your mother she is very wise.'

He has a knack of diffusing every awkwardness and I am grateful for it, because I'm not accustomed to feeling awkward. The situations of my life are always smooth and predictable. I am the queen of the social dance but I have never encountered a person quite like this. Because he is foreign, I cannot assess him. His speech is imperfect, but English is not his language. His role sounds modest – assistant to an artist – yet he carries himself with great assurance. His golden hair is longer than I would expect in a gentleman, but perhaps the fashion is different where he comes from. For an artist, he is very well dressed and even from our appropriate distance I can smell the clean, wholesome smell that rises from him, not a note of sweat or whisky in the whole bouquet.

Once again, I recover my manners. 'Mr Bartek, forgive me, it is a little earlier than I am accustomed to being social. Please, take a seat and tell me about yourself while we wait for my mother.' If I ring for the parlour maid, she will fetch Mother in a trice, but I'd quite like a few minutes alone with the enigmatic Mr . . . whatever it was. I realise that Bartek is a variation on his first name, yet I persist in calling him Mr Bartek because we *cannot* proceed to first name terms so quickly, especially some sort of . . . *nickname*!

'What do you care to know, Miss Blythe?'

Everything! I am tongue-tied for a minute then the questions pour out in a rush. 'Are you an artist yourself, Mr Bartek? Tell me about . . . your country. What brought you here? Do you have a family of your own?' Oh, mortifying! Why did I ask that last?

He laughs again. 'Story of my life, then! My country has long history, Miss Blythe, too complicated for daytime conversation. It takes candlelight and a great deal of red wine.'

'Oh! I see!'

'Yes, we hope every day for the restoration of an independent Poland. Then my father's title will be restored and—'

'Your father is titled?'

'He was a count. I wish to be artist. My father not approve but I am twenty-one. So I come here, the land of the masters, Constable, Turner, I apprentice to Lethbridge. Between you and me, Miss Blythe, as a man I not respect him all that much. But he has talent and I can learn and I can make . . . how do you call the people of influence?'

'Connections,' I say faintly. 'I have never had a conversation so interesting.

'Yes, connections. I work hard and one day *I* will be summoned to fine homes to paint pillacles of society.'

'Pinnacles,' I murmur. 'Or pillars.'

'Yes. Thank you. My English not so good.'

'Your English is excellent. I could never get by so well in . . . your language. I don't know a word of anything besides Italian and French. And they are rudimentary, I'm afraid. I wish you luck with your ambitions, Mr Bartek. I'm sure you are a very fine artist.'

'So kind.'

Just then Mother surges in, shocked to see me alone with a young, handsome man. 'Ah, Mother, there you are at last. This is Mr Bartek. He has come on behalf of Mr Lethbridge, who is unwell today.'

Mother looks at Bartek with something like horror. 'Mr . . . Bartek, was it?' she queries, dripping with disapproval.

He greets her smoothly, again giving that courtly bow, explaining himself. I can see that although Mother is not happy, she is somewhat mollified. She quickly launches into a detailed explanation of her vision for the portrait. She has it all planned out. I am to be painted standing at the foot of the grand staircase, wearing this champagne silk-satin. Hair up, diamonds, hand on banister . . .

Bartek listens respectfully and tells her that her ideas are *wonderful*, that she is a very clever woman with exquisite taste. But Mr Lethbridge is a law unto himself, he explains regretfully. When it comes to composition, he will insist upon having the final say in such matters. Therefore Bartek must sketch me in different rooms and positions. He will take note of the light, the decor and so on. Including the grand staircase, naturally. He's so firm, yet so charming, that Mother is quite disarranged.

'I see!' she says, feathers ruffling. 'Mr Lethbridge sounds very . . . exacting! I suppose artists are known to be difficult.'

'He has strong artistic passion. I apologise in advance for my employer. He is very successful. Sometimes it make him forget a little bit his good manners. Please, my dear lady, never tell him I said such a thing. But he is genius, yes? And he will give you best portrait of your daughter you could ever wish.'

'And you, Mr . . . you will put in a strong case for the grand staircase?'

'I will recommend most strongly.'

'And to the gown, at least, he will agree?'

'Ah.'

'Oh, for goodness' *sake!*' cries Mother. 'Are we to pay Mr Lethbridge's considerable fees for something we have no say

over? It seems absurd! Rowena, was it like this when Mr
Lethbridge painted Verity?'

'I . . . I think so.' In fact, I have no idea. All Verity ever told
me was about his unpleasant habits and how beautiful she was
in the finished portrait. 'It's very flattering.'

'Yes, I've seen it.'

'If you feel more comfortable cancelling Mr Lethbridge, I
would understand, Mother.' Although Bartek is here today, in
a few days it will be Lethbridge after all.

She frowns and I resist telling her that it is ageing. 'No, no.
When the thing is finished, I want to be able to tell people it's
a Lethbridge.' She turns to Bartek. 'Explain to me about the
dress.'

'Dear lady, the choices that in real life look to perfection, like
this you have chosen . . .' – he sweeps a hand towards me –
'they not always . . . transfer, with same success, to canvas.'

He goes into great length about oil paint and pigmentation
and the drying process. I'm certain Mother understands none
of it, and nor do I. 'Most esteemed lady,' he concludes, 'Mr
Lethbridge will want consider five or six different gowns. He
will consider gowns, consider background, and he will pick the
combination that show to perfection your daughter on canvas.
Please understand, not only art, but science.'

I absolutely cannot bear the thought of parading before
Lethbridge in six different gowns. 'Can you not make that
choice for him?' I ask abruptly.

'Rowena!' Mother exclaims. 'Whatever next? I apologise for
my daughter, Mr . . .'

'No, Mother, please. I was only thinking that if Mr Lethbridge
is ailing for several days, and then, when he does appear, he
has to sit through an interminable fashion parade, it will be
for ever before he can properly begin.'

Mother tilts her head, conceding the point. 'Just how sick *is* Mr Lethbridge, Mr . . . ?'

I jump in. '*Very* sick, you said, Mr Bartek, did you not?'

'Very sick, yes. Very unpleasant.' Bartek makes a face.

'Hmm. I certainly don't want him coming here before he's fully recovered. I don't want him bringing a germ into the house.'

'Germ very bad,' agrees Bartek.

'Is this a choice you could make for him? Are you qualified? Do you know enough about the colours drying and so forth?'

'I know it, yes. He will make final decision but I could bring paints tomorrow, make preliminary colour sketches to take to him. If you like, I wish to help mostly.'

'Then bring your paints and let us make as much progress as we can in the absence of the maestro.'

Bartek flashes his dazzling smile at Mother. 'Maestro, yes. I bring paints. Now, which exquisite Blythe lady to show me house and garden so I can make notes for maestro?'

'Well, *I* don't have time,' says Mother, exasperated. 'And Rowena, you cannot do so unchaperoned. I shall ring for a maid. And you should change. That's hardly the gown for wandering about the place.'

I go to change into something warmer and I can't stop smiling. Unexpected reprieve! Far from being the ordeal I had expected, this promises to be a very pleasant week indeed.

Five

Olive

Interesting creatures, men. Across my office I'm surreptitiously watching Mr Harper, a trustee of my charity, the Westallen Foundation, as he confers with Mr Gladstone, its manager. Mr Harper's intent expression is interrupted by repeated glances in my direction, which amuses me. Men! They do their level best to rule the world, hold cast-iron opinions about the role and qualities of women and are firmly persuaded that the world revolves around *them*. One of my greatest enjoyments in life is confounding them whenever I am able. I do not catch his eye. I have better things to think about.

The weather is not one of them! The February rain bashes away at the windowpanes as if it holds a personal grudge towards each and every one of us. The sky is dark and lowering at three in the afternoon. The wind is doing that parlour trick where it pours itself through every crack and cranny it may find, just for the fun of emitting startling, eerie moans.

But the weather shan't defeat *me*! No, I am feeling most satisfied with my life at present. Of late, I have achieved Great Things; everyone says it. Of course, in terms of all I *wish* to achieve, I have only reached the foothills of the mountain. Nevertheless, after an arduous climb, I think it fitting to pause and take in the view. A little self-satisfaction can be most enjoyable now and then.

Sixteen months ago I resigned myself to the fact that love and marriage were not to be part of my lot. I am wealthy, clever and the only child of Captain Westallen, a man universally admired. However, I am also headstrong, unconventional and outspoken – no man's ideal choice for a wife. Having come to terms with this, I decided I would not let it stop me doing anything else I wanted in life, including motherhood. Therefore, I went to a local orphanage and adopted a daughter, Clover, a darling angel now nearly six years old.

Sometime later I took in a small companion for Clover. Angeline is the sister of Mabs, a friend of mine who hails from a desperately poor family. As I told Mabs at the time, I do not consider Angeline another daughter, for she has her own family, a loving father and the memory of a dear mother, now dead – not to mention a host of brothers and sisters! But as her siblings one by one went out into the world, Angeline would have been left alone. Young as she is, she could not have worked or fended for herself. By having her to live with us at Polaris House, I can ensure that she is cared for, educated, protected and loved as if she *were* my daughter. And we benefit from the arrangement quite as much, for she is a delightful child and provides invaluable companionship for Clover, who is often excluded from neighbourhood gatherings on account of her dubious origins. People can be quite unbelievably stupid and cruel. That is why I like to go my own way, and not be troubled by them.

Altogether, I found positions for several of Mabs's siblings last year, for I do love fixing the affairs of others. This meddling, added to my daily observations, convinced me that insufficient is being done to help the poor folk of London. So, six months ago, I founded the Westallen Foundation to do exactly that. I'm immensely proud of it. We serve as emergency supply provider, educational resource, a source of connections and a font of inspiration, all rolled into one. I believe it to be unique among charitable institutions in this last function.

It was launched last August with a glittering ball. As I cast a baleful eye at the weather outside, I sigh, nostalgic for that hot summer night swathed in the scent of jasmine, glittering with jewels and heady with champagne. No matter. Spring will come again.

These are some considerable achievements, I allow. Hence my quiet moment of pride. Even so, I shall not rest on my laurels. People tell me repeatedly that I am remarkable and inspiring. It makes me envision a helmeted knight in a medieval tale: Olive the Remarkable! But really, am I? Surely that is the whole *point* of being filthy rich? What else should I do in my position? Sit around eating candies and gossiping? People of my background do, I know, but I cannot imagine it. Even now that we are up and running, helping a large number of people to better their situation, I remain painfully aware of all that is *not* done, the injustices that have yet to be righted.

I look around. My office is situated on the first floor of an old warehouse in Euston. It is large and draughty but I love it, for it is the scene of so many worthy endeavours and, already, so many happy results. On this dark and dreadful day we have lit many lamps to brighten the gloom and long shadows stretch across the wooden floorboards. It would be eerie except that it's filled with good people and purpose, which makes it feel like home. It belongs to Mr Harper and he has kindly given it to the foundation for use in perpetuity. He was the very first trustee of the charity and I will always be grateful for the aid he has given us. That gratitude, however, is somewhat complicated by a small amount of personal history that exists between us.

He comes towards me now. He is tall and attractive. Society at large considers me the eternal spinster – but this does not stop me from appreciating a handsome face when I see it. From our first meeting I have liked his calm grey eyes, his neat brown beard and his obvious intelligence. He is mannerly and a keen businessman. Our early conversations suggested that he was similarly impressed by me – but then he found out about Clover. Adoption is not generally considered quite respectable and an unwed mother, no matter the circumstances, cuts a marginal figure in society. Women who want children are meant to languish and pray until they find a man to give them one, and if they do not, they are meant to weep for the rest of their days. That is not my style. So I went and got a daughter for myself and Mr Harper was very shocked when he discovered it. He is a clever man, there is no question of that, but his mind is not always as open as I would wish. One can only assume he has overcome those scruples now.

'Miss Westallen, I've spoken to Mr Gladstone and we've agreed that I will take on young Will Brown as my apprentice for a month, beginning as soon as he likes. He's a promising lad, as you said. But of course, you're always right.'

He twinkles at me and I acknowledge the compliment with a smile. 'Thank you, Mr Harper, I'm so pleased. Will is the very sort who will seize the opportunity with both hands. Will you tell him yourself? He's calling in this afternoon to see if there's any news.'

'No, I must go. We received a shipment of rubies earlier and I intend to check each and every one of them myself before I go home. You'd be surprised how often suppliers slip in a few paste baubles or garnets to make up the number.'

'Shocking,' I murmur, pleasantly diverted by the image of Mr Harper sitting in a pool of lamplight well into the night, surrounded by rubies. How very picturesque. He runs a successful business importing gemstones that he sells on to bespoke jewellers. Recently he has branched out and opened a small jewellery workshop himself. The wish to grow, he claims, was kindled by my own achievements. Mr Harper can be really very charming when he wishes.

I enjoy his praise but neither do I forget that last year, just when he had come to terms with the fact of Clover, he became briefly infatuated by Rowena Blythe, a famous society beauty who lives across the heath in Highgate. It was at the foundation ball, in fact. He and I were midway through a conversation when Rowena walked in and his eyes lit up like a child watching fireworks. I did not see or hear from him for a few months after that.

Now, he shows some interest in me yet again. Either *he* has decided against Rowena for really, they were not remotely suited, or *she* has spurned him – more likely since, even though he is a wealthy merchant from an excellent family he is not sufficiently grand for the Blythes to entertain him as a husband for their only daughter. The Blythes are notorious for their pride. All I know is this: Mr Harper has many excellent qualities and, overall, I admire him. However, he is a man of his time and if *I* were ever to marry – which I still consider doubtful – I should require nothing less than a visionary! *And* he is fickle in the face of great beauty, which I concede most men are, but still, my vanity was plucked.

In general, I consider myself both rational and compassionate. I'm a great believer that we can never judge another till we have walked a mile in their shoes. I try to remember that there is good in everyone. However, everyone has a weak spot where they simply cannot live up to their own principles; that is simply part of the human condition. Everyone has a chink in their armour; Rowena Blythe is mine. If you ever hear me gossip or pass judgement, it will be about her. If I ever think an unkind thought, it will be about her. I do not like it in myself but there we are. In short, she is my nemesis. I dread the day she marries for the society pages will be full of her and there will be lengthy descriptions of her great beauty that I shall not be able to resist reading. The celebrations will be nauseatingly extravagant and, no doubt, angels will sing.

I could allow Mr Harper to call on me, I could flirt, and I could overlook his faults, continue to get to know him. But I would always remember that, when faced with her dazzling blonde divinity, he forgot I was even present.

He takes his leave with a lingering backward glance. I'm heartily glad about Will, though. He came to us a month ago in such dire circumstances. His father had been thrown in the debtors' prison, his mother was up to her ears in scrubbing, the only work she could get, and he is the eldest of four. He heard about us through a friend of his, which is good news; it means that word of the foundation is reaching the people for whom it's intended. Will had left school to labour in a builders' yard but they pay him a pittance and the family is starving. We gave them some practical assistance. Will started coming to us after work for an hour at a time to continue his study. He talked to a number of our supporters about a range of different employments and decided he wanted to learn about international trade from Mr Harper. The next step will be to buy him a suit. He is only thirteen but so full of promise. He exactly epitomises why I started the foundation.

I hear laughter and jovial voices in the corridor outside. In bursts my friend Mabs, who is now the assistant manager of the charity. She has her arm around none other than Will, whose narrow, white face is aglow. Behind them is Mr Harper, who tips his hat across the room at me. 'I ran into Master Brown and I couldn't resist telling him the news,' he calls.

'Quite right, too,' I decree. 'I'm so pleased you saw each other.'

Will shoots into the room and hovers by my desk, brimming with pride and excitement. 'I'm to do a 'prenticeship, Miss Westallen! Only a month, see if I like it an' all, make sure Mr 'Arper ain't gonna get sick o' me. But it's a chance! Oh, but I got to hand me notice in at the builders'. What if I don't cut it at Mr 'Arper's, miss? What if I mess it up and then I got no coin comin' in?' His face falls with the sudden realisation of the possible real-world consequences of taking a chance. It's the sword that slices many a poor person from their chance at something better.

'Will, you should know by now that if the worst comes to the worst, we shan't let you fall. The foundation is here for you. But it won't come to that. Believe that this is the start of something good for you, something you deserve.'

Relief works a little colour into his sallow cheeks. 'Yes, Miss Westallen, thank you, miss. I want this so bad.'

'And you shall have it, Will.' I feel like Cinderella's fairy godmother. I love this. I love making things possible. I look up, beaming, but Mr Harper has gone. Mabs waves at me as she takes off her navy winter coat and settles in at her desk. Will hurries home, light of step, and I think again about Mr Harper.

I suppose to indulge him a *little* would not hurt. Not every businessman would take a chance on a boy like Will. And, for

all their shortcomings, men can be diverting. There is no reason
I shouldn't enjoy a little male company, providing I do not take
it too seriously. Oh yes, I am feeling most satisfied with my
life at present. And I am determined that things shall only get
better.

Six

Pansy

*J*ust *when you think things can't get any worse*, thought Pansy, *they do. And then they keep getting worse after that.* It was bad enough that she'd missed her day off. She missed her mother and Elstree so much it scalded. Then, because Charlotte was still unwell, the other girls had to cover her duties. Charlotte was an upper housemaid, with duties to Miss Blythe, and today Pansy was to carry them out, just when she was sicker than ever of the very thought of Rowena Blythe.

In the cruellest of ironies, today was no ordinary day. The whole household knew that Rowena was having her portrait painted. Today, apparently, the artist fellow was coming to see her in different dresses, and guess who had to get her in and out of them? Not only did Pansy have to be in the same room as Rowena all morning, but she had to dress her hair and fasten her necklaces and see her in a succession of stunning gowns at close quarters, growing seemingly lovelier as the day progressed. As if that wasn't torture enough, Rowena hardly submitted to the attention with good grace. She scowled and flounced and sighed. She grew restless when Pansy was dressing her hair and walked away halfway through so that all the carefully arranged coils tumbled down and

Pansy had to begin again. She called Pansy 'girl', and pinched her when she was feeling too smothered. Once she even slapped her.

Pansy stepped back then, shocked. Tears sprang to her eyes. Not through pain – it hadn't been a hard slap – but through humiliation and fury. She couldn't afford to be angry in her position.

'Carry on, Tilney,' said Mrs Blythe. 'Hurry up!'

The artist was some young foreign chap, not the great man they'd all been expecting. Apparently *he* was ill too. Always something going around in February. The assistant was set up in the drawing room with a sketchbook on his lap and a tray of little paint blocks at his side and when Rowena appeared in each new outfit, he spent half an hour or so mixing colours with water and making little paintings of her with a great many notes beside.

Maude Blythe was with them, which made the whole ordeal worse. She wasn't easy at the best of times and her nose was out of joint because she wasn't automatically getting her own way about the dress for the portrait. She made up for the disappointment by managing every little detail to the nth degree.

'Tilney, not on that link! The sapphires must sit on the collarbone!'

'*No*, Tilney, leave some tendrils about the face.'

'Tilney, what are you *thinking*? That pin is far too low.'

Why don't you just do it yourself, you daft old cow? thought Pansy, but she gritted her teeth and followed every instruction, completely dispirited by the sight of Rowena in her undies, as slender and curved and silky as any man could dream. Pansy couldn't help thinking of John. Rowena's skin, her figure, were perfect, all clad in wisps of lace and silk, nothing like the cotton chemise Pansy wore every day under her dull uniforms.

'Tilney, pull the stays another notch!' commanded Maude and Rowena's waist grew even tinier, her breasts just about to pop out of the top. Pansy closed her eyes and felt a dull headache blooming; this was just too much Rowena Blythe.

First, the blond artist painted her in the champagne silk-satin that was her mother's choice. Then Rowena, Maude and Pansy ran upstairs and got her into her apricot chiffon. Then the sky blue, then the eau-de-nil, then the silver lace and finally the ivy green.

At last the artist packed up and left. Pansy followed the Blythe ladies up the stairs one last time and helped Rowena out of the ivy dress and into a lemon-yellow day dress. 'Thank the *Lord*!' gasped Rowena when her stays were loosened. 'I couldn't have tolerated it a moment longer. I've the most fearful headache, Mother. I'm going to lie in the snug with a glass of water and a magazine. Bring me a cool flannel for my forehead, girl. Then clear all this.' She waved her hand at the mound of silk and stockings and jewels flung on her bed.

'I'm going to my room,' said Maude. 'Rowena thinks *she's* tired but no one knows the strain of making the decisions. Bring me a pot of Assam, Tilney, and then I'm not to be disturbed.'

With both of them gone, Pansy took a deep breath. No word of thanks and, of course, no recognition that the donkey work had, in fact, been carried out by *her*. But at least the worst was over. In many ways it hadn't been the hardest of mornings, not physically at least. It was the mental torture that had made it so hard on Pansy. She saw to the cold cloth, then to the Assam, then returned to Rowena's room to get it all straight. She placed the jewels back in velvet boxes and shook out and hung the dresses. The shoes went back into their boxes and the corset into its drawer. She straightened the bedspread and opened the window a crack to let in a little fresh air, though she would have to remember to close it soon as there would be hell to pay if Rowena found her room too chilly.

Pansy would be haunted for months to come by the sight of Rowena's satin shoulders, her slender legs in pearly stockings, her pink lips parting for each new application of lip stain. Would she tell John about this? she wondered. Never in a million years. Perhaps she would tell him that Rowena was covered in boils and scaly patches of skin! No, even that wouldn't put him off, devoted as he was. Sighing, she knew she would keep this morning's ordeal to herself and wait for the memory to fade with time.

There was one other thing that Pansy had noticed about Rowena, though. It was the way she had looked at the artist, with more than the usual number of stars in her pretty blue eyes. Pansy paused in the middle of dusting Rowena's room. Rowena was a coquette, everyone knew it. And the artist was a handsome fellow with an air about him, a sort of a dash and a flourish. Pansy could see why Rowena would enjoy his company. But there had been a breathless, glittering air about her in his presence, now Pansy came to think of it. She frowned. Rowena couldn't have feelings for him, could she? She was aiming so high, the staff made jokes about mountain views. It would surprise no one if Rowena married a prince.

Pansy closed the bedroom window with a bang. She felt all churned up. On the one hand, wouldn't it set the cat among the pigeons if Rowena fell for such a lowly fellow? Wouldn't the Blythes just love that? Pansy could relish the prospect of Rowena taking a mighty topple. On the other hand, any foolish fancy on Rowena's part could get in the way of her choosing a husband. Pansy couldn't bear any further delays; she'd already been waiting quite long enough! *Don't be stupid, Rowena*, she thought as she walked past the snug. *He's not for you. Marry a lord and have done with it.*

Seven

Rowena

I never thought it would be possible to see more of Verity than I always have, but now that she is family, she is here all the time. The moment she heard that not Lethbridge, but an exotic and beautiful assistant was beginning the work on my portrait, she swept through our front door with the speed of a prize-winning racehorse and the tact of a baboon. She stayed all morning, chattering to Bartek and me while he drew me, and she is here still, hours after he departed. We are ensconced in the cosy corner in the snug, with our shoes kicked off and our feet next to each other's bottoms, the way you can only sit with the oldest of friends. It is a dark grey afternoon once more and the oil lamps are burning. We have scones.

When I think back over the years I have known Verity, they are full of memories to make me smile. We met when we were five years old and have been inseparable ever since. We played at tea parties together, we attended our first ball together. We have whispered and giggled and confided every silly secret in one another. When she married, Felix rented for them an exceptionally smart townhouse in the village and I thought she was sure to spend some time attending to her own home. I wondered if she would become dull and talk about house-keeping. I needn't have worried about that.

When she is not lording it over me because she is married and I am not, Verity loves to gossip. She prattles on and on about people we know, even people we *don't* know, or know only a little. Her favourite topic in the latter category is Olive Westallen. Verity *loves* to discuss Olive Westallen.

'Do you know,' she is saying now, licking cream off her fingers, 'she doesn't even employ a nursemaid! She has two small children in her home, and no *nursemaid*! Why, do you suppose? Is she thumbing her nose at convention? Is she making a point? If so, what is it and who cares?' Verity shakes her head ruefully. 'She must be worth, what, forty, forty-five thousand a year at *least*? The *husband* she could catch! It's *wasted* on her.'

Olive Westallen has ever been a thorn in my side. She is the daughter of James Westallen, sea-captain-turned-merchant-trader, former best friend of my father. Something poisonous happened between them and they have been estranged ever since. No one knows the cause of their falling-out. The two of them have carried the reason in secrecy and grim-jawed silence for twenty years now so I suppose no one ever will. The point is, they went from almost-brothers to mortal enemies overnight. Whatever happened, I shall never under-stand how they could just slice out all those years of affection and shared adventure. How I hope the same thing never happens to me and Verity. But women are more sensible than men, I think.

Olive and I are both only daughters; she is my counterpart, I suppose, in that other grand family across the heath. And it always feels to me that I measure up very poorly. She is no beauty, so I have that over her, for whatever beauty is worth. Even so, I do not consider her appearance tragic, as Verity does. In some lights she is even rather handsome. The thing about Olive is that she is clever. So very clever. In every conversation I've ever had with her I have found myself at a loss, so I'm glad we don't cross paths very often. She is famously learned, vastly independent and seems to live life according to her own dictates. Verity and I have always watched from afar and condemned, since Olive is a living affront to all the rules we live by. Yet lately, for me, this is another thing that has started to change. Sometimes I even feel I admire her.

'Do you suppose she *bathes* them herself?' Verity returns to the matter of Olive's small wards, tucking her lower lip firmly inside her upper one, and frowning as she considers it. 'Surely she does not prepare their meals? I mean, she *couldn't* wash their clothes . . . so why *not* just employ a nursemaid? Does she not realise that convention is a *good* thing? It *helps* us! *I* shall employ a Norland nurse as soon as I am *enceinte*. They are the very best, you know.'

'Norland nurse?' I ask vaguely, patting some raspberry jam into place with a fingertip. Motherhood is only a very distant and hazy prospect on my horizon.

'Yes! A girl trained by the Norland Institute. *You* know! It opened a few years ago. The girls are not terribly bright but they are *gentlewomen*, and they have a very specific training in the new thinking about child-rearing . . . German, you know.'

'The girls?'

'The *thinking*! They function as a . . . moral mentor and educator.' Verity casts her eyes up to the ceiling, obviously recalling a phrase from a pamphlet.

'That sounds very impressive. Why, Verity, you're not expecting, are you?'

'Heavens, *no*! I wouldn't be half so cheerful if I *were*, I can assure you! Perhaps I should not say so to *you*, since you are unmarried and Felix's sister, but there are certain steps one can take to prevent . . . but I should not share the married women's lore outside of the sisterhood.' She giggles, a trifle smugly perhaps. '*Anyway*, the point is that Olive Westallen can well afford to hire a Norland nurse yet she obstinately persists in this outlandish mode of parenting . . .'

I was Verity's bridesmaid, of course. Mother was put out by the haste of the occasion. One moment we didn't even know that Felix was *considering* Verity, and the next they were engaged! One might have suspected a certain reason for the haste except that Verity is, as she is fond of telling me, *far* too sensible to be caught like that. She always dissects every scandal that crosses our ears and her stories usually conclude with a salutary reason why *she* would *never* have made that mistake. Verity's certainty about her own rightness has always made her bolder than I. Anyway, in September they announced it and in December I trailed up the aisle of St Michael's in yards of blue satin.

I hope they are happy. Verity doesn't talk about Felix much. Sometimes I think she wanted to be a Blythe more than she wanted to marry Felix, but I'm sure that is nonsense. I love my brothers. Felix is special, because it is only to him that I am 'little sister'. To Crispin and Ignatius, I am 'big sister', an altogether different role. My brothers all have affectionate dispositions, an abundance of silly jokes and interesting aspirations. Really, I hardly know where they came from. Our parents are the most tradition-bound of people, stiff and unbending, capable of holding a grudge for ever. We have been brought up *very* strictly, yet the boys have an openness and an easiness that I admire. If I'm honest, I think I'm more like Mother and Father: stiff, aloof. Perhaps it's because I'm a girl, and trained to comply. I cannot afford to put one step wrong or my spotless reputation, my *value*, could be lost for ever. Our world is a treacherous place for women.

I know I shall have to marry very soon now; people are starting to speculate. What have I been waiting for? The truth is, I hardly know. People *say* that I'm waiting for a king but I have money and station enough. Perhaps I'm reluctant for childhood to end. That might sound laughable when I am now nearly three-and-twenty but I like my house, my position, and the security that comes from knowing what every day will bring. I have three brothers to bring me a little laughter and a best friend always at my side. To leave all this for the unknown, I will need considerable inducement. Or perhaps all I am really waiting for is to *feel* something.

It occurs to me sometimes that, wealthy and cherished as I am, I don't *need* a husband, I could just stay here for ever. Mother says that is impossible, but *Olive* is unmarried and she is some seven years older than me.

Mother is hoping for an engagement around my birthday. But of all the men I know, there isn't one I regard more highly than the others. Verity suggested I make a list of their various merits and drawbacks. She says that as my heart has no preference, I may as well choose from a purely logical standpoint. But something in me shrinks from a list.

Verity is *still* talking about Olive. 'But then she *will* take in all manner of waifs and strays, so perhaps *Norland* will not consider *her*,' she muses, as if the domestic arrangements of someone we barely know could really matter to either one of us.

'Two,' I interject. 'Just two waifs and strays.'

Olive goes walking alone. Olive is unmarried, yet adopted a small girl to be her daughter and acquired a small companion for her moreover. Olive befriends people of the servant class! Would I want to be Olive? Emphatically *not*. She scares me. Only, her way of living does beg questions. Perhaps it is *she* who creates the lurking question mark in the shadow of my days. Damn her! I was perfectly content before.

'Verity, darling,' I say at last. 'Please can we talk about something besides Olive Westallen now?' I give her hand a placatory squeeze.

Verity dimples. 'I've run on again, haven't I? Felix always says I'm like a *magpie* chattering away. I know, let's talk about Bartek! Isn't he *delicious*? I assure you, I would *far* rather have had *him* taking liberties with my bodice than ugly old Lethbridge.'

'Bartek takes no liberties.'

'Well, *no*, because I was there! What better chaperone could you ask for?'

'You were delightful, my dear, but even when you are not there, he is a perfect gentleman.'

'Oh, I think that rather overstates the case. I don't think you can apply the world *gentleman* to an impoverished artist with too-long hair and paint on his cuffs. But he's ornamental, I grant you. I suppose you could have a *flirtation* with him; you are not married yet. Though you would have to be careful. All artists are *rogues*, you know, with the morals of dogs.'

'*Verity!* Of course I would not! Quite apart from anything else, Mother would kill me. I assure you we are both quite proper. And you know, at home in . . . wherever he's from, his father was a count. So he *is* a gentleman by birth. Yet he seems perfectly content to forge his way in life by using his talent. What do you think it would be like to have a purpose?'

'Rowena, we don't need a purpose, we have *husbands*! Well, I have one and you will too, very soon. Now come, dear, let me help you with this. I have chosen exceedingly well after all! If you really won't make a list, then think about who will make the most pleasant fourth when you come to dine with

Felix and me. No, don't laugh, I think an everyday situation like that can tell you a great deal about yourself. Close your eyes, dear, humour me.'

I oblige and listen to Verity as she adopts a soothing, mesmerist-type voice. 'You are leaving your home,' she intones. 'You are wearing your beautiful blue mantle and your Caroline Reboux hat with the feathers. You are walking through the village towards Theodore Place with your husband at your side.'

'Why have we not taken the carriage?' I wonder.

She tuts. 'Because there is no call for it. You are in love and walking is romantic. It is a beautiful summer evening.'

'Then why the blue mantle?'

'*Rowena!*'

'Sorry.'

'It is warmer than you had realised, so you take off your mantle and drape it over your arm. At once your husband takes it from you, for he wishes to ease your every burden. You enjoy the summer air and the singing of the birds. You arrive at our house, Felix's and mine, with a pleasant sense of anticipation. We – the two couples – enjoy many such an occasion together and you are very happy. You have brought me gifts and flowers. You pause on the doorstep, the two of you, and before you seize the knocker, you turn to one another and smile . . . Who is he? Who do you see?'

I open my eyes. Verity is leaning forward, staring into my face as though she might see what I have just seen. I'm glad she cannot.

'Did you see someone?' she bubbles. 'Was it Algernon Delauncey? I always think he is very droll. Was it Sir William? *So* refined. Or Whitford Sedley, or Lord Merrihew? *Tell* me, Rowena!'

'I'm sorry, V,' I say and her face drops. 'I didn't see anyone. But it was a good idea. Can we try again tomorrow?'

But I am lying. I did see someone, vividly. It was Bartek. Instead of the men that Verity has named, all choices that would make Mother wildly happy, all men with titles and fortunes and connections, I saw a man I can never have. A man so far outside of respectable circles that he may as well live with the gypsies. A man with paint on his cuffs and a surname like a sneeze.

Eight

Pansy

The days had dragged their weary way one into another, but Thursday morning was here at last. Despite Lou and Maisie's best efforts to be quiet, Pansy woke at five and didn't go back to sleep. When the girls left the room, she blew them kisses then sat up. She couldn't relax; the memory of last Thursday was too sharp. She wasn't going to risk old Clarendon looking out for her today at the time she knew Pansy would be leaving. She washed and dressed, then ran downstairs.

It was too early for the family and too late for staff still to be wandering the staircases. Pansy made it through the house without seeing anyone, then she put her head down and looked at no one as she rushed through the bustling kitchen to the world outside. Pansy never stopped for breakfast on a Thursday; everything tasted a hundred times better in her mother's kitchen, even if the Blythes did employ the best cook in all of London.

Pansy hurried through quiet streets to The Garden of Eden Fine Foods and Wines in Highgate village, where she would get a ride on the delivery cart to Elstree. Mr Ollander, the proprietor, had grown up in Elstree and owned a second, smaller store there. It was still February, still dark and cold. But Pansy thought she could smell spring, far off, as she hurried up the steps to the street – and wasn't that the sound of a blackbird?

At The Garden of Eden, Pansy peered through the window – Mr Ollander was sorting out tins of luxury teas on the counter – and rapped at the pane to get his attention.

'Good morning, Pansy, you're very early!' he exclaimed when he'd unlocked the door and let her in.

'Didn't want to risk hanging about after last week. I'll help out while I wait. How are you, Mr Ollander?'

He was well and set Pansy to work arranging tins of tea on the shelves, which she did with the aid of a small stepladder while Mr Ollander unpacked crates of heavier goods, like bottles of port and shining jars of rum-soaked apricots. When Pansy had finished, she helped Hipólito, Mr Ollander's delivery man and unseen assistant, to load the cart. Sometimes Mr Ollander made the delivery and sometimes Hipólito, so that neither of them got bored with the same old routine.

Hipólito was from Santo Domingo. He had rich brown skin and dark eyes that were often watchful and sullen, but which danced with warmth and merriment for a very few people. Mr Ollander and Pansy were two of them. Mr Ollander had come across Hipólito in dire straits a few years back – he had been beaten and robbed – and gave him a place to recover and a job. The world wasn't such that Hipólito could work at the shop counter, not if Mr Ollander wanted to keep any of his custom, so he worked in the storeroom, and in the upstairs room balancing the accounts. Highgate was full of families like the Blythes, with opinions about who constituted the right sort of people, opinions that they held as truths. To them, Hipólito was definitely not the right sort of person.

In Elstree, however, they were used to his regular appearances on a Thursday and Hipólito, who was gregarious when he didn't have to stay invisible, enjoyed delivery days. With Pansy's help they set off a little earlier than usual.

'That's a smart hat, Pansy,' commented Hipólito, winking at her as they rattled off. Mr Ollander's horse was a pretty white gelding called Steed.

'Thanks, it's new. Trying to cheer myself up.' She shouldn't really waste her money on hats, but Pansy did believe that the right headwear could transform any girl into a lady. There were few things in her life that really cheered her and hats were one of them. And, it was a reaction against that damn Sunday bonnet. The hat was a soft blue with a very plain shape that did nothing to detract from its innate stylishness. Worn at a tilt on the soft chestnut waves of her hair, it was very becoming and somehow made her eyes look more, not less, green.

'Why don't you get another job?' demanded Hipólito, as he did most Thursdays.

Pansy groaned. 'You, John, Lou, Mr Ollander, my mother . . . !' *Because of John*. The answer was always clear and simple in Pansy's head but she never actually said it. She had a feeling it would sound a bit feeble spoken out loud.

'Ever think there's a reason why *everyone* says it?'

Pansy decided to be selectively deaf and turned to watch the countryside emerging from the morning shadows. It was a relief to leave Highgate behind and feel the usual sense of opening up as London dropped behind them. To enjoy her weekly return, and reunion with the lost parts of her own self.

Hipólito dropped her at the end of the lane that led to her mother's cottage then carried on to Mr Ollander's local shop, The Tree of Life, with a wave and a rattling of precious and delicious cargo as he and Steed jolted along the country road. Pansy hurried between the sparse hedges. Now that she was nearly home, she couldn't wait another minute. It was a walk of five minutes to the little house in the woods and she soon found herself running.

'Mums!' she cried, using her pet name for her mother, an instant connection to childhood, as she hurtled through the front door.

Laura Tilney appeared from the kitchen, wiping her hands on her apron, the delicious smell of the traditional Tilney family breakfast drifting out with her. 'Pansy! Oh, my darling, you're here. I'm so glad to see you!'

Pansy was engulfed in the warmth of her mother's hug. Was there any safer, happier feeling in the world? 'I'm so sorry about last week. Charlotte was sick and they made me work. Clarendon wouldn't even let me out for ten minutes to tell Mr Ollander so that he could send word! Were you worried?'

'Disappointed mostly. I did wonder if *you* might be ill but I guessed it would be something like that. Your life's not your own, working there, Pansy. You know you really should—'

'Mums! Hipólito's already told me. Can I have breakfast *before* the lecture?'

Laura laughed. 'I'll save it,' she promised.

Pansy loved breakfast at home more than any other part of the day. The whole day stretched ahead of her, with Garrowgate Hall no more than an ominous smudge on the horizon, and her mother could cook like no one else. Her younger sister Eveline was nowhere to be seen yet. Eveline was sixteen and soon to finish school. Meanwhile, she had discovered a great love of bed and never emerged until the last possible moment.

The Tilneys had been 'gentleman farmers' until seven years ago with a modest but comfortable life. But Tom Tilney's heart had given out without warning just weeks before his fortieth birthday. The agricultural economy wasn't robust and the farm had debts; there was no way to keep it going without Tom.

Laura and her three children had moved quickly to this cottage, with a large enough garden that they could continue to grow food and keep chickens and even a pet sheep called Eustacia who kept the grass in check. Pansy's brother Matthew, then nineteen, had gone to labour on another farm and Pansy, at the age of sixteen, had gone into service at Garrowgate Hall. Laura had continued to raise Eveline and keep heart and home together for them all.

Despite missing Tom every single day, they had somehow managed to make a new home that *felt* like home. Pansy admired her mother more than anyone she knew. The echoes of their farming past were all around them, in the herbs drying in the kitchen rafters, the sound of Eustacia bleating outside the window and above all in the hearty farm breakfasts that Pansy loved so much. Bacon and eggs, freshly baked bread with thick butter and glasses of cold, creamy milk. Pansy didn't need to eat for a week after one of Laura's breakfasts, despite which she managed to step up to the mark for lunch and then for afternoon tea in Primrose Cottage.

When she'd devoured her fill and sat back wiping her mouth appreciatively with her napkin, Laura pounced.

'Pansy, my darling, I'm worried about you. You never look happy when you leave here at the end of the day. It's natural to miss your home and family – we miss you too – but you look as if you have *nothing* to look forward to for the next six days. You look as if you're going back into chains!'

Pansy looked down at the table and dabbed at breadcrumbs with a fingertip. She had never told her mother or Eveline exactly how much she hated her life, not wanting to make them unhappy, but she obviously wasn't as good at hiding her feelings as she thought.

'I've asked you before, and I know your friends have too,

why do you stay there? You could do so much more. It's time to tell me, Pansy.'

Because of John. The answer ran through Pansy's head silently once more. Close as she was to her mother, Pansy had told her all about John, Lou, Maisie and the rest, but when Laura had teased her about John, she'd insisted that he was merely a friend, like the others. But she couldn't fob her mother off this time. What was it that had finally nudged Pansy towards the end of her tolerance? Was it the humiliation of dressing up Rowena Blythe on Tuesday to make her more beautiful than ever for her portrait? Was it missing her day off last Thursday? Or was it simply that she'd run out of hope? Whatever the reason, she suddenly wanted to unburden herself to her mother so she said it aloud.

'Because of John. I love him, and he loves Rowena and it's all impossible. But I love him and I keep hoping that she'll get married and he'll start to forget her and then . . .' She'd been right. It did sound feeble when she said it out loud.

'And then settle for his long-suffering best friend? Turn to you as second choice?'

Pansy winced and nodded miserably.

'I see. Well, at least it explains your determination to stay in a place that clearly makes you miserable.'

Laura was quiet for a moment, gently scratching her finger-nails over the wooden tabletop, as she always did when she was thinking. Then she spoke, looking Pansy right in the eye. 'Now you listen to me, Pansy Tilney, and heed my words,' she said.

Pansy swallowed and nodded. Her mother was wise, she knew that. Now that she had told her, there was no going back.

'I understand that love is a powerful force. John sounds like a lovely man and if he loved you too, it would be a wonderful match. But he doesn't. Please don't think I'm not sympathetic. I know that love isn't easy to set aside. But this is no way to live a life. Love is supposed to be a good thing; yours is keeping you prisoner. You hate that place! We all see it. I want to see some big changes in your life before summer, Pansy, or we'll be having words.'

'Yes, Mums,' croaked Pansy, her throat full of fear.

'Don't you *Yes, Mums* me! I don't want lip service, Pansy, I want you to be *happy*. I want you to have a fulfilling life. John's a good man but he's a fool and you're too clever to be with a fool. He's not your match. Rowena Blythe, indeed! You're a beautiful young woman, Pansy, and I won't stand for you wasting any more of your precious life. It's not enough to be happy only one day a week. You're not to come here next Thursday . . .'

'Mum!' cried Pansy in outrage.

'I mean it. I don't care where you go or what you do but do *something* to start yourself thinking about how you can make your life better.'

'I can think here!'

'No. There are different types of happiness, Pansy. There's the happiness of family. You're lucky, you know what that's like. Then there's the happiness of married love. I lost mine, but I had it, and that makes me blessed. You're desperately clinging to the hope of having it with John, but you can't, Pansy. You need to find the third type, the happiness that's all for you, the happiness of knowing who you are and why you're in this world, what lights you up, what drives you forward.'

Pansy frowned. 'I can't think of anything that makes me feel like that.'

'Of course not! Because there's been nothing for you for years now but mindless drudgery and empty dreams of John. So next Thursday, go and do something that doesn't revolve around me and Eveline, and doesn't revolve around John. Something for *you*, Pansy. Think of it as a quest!'

Nine

Rowena

As the week progresses, it occurs to me that I feel strange – different. I have a lightness of heart, a keenness of mind and an eagerness of step that are unfamiliar. I wake with more zest than is usual, and once or twice, I hear myself humming. I suppose then, I am happy. I thought I was before.

Despite being chaperoned every day, Bartek and I have talked of many things. He has told me the history of his land, which I did not greatly understand and readily forgot but enjoyed hearing all the same. He has spoken of art and the ideals that impassion him. He described the different countries through which he has travelled and there I had something to offer; we spoke of France and Italy for a little while. Having Bartek in a room makes it brighter, not just because he is handsome, but because he has an energy and a vision that is not found among those of my own circle. He is poor, and far from home, yet I don't think I've ever seen anyone so cheerful. When he leaves, I think about our conversations all the rest of the day.

On Friday he bears the news that Mr Lethbridge is recovering and will come on Monday. Today is the last time I shall ever see Bartek. Fate is kind and this morning we are alone. Verity has another engagement and although I ring for a maid, no one comes. I expect they are all busy; if I rang again, someone would come in a trice. But I do not.

This morning he wishes to paint me in the silver dress, seated. He already has plenty of sketches of different backgrounds, so we simply stay in the parlour. 'So, Mr Bartek,' I say when he is underway, 'today is your last visit to Garrowgate Hall. I wish to thank you most sincerely for your courtesy and excellent work on behalf of Mr Lethbridge.'

They are thin words compared with all I feel. Like many proper young ladies, I am conversant with the language of flowers though I believe few love them as I do. Today I've arranged carnations from our conservatory in the vase at my side. They say eloquently all that I cannot. The pink carnations mean *I will never forget you*, the red *My heart breaks* and the magenta and white striped carnations are a reminder to myself: *I cannot be with you*. I doubt he will understand any of it, but this is the only language I have.

He pauses, wet paint gathering on his brush and threatening to fall on the page until he carefully lays it aside. I have never noticed the colour of his eyes before, only ever his gilded skin and hair. His eyes are green, the crystal green of lakes in summer. My head swims a little.

He clears his throat and frowns. 'It was pleasure, Miss Blythe. Such enjoyable week of work for me. That I must hand work to maestro, that is not pleasure. Not to see you again . . . is not pleasure, for me.'

I feel my face flood scarlet but I am glad he said it. 'Nor for me,' I whisper, hanging my head and grateful with every fibre of my being that Verity is not here. For then I would not have the opportunity to speak true.

'Please not to put down your head.'

'I beg your pardon, I shall ruin your watercolour sketch.'

'Is not for sketch. It is for to see a lady such as you in distress is most hard for me. To see you anything but proud and happy, this is most hard for me.'

I can't speak. But I look at him. What can we do? There is no way that Bartek and I could be together and I am not the bold sort to defy expectations. I barely know him. I only know that he brings a joy and an excitement to my days that I hardly know how to live without. All that without ever leaving the confines of Garrowgate Hall.

'I bring for you something,' he says, to my surprise. 'Please.' He reaches into his artist's satchel and rummages, drawing out a battered book, much thumbed, with binding that sags. He holds it out to me hesitantly and I take it as though it is a smouldering coal.

'*Scènes de la vie de bohème*,' I read. 'By Henri Murger.' I look at him enquiringly.

'Your French pronounce exquisite.'

I wrinkle my nose. 'Thank you, but I fear my pronunciation is the only thing about my French that is. I have ladylike contemporary French that allows me to get by as a tourist. I'm not sure it is up to a . . . is this a novel?'

'Yes, a sort of, though based on life of writer. No expectation for you to read, but help you understand me a little better perhaps. Is old book, forty, fifty years, but perhaps you know the opera?'

'There is an opera?'

'*La Bohème*, of Puccini.'

'Why, good heavens! I had no idea it was drawn from a book. How ignorant I feel. Have you seen it?'

He shakes his head. 'No, I cannot pay for opera, but the book has been my friend long time. I loan it to you only for I must have it back.'

'Well, of course! Thank you, Bartek, I shall be fascinated to read whatever I can understand. Only, how shall I return it to you? I could send it with Mr Lethbridge next week?'

'No, not him. I would not entrust to him a treasure. That is why next week, for me, very hard.'

I blush again. 'I have heard . . . I am not looking forward to it, suffice to say. Especially after you have been so very . . . chivalrous.'

'Be firm with him, Miss Blythe. He is not monster, only he takes chance where he sees.'

'I see. Thank you.'

'And book, you could return at studio by post if you wish. But I wonder, would you care for a walk some time with me? Only a walk, I presume nothing. I know . . . how things must be. But I cannot stop thinking how beautiful to be to walk with you. Beautiful to give lifetime of happy memories.'

No point suggesting a chaperone, for a full army would not reconcile my parents to any unnecessary interaction with Bartek. No point in agreeing to a walk that would almost certainly make us wish for more. No point at all. Yet I find myself agreeing. 'It would need to be . . .' I look at him with deepest apology, for it is not easy to say to a man that he is not good enough.

'Secret. I know,' he says matter-of-factly.

'I think the best way would be to go very early in the morning. My family rise late. Would that be possible?'

'For you I rise with sun. You do me greatest happiness, Miss Blythe.'

We agree to meet on a quiet corner of Hampstead Heath a week from the following day. I have never taken such an enormous risk in my life. If I should be *seen*! We conduct the rest of the session in silence while my mind churns and worries and plans and hopes and chastises. And Bartek cannot stop smiling. His joy is ill-contained and he is even more beautiful like this than when he is professional and decorous. *I have done that*, I think. And it strikes me, perhaps fatally, that although I have spent my whole life living to please others, I have never before made anyone look so happy.

Ten

Olive

The following Monday I am glad to arrive home from the office. It's been a productive day, but a long and tiring one, and the weather is improved, but not by much. I'm glad to step inside, take off my wet coat and shake out my hair, which is cold and clings to my neck. Clover comes racing into the hall when she hears me. 'Mama!' She hurtles down the vast, mosaicked expanse and throws herself at me. I catch her up and swing her around, pretend-groaning at her weight.

'My goodness but you're growing!' I exclaim. 'Do you sprout every time I leave the house?'

She laughs, kicking her feet in the air. For all she is getting taller, I can still lift her clean off the ground. Thank goodness. When I adopted her I had first intended to take an older child but that didn't work out. The first girl, Gert, didn't want me. It seems she was just too damaged by her life to open herself to the possibility of kindness. Now, though my heart still bleeds for poor Gert, I am glad of it, for every day with Clover is precious and already almost-six feels too old. I want her with me for ever. Her laugh is a gurgle, her long honey-coloured hair spills down her back in curls, caught up in a purple ribbon. Clover is as fair as I am plain. 'I do!' she boasts. 'Every time you go out, I eat some Eat Me bread and

I get bigger.' We have been reading *Alice in Wonderland* together.

'Well, that explains the mystery. Where's Angeline? What have you been doing today?'

Chattering, she tows me into the drawing room where I find both my parents and Clover's companion Angeline much engrossed in mugs of cocoa. Like all of Mabs's siblings, she'd been hungry for too long to stay indifferent to food. Now she eats and drinks as if making up for lost time. We had Dr Stickland examine her for a worm but there was none. Now neither Mama nor I nor any of the maids can deny her any snack or treat she wishes for. When she came to us she was a wisp, a little malnourished fairy. Now there is a decided chub to her frame, which I will only worry about if she starts to look unhealthy. Just now her plump little tummy and round, rosy cheeks look so beguiling with her dark, glossy hair, which she always begs to wear in ringlets. She looks just like a doll I had when I was small.

Both my parents are watching her fondly. Considering they were originally against the idea of me adopting a child, they didn't take long to fall in love with Clover when she arrived, and then with Angeline a few months later. I don't like to say I told them so – but sometimes I do.

I give Angeline a hug and kiss my parents. My mother wipes the trace of a cocoa kiss from my cheek. 'How was the day, darling?' she asks. Both my parents are inordinately proud of my work at the foundation. My mother in particular often weighs in with ideas and counsel.

'Very good,' I tell them, sinking gratefully into a comfortable chair at the fireside. Clover clambers onto my lap with a book which she waves hopefully under my nose. 'In a while, my darling. Let me talk to Grandmama and Grandpapa first. We received a small donation from Adrian Gibbs. Remember him?'

'Good Lord, yes,' says Papa. 'My old banker of many moons ago. How the devil is he?'

'According to his letter he's well and retired to Brighton. His daughter told him about the Westallen clan's latest eccentricities. He asked for his regards to be conveyed to you.'

'Splendid fellow,' Papa murmurs. The number of worthy men and women Papa knows is testament to his sterling character and the esteem in which he is generally held. No wonder I am unmarried; no man could ever measure up to my papa.

'Then that street-thief masquerading as an unfortunate came back again. I don't know why he bothers. He must know we'll recognise him.' Our policy for criminals is to offer them support and education to help with a new start, but not to give foundation funds that could benefit others. He's not interested in a fresh start but seems to be operating under a conviction that we give away free money to anyone who asks for it. We sent him away yet again.

'And then Mr Gladstone talked me and Mabs through the month's accounts. Not the most interesting activity but essential, and, of course, it's gratifying to see that it's all working like clockwork and our work looks sustainable.'

Mr Gladstone is the manager of the charity. He saves me from troubling my head with uninspiring things like finance and administration and Mabs is learning all the ropes from him. He is of retirement age and swore he would only stay with us a year, but Mabs and I hope he will stay for ever.

Our maid Anne brings me some hot tea and a scone, which Angeline eyes covetously. 'I'll bring you one in a minute, poppet,' says Anne, putty in her hands. 'Can I get you anything else, Miss Olive?'

'No, dear. This is perfection after a long, cold day. Thank you.' I wrap my hands around my teacup and sigh luxuriously.

How I do love home. It is full of the people I love and Mama has made it so beautiful. Everywhere I look there is something lovely – an oil painting, brightly coloured wallpapers, a graceful fall of drape in some lustrous fabric. She has the gift of making interiors fashionable yet timeless, beautiful yet entirely comfortable. There is nowhere in all the world like Polaris House, so-named for the guiding star that brought my sea-captain father safely back to us, again and again.

A knock at the door interrupts our peaceful family reverie. Another of our maids, Jenny, who is also one of Mabs's sisters, announces Mr Harper.

'Show him in, Jenny, by all means,' says Mama. 'Is that all right, Olive? Will he mind being confronted with the entire family?'

I shrug. 'I am too tired to move. The cold in that office creeps right into your bones. It gives me an inkling of what it's like to live somewhere that doesn't have fires or hot water. Let Mr Harper find us as we are.'

Jenny nods, winks at the girls and returns a moment later with Mr Harper, who maintains his composure when faced with a chorus of greetings. 'And which of these is your little girl?' he asks, gamely confronting the children. 'This is Clover,' I tell him, hugging the darling on my lap. 'Please forgive me not getting up, Mr Harper, but I have a warm, heavy impediment. And that is Miss Angeline Daley, Clover's companion.'

Angeline jumps to her feet and performs a divine little curtsey, pointing her feet with balletic grace. In the slums of Saffron Hill she often went shoeless. Now her black patent pumps are the one possession she would save from a burning building and she misses no opportunity to show them off. 'Good evening, Mr Harper,' she declaims. I smile at her. Good girl.

He bows. 'Good evening, Miss Daley. Oh! Daley? Any connection to . . . ?'

'Her sister.'

'Ah.' Again, he is confounded. If I do say so myself, I have a real flair for unconventional living arrangements. In addition to Mabs's sister Jenny coming to work as a maid here at Polaris House, her brother Jem was placed as an errand boy and general helper with my good friend Julia Morrow, though he is more like an adopted son to her than an employee. If people can be happy living together, and have all their needs met, what does it matter whether or not they are related, whether or not society would have put them together?

My parents make Mr Harper welcome. He takes a seat but declines tea and cake. 'I've come unannounced and I shan't stay long. I only wanted to tell you about Will Brown's first day with me. I thought you'd want to know.'

'You thought aright, Mr Harper. Please tell me everything.'

'Well, he's a promising lad. He was cock-a-hoop to be there, you may imagine. I set him to some very simple tasks, ordering paperwork by subject, sealing letters and so on, but as he carried them out, I explained their function, so he might learn. Several people came for meetings, a supplier, the representative of a firm I sell to and a fellow about our new contract . . . I had Will sit in on them all. He listened with a keen attention, Miss Westallen, and asked me a great many questions afterwards. His interest was rewarding, I must admit. Tomorrow I plan to show him the jewellery workshop, then on Wednesday I thought he could go out with my associate Mr Branden when he visits another jewellery firm. He must make himself useful, of course, but he will not get an overview of the business by sitting in my office shuffling paper for a month.'

'It sounds splendid,' I tell him. 'Better than I could have imagined.'

'Exactly what we hoped when we first began to conceive of the foundation, in fact,' interjects Mama. 'It is most kind of you, Mr Harper.'

'Well,' he fudges. 'I don't know about that. Merely as, er, a trustee, you understand . . . But the thing is . . .'

'You enjoyed having him,' observes Papa. Always he is a perceptive reader of men. 'It does you credit, Mr Harper. Nothing is more rewarding than nurturing the next generation.' He smiles fondly at his two small girls, who have now crept towards him and are sitting at his feet stuffing their hair ribbons into his socks. He affects not to notice. 'Will you stay for dinner?'

'Sadly I am promised to my aunt tonight, but thank you, sir.' Mr Harper stands and bows.

'Another time.' Papa rises and shakes his hand, then pretends great amazement at his beribboned ankles, sending the girls into gales of giggles.

'Show Mr Harper out, Olive,' Mama instructs me, with a meaningful look.

I raise my brows haughtily and stand with great state. 'I was about to, Mama. Mr Harper, thank you for calling and for your report. It's much appreciated.'

I show him out and he looks around the hall with its brightly coloured geometric tiles and the golden sprays of forsythia that brighten the corners. 'A welcoming prospect,' he comments.

'Well, my family welcomes you whenever you wish to call. Goodnight, Mr Harper.'

'Miss Westallen . . . we have known each other some months now. Might you consider calling me Lionel?'

'Well, certainly! So long as you call me Olive.'

'Olive. I wonder . . . would you care to accompany me to dinner in the West End some Saturday evening? I know a very tasteful little place and I believe it would interest you.'

I pause. If I say yes, will I give him the wrong impression? For that matter, what is the right impression? I do like the idea of dinner in the West End. My life of late has been small children and big ideas; some of the more usual pleasures people enjoy have got rather lost in the middle. A dinner is not a marriage contract. I only worry that he may think we are courting; I would not like to lead him down a garden path. But dinner would give us ample time to talk more frankly.

'Thank you, Lionel. That sounds most enjoyable.' He smiles and tips his hat, then disappears into the cold, grizzling night.

Eleven

Pansy

When Pansy awoke the following Thursday, she felt all at sea. If she wasn't to hurry to Mr Ollander's and jump in the cart to Elstree, what on earth was she to do? She felt a little worm of unease in her tummy. Her mother had banned her – not for ever, but for some weeks to come. Pansy had her quest – she just didn't know where to start.

Last Thursday, Eveline had come down in her school dress just as they were finishing their conversation, rubbing sleep from her eyes, blonde curls sticking up every which way. She had left herself time only for a slice of thickly buttered bread and a gulp of milk. 'What's happening?' she'd demanded, sensing the atmosphere.

'Pansy's not going to visit us next week,' Laura had said calmly, clearing their plates and loading up a new one for her younger daughter. 'She's going to leave the Blythes and find something that makes her happy.'

'Oh, thank God!' Eveline had declared. 'You must tell me all about it when I get back from school.' She hugged her sister and Pansy felt the sleepy warmth of her body and the familiar scent of her skin. It tugged her heart back to a blissful remembered childhood but her mother was right. She couldn't go back. She could stay at Garrowgate Hall or she could go forward into the unknown; those were her only two choices.

'I have news too, Pansy. I applied for a job!' Eveline came fully awake then, brimming with excitement. 'I'm going to teach piano to young children at a music school in Camden when I finish school in June. I'll have room and board and I'm going to study music in the evenings so that I can improve and get an even better job one day. We'll talk more later.'

Remembering her lovely day off last week, Pansy sighed. Her mother *and* her sister were both doing a better job of life than she was. She couldn't spend her days in drudgery and resentment any more. It was a terrible choice to make. Very well, she thought now, from the warmth of her bed, if she wasn't cleaning out fireplaces, and she wasn't going home, what could she do with herself? Ahead of her was a day completely unknown.

She went downstairs, feeling she wouldn't mind if she *was* waylaid because at least then her decisions would be made for her. Already she was missing her mother's breakfast. It was too early for a coffee house. She didn't want to spend more time than necessary in Garrowgate Hall so she asked Mrs Andrews, the cook, if she could have some breakfast to take with her. Mrs Andrews grumbled a bit but packed up a few bits and pieces and gave them to her in a string shopping bag. Then Pansy stepped outside into the hush and lightening sky of earliest March. What now?

Pansy decided to do some thinking on the heath while everything was closed and she had nowhere else to go. It was dry and she was warmly dressed; she could have an outdoor breakfast and try to make a plan. The air was fresh and tingling; green shoots were bursting through in great clusters beneath the trees. It was, Pansy acknowledged, a good time for a new beginning. Could she really do it? Break away from all that was familiar and start again – away from John? But dear as he was, Mum was right: one day a week wasn't enough to be happy.

Pansy walked over the scrubby, open heath, all the way to Parliament Hill and decided she'd waited quite long enough for breakfast. She sat on the grass at the top of the hill and investigated the string bag. Bread, cheese, cold ham, apples, a stoppered bottle of apple juice, a piece of meat pie and a crumpet dripping with apricot jam. Bless Mrs Andrews, there was lunch in here, not just breakfast. There was a kind heart beneath her grumbling exterior.

Pansy feasted on the crumpet, then the bread and ham, and pondered. What could a woman *do*? Work in service, work in a shop, or work in a factory. Those answers came easily and held no appeal. Nursing? Pansy had no taste for blood and worse things. Teach, as Eveline was to do, or become a governess . . . ? There weren't many things, really, if you weren't a wife.

She'd recently heard something about office work, women starting to do the job of clerks. She didn't know much about it but she'd heard that men didn't like it when women took their jobs. How was she supposed to *know* if she might like working in a shop, or using a typewriter? Trying things out was the best way, she supposed, but Pansy was twenty-three. It was a bit late to start trying out this and that. Everyone else just got a job and stuck to it if it kept a roof over their head. Then again, everyone else didn't have Laura Tilney for a mother.

She got up and started walking. She could hear church bells rolling across the heath from Hampstead in the west and Highgate just to her east. Somehow it was already nine o'clock. When had Pansy ever spent so long in reverie? Already she felt different. She missed her mother and her brother and sister very much, yet the anger that had boiled inside her for so long was quieting. Perhaps even the *thought* of leaving the Blythes was lessening their hold over her. She was asking herself questions that she probably should have asked years ago.

What made her happy, besides home? John – but she mustn't think of him. Hats. She laughed. Hats weren't any help. She couldn't make a living out of hats. Unless she went to work in a milliner's. Could you make much money there? Perhaps she could find out.

What was it that made her days in Elstree so wonderful? Her family, of course, the good food and that sense of just being herself. Every Thursday, Pansy fed the chickens with Mums, petted Eustacia, visited her old school friend Elsie. After lunch she would go to the nearby farm to see her brother and take him treats from Laura's kitchen. Leaving was the worst part of the day.

Pansy's thoughts darted all over the place, like dragonflies. Congenial company. A sense of being at one with herself, not harried and pulled every which way by folk who were utterly indifferent to her well-being. In what sphere of work might she find those things? Or was it simply a question of finding work that was the least of all evils? She frowned. If she learned to type, how much would it cost? Would she struggle to learn? She hadn't minded school but she hadn't shone either; she'd never really tried. She'd been complacent, she supposed. What was she capable of? Oh, *why* had she spent so many years pining after John? If she was only married now, she wouldn't have to think about any of this!

Lucky Rowena, not to have to trouble herself. When *she* was ready, she merely had to click her fingers and a husband would appear to take care of everything for her – dropping into her hands like a ripe plum.

Twelve

Rowena

Having Lethbridge here, seated behind an enormous easel, instead of Bartek balancing his sketchbook on his knee, is a sorry contrast, but thanks to Bartek, I am bolstered through the week.

Lethbridge tried his old trick with the hair ornament on the first day, but I was prepared and moved away from any unwelcome touch. Seeing the disappointment on his face, I held his eyes in a challenging manner. At least, I thought I did; I had never been challenging before so I may not have achieved quite the effect. Perhaps not, for he tried it again.

'Mr Lethbridge,' I said firmly. 'I think that is quite unnecessary, don't you?' And that was the end of the unpleasantness.

During our sessions we converse little and I insist on a chaperone each day. Verity is scarce – Mr Lethbridge has neither looks nor novelty value to attract her. A different maid each day performs the duty: the timid blonde maid, then the tough-looking one whom I've heard speaking in a shockingly low-class way when she thinks none of the family can hear, then the sulky chestnut-haired one . . . She sits in my eyeline but does not look at me. I wonder if she is miserable. My heart sinks now when I see her. I sometimes wonder if she dislikes me.

The hours have passed surprisingly quickly. I've been miles away, in 1840s Paris with Mimi and Rodolpho. In the evenings I go to bed early, telling Mother it is to look my best for the sittings. In truth, it is to read whatever I can understand of the book Bartek lent me. I dip in and out of it; my French does not permit a thorough reading, yet I understand more than I thought I might. It helps that the story is loosely familiar to me: I saw *La Bohème* at the Royal Opera House just a few months ago. A brand-new opera is a must in our circles, even if we are not fond of music or theatre; even if we are bored to tears, we must be able to say we have seen it, we must have an opinion to contribute at social gatherings. All *I* said about it was, 'very powerful,' and, 'quite tragic'. Hardly ground-breaking insights but I don't suppose anyone expected more from me.

Now, reading Bartek's book, I find myself fascinated by these glimpses into a whole world of people who live outside polite society – by *choice*! Choosing art instead of respectability, following their inclinations rather than the rules. Actually, I find it rather scandalous, rather alarming.

If a slice of fortune falls into their hands, you will see them at once mounted on the most ruinous fancies . . . never finding sufficient windows to throw their money out of. Then when their last crown is dead and buried . . . hunting from morn till night that wild beast called a five-franc piece.

And this is only the preface! I could never live like that. I could never endure such a hand-to-mouth existence. I shudder. How do poor people *manage*? The phrase 'ruinous fancies' haunts me.

Soon it is Saturday morning and I awake in the grey dark of earliest March. I feared I might sleep through the appointed hour but I slept only fitfully all night. My chance to send my apologies in a note has been and gone. I am committed now.

It is strange to dress myself but I manage passably well. A glance in the mirror shows me an unusual Rowena, dressed for once in the plainest garb I own – I do not wish to draw attention to myself – but a face glowing with . . . well, I do not want to put a name to it.

As I expected I pass none of my family on the way out but see three or four maids. I would never have imagined so many of them to be early risers and already they are hard at work! They look so surprised to see me that they don't even murmur a good morning. I try to look as if this is perfectly ordinary behaviour for me.

Mrs Clarendon, the housekeeper, is in the hall so I swerve into the ballroom to let myself out by the terrace doors. The maids would never say anything to Mother but Mrs Clarendon might. To my surprise, the doors are unlocked and, when I step quietly outside, I see one of the footmen doing some strange exercises on the terrace.

He is clad in just breeches and a loose shirt and he is jumping his legs backwards and forwards whilst supporting himself on his hands then standing up and reaching for the sky before doing it all over again. He sweats and gasps, completely unaware of my presence. I have never seen a man carrying out such an activity and I'm transfixed for a moment by his sheer strength, by the way his muscles are working, then I realise it is not good manners to watch someone unawares.

'Good morning, Henry,' I say since I cannot leave without walking straight past him. I do not know his actual name; we call all the footmen Henry, it makes it easier for Mother to keep track. It's the young, good-looking one, who has brown hair, blue eyes and a sweet smile. He practically explodes with shock, staggering for a minute and almost losing his balance. He gazes at me with something like horror.

'Miss Blythe! Good God! I mean, I beg your pardon. Good morning. I had no idea you would be coming this way or I would not have . . .'

In a trice he's transformed from a powerful being concentrating on his own physical strength to a footman, concentrating on me. Even though his hair drips sweat into his eyes and he's not wearing livery, his whole manner and posture are suddenly deferent, dignified. I had never thought how different a footman's demeanour might be in his private moments. I wonder if the change comes easily.

'Please don't apologise, Henry. I should apologise for startling you. I'm rarely out at this hour.'

'Is everything all right, Miss Blythe? Can I assist you with anything?'

'Thank you, no. I'm simply meeting a friend for an early walk. I've often been told these are the best hours of the day.'

'That they are, Miss Blythe.'

'Henry, what . . . are you *doing*, if I might ask?'

'My morning calisthenics, Miss Blythe. Your mother requires us to keep a certain . . . shape.' He blushes scarlet and I smile. I'm glad I'm not the only one who wears my embarrassment for all to see.

'My mother? So this is a requirement of your job?'

'Yes, Miss Blythe.'

'And do you do it every morning?'

'Every other, Miss Blythe.'

'Well, I commend you. It looks very . . . strenuous.'

'Thank you, Miss Blythe.'

'Well, I must go. If I keep my friend waiting, she will start the day cross.'

He smiles that soft smile and it makes me want to smile back. 'That wouldn't do, miss. Have a good day.'

'Thank you. Oh, Henry? Don't mention to Mrs Clarendon that you saw me. My parents worry about me going even the shortest distance alone.'

'Of course, Miss Blythe. Do you have far to go? May I escort you?'

I think being seen with a lightly clad, dripping male of a 'certain shape' would be more damaging to my reputation than being seen alone, or with Bartek. So I decline and hurry on my way. If I'm not mistaken, I can feel him watching me go.

I have never been out so early and never walked through Highgate without a companion before. There is such a hush in the streets and not a soul to be seen; I fear the silent windows are watching me! I feel exposed and nervous but tell myself not to be silly. This is a very genteel area and many people enjoy an early morning stroll. As I approach the heath, how I hope he is there . . .

And he is, of course, his face lighting up when he sees me. I feel suddenly shy, but oh, how glad I am that I've come. The air is invigorating and sweet, the heath quiet and empty. Bartek shakes my hand, perfectly formal and proper, and it gives me a little thrill. 'Thank you for to come, Miss Blythe. I am very happy to see you. The portrait, it is done?'

'All done, thank heavens. I enjoyed it when *you* were . . . explaining the artistic process and so forth, but Mr Lethbridge is not so informative. Two weeks is a long time to sit still all morning.'

'Yes. Very long. Pleasure for me and Mr Lethbridge to gaze on beauty, but not for the beauty herself, I think.'

I dip my head, feeling the rush of colour in my face. He thinks I'm beautiful! Well, so does everyone, but I'm gladder of it when Bartek says it.

We walk a little and he points out things I have never seen on my many summer promenades with Verity: a native crab apple tree and then one that is a wildling – he tells me that is a tree growing wild but seeded from the pip of a domestic apple. I like the word 'wildling'; I had never heard it before. I think that Bartek is a human wildling. He points out a bird's nest high in the branches of a tree and some fresh yellow-green spears shooting forth among the dull brown foliage. Daffodils, for new beginnings.

'You know this place well, Bartek. Better than I, and you a newcomer!'

'When I arrive in new place, I like to explore, to see every detail, little and precise. The painter in me, I think. But also the explorer. Get to know a new place is to have . . . relationship with it, yes?'

'Yes, I suppose it is.' I think of the dearth of exploring I have done in new places. When we summer in France we simply replicate our exact Highgate life there but with better weather. Perhaps next time, *I* shall explore a little.

Bartek asks me what I thought of the book and I'm glad I could understand enough to pass comment. 'I found it fascinating,' I say truthfully. 'A world entirely different from my own, values and characters I never encounter in real life. In fact, it seems utterly fantastical to me, but it is autobiographical in theme, I believe you said.'

'Yes, and I too think some of those thoughts, admire some of those attempts to live more good, more free.'

'But, Bartek, some of the characters hold very extreme positions. Do *you* think it is better to starve than to be part of society?'

He laughs a deep belly laugh. 'I would not tether my soul for to be secure. But I do not hope to be poor always. I wish to be success at art, like maestro. I hope there is way to combine to be true to self, and to have certain . . . comfort. I do not wish to die in attic.'

I smile. 'I'm glad to hear it.'

Unbidden, I think of Olive Westallen. She certainly could not be further from starving in a garret, yet she shakes off convention when it suits her; she seems to make things up as she goes along so that her life is the way she wants it to be instead of the way everyone else would have it be. Surely she knew, when she adopted that little girl from the gutters, that it would prevent her ever from marrying? I wonder if she simply didn't care, or if she did care but went ahead anyway. Bartek, the sulky maid, Henry, Olive: I have never wondered so many things about so many people before.

We walk and talk until I must go back, before my absence is noticed. It is only as we take our leave that I realise I've forgotten the book, the whole purpose of the meeting. We arrange to do the same thing next Saturday and I promise I will not forget again.

Thirteen

Olive

The following Monday, Mabs and I decide to squeeze in a quick lunch together. It isn't often we can do so; the office is busy and needy folk drift in and out all day long. It isn't pleasing that so many are in need, but it is pleasing that they find their way to us when they are.

We prefer for one or both of us to be there for them; Mr Gladstone is an excellent man but he is very senior, and can appear a little stern. Often the people who come to us need a great deal of encouragement. They are hesitant at taking this unusual step, for daring to entertain the idea that anyone or anything might help. Mabs and I offer a softer, more reassuring welcome, Mabs even more than I, because I am older and grander than she. I first met Mabs when she had just left her dire home situation to work for a local family; there she spent a great deal of time with the youngest daughter, Ottilie. I befriended Ottilie when she rescued Clover from a tight scrape up a tree, and Mabs followed soon after. My life has been immeasurably improved by knowing them both. Mabs's speech is a hundredfold better since we met but the accent of her childhood in the slums of Saffron Hill still hovers and she can accentuate it when she wishes. This is reassuring to the people we help.

But March is here and although it is still bitter cold, the air is diamond-bright and the morning has been quiet. The temptation to go out is great; spring lures us. Then my friends Julia and Jem call in, an unusual pleasure since Julia does not go about a great deal. She is a divorcee, and spurned by many of the self-righteous of Hampstead, so she has developed the habit of living quietly. Jem, Mabs's brother, is a bright boy of ten. Julia is fascinated by the work of the foundation and has come to see for herself, Jem determined to join her, that he may see his sister at work.

'I never thought it, mind, Mabsy,' he says, standing back and viewing her at her desk with an air of a gallery-goer inspecting a great painting. 'Look at you. Proper toff. Who'd have thought it back in the day?'

'Who indeed, Jeremiah?' I agree. 'Your sister is achieving great things and you shall too!'

As we chat, we decide that they will stay for a while so that Mabs and I can have our lunch. Mr Gladstone will be happy to have someone to talk to any comers while he continues his paperwork and I trust Julia and Jem as I would my own family. So the two of us head out into the throng of Euston. It is pleasing to step into a coffee house where we order sandwiches and spend a pleasant half hour gossiping. It is long since we did this.

The first subject of the gossip is myself: Mabs demands to know what is going on with Mr Harper.

'Going on? Nothing is going on, young Mabel.'

She laughs and bites into her ham sandwich. 'You can't fool me, Olive. I've seen the way he looks at you. And you look too, though you're more careful about it than he is.'

I take my time before answering, procrastinating with a bite of my own sandwich – cheese – and think about what to tell her. 'You know my reservations about him, Mabs,' I say when I have swallowed it. 'He was so dreadfully disapproving about Clover. And then that business with Rowena Blythe.'

'But you like him anyway?'

'I like him, of course. Not as a suitor, I couldn't entertain that, not after everything. And yet I've agreed to have dinner with him.' I frown. It sounds inconsistent, put like that, and usually I am anything but.

She grins. 'Dinner, eh? That sounds nice!'

'I hope and trust it will be. But, Mabs, am I doing the wrong thing? We shall be unchaperoned. We are simply two colleagues, friends, wishing to discuss all the matters that we otherwise have no time to discuss. But how will it appear?'

'When did you ever care about that, Olive? He knows you. He won't expect anything just because of a dinner. I'm sure it's fine. I do like Mr Harper. I know he ain't . . . isn't perfect, but who is?'

'Well, me.' We laugh. She knows I'm joking; my faults are legion: headstrong, stubborn, overambitious, meddling, quick to scorn those who do not think for themselves like Rowena Blythe . . .

'Well, obviously, you. But you could be great friends, the two of you. I know he had a shock about Clover but he thought again, didn't he, and admitted he was wrong. That's something.'

I nod and fiddle with my coffee spoon, pursing my lips. 'It's Rowena Blythe, isn't it?' says Mabs, who knows me well. 'You're still stinging about that. I understand that. It wasn't his finest hour, that's for sure. I still can't believe a smart man like Mr Harper got pulled in by her.' She tuts. 'Just because she's pretty!'

'Oh, she's more than pretty. She's a siren, a goddess, nectar to bees, the moon to the tide, the star to every wandering—'

'Olive. She's human. She's a woman, that's all, just a very, very pretty one. Does he mention her ever? Surely there's nothing between them now?'

'I don't know what happened and I don't care to. But no, I do not believe Rowena Blythe features in the life or thoughts of Mr Harper now.'

'It's her birthday soon, Lou told me.' Mabs's friend Lou is a servant in the Blythe home, Garrowgate Hall.

I sigh. 'Yes, in a couple of weeks. Then the papers will be full of her for another week, feting her beauty, her grace, her poise . . .'

'Lou says the mother's giving her grief about naming a husband. There's gossip at the house that she'll announce an engagement any day now.'

'Well, she's of the age, I suppose, and there'll be no shortage of willing swains.'

'I wonder what it's like, being her,' Mabs muses. 'How will she pick someone? Will she just go for the richest? Or don't that matter so much when she's so rich herself? She's so perfect and polished it's hard to imagine her having a laugh with someone or giving them a hug.'

'I have no idea how Rowena Blythe thinks, or even if she does,' I snip. Then I repent. We had a short conversation at the ball last summer, and it was less uncomfortable than our encounters usually are. She asked to meet Clover and Angeline and for a few minutes I saw a softer, smiling Rowena that I almost thought I could like. Then Verity Crawford claimed her and she was gone.

Fourteen

Rowena

My birthday is approaching fast and I'm not in the mood for a big party. But Mother insists upon one and it must be at the house; the new portrait will be with us by then and she wants to show it off. Mr Lethbridge chose the silver dress in the end and Mother has grudgingly admitted that it is spectacular against the dark backdrop of the grand staircase.

She draws up an impressive guest list and shows it to me more as a courtesy than for my approval. I suggest inviting Mr Lethbridge and Bartek, since they are responsible for the portrait, but Mother says it would not be appropriate, that she couldn't bear to have 'people of that sort' in her house. Verity, who is with us at the time, eating chocolates, agrees with her.

'What *are* you thinking, Ro, dear?' she tinkles, as if I'm simply too, too silly. Then she is distracted by the appearance of a blonde-haired maid. 'Oh, girl,' she trills, 'I've dropped some crumbs, come and sweep them up.' She has done nothing of the sort – Verity would never allow the smallest flake of chocolate to escape her – but she delights in seeing staff scurry towards her to do her bidding. I turn back to Mother.

'But, Mother, one or other of them was here every day for the last two weeks!'

'Yes, Rowena, but they were being *paid*.'

On the morning of my second early heath walk with Bartek, the terrace door is bolted and there is no sign of Henry. Cherry blossoms bloom in great pink clouds all through Highgate; cherry blossom for impermanence. The air is truly spring-like now, though cold, and there is a brightness that gilds everything. I'm not sure if it's the March sunlight or Bartek. It's wonderful to see him again and I remembered his book this time. I felt mortified all week that I forgot it. I still remember my great-aunt Althea – a terrifying crone whom I haven't seen since I was a child, to my relief and hers – saying to me once, 'Nothing happens by chance, Rowena,' and I shrink from myself. I give it back to him at once and he slips it into his satchel.

'Thank you, Miss Blythe. I am glad for to share with you.' But he looks solemn today and after a while I ask him what's wrong. He sighs.

'Miss Blythe.' He looks at me with a universe of adoration in his eyes. 'We always knew we could not continue for to do this. I should not have asked you; the risk is great for you, I think. Yet I feel sad to think goodbye. In one month I leave London. I will not see you, and this makes me sad.'

'It makes me sad too,' I say, unable to be coy or appropriate. I meet his eyes. 'Will you go far, Bartek?'

'I go to Cumbria. My place with Lethbridge, it ends. I apply for, and am granted, apprenticeship with very great artist of north of England. I will paint mountains and lakes and this is new for me. Excellent chance.'

I swallow. So very far away. Around me, daffodils are opening; they nod and sway. Inside, I feel as if something in me might stretch to breaking. 'It sounds wonderful,' I say, after a deep breath. I cannot ask him to pass up this opportunity and stay here for me when I can offer him nothing. I cannot be selfish.

This too, I fear, is new for me. 'You will learn so very much and paint such exquisite landscapes.'

'Yes. Many reasons for excitement. Only one thing missing, Miss Blythe. But perhaps I should not say.'

'No. But I'm glad you did. We are an ill-starred pair but it is comfort at least to know that you . . . feel as I do.' Would I have said that if he weren't going away? His leaving is dreadful, but it frees me.

His eyes burn with green fire. He takes my gloved hand and kisses it. 'Beautiful Rowena, you have given me so much. Such memories and now kind words.' He bows again, that same courtly bow that struck me the first time we met. I feel utterly woebegone. This new doorway that opened up in my life, letting in light and fresh air, is to close far too soon. But perhaps it is better this way. My path is set after all.

'Miss Blythe, I have in my heart a question. I will ask it. You said once that your favourite flower is lilac. When you tell me, I do not know this word so when I leave, I look up. I know special place, a place you would adore. I would beg you to give me, just once, an afternoon. And I will show you the most beautiful thing. If you say no, I understand. I should not ask.'

He should not. And yet, I cannot resist. Foolish girl. But to see a 'beautiful thing' with Bartek – a thing he has conjured in a daydream when we were apart. No, I cannot resist.

It must be April for the lilacs. The Greeks call them *Paschalia*, for Easter, a pretty name. We arrange a date then return to our lives. I go home and lay the groundwork for my afternoon with Bartek. I tell everyone that I'm going to meet Susanna Heatherton, an old school friend of mine. Susanna moved two years ago to Derbyshire. According to *my* tale, she is in London for just two days and begs to steal me away for an afternoon. I do not know where we are going; it is to be a surprise, somewhere beautiful that I will love. I write to Susanna and receive a reply so that, when asked, I can convey truthful news of my old friend and the arrangements seem real. Whoever would have imagined me so gifted at deception?

My birthday arrives and with it Mother's grand party. It is lavish and formal and exhausting. The portrait is much admired. Verity is more enthusiastic about the party than I am and begins every sentence with, 'When Lethbridge painted *me* . . .' I cannot say I truly *enjoy* the evening, not the way I enjoy talking to Bartek or even the brief conversation I had with Henry that morning. Bless him, whenever I see him now, he blushes. I wonder if he has a small crush.

I cast about in my mind for other conversations or situations I've similarly enjoyed, and I'm appalled to find there aren't many. One instance was at the Westallen Foundation ball last August. I was being pinioned, conversationally speaking, by a particularly dull admirer when Olive Westallen came and rescued me. Then I found myself in a new discomfort, for our previous conversations had ever been hard work. But this time I asked after her adopted daughter, who was at the ball with her little companion. Olive took me to see the children; they were playing on the terrace under a climbing jasmine and they made me a crown. It was all rather charming and I envied Olive, for a moment. I said nothing of it to Verity, but I often thought of that odd little tableau over the subsequent weeks and it made me smile.

At my birthday party I wear a cobalt-blue gown with dramatic scarlet trim and I receive my ninth proposal of marriage, this time from Sir Charles Herrangrove. Sir Charles Herringbone, Verity calls him. I'm not sure that I wish to be Rowena Herringbone, but I must admit that Charles is perfectly nice.

He is suitable and pleasant and I would have a very good life, the sort of life I already know, at which I excel and in which I am a prize. He has all the attributes about which I'm supposed to care, and has no disconcerting mannerisms. He would do quite as well as anyone and I *must* pick!

So instead of my usual appreciative but flat refusal, for which I'm famous, I believe, I ask to think about it for a week or two. He looks so delighted one might think I had said yes there on the spot.

I have questioned so much about my life lately, in a repetitive, niggling sort of a way that creeps into my idle moments and unsettles them. Already I have broken the rules twice and plan to do so again. It is reckless and misguided and I am neither of those things. Yet I cannot forego my afternoon with Bartek. I will not accept Charles until that is over, for I could not promise myself to one man then keep an assignation with another. It is not so much to ask for myself. I will go walking with Bartek, somewhere beautiful, for three or four hours. Then he will leave my life for ever and I will marry Charles and keep that memory tucked away secretly, like a rose petal in a book.

Fifteen

Pansy

Pansy spent the next couple of Thursdays at The Garden of Eden. She knew it wasn't what her mother had had in mind, but she couldn't really think of anything else to do. When she first told Hipólito and Mr Ollander, with some indignation, about the quest her mother had set for her, they were sympathetic.

'This is why women marry!' she had concluded at the end of her woebegone tale. 'It's *hard* to find a purpose.'

Mr Ollander had agreed that life was very hard for women without a husband. Hipólito said he'd marry her himself except that it would create a barrel-load more problems for both of them.

Working in the shop was a pleasant way to pass the time, but only because she knew Mr Ollander and because it was all new. As she wrapped jars of glowing peaches or bottles of rare liqueur in fine sheets of muslin, as she rang each purchase through the till and noted the sale in Mr Ollander's ledger, she was under no illusion that she would find it fascinating day after day. It was *something* to report back to her mother when she saw her but she would need to think of something else to try soon.

This particular Thursday, when Mr Ollander turned the shop

sign from *Open* to *Closed* at lunchtime, she took off her apron and asked him if he could spare her that afternoon. 'It's too nice working here with you,' she explained. 'Too nice and too easy. I've learned a lot but . . .'

'But you won't learn much more,' he finished for her. 'And a career in fine edible goods isn't where your heart lies. You can work here whenever you like, Pansy, but there must be something else you can do with your time. Have a little lunch with me before you go?'

Pansy accepted happily; lunch at The Garden of Eden was a fine thing: flaky cured ham and salty Caerphilly cheese; red grapes as large and sweet as apricots, with satin skin that burst beneath your teeth, and all washed down with a sparkling elderflower drink. They sat in the little room at the back of the shop.

'No Hipólito,' frowned Mr Ollander as they finished their meal. 'He's usually back by now. I don't remember that he had any extra errands to run today. Perhaps they're giving him lunch at The Tree of Life.'

'Hipólito does love a good chat,' agreed Pansy, leaving with some reluctance. She took a long, circuitous route around the village in search of inspiration. If no other ideas presented themselves, she would buy a newspaper and settle herself in a coffee house to scan the situations vacant.

But when Pansy passed the police station, she saw a surprising thing outside: the cart from The Garden of Eden, with Steed stamping in its shafts. Pansy frowned. What was Hipólito doing in the police station? She hesitated, nervous to go inside. It was perfectly possible that Hipólito had legitimate business there and she didn't want to intrude on his privacy. But she had a bad feeling about it.

Reluctantly, she went to the open door and peered inside.

On the outside, the police station was tall and severe, with an imposing chimney on the roof that could be seen above the rooftops for some distance around. On the inside it smelled of bricks, vinegar and fear. And there was a commotion going on. Pansy hovered on the threshold, wary of running into a ruckus of hardened criminals, but instead she saw two constables holding a struggling man in handcuffs and a small boy standing by, yelling; his voice was so high-pitched and anxious she could hardly make out his words. The man in handcuffs, she saw with a shock, was Hipólito.

'Hipólito!' cried Pansy without thinking. 'Whatever's happened?'

The hubbub subsided and everyone stared. Even the boy stopped shouting and gazed at her with wide eyes, his dark hair standing up in a shock.

'Pansy?' The relief and hope in Hipólito's voice tugged at her heart.

'You know the culprit, miss?' asked one constable in a nasal voice, full of disdain. Suddenly Pansy remembered a thing that never made an iota of difference when they were at The Garden of Eden: Hipólito was black. Lots of people, maybe most, would hate him just for that. And they wouldn't think much of *her* if they thought she was his friend. Her head spun for a moment but she knew she wouldn't be much help to Hipólito if she let her fear get the better of her. Oddly, she thought of Rowena Blythe and drew on everything she knew of her. She stepped forward, head high.

'I demand to know what's happening,' she said in a clear voice. 'I know this gentleman and I can assure you he is no common criminal to be arrested. There must be some mistake.' *Gracious, I even sound a bit like her*, she thought, congratulating herself briefly. It wasn't often Pansy wanted to be like Rowena.

'I don't see no gentleman, miss. This darkie was found
robbing and beating this child.' The other policeman, plumper
than his colleague, was perspiring from the struggle.

The boy started wailing again. 'He *weren't*, miss, he *weren't*
robbing me, it were another feller. I keep tellin' 'em but they
won't *listen*!'

'This can't be,' said Pansy. 'I know him and I can vouch for
his character. He would no more set upon a young child than
I would!'

'How would a young lady know an unsavoury sort like this?'
asked the thin one with the pinched, narrow nose. 'You one
of Mrs Foggarty's girls?'

Pansy gasped. Mrs Foggarty was a notorious name in the
north of London. She ran a brothel not three miles from
Highgate, near the canals. The only reason Pansy had heard
of it was because of servants' gossip; you often heard of maids
dismissed from Garrowgate Hall for some minor infraction
who ended up working at Mrs Foggarty's because, without a
reference, it was that or starve. The implication that she might
be a . . . that the only way she might know someone like
Hipólito was because he would . . . It made her head spin.

But she thought of Rowena again and spoke as crushingly
as she dared. 'How *dare* you? Since when did the police force
insult ladies? We must clear up this mess. I've told you already,
I can vouch for Mr Cruz. And it sounds as if the boy is saying
the same thing. Is that right, child?'

'*Yes*, miss. Me name's Jem, miss. I was set upon an' robbed,
they got that right, only it weren't this feller, it were some
other one. Only *he* run off and this one 'ere, he were passin'
an' he stopped to see me right. Then the peelers come along
and think it's him what done it! He was '*elping* me!' he
concluded, turning again to the constables.

'I don't understand,' said Pansy. 'If the victim of the crime has told you this man is not responsible, why do you insist on . . . on insisting that he is?' Here her Rowena words and her Rowena manner deserted her. It was simply too frustrating and frightening. She felt as if she were in a world turned upside down.

'Sirs, you have no case against me,' said Hipólito in a respectful voice. 'This will stand up in no court. I have done nothing wrong and I do not stand accused.'

'He don't!' shrieked the boy. 'He don't stand accused!'

'But we can teach you a lesson all the same,' said the second constable, the tubby one. 'A night in a cell will teach you to be out and about in a smart cart you probably stole, in a nice neighbourhood where no one wants to see the likes of you.'

'That's ridiculous!' cried Pansy. 'It's his job to drive the cart. He works for Mr Ollander of The Garden of Eden. I'm sure *you* know it,' she added to the rounder of the two. 'Shall I go there and fetch him? He has a solicitor, you know.'

The constables exchanged a glance. They dropped Hipólito's arms and looked at Pansy. 'Why would a gent like Mr Ollander have one of this type working for him?'

'That's his business. Would you like to ask him?' They hesitated. 'I assure you Mr Cruz is his assistant. But if you can't believe an employee of the *Blythes*, I suppose you—' That was the name that did the magic trick.

'All right, all right,' said the nasal one. 'You'll sign a statement, I suppose? That he works for Ollander and that you work for the Blythes?'

'*Yes!*' cried Pansy. 'Just let him go.'

Ten minutes later the paperwork was done. Pansy, Hipólito and the small boy Jem were standing on the pavement outside the police station, getting wet in a purposeful grey shower.

'Thank you, Pansy,' said Hipólito in a low voice.

'You're welcome,' she replied distractedly. It was hard to comprehend that she'd just waged a battle with the police and won – that was quite gratifying – and that she'd witnessed what she had. There was nothing gratifying about that. 'Hipólito, why . . . ?'

'You know why.'

'Yes, I suppose I do. Only it's . . .'

'*I* don't understand why,' piped up Jem. 'They didn't seem a bit interested in finding the villain what really robbed me. Now that ain't right.' He pushed his wet hair furiously out of his eyes and it stood up in a crest.

'No, young sir, it isn't,' said Hipólito. 'I thank you for speaking on my behalf.'

'Well, it was only fair! *Why* was it, sir, if you don't mind me askin', that they treated you like that?'

Hipólito and Pansy exchanged a glance. 'It's how I look,' said Hipólito simply, 'because I am different.'

Jem nodded wisely, then scrunched his narrow nose sideways. 'Wait, that can't be all. I mean, I know some folk – most folk – don't like people that are different. But this was serious! It oughtn't matter that much.'

'You're right. Yet many people think it does, and when enough people think something it becomes . . . not true, but solid.'

Jem pondered this, kicking at a lamp post as he did so. 'I don't like that,' he said. 'I'm glad you come along, miss. They wasn't listening to either of us.'

Pansy began to gather her thoughts. The boy had been robbed, they'd said. He was too young to be out on his own after something like that. He talked roughly but he was well dressed and clean; clearly somebody cared for him. And it was raining.

'Where do you live, Jem? I'll take you home. Are you hurt? Were your losses very great? You must have had a terrible shock.'

'I'm all right, miss. I live over in 'Ampstead, I wouldn't want you goin' out of your way. I didn't have much, if I'm honest. Only a few pennies in my pockets. 'E took those, and the other thing was me mistress's bonnet. She'd sent me over 'ere to fetch it for 'er. Ever so disappointed she'll be.'

'Will she be angry?' asked Pansy, thinking of the Blythes, who took a dim view of errands gone wrong, no matter where the fault lay. You could be punished for something like a stolen bonnet. 'You won't get in trouble, I hope?'

'Who, me? Lord, no, miss, she'll be worried about me is all. I just feel bad I couldn't 'ang on to it. She can't afford another, I don't 'spect.'

Pansy thought. 'Perhaps something can be done. Would you like me to come with you to the hat shop now and see if they can help? And then I insist on taking you home. You're too young to walk alone after such a horrid event.'

'Would you, miss? I'd be ever so grateful – for the 'at shop, I mean. I thought maybe I should talk to them but I didn't know if they'd believe me.'

'Come to the store when you've finished,' said Hipólito, 'and I'll drive you both to Hampstead, then bring you home, Pansy. It's too far to walk.'

'I think you've been out and about quite enough for today,' said Pansy. 'But we'll come to the store, yes, and check you're all right.'

Hipólito climbed into the cart and saluted Jem, who saluted back, then drove off, snapping the reins and disappearing at a stiff pace. 'Poor Hipólito,' murmured Pansy. She knew why he didn't work in the front of the shop but now she understood a little of what it was like to be Hipólito living in this world. Because his interactions were limited, she'd only ever seen him around people who liked and trusted him. This was something quite different. Then she shook herself. She had a child to look after.

An hour later, Mr Ollander was driving them to Hampstead. Their trip to Esther Gray's exquisite millinery had been successful. With Pansy's support, Jem's story was believed and the woman behind the counter said that her milliner was working on another very similar piece. She would sell it to Jem at half price if his mistress was willing. Pansy had spent long hours gazing into the window of that very shop, she realised, and a modest amount of her money inside it. Perhaps the sympathetic proprietor would allow her to work an afternoon or two here, as Mr Ollander had done. Jem was looking pale and tired so she hadn't asked. But she would come back next week.

At The Garden of Eden, Hipólito had already recounted the day's events to his employer. Mr Ollander closed the shop to take Jem home. He ordered Hipólito to rest, eat and collect himself after a highly unpleasant day.

It was fun riding around the curving edge of the heath, watching through the trees for glimpses of Parliament Hill or picnicking parties. Steed kept a lively place, tossing his mane as though shaking out the frustrations of the day. Jem told them that he lived in the Vale of Health, a place Pansy had never heard of and was very oddly named, she thought, but Mr Ollander knew it and soon they were drawing up in a quiet crescent at the very edge of the heath. Jem leapt out of the cart while they were still scrambling down and raced up the steps of a tall white house. He barrelled inside hollering, 'Mrs M! Mrs M! Come quick, there's people to meet. Ain't I 'alf had a day!'

By the time Pansy and Mr Ollander reached the doorstep, a slender blonde woman with a drawn face and sad eyes had appeared. 'But are you all right, Jem? Are you quite all right?' she was asking him.

'Right as rain, Mrs M, no harm done, least said soonest mended an' all that. But that's thanks to these folk.' He waved an arm expansively at his new acquaintances and rattled off a summary of his afternoon's events at great speed. When he reached the part where he'd been robbed, she gasped and pulled him in close to her side. When he explained about Pansy appearing – in his telling much like an avenging angel – she lifted her eyes to the visitors as if noticing them for the first time.

'Thank you,' she said. Pansy thought she sounded like an oboe, resonant and sad. 'Where are my manners? You helped my Jem and I leave you standing on the doorstep. I was just so worried as the hours wore on. Jem is precious to me. Please come in and let me thank you properly.'

But Mr Ollander was anxious to get back to Hipólito and Pansy was exhausted. When this was explained, Mrs M – Mrs Morrow as she introduced herself – took her hands and thanked her again. 'Then please come and visit us at your earliest convenience and allow me to shower you with some home baking. It's the best way I know to show gratitude.'

'Ain't that the truth?' piped up Jem. 'Do come, Pansy. 'Er cherry buns will make you cry they're so good, that's what. Make yer cherry buns, Mrs M, if you want to say a proper thank you.'

Mrs Morrow smiled. 'Indeed I will, and a great deal more besides. You too, Mr Ollander, you're always welcome. And please extend the invitation to your friend too – Mr Cruz, was it? For he helped Jem too.'

That would be something to tell her mother, thought Pansy as they drove off, waving. A new acquaintance, an educated lady. Mrs Morrow intrigued her. For one thing, she was Jem's mistress, yet to see them together was like looking at mother and child. For another, there was a strange, complicated unhappiness written all over her face, yet she seemed warm and caring. Pansy was already looking forward to visiting.

Sixteen

Rowena

The day of my outing with Bartek arrives. My heart is doing strange things. Because I'm supposedly going out with Susanna, I can take trouble over my appearance. I wear my favourite day dress of apricot and cream. I gather some sprigs of lily of the valley from the damp, shady corners of the garden and tuck them into my hair and bodice. I want to wear all the flowers that declare love and passion: tulips, red roses, myrtle, but they are not in season and I would look ridiculous. I content myself with lily of the valley, signifying a return of happiness. What do I hope for? That Bartek will somehow return to me, or that I can find a way to be happy after he has gone?

A slight problem arises when Mother realises that I intend to walk to the heath to meet Susanna. 'You cannot go alone,' she says at once.

'Mother, it's five minutes, seven at most. It is broad daylight.'

'You will take the carriage and Crispin will go with you.'

'*Go with me?* But Crispin will not care to listen to us prattling away all afternoon!'

'Not on your *outing*, just to your meeting point. He can see you safely into the carriage. I can't think why you didn't arrange for Susanna to call at the house. It wouldn't kill her to exchange a polite word with your father and me after all this time.'

'I told you, Mother, she has something planned. Perhaps she will call when she brings me home.' I can feel my cheeks burning so I turn away.

When my brother and I arrive at the gate, I climb out at once. 'You should wait in the carriage, Ro,' he says. 'There's no sign of Susanna.'

'But it's a beautiful spring day! Climb down, darling, and wait with me.' I want Crispin clearly in view when Bartek arrives so he will see my dilemma. How can I get rid of my brother? We wait a few minutes then a smart carriage appears and pulls to a halt a little way down the street.

'That must be her!' Crispin remarks.

But I cannot imagine Bartek in such a grand conveyance. What to do? 'Let's wait and see if she comes out,' I say, and of course she does not. I bite my lip for a minute, then tell Crispin to wait while I go to see the carriage.

'I'll come with you,' he frowns, 'say hello.'

'No, no. She's sure to be in a great haste!' I run off before he can stop me and stand on my toes. Inside the carriage waits Bartek, with a perplexed expression. 'It's Susanna!' I call over my shoulder to Crispin, who is following. 'We must go, goodbye!'

I scramble up indecorously and Bartek reaches across me to slam the door. Even in such a fraught circumstance, his proximity is thrilling and I breathe in involuntarily, dizzy with his warmth and clean, airy smell. He knocks the roof of the carriage, hard, and we jerk into motion. He smiles and sits back.

'Apology. Much speed. Who was gentleman?'

'My brother. Sent to see me safely into my friend Susanna's carriage.'

'Ah. Now I understand. You think he suspects?'

'No, I'm sure he doesn't.' It's true. Dear Crispin would never imagine that I'd lie in order to meet an unsuitable man. My behaviour has always been beyond reproach and something in me feels sad that that has changed.

We don't talk again for the length of the journey, which is about twenty-five minutes. The carriage draws up at the edge of some pretty woodland and Bartek jumps down then comes round to open my door. He helps me out, thanks the driver and the carriage drives off. 'Now we walk,' he says and because we are all alone, he takes my hand. It is utterly blissful. We walk the dappled avenues in the deep green light. It was all for this.

We meander slowly and the smell of the leaves is fresh. 'The carriage, he comes back in three hours,' says Bartek.

'How did you come by it?'

'It belong to a friend who owe me favour.'

'Ah, the best sort of friends,' I say with a smile.

'I want to make journey pleasant for you.'

'It was very comfortable, Bartek, thank you. And this wood is lovely.'

'Yes, but not special place yet.'

A few minutes later he pauses. The air smells even headier, with a scent I immediately recognise. Lilac. My favourite flower. Another that symbolises love. Bartek turns and smiles at me. '*This* is special place.' He leads me forward and I find myself in a grove of seven or eight lilac trees.

I've never been surrounded by so many before. They're in full flower, voluptuous cones of purple made from tiny, delicate stars. The fragrance is sweet and intoxicating, like fairy flowers. I turn around and around, absorbing the wonder of lilac everywhere I look. 'Oh Bartek!' I sigh. 'It is *so* beautiful. Thank you for bringing me.'

He looks down. 'You like. I knew you would like.'

'I love it. After this, I will always imagine heaven to be a lilac grove.'

Bartek reaches into his satchel and spreads a blanket over the soft, emerald grass. We sit upon it shoulder to shoulder. Then he brings out some bread and cheese wrapped in cloth, some perfect, tiny tomatoes and two flasks. 'Water. Cider,' he says, brandishing each in turn. 'Picnic.'

I laugh in delight. 'How charming!' The picnics of my experience were never like this. They always involved hampers and cutlery and champagne and tiny, crustless cucumber sandwiches. I have never tried cider.

We sit and talk of many things while the lilacs bloom around us like blessings. The gentle April sun caresses us and I have never felt more beautiful. Gradually our excited conversation slows and falls silent and we can do nothing but gaze into each other's eyes. When Bartek kisses me, I feel the whole world stand still. It is a physical feeling akin to the sight of sparkles of sunlight playing upon water. My whole body starts to shake. I am the most famous beauty in London, I am twenty-three years old and I have been proposed to nine times. But I have never been kissed. No one would dare! And this is no stuffy drawing room peck, but an opening, a searching, a question and an answer. Without intending it, my hand floats up to rest on his face, in his hair.

He draws back with a sigh and looks at me wistfully, worshipfully. I try to resist his gaze. 'I wish it could be different,' I say. 'With all my heart I wish it.'

'Can it not?'

'What do you mean?'

'My Rowena. My love. Never have I known woman such as you. You make complete my heart. I would speak to your father and if he would not give permission, we could run away . . .'

'Permission?'

'I have no right to ask. I have nothing to offer now. But I

will, Rowena, and I can marry no other woman now I have met you. Angel, I go to Cumbria in ten days. The first part of journey I take by boat on canal. I dream sometimes of you beside me, sitting on deck in late afternoon sun, wind in hair, water shining, of reaching to kiss . . . We would go first to Gretna Green and marry, then on to Cumbria. I am apprentice, you are my wife. Soon, I am great artist and all my fame I share with beautiful wife . . .'

He is talking about marrying me. About speaking to my father and *marrying* me! And I . . . *still* cannot imagine it! But I can imagine the boat, the water, the sun. A true scene of Bohemian life! And I cannot imagine life *without* him any more. But what would it take? We would have to run away, for my father would never, ever consent to this. I would have to sever ties with everyone I love, relinquish my wealth, my position; it would cause a scandal the likes of which even Verity has never heard. It would mean living a life inconceivable to me: poor, romantic, outside the margins of the world as I know it, as alien to me as going to live in a desert. I cannot. I am not adventurous, I am not foolhardy, and I am not tempestuous. I am not a heroine in a romantic novel. I am Rowena Blythe.

All of a sudden, as beautiful as Bartek is, as enchanted as the grove of lilac trees might be, I want nothing more than to go home and pen a note post-haste to Charles Herrangrove telling him I accept. But just as swiftly, the impulse is gone. It would be a grey existence, when here all is lilac, green and gold. Unable to say yes, unable to say no, I stare at Bartek mutely and he kisses me again and I feel every conflict in my body dissolve. Our kiss deepens. Somehow we are lying down and his hands are in my hair and our bodies are stretched out close.

Desire and curiosity are stronger than my rational mind. It is all wrong and yet I have never known such sensual pleasure, the colour and the scent all around us, the taste of his mouth on mine, the feel of his hands running down my body now and, I think, unbuttoning my bodice. My hands are full of wonder as I explore the contours of his chest, so hard and warm and lovely. I am in a dream and the will to stop fades further. What harm can come to me in a dream?

I feel as if we are suspended in mid-air, surrounded by light. A sharp pain beneath my skirts brings me down to earth with a bump and my eyes fly open. How have we got here? How have I let this happen? And yet the pain is gone and now I'm floating on warm waves and I cling to Bartek for I love him and he loves me and this afternoon is all we can ever have . . . I wanted to *feel* something – well, Bartek has made me feel. And he holds me so cherishingly. For a while I am simply cradled in sensation and all is well.

At last he sits up and I do likewise, reassembling my costume, re-pinning my hair. The mundane tasks bring me back to myself and I am hit by the enormity of what I have done. My hopeful lilies of the valley are thoroughly crushed. My heart starts racing, bubbles of fear shooting through me. 'Oh God,' I whisper, breathing rapidly. 'Oh God, I shouldn't have. What have I done?'

He cradles me. 'My darling! Don't be afraid. I do not seduce you for to abandon you. We will leave together. Now we must, is only right thing. We will be man and wife. We will make beautiful life, I make you happy.'

Happy. Yes. He has made me happy, but I do not feel happy now. Tears blur my eyes. How could I have been so *stupid*? How can such an enormous thing have happened almost without my noticing? I have undone my whole life in an instant. I am ruined.

Seventeen

Pansy

For once, the days at Garrowgate Hall passed quickly. Pansy dusted rooms and cleared grates with a new energy. Her thoughts were elsewhere the whole time. They were back in the police station with Hipólito, or they lingered in the Vale of Health. Sometimes they strayed to the hat shop. For once she was glad her work was mundane and repetitive: it allowed her thoughts to wander. By now Pansy could clean Garrowgate Hall in her sleep – and often did so in her dreams.

Caught up as she was in her new thoughts and experiences, she scarcely noticed that Rowena Blythe was quiet and pre-occupied, that Mrs Blythe was more than usually impatient – still no engagement had been announced – and that John was worried. His adored one was under pressure and he poured his heart out to Pansy – under usual circumstances it would have driven her to distraction. As it was, she was too preoccupied with her new experiences to care much about the tedious, tangled emotions at Garrowgate Hall.

She thanked her lucky stars every day that she'd passed the police station when she did. She'd never thought of herself as the heroic type. She'd been an ordinary girl, indifferent to school and with no particular dreams. Then she became a maid. And nothing had happened to her in a long time that made her feel she was worth very much. But standing up to the peelers as Jem had called them – the word made her giggle – had made her feel differently about herself.

Early on Wednesday morning, Pansy was sent to sweep and dust the ballroom, an assignment she would take her time over if John was outside doing his exercises. Their unrequited love, hers and his, and the drama in which it had trapped them had seemed never-ending. But now, at some point, it would end – because of her. She was proud of that. She found the broom and duster and hurried to the ballroom, but she stopped when she saw Rowena Blythe slip inside before her.

Pansy frowned. What *was* that woman doing up and about so early? She suddenly remembered spotting Rowena upstairs a few weeks ago at the same sort of time. Had the indolent young lady of the house developed a taste for early rising? Pansy would bet money that wasn't it. But Rowena wasn't the sort to have a secret. In addition to her great, great beauty, she was annoyingly good. That was why John's adoration exasperated Pansy so; Rowena was nothing but an animated doll, hardly a real girl at all.

Then an awful thought struck her. Had Rowena discovered John's morning exercise habit? He was a good-looking man after all. Had she finally found some sense and noticed how wonderful he was? For a moment, Pansy couldn't move. The thought of some sort of . . . *friendship* developing between John and Rowena filled her with a terror she could hardly fathom. It made her realise that she still loved John, for all that her horizons were expanding and her mood was lighter. Alongside her hopes of moving on, the old story ran persistently on. John loved Rowena, Pansy loved John. One day John would realise he loved Pansy instead . . .

She pushed open the ballroom door, bracing herself for what

she might see. Rowena and John talking? Rowena and John *kissing*? But when she reached the doors, Rowena was already hurrying across the grounds. He was standing looking after her, and the expression in his kind blue eyes made her heart twist.

'John,' she said quietly and he jumped.

'Morning, Pansy. They've got you sweeping again?'

'Yes. Where's she off to then?' Pansy nodded after Rowena, who had disappeared behind some larch trees.

John sighed. 'An early morning walk with a friend, she says. She's done it a couple of times now.'

'Which friend? Verity Blythe?' Pansy snorted at the idea of Verity enjoying an early morning stroll.

'How should I know? Don't tell anyone, will you, Pansy? I don't want her to get into trouble.'

'I won't. Did you get a good morning from her?'

'Yes. Each time she sees me she says, "Good morning, Henry," and gives me the prettiest smile.'

Pansy snorted. Of all the lunacies and indignities of life at the Blythes', the calling of every single footman by the same name because they couldn't be bothered to remember their real names had to be the most absurd. Or the fact that when they employed footmen, they actually measured the circumference of their calves with a tape measure, to ensure they'd show a shapely leg in stockings! 'She looked unhappy this morning, though,' mused John.

Pansy rolled her eyes. 'According to you, she's always unhappy.'

'But recently she's been smiling, sparkling. She was pale this morning, Pansy, and dark around the eyes, as if she's worried.'

'Well, she's welcome to life as the rest of us know it,' said Pansy, her sympathy levels for Rowena Blythe non-existent. 'I'd best get on. And so had you, John Hobbs. Stop mooning.'

She started sweeping, reflecting on how Rowena brought out a hardness to her character that she didn't like. She'd always thought of herself as quite a nice person. Not a saint, but decent enough. But the very thought of Rowena seemed to turn her into a hard-hearted harpy. The sooner she was away from here, the better. She swept briskly, as if sweeping herself into a better life, pushing the dust over to the terrace doors more often than efficiency dictated. John was doing his calisthenics now and the sight of his well-muscled body sweating in nothing but light trousers and a clinging shirt was a nice way to set a girl up for the day.

Eighteen

Rowena

After the momentous day in the lilac grove, Bartek and I *had* to meet again, to discuss what had happened and what, if anything, we would do about it. I am more relieved than I can say that he did not simply shake me off; even so, I've been dizzy with confusion ever since. I haven't slept, I eat only a little, I cannot fully believe what we did. My head throbs ceaselessly and the wheels of my mind turn in fruitless circles. Everyone asks me what is wrong, especially Verity, but I can speak of it to no one but Bartek. This, then, is why chaperones are necessary.

He is adamant that I must leave with him, and truly I can think of no other way forward now. He is my first love. Surely, surely he is my true love, else I would not have done what I did? And how could I marry another man now? I do not know if a man can tell whether a woman has given herself previously or not – but if so, I would be cast off before my wedding night was over! But it's not just the thought of being found out. It's the thought of beginning a new life in a dishonest way.

Although I'm not worldly, there is one thing I do know. I might, now, be with child. I do not know the exact mechanisms and I suppose it *might* be possible to enjoy such intimate acts without a child ensuing – I would guess as much, else there would be a lot more children in the world. But which factors govern whether or not the act reaches that particular outcome I have no idea. I could ask Verity, of course, with her superior knowledge of such matters. I *should* be able to ask Verity, my best friend . . . and yet I cannot. What she would say does not bear thinking about. So, in conscience and to save my own skin, what can I do but go with Bartek?

I do love him. How could I not love a man of such beauty and light, who adores me so completely? If he were a cad who had run away as soon as he had what he wanted from me, I would be in an entirely worse position, forced to stay here with my questions and fears, wondering how and when my shameful secret might be revealed. But he is not. There was never any hesitation on his face about what should come next. And we were in a grove of lilacs, which symbolise love. I try to draw comfort from that. It is how it's supposed to be – two people fall in love, and unite their lives. If only, in our case, it did not mean exile.

Desire is a cruel trick. I have heard of insects that numb their victims in order to feed off them. Desire is just like that: it numbs a person to any sense of reality, intoxicates her, and only when the frenzy is passed is it possible to see how vastly everything is changed. I'm reminded of that phrase from his book: *ruinous fancies*. Bartek is mine.

So I send him a note telling him I shall go with him. On a boat. To Gretna Green and then to Cumbria. How do I plan? What do I pack for a trip like this? For a new life unlike mine in every respect and which must, in the first instance, fit inside a boat. My poor roving brain can find no way to anchor itself. Summer is coming. Will I need cool clothes for the season or is life on a boat cold? I will not be able to carry much. How long will the journey take? How long before I become Mrs Woźniak and free from the fear of an illegitimate child? What manner of county is Cumbria? How long will Bartek's apprenticeship last? Where might we go afterwards? How long before we are settled? My questions are legion and I realise how little I know of the wider world.

There is no point in Bartek speaking to my father and asking for my hand. Father will say no and I will be watched like a hawk. The only way I can leave is by running away. For the sake of one afternoon amongst the lilacs with Bartek, I will break the hearts of everyone I love. I hate myself.

Nineteen

Pansy

The next Thursday Pansy went to The Garden of Eden to check on Mr Ollander and Hipólito. Their little world had settled down again and Hipólito was back to his usual self. Reassured, she went next to the hat shop. The woman who had talked to Jem and Pansy last week – Esther Gray herself, it transpired – was happy to let Pansy work a few hours with her to see how she liked it. She had a busy day ahead and would value a helping hand. Easy!

At first, Pansy felt a shimmer of good luck. Hat shops had always, for Pansy, felt like some sort of promised land. She was surrounded by hats and bonnets of all styles and sizes; everywhere was colour, shape, elegance. Every curve of buckram, every curl of feather, every ornamental rose, was pure delight to Pansy.

When there were no customers, Esther explained as much of the job as she could. Besides the hats, they sold gloves and ribbons, aprons, hoods and handkerchiefs, muffs and buttons – it was a treasure trove! If she went to work in a hat shop, Pansy could expect to do bits and pieces of sewing, hemming the handkerchiefs, for instance, before setting them out for sale, or trimming the gloves. She would roll ribbons and fold aprons.

At first it was all a novelty and Pansy wondered if here might be the key to finding the personal happiness of which her mother had spoken. As the morning progressed, however, her enthusiasm wilted. It wasn't the hats that disappointed; it was the people who bought them. Some of the customers were pleasant but many were haughty and condescending. At one point, two friends of the Blythes came in. They didn't recognise Pansy, which was a blessing; she suddenly realised that the Blythes wouldn't like the idea of their staff working elsewhere in their spare time.

Imagine if Verity Crawford-Blythe came in! *She* would recognise Pansy; all her life she had taken an inordinate interest in all matters Blythe. Pansy hated working with Verity's sharp eyes upon her. She hated the pregnant silence that fell when she walked into a room and Verity and Rowena brought their conversation to a halt as if Pansy were only there to eavesdrop and spy. As much as Pansy loathed Rowena, it was possible that Verity was even worse. *She* mustn't get wind of Pansy's desire to leave until Pansy was good and ready.

Mrs Sedley spent two hours dithering between two bonnets. Pansy lost patience after about twenty minutes but Esther had impressed on her the importance of deference to the customer no matter the circumstances. Mrs Alderton was downright rude, making derogatory comments about the items for sale, impatient when Esther or Pansy fetched something from the storeroom. Eventually she flounced out proclaiming them 'amateurs', declaring she would tell all her friends to shop at Willets in Bayswater hereafter and leaving a strewn rainbow of discarded accessories in her wake. Pansy cleared up, slowly restoring the shop to order, recreating its lovely displays from memory.

'After just a few hours you remember where everything goes,' Esther commented. 'Impressive. You've quite an eye.'

Pansy smiled and didn't say that the hats themselves were the easy bit. She didn't want to spend her days dancing attendance on the wealthy and entitled of Highgate. She could stay at Garrowgate Hall and keep doing that. All in all, Pansy was glad when two o'clock came and she could leave.

'Thank you, Miss Gray, for giving me this chance,' she said when they took their leave. 'I appreciate your trust and encouragement.'

'You've been a boon,' said Esther. 'You can come here any Thursday you wish.'

'Thank you, that means the world to me. But I'm not sure that shop work is quite right for me. I like the hats better than the customers and that's not right, is it?'

Esther shrugged. 'As long as you can disguise it as well as you did today, you'll do fine.'

But Pansy didn't want to spend her life pretending. She'd spent enough of her hours and years swallowing down resentment, pasting a serene exterior over a seething inside. She didn't like the person it was making her.

'You can be a milliner,' suggested Esther. 'Women do, you know – it's one of the few trades open to us. Not everyone thinks it's respectable – just last week there was an article in the *Highgate Courier*: "The Five New Faces of the Old Profession" it was called. Millinery was one of them, if you can imagine that! That aside, you've an excellent eye, it could be something for you.'

Was there *anything* a woman could do without being accused of being a prostitute? It was starting to make Pansy hopping mad. Even so, millinery sounded promising. 'How would I go about it? Where would I start?'

'You'd need to do an apprenticeship. They're quite informal these days, but still, you learn on the job.'

Pansy bit her lip. Even if she worked in a shop to save up the money for an apprenticeship before disappearing behind the scenes for good, it would be hard. Esther had said that shop wages were low, lower even than service and there you had your food and board included. Pansy sighed. 'I'll think about it,' she said. 'Thank you again.'

Pansy strode across the heath. It was a grey day for April but not cold and although the rain threatened, it never quite fell. Her tummy rumbled and she hoped those cherry buns would be all that Jem had promised. She arrived at the Vale of Health shortly after three and climbed the white steps to the dark green door. Jem opened the door and grinned when he saw her. 'You came! And you timed it just right, she's just making shortbread. *And* the chicken pie's almost ready. Come on in!'

Pansy followed him into a high-ceilinged hallway and thence to a parlour with yellow curtains drawn back on either side of French doors that looked out on a long garden screened by trees. Was that silver gleam through the trees a stream or a pond? Everything in the room was old but lovely.

A moment later Mrs Morrow appeared, drying her arms on a towel and smiling. 'Pansy, welcome. We hoped you'd come. I've taken the precaution of cooking everything Jem tells me you must sample, so I hope you've brought an appetite.'

Pansy smiled. 'As a matter of fact I have. Thank you, Mrs Morrow.'

'Call me Julia. And if we're dispensing with ceremony, would you be horrified to join us in the kitchen for lunch? Jem and I only use the dining room when we have company but I'm happy to lay the table if you'd be more comfortable.'

'I'm always comfortable in a kitchen. My mother's is my favourite room of any house anywhere.'

It was the most glorious afternoon. Pansy had only imagined staying an hour or so but time just slipped away. They had a late lunch and talked in the kitchen around a scrubbed table. They went out to the garden and talked over a pot of tea, where an old oak and a couple of chestnut trees held a rustled conversation of their own. When the clouds massed and rain looked probable, they withdrew to the drawing room and talked indoors, with more tea and some of the homemade cherry buns. They were every bit as delicious as Jem had claimed. In the manner of instant friends, they never ran out of things to talk about.

Julia was a divorcee, Pansy learned. She guessed that it wasn't something Julia usually shared with new acquaintances but Jem volunteered the information in his cheery way when Pansy asked about Mrs Morrow's husband, not the most tactful enquiry in hindsight. Julia looked terribly uncomfortable and Pansy would have changed the subject except that Jem, swinging his legs in a wing chair far too tall for him, piped up, 'She's divorced. That means she used to be married but now she ain't. Some folk think bad of a lady for that but *I* don't.' He looked at Pansy a little challengingly.

That would account for the great sadness Pansy sensed about her. She smiled. Julia had a small but stout-hearted defender of her honour. 'Nor do I, Jem. People have altogether too many opinions about women if you ask me. We'd all be a great deal better off if we were just left alone to get on with our lives.'

Jem nodded, satisfied, and took an enormous bite of his bun. 'I'm sorry to hear that,' Pansy said to Julia.

'Don't be. It's for the best, despite the many difficulties it brings. I'm sorry Jem has burdened you with something so personal on our first proper meeting. I've learned to be reticent on the matter but Jem's a straightforward soul, aren't you, Jem?'

Jem nodded. 'I guessed she was a right-thinking sort,' he explained through his great mouthful, jerking his head in Pansy's direction.

'Indeed so. All the same, would you refrain from mentioning it to new acquaintances in future, Jem, dear?'

'Right ho, Mrs M.'

Pansy smiled. She loved the easy accord between them; this was a lovely home. It made Pansy linger and accept more cake than was good for her, reluctant to return to Garrowgate Hall before she had to. When the sun came out again, they thought about returning to the garden but even as they considered it the golden wash in the sky shrank and purpled over. It was one of those changeable days of spring.

Julia asked Pansy about her life at Garrowgate Hall and Pansy found herself confiding about her mother's challenge. She skipped over the reason she'd stayed with the Blythes for so long; she didn't feel like talking about John on such a happy day. Besides, Jem was a little young for tales of romantic anguish. Instead, she confessed how she had truly come to hate her working life and yet felt afraid to leave.

'It feels rather late in life to make such a change. I've always been an ordinary girl, you know? Not beautiful or ugly, not clever or stupid, not adventurous or dull. Just . . . me. Yet my mother seems to think I have some wondrous path before me. I'm afraid she's overestimating me.'

Julia shook her head. 'Do you know that your name means thought?'

Pansy frowned. 'Isn't it just the name of a flower?'

'That too, but the name comes from the French word *pensée*. It means thought. So perhaps you're destined to think deeply about things, differently. After all, who knows you better than your mother?'

'And,' added Jem, between mouthfuls, 'you didn't turn a
hair about Mrs M being divorced. You stood up somethin'
fierce for Mr Cruz last week and not everyone would do
that . . .'

'Jem makes a fair point,' Julia agreed. 'I believe there's more
to you than you think, Miss Tilney.'

It wasn't until the clock in the parlour chimed six that Pansy
remembered that this wasn't where she belonged and she had
to work the next day.

'But come again!' Julia invited her. 'Any Thursday you like.'
Pansy thanked her eagerly and promised to come when she
could. 'Perhaps I should mention a friend of mine,' Julia went
on. 'Her name is Olive Westallen – I have her to thank for
Jem being here with me, in fact – and she runs a charitable
foundation to assist the poor. I know you don't exactly fall into
that category but she does help people learn about work they'd
never otherwise be able to try – which is exactly what you're
trying to do. If you'd like to talk to her, I'd be happy to arrange
it.'

Pansy thanked her effusively. She had heard of Olive
Westallen; everybody had. She was clever and influential. She
was as rich as the Blythes but nice, by all accounts. But the
very best thing of all – she was someone that Rowena and
Verity considered a deadly foe. Pansy could hardly believe her
luck. As she walked back to Highgate, the rain came at last,
soaking all who were abroad in it to the skin, but Pansy didn't
mind. She was going to meet Olive Westallen, and Julia believed
there was more to her than she thought.

Twenty

Olive

On Friday evening, I go to dinner with Lionel. It feels strange to tuck in my little ones and then, instead of sitting downstairs in my house dress with Mama and Papa, to dress in something more formal and wait for his carriage. It's not that I never go out, but it's a long time since I have done anything that could conceivably be classed as courting. Are we? Aren't we? I don't know what to hope for.

He arrives promptly, a mark in his favour. I cannot fathom those who are unable to keep track of time. His carriage is smart and spacious. 'A whole evening to enjoy your company, Olive,' Lionel beams, pulling the door closed behind me. 'Thank you for coming.'

'My company *is* a very great boon, it's true.' I smile. 'I try to bestow it fairly and equitably as part of my charitable works.' I'm making fun of myself and he laughs appreciatively. 'I jest, of course. The pleasure is mine. Tell me about this dining establishment.'

I'm largely unfamiliar with restaurants. I visit a coffee house sometimes for lunch with Mabs. I take Clover and Angeline to a tea room on afternoons when I wish to treat them – their favourite is Astrid's in Hampstead for the pretty bay windows and the pink macaroons. This will be a pleasant adventure.

'In truth, it is more of a supper room.'

'A supper room? Is that not where . . . ?'

I don't know what I'd been imagining. Somewhere quiet and discreet. Perhaps with candlelight. Mr Harper and I talking confidentially. Whereas a supper house, if I am not wrong . . .

'Where everyone sits around a communal table, yes. I assure you, the food is excellent. It's a place that's popular with the workers of the area, in a quarter where there are a great many jewellers.'

'I see!' At once I understand. He wishes me to meet some of his business associates, people who will meet Will and be a part of all he is learning. 'It sounds fascinating, Lionel. I assume I shall meet some of those you've told me about, with whom you have regular dealings?'

'Indeed, yes.' He proceeds to list several names I've heard him mention before and to remind me of their roles. I confess I am a little preoccupied, adjusting to this new prospect before me. It seems, then, that his intentions are *not* romantic. This evening appears to offer a continuation of our working rela-tionship, because he knows what an interest I take in everything pertaining to the foundation's work. I'm not disappointed, but I must rearrange my context.

Micklethwaite's Chop House is rough and ready in appear-ance, the ground floor of one of those old Tudor buildings you find here and there in London still. The floor is made of uneven wooden planks and slopes from rear to fore; the long wooden tables and benches appear to be hanging on grimly so as not to slide out of the door. Lanterns hang from rafters and swing in inexplicable drafts. I have the amusing impression that I am on a ship.

The building in which the supper room is housed stands at the confluence of a great many streets near Covent Garden.

The clientele is all male, and even I, bold though I fancy myself to be, hesitate to enter and join *so* many men, all strangers. The air is cloudy and rich with cigar smoke and the only other women to be seen are the serving girls, who run up and down the long lines of tables with loaded plates and brimming jugs of red wine. They bat away the attentions of the diners with varying degrees of ease or annoyance and I'm glad I'm not in their shoes. I enjoy the company of men and I know some very fine examples, but *en masse* like this, they are a prospect that make the hairs on my neck bristle.

But I am with Lionel and he takes my arm. He steers me to a table of colleagues and introduces me all round. At closer quarters they all look very respectable: professional men snatching a good meal after a busy day, not idlers bent on trouble.

We sit opposite one another at the end of a long table. Next to me is Mr Kemp, who owns a jewellery shop in Highmarsh Street and met Will only yesterday. 'Promising lad, young Master Brown,' he beams through some enormous whiskers. 'Had him serve a customer or two – thought they'd be amused by it. Lovely little manner he's got on him, and a real interest in jewellery, that's apparent.'

'I'm delighted to hear it,' I say, slicing into my chop. 'Thank you for assisting our foundation, Mr Kemp.'

'Interesting initiative, very enterprising. Excellent idea altogether, Miss Westallen. Hats off, and all that.'

Opposite Mr Kemp is Mr Sloane, a competitor of Lionel's, another trader of gems. He is understandably less effusive than Mr Kemp, though civil. I learn a great deal about Lionel's business as the evening proceeds and I can see that he is liked and respected by all. That is something to know about a man.

The food, as promised, is simple but excellently cooked, the

chops tender, the gravy savoury and the roast potatoes pleas-
ingly browned around the edges. The wine is a little rougher
than I am used to and I soon beg for water but altogether it
is an interesting evening. My brain is stimulated and that is
always the most rewarding thing for me.

'Miss Westallen has a remarkable grip on economics,'
remarks Mr Sloane at one point and I inwardly growl. Must
men be eternally surprised when women understand something
other than needlepoint? I long to put him in his place. The
truth is, my parents have indulged my intellectual curiosity
and gave me a most unconventional education for a girl. I
know full well I am cleverer than most people here and at
least as knowledgeable on a wide variety of subjects. But I am
with Lionel, I shall not make things awkward for him, and
besides, it is not gracious to boast of one's accomplishments.
Let my education speak for itself and perhaps make some of
the men here think twice about the capabilities of women.

Five minutes later, however, I forget all about Lionel's
comfort and speak up I do, not on my own behalf but in
defence of one of the serving girls.

'Fill up my glass, Molly!' 'Here, my beauty, bring me another
chop!' 'Don't stint on the gravy, Molly!' The cries ring out all
around me. I do not believe that so many women and girls,
all in one establishment, were christened Molly. It appears to
be a pet name of sorts. As they bend over the tables to clear
plates or pour wine, the men stroke them fondly on the arm,
pinch their cheeks, and slap their backsides. It is all done with
a hearty good cheer as if it's the most natural thing in the
world. Perhaps it *is* the done thing; I wouldn't know for I've
never been in such a place before. Their assurance makes me
wonder if I am being prissy but I try to imagine if *I* would
like it. I would not. Of course, they would not dare handle me

thus because they know me to be a person of stature and wealth. They recognise my father's name.

As the evening has progressed, the wine has flowed. Now, a little way from where we sit, one of the men has his arm fast around the waist of a young server who is pulling away and saying, 'Please, sir, I have to get back to work!' She can't be more than sixteen – Clover in a mere ten years – and her face is alarmed and tearful.

'Come and sit on my lap, my beauty! Don't be shy now, Molly, how about a little kiss?' He pulls her firmly onto his knee without waiting for her answer and the look of revulsion on her face has me shooting to my feet.

'Sir, please release that young girl at once!' I command. I can feel my face flaming with rage and I jut out my chin at the man, who looks at me in amazement.

'Who? Me?' he asks in amazement. 'I mean no harm, ma'am. Molly knows that. It's just a bit of fun.'

'What's your name, child?' I ask.

'Edie, ma'am.' She takes advantage of the interruption to stumble to her feet.

'Very good. Well, Sir, *Molly*, as you call her, is not her name at all. If you mean it's fun for *you*, I concede you are right. If, however, you wish to know whether it is fun for *her*, you might take the simple step of looking at her face. You observe the harassed expression, the tearful eyes? They suggest that indeed this is *not* fun for her. Unless the matter of how *she* feels is of no importance to you, which I imagine to be so. But in that case, I challenge your original statement that you mean no harm. To take your own enjoyment irrespective of the feelings of another is indeed harmful.' I take a deep breath. I realise I am voicing opinions utterly out of the ordinary and probably come across as a madwoman. But my blood is roaring. It is what I feel. It is what I suspect every woman feels, only we are bred not to speak up.

He gapes at me and so do several other faces. No man likes being told what to do by a woman. But I am with Mr Harper. More importantly, I am Captain Westallen's daughter. There is not a man in London who would cross my father. I wear my identity like a protective mantle. Most women do not have that. I have endeared no one towards me except poor Edie, who bobs me a curtsey, gratitude in her eyes, and scuttles off.

'Thank you, sir. A little basic respect for one's fellow man – and woman – can never be a bad thing, I find.' I sit down and continue my meal. Mr Kemp, Mr Sloane and Mr Harper all regard me cautiously, as if I am a lion in their midst. I shall not apologise. A moment or two later I finish my plate, lay knife and fork neatly together and smile. 'Delicious, gentlemen. What's for dessert?'

One dish of treacle pudding later, Lionel and I take our leave. My outburst is not mentioned. Several of the men shake hands and pledge donations for the foundation. At the door, a tug on my arm. It is Edie, the serving girl.

'Thank you, Miss Westallen,' she says. 'They told me who you was. I'm so grateful.'

'It wasn't really my business but you did look unhappy. Have you done this work long?'

'Two weeks only. I don't much like it but it helps me ma.'

I hand her my card, the one with the foundation's address on it. 'Call on me, Edie, if you should ever want to talk about alternatives. There are many ways I can help. I hope your mother is very proud of you.'

We step into the night and walk a little, without conversation. I cannot tell if the silence is comfortable or resentful; Mr Harper is such a mix of open-mindedness and conservatism.

'Are you happy to walk a little, Olive?' he asks me at last. 'Or would you rather go straight home?' I tell him I'm happy to walk. 'I thought we might go to the river and catch a cab from there,' he suggests. I agree that to see the river would be lovely.

Soon we are strolling along the Embankment next to the inky water, counting bridges. London's great history is laid out in bridges along this stretch of the river. We linger and gaze at the night-time vista and it feels a little romantic after all.

I had better say something. 'I hope I didn't embarrass you at the supper room. I don't want your colleagues to think you consort with unpredictable firebrands. But I saw that girl's face and . . . well, I had to.'

'No, you didn't embarrass me. You caused me to think, though. You always make me think, Olive. You weren't wrong to step in but really it should have been me – or any of us. But we didn't, because we're so used to it. Old Norden – that's the chap you berated – isn't a bad sort. He wouldn't have assaulted the girl or anything of that nature. He just grows foolish when he drinks. We all just accept that some of the fellows talk to the girls like that. We know they don't need to be afraid, but the girls don't know that, do they?'

'No, they do not. There are many degrees of indignity and discomfort short of an actual assault, Lionel. Imagine if someone had spoken to me like that, grabbed me around the waist . . .'

'I should have pulled my pistol,' he says, tongue in cheek. I doubt very much Lionel owns a pistol.

I shrug. 'There's no difference between me and her, except that I am rich and my father is a man of renown.'

'You know, I really can't imagine anyone behaving like that with you,' he grins. 'Molly.'

Is he teasing me? I have never known him to tease before. He's always so purposeful and serious. I raise my eyebrows to show him I shan't be answering to 'Molly' any time soon. I want to say more, but I know I can be like a dog with a bone when I'm indignant so I leave the subject. 'At any rate, it was a splendid evening. It has set my brain cogs a-whirring as no doubt you thought it would.'

'I hoped as much. I knew you'd enjoy the conversation and that you'd doubtless come away with many ideas for the foundation. And . . .'

'And?'

'It was a way of spending some time with you without it seeming . . . inappropriate. I enjoy your company, Olive, but we're colleagues and I don't wish to overstep any boundary you wish to preserve. But whilst we're alone together, I wanted to tell you, in case you're in any doubt, that I admire you. You're a remarkable woman. No, *that* is not what I wanted to say – I know you hear that all the time. What I *wanted* to say is that I find you intriguing, inspiring, good-hearted . . . and beautiful.'

'Beautiful, Mr Harper?' I laugh. I should not laugh when the poor man is making a declaration. Awkwardness, I expect. He's right, I hear 'remarkable' a good deal more than any other compliment. I sometimes garner a 'handsome' or a 'striking' but never a 'beautiful'.

'Yes, beautiful,' he insists. 'Inner and outer beauty in complement, a rare combination. I hope you don't mind me saying so.'

'How could I?'

'That I feel this way, that it sits alongside our most valuable working relationship – does it cause you any discomfort?'

There are so many things I want to ask him that I have

wondered for some time. About Rowena, about his reaction to Clover . . . The fact that I apparently inspire him to change his more rigid assumptions for the better is flattering, of course, but how much can a man really change? And what does he *want* of me? But in this moment, with the purple-black river snaking sighingly past and the reflections of the gas lamps bobbing in the water like golden balls thrown up from an underwater kingdom – with Mr Harper showing me a softer side to him than I have seen hitherto, casting compliments about me like spells – all I can manage to say is, 'No, Lionel. It rather intrigues me.'

He raises my hand to his lips and kisses my glove, holding my gaze with his earnest grey eyes. He releases my hand and smiles. 'Let us call a cab,' he says.

Twenty-one

Rowena

O nce again I find myself creeping through the house while my family is asleep. But this is no early morning escapade – an hour of gleeful stolen liberty before returning home again. It is three o'clock in the morning on Thursday the twenty-second of April 1897 and I am leaving. In years to come the history books will not mark the date but for me it is as significant and final as the outbreak of any war.

The house is completely dark. I steal along corridors and down staircases like a girl in a fairy tale, escaping to meet her prince. Except he is not a prince, he is . . . a man I hardly know. A man from another world. I tell myself it is romantic.

The last few days have flown by, their precious moments spent. Unsatisfied though I have been with my life of late, I have spent them drifting from room to room with an aching head, mourning every small detail of the life I am to lose. The gleaming chandeliers that throw seeds of light about the rooms, the fine silks that jostle together in my armoire, the thump of Ignatius's feet as he hurries up and down the stairs on endless errands of his own designing. My parents, reserved and exacting though they are, my brothers, lively and warm, the servants – silent presences who sweep and polish and . . . do all sorts of things to keep the house the way that we like it. However will I do without all this? Even the hated portraits of me, at ages eleven, eighteen and almost-twenty-three, look dear to me now. They show me in more innocent times, when I was the daughter they thought me, when I was safe in this privileged life. If anyone had told young Rowena that I would find myself in this invidious position, she would not have believed it. She would not have thought it possible.

I have left two letters on my bed, one for Mother and Father, and one for Verity. I pored over them last night with more effort and attention than I gave to any schoolroom assignment when I was younger. I've never cared much for writing but I wanted them to understand, if understanding is possible. I try not to think of the words that I wrote or I might sink down here on the stair and never move . . . The thing is done. I must go.

I slip into the ballroom once again and glide across the floor for the last time, a solitary trajectory so different from the whirling circles I have danced over the years in the arms of countless partners. In this depth of night there is no Henry conducting his exercise on the terrace, the door does not stand ajar to let in the spring air. I struggle to unbolt it; I need to climb on a chair to reach the top lock. Then I set the chair carefully back in its place because this, the disarrangement of a chair, is one small inconvenience I can spare my family. Although, when did any of us ever move a chair? It would be some servant who would find it out of place and wonder why.

I pull open the door and step outside. Indoors, darkness is restful, a warm presence that ushers me to sleep. Out here, in the world, it stirs around me and seethes like some monster of the deep. I am filled with foolish, instinctive fears. I close the door behind me. With a quiet click and the soft sigh of a night breeze, I rip myself from my life.

Twenty-two

Pansy

Pansy opened one eye to the darkness of the attic and beamed. Finally the day had come: she was going home. Her new experiences were rewarding – but they could wait.

Soon she was bouncing along the roads with Mr Ollander as the sky turned yellow then peach and the sparrows went busy about their day. For the last four weeks, with every new thing that she'd done, she'd wondered, *What would Mum think?* Now she was going to find out.

Home looked dearer than ever. Bluebells and primroses were everywhere in the lanes, thrushes darted to and fro, nesting, and the cottage was washed in pale golden sunlight. Pansy rushed in and threw her arms around her mother. They held each other for the longest time.

It would be as easy as anything, thought Pansy as she sat at the kitchen table to wait for her breakfast, just to leave the Blythes' and move home. They could live together perfectly happily; Pansy could get a job in the village, perhaps at The Tree of Life – Mr Ollander would recommend her – and she could see Matthew all the time, Eveline too when she visited from Camden. It would be blissful. But purposeless. She sighed. Mum wouldn't think much of that.

When the two of them were seated with heaped plates,

Pansy told her mother about working in Mr Ollander's shop and the hat shop, about rescuing Hipólito, meeting Julia and the chance of meeting Miss Westallen. Laura asked her searching questions about what she had liked and what she hadn't and Pansy did her best to explain.

'You're taking this seriously,' Laura noted, her hands cupped around a glass of creamy milk. 'And the way you defended Hipólito, and helped Jem – I'm very proud of you. I hope you're beginning to think about yourself, and your life, differently.' Pansy was, and when Laura waved her off at the end of the day, she knew her mother's pride would sustain her over the weeks ahead.

When she returned to the servants' entrance to Garrowgate Hall she stood for a long moment looking up at the large white building. She hoped she would find her happiness soon. She was tired of coming back here after every day off, after every errand, knowing that inside, Rowena drifted in beauty from room to room while her father spun money from air. Mrs Clarendon was there, running her tight ship, Verity Crawford-Blythe blew in, prickling with malice, and Maude Blythe ruled over them all . . . What a perfect, unassailable world they had built, and Pansy did not belong.

The moment she pushed through the kitchen door she knew something was wrong. The kitchen was empty and the house had an atmosphere, one she couldn't name. Pansy tensed. Garrowgate Hall never changed. What on earth . . . ?

She made her way up from the basement to the main house – silent, empty – and walked to the stairs. On the first floor she heard a door slam. She stilled, listening, and heard raised voices, the family's voices, but she couldn't hear the words. A creeping unease claimed her. Had somebody died?

She peered into a couple of rooms, expecting to find somebody *somewhere*, doing *something*. The work never stopped at Garrowgate Hall. But all the rooms were empty, as if the entire staff had blown away in a hurricane. Pansy ran up to the attic. A moment ago she'd been tired as tired but she wasn't sure she could sleep now. This ghostly place looked just like the Blythes' house but it didn't feel like it, not at all.

She pushed open the attic door and felt monumentally relieved to see Lou and Maisie sitting on their beds. 'Thank God!' Pansy cried. 'I was starting to think the place was under some sort of spell. Where is everybody?'

'You haven't heard then?' asked Maisie in a faraway voice.

'Obviously not,' retorted Lou, her work accent slipping. 'Pansy, love, sit down. Yer'll never believe what's 'appened.'

Obediently, Pansy sat beside Maisie, facing Lou, and pulled off her hat. 'What is it? Tell me, girls.'

Maisie gave a long sigh. 'I can't believe it, that's all. I just can't believe it.'

'Rowena's gone,' said Lou.

'Gone where?'

'Run away. Gone for good. I swear I thought Mrs B would 'ave an 'eart attack when she found out.'

'*What?* Gone for good? How could anyone know that?'

'Oh Pansy, it was terrible,' gasped Maisie and the story came tumbling out. 'Mrs Blythe, the new one, Miss Crawford as was, came calling and Rowena wasn't there to greet her. Mrs Blythe – the old one, *our* Mrs Blythe – was having a fit, annoyed that Rowena was late, disrupting everything. She ordered Sarah – thin Sarah – to go and fetch her at once, even to wake her up if she was asleep. Sarah didn't want to, because you know what Rowena's like if you try and rush her, but Mrs Blythe was on the warpath so it had to be done. There was no answer when she knocked on the door so after an age she went in. And Rowena wasn't there! There were two letters on the bed and Sarah said she knew right away there was nothing good in either of them. She was afraid to even touch them. She went downstairs and told them. Apparently the mistress went white – the colour drained right out of her, in front of Sarah's very eyes.'

'Good God!' said Pansy. 'Then what?'

'Old Maude went charging off to Rowena's room 'erself.' Lou continued the story. 'Like a thief with the bluebottles on 'er tail, she was. By then, o' course, we'd all got wind of it. A few of us went after the mistress and got busy with dusters or polish in the corridor while she went in – madness when you think about it, at such a time as that – but it was like we all sensed it, that something big had happened. Five minutes later, she was screaming.'

'Malvern! Verity! Crispin! Ignatius!' Maisie mimicked her mistress. 'She was calling for them all. And her voice . . . Ooh Pansy, it would've made your blood run cold.'

Lou nodded. 'It was bad, Pans, I never 'eard nothin' like it. So bad, all of them come running. They come thundering up the stairs and I thought we was going to get it for not minding our own business but no, in they went, didn't even notice us. I couldn't help it, Pans, I went and took a good look through the doorway. Maude Blythe had tears pouring down her face, and she said, "She's gone, Malvern, our precious diamond has gone. Run off with that artist fellow like a common chorus girl."'

Pansy gasped. Truly? She had *wondered*, but she'd never really thought . . .

'She handed 'im the letter an' he started to read it but then Maudie fainted clean away. 'E tossed the letter, caught her and dragged 'er out himself. Didn't look at no one, just marched

down the corridor to her room, her lolling against him like a
rag, and slammed the door shut behind them. Meanwhile, old
Crispin's hangin' on to the door frame looking like he might
faint 'imself, muttering, "Dear God, no, not Rowena," and old
Verity's rippin' into her own letter and reading as avid as if it
had the secrets of the world in it . . .' Lou took a deep breath.
'Then this *look* come over her face . . . contemptuous it was.
She shoved the letter in her pocket and marched out without
a single word.'

'Oh my God,' whispered Pansy. 'I can't believe it. I really
can't!' She could picture that very expression of Verity's. What
on earth would her husband say when he heard the news? All
three Blythe sons adored their sister, Felix most of all, perhaps.

'Oh, how I'd love to know what was in those letters,' Maisie
sighed. 'But none of us ever will.'

Lou looked shifty. 'Not in old Verity's we won't. It's gone
with her an' that's that. But the other one . . .'

Pansy frowned. 'Lou, what did you do?'

'Went in there, didn't I? Crispin and Ignatius 'ad floated out
like ghosts, and I went in and the letter was there on the floor
where old Blythe had flung it. So I picked it up. I know it was
stupid, but you know what I'm like. Couldn't resist! It was all
a bit of a tizzy then with Clarendon trying to get us back into
some sort of routine but by late afternoon, we'd all given up.
Pointless, weren't it? So Clarendon sent us all to our rooms
and said not to show our faces till morning.'

'You took the *letter*?' Lou had always been the boldest of
all of them. Even so, Pansy couldn't believe her gall. 'Where
is it now?'

'It's here.' Lou pulled a sheet of paper from her pocket.
Maisie squeaked. They looked at one another a long while.
'I'm not proud I took it,' said Lou eventually. 'And I could get

fired for this. I'd better put it back right away. I expect we shouldn't read it. It's ever so private.'

'Of course,' agreed Pansy. 'Put it back, Lou, while it's all quiet out there. And no, we certainly shouldn't read it.'

'It would be very wrong,' whispered Maisie.

The three of them looked at the folded paper on Lou's lap. Rowena Blythe's last words to her parents before running away with the artist's apprentice. Pansy wanted to be the sort of girl who was honourable and would always do the right thing. But the truth was that she didn't give a damn about a single one of the Blythes and it would take a better woman than her to resist this temptation. She grabbed the letter and started reading.

Twenty-three

Rowena

The canal boat is called the *Supreme Monarch*. This seems to me both tautological and deluded. It is *small*! At least from the bank it appeared sizeable; long, narrow and rather graceful in appearance despite its considerable bulk as it waited on the water. Altogether less so when one attempts to live on it! The cabin, which Bartek and I share, is no more than nine feet by six. I am living in a space only as wide as my brother Felix is tall, as long as one and a half brothers.

The boat is scuffed and chipped on the outside, its black paint dull, the once-gaudy roses and castles painted thereon scratched and faded. The second *e* of its name has worn away altogether, rendering it a *suprem* monarch. On board it is dirty: unswept and messy. Its deck and scant furniture are crusted with dried mud.

And yet, this first morning, as the sun rises and the boat slips along the green canal, I can glimpse the poetry I imagined when Bartek first spoke to me of his plans. A way of living all new to me, free of everything I once thought important. Guy Flack, whose boat this is, is even now on the towpath leading the horse and we glide, glide onwards. That was a shock, realising this journey was not to be the romantic idyll I had expected but shared with a gruff, bearded man in late middle age with an accent so thick I cannot decipher it. I do not even know where the accent is from. Meanwhile Bartek is asleep in the cabin. I have come onto the deck so that my fidgeting does not disturb him. To watch the morning brim into fullness, to be alone in my strange new surroundings, soothes me. And Lord knows I need soothing.

My night-time walk to the heath to meet Bartek was terrifying. I saw strange trotting creatures with eyes like lamps and heard terrible noises, rough shrieks that could well have been a crime being committed. The night world is not my domain, unless I am returning from a ball in the carriage, dizzy from dancing, clouded by champagne, with Verity chatting incessantly at my side. Or perhaps the night of my flight was simply cursed. Perhaps the world itself was shrieking at the wrongness of Rowena Blythe leaving her rightful place.

I walked, stiff and burning with fear. It occurred to me that if I turned and ran back then, I could let myself in and steal upstairs before anyone was up. I could return to my room, unpack my bag and it would be as if I had never run away. But that life vanished the moment I allowed Bartek to make love to me.

I was so relieved to see him waiting for me! I fell into his arms, sobbing. And I babbled, desperate: 'I love you and I want to be with you with all my heart but I can't do this, I don't think I can do this. It's too hard.' I'm not even sure why I said it. I *don't* want to be with him with all my heart. My heart was and remains conflicted. In fact, the larger part yearns to be Rowena Blythe again.

Bartek patted my arm and did not seem overly disturbed that his love was distraught to the point of hysteria at the prospect of yoking her life to his. 'Is emotion, will pass,' he said. How does *he* know?

He took my hand and we began walking. We walked for almost an hour to the canal and spoke very little. When we reached the boat, moored amongst others at the harbour or dock or whatever the terminology is for canal boats, Bartek gave an expansive gesture. 'Here she is,' he beamed and I could see his teeth white in the darkness. '*Supreme Monarch*, boat fit for my queen. Let us begin our life together, my beautiful Rowena.' With a certain ceremony, he handed me on board and I looked around in a daze. All was shadowy and indistinct and when a man emerged from the darkness I shrieked. They shushed me and Bartek laughed softly. 'Hush, my love, they will think I have stolen you, not that you come willing,' he chided.

Bartek towed me to the cabin. 'We sleep,' he said. 'Is late. Guy will take first turn with horse, we make early start to leave. To the North!' He kissed me passionately, pulled off his clothes and dived into the small bed. I stood, paralysed. 'Rowena, come,' he whispered. 'You need sleep.'

'But I *can't* sleep!' I exclaimed. 'Bartek . . . where do I wash? I don't think we can both fit in that bed. And is there no tea? I know it's late but I don't think I can go from running away to sleep with . . . nothing in between!'

He jumped from the bed again and I blinked. A lamp was burning and I was embarrassed by the sight of his naked body. Of course we had already . . . *been together*, but in truth, most of our clothes had stayed on then. I had never seen a man naked before. 'Ah, my Rowena,' he said, stretching out his arms, vastly uninhibited. I took his hands as one in a trance. 'I forget how different all this from what you know. You will need explaining of how things work on boat and reassurances.

I am beast! Forgive me for I am excited only. My darling, we must sleep now, but never fear, we talk in morning. Here is chamber pot if you need.' He reached under the bed and brandished it. Oh, dear God!

I shook my head dumbly and he stuck it back under the bed. 'Bed fit fine for two who love each other as we do. Come, my angel, come to bed.' As he talked he unbuttoned all my clothing – even my maids were not so efficient – and led me to the bed in just my chemise. Oddly I was glad that I was not also naked. That thin layer of muslin was all the protection from reality I had. He hopped in after me, pressing his body close so that I was jammed between him and the wall. 'Sweet dreams, my Rowena. We will wake to a new world!'

And, in fairness, I did. The air is cool but not chillingly so. The world is entirely green and gold: water, trees and sunlight. The only sounds are the splash of ducks, plangent birdsong swelling the air, the thud of the horse's hooves on the hard earth and the creak of the harness, the low murmuring of Guy talking to his beast. The horse probably stands as much chance of understanding him as I do. His soft voice makes me hope there is a kinder side to him than the one I witnessed when we boarded. He was not rude to me, just indifferent. I have never been treated thus. *Don't you know who I am?* I wanted to ask. But, of course, it's best he doesn't.

I cannot give in to self-reproach. No doubt there is plenty of it in my future but for now I need all my strength to adjust. Imagine my horror when I discovered that there is no lavatory! Bartek woke briefly this morning when I clambered over him and I took advantage of it to ask a few questions. We must empty the chamber pot *ourselves*! Into the *canal*! Bartek laughed at my horror – I see nothing funny about it. I used

it this morning when he went back to sleep; I was crouched
and tense lest he wake again and see me! But I could hardly
use it on deck in the bright morning air! With Mr Flack asleep
on the wooden boards! It was the lesser of two evils; even so,
I am humiliated. Unpleasant, enforced intimacy. What a beginning to my life with Bartek. I cannot *imagine* what Verity
would say.

Thinking of my best friend brings tears to my eyes. True,
in recent months I've found her overly cutting, sometimes
unkind, and terribly suffocating. But now, most probably, our
longstanding friendship is over. I shall write to her, of course,
and rely upon a correspondence with her to keep me cheerful
in my new life. But that is not the same as seeing someone
every day. I shall miss our endless small confidences, her ready
wit, her vivacity and confidence. Now she is a member of the
Blythe family and I am not. She will become their daughter
in my stead. She will probably do a better job of it.

In the letter I left for her, I confided a little of my inner
turmoil. In the letter to my parents, I could not. To them, I
had to stand by my choice; I gave the only explanation that
could make any sense of this: true love. To Verity I wrote:

Dearest V,

*I am so very sorry for the trouble I have caused. I hope
and pray that you will not think too badly of me.
Remember that day in the parlour, dear, when you
asked me to imagine myself coming to dinner with you
and Felix, with a husband at my side? I told you I did
not see anyone, but the truth is, I was shocked by who
I saw. Bartek. It was involuntary, yet there he was. I
hope that you can sympathise. You have met him,*

*you've seen how handsome, how clever, how gentle-
manly he is. The truth is that since we met, I could
consider no one else for they all seemed dull and grey
in comparison. And yet I am torn, my dear. Every bit
as much as I love and admire him, I shall miss and
miss and miss you all. I wish it had not come to this, I
wish our world were different, that it did not have to
be either Bartek or my life and family. The choice does
not sit easy with me and yet to stay is impossible. You
are my best friend. I shall think of you with the greatest
fondness always and hope you can think of me likewise.
I shall write to you when we are settled. Please write
back. It will mean everything to me.*

With love,
Ro

I cannot begin to imagine Verity's reaction. Will she be
offended that I did not confide in her? Angry? Worried? Sad?
She's always been one for a scandal – quick to judge and avid
in her recounting of salacious news. Yet she loves me, I have
no doubt of that.

I close my eyes and the sun warms my face. I'm seated on
a rough bench, and the splinters that catch my silk skirts are
the least of my worries. How has it come to this?

I do not know how far we have come and I've little concept
of the world outside London. I know we are to take one canal
a certain distance and then we are to join another that will take
us north, because Bartek has told me so, but I cannot remember
the details. All I see is a long, straight road of water, a cloud
of trees at either side, brick-built bridges and sometimes the
roofs of small, mean houses. I, who have always lived such a

controlled life, always with appointments in my diary and the parameters of respectability dictating where I go and when. Before, there was never a time when countless others did not know exactly where I was. Now *I* do not know where I am! I am adrift, in every sense of the word.

Twenty-four

Pansy

Downstairs was still in disarray. Mrs Clarendon marshalled the servants to do the basic cleaning but no one rang for breakfast or requested help to dress. Without the usual cast-iron routine, it was impossible to tell what the Blythes might need. Water was kept boiling at all times, a simple breakfast prepared so it might be served at a moment's notice. But even Mrs Clarendon, she of twenty years' faithful service and apparently of one mind with Maude Blythe, hesitated to go and enquire. The family's doors were shut fast.

Pansy did a few jobs in a desultory manner, at half her usual pace, then wandered off to find John, because no one seemed likely to stop her. Did he know? He must. No one living at Garrowgate Hall could be unaware of what had happened. How had he taken the news?

She found him in the hall, standing guard against any callers. There were unlikely to be any at this time in the morning but no matter what, John would carry out his service to Rowena's family. He was immaculate in his wig, white stockings and black livery, a tall, strong figure against the vast, white columned hall with its cascades of spring flowers and stretching, spotless floors; even so, John wore the air of a dog lying on his owner's grave.

'You've heard, then?' she asked.

He turned miserable eyes on her. 'Oh Pansy. What has she done? Is she all right, do you think?'

For once, Pansy didn't have the heart to make an acerbic comment. She shrugged. 'I don't know. I hope so. I'm sorry, John.'

'It wasn't meant to happen like this. Oh God. She wasn't meant to be with *me*, I know that. But she was meant to marry someone fine, to have a *good* life. Everyone's saying the family will never speak to her again – even if she does come back. Though she probably never will, now.'

Pansy nodded. No more Rowena Blythe. 'She's cut herself off from everyone and everything. It would need to be a very great love indeed to make that worthwhile . . .' She trailed off as she saw the look on John's face. His outward composure could not disguise that he was breaking inside.

'I hope that's how it is,' he said, his voice unusually thick. 'That's the only thing to wish for now.' Pansy wanted to hug him for his unselfishness. It only made her love him more, emotions rocking through her like a storm. The repercussions of Rowena's flight would unspool for a long time, she realised, not just for the family but for herself and John. Suddenly she had a horrible feeling that those consequences had only just begun.

'They're saying it was that Polish fellow,' said John, in the same dull voice fattened by unshed tears. 'Do you think it's true?'

'I know it is.' Pansy took a quick glance around the white marbled hall but there was no one in sight. She stepped closer and whispered. 'Lou took the letter she left. I read it, John.'

His blue eyes widened. 'What did she say? Did she sound happy?'

Pansy wasn't sure. She had read it out of curiosity, not concern. The letter had been astonishing.

Dear Mother, Father,

I am so very sorry to cause you hurt and pain. Please know that I love you with all my heart. I love my life here at Garrowgate Hall. I am full of gratitude for all you have given me. But I had no choice. I have fallen in love with Bartek Woźniak, the artist who came in place of Mr Lethbridge for a while. He has asked me to marry him and I have accepted. My feelings for him have made any other match quite impossible. I wanted to ask your permission, I wanted to tell you. But I did not believe you would accept the match. You could not even countenance him attending my birthday party. Had I believed for a moment that you would give us your blessing, I would not have taken this step. I'm so sorry – I had no choice. If I have misjudged you, as I hope and pray that I have, I am sorry for that too. I wish nothing more than for my husband-to-be to be welcomed into the family and for our lives to continue on as always. When we are married and settled, I shall write to you and hope you will write back kindly. He is a gentleman after all, aristocracy in his country. It is not such a poor connection. Give my love to Felix, Crispin and Ignatius. I love you all, so very much.

Your daughter, always,
Rowena

Now, Pansy tried hard to remember as much of it as she could to tell John. They had only read it the once, then Lou darted off to put it back on the floor of Rowena's room, where it had fallen. Thankfully, she hadn't been seen.

'That's that, then,' said John when she finished. 'At least he's marrying her, at least his intentions are honourable.'

'It hasn't happened yet . . . Sorry, John, I shouldn't have said that. Please don't worry. He seemed like a nice person when he came to the house, I'm certain he's genuine.' She wasn't, but she didn't want to make John feel even worse.

So he'd told her he was nobility, had he? Pansy wondered if it were true. *I had no choice*, she'd written, and she'd written it twice – Pansy could remember that much. She could hazard a fair guess what that meant and Lou and Maisie had thought the same last night. But she wasn't going to say that to John either.

'No matter what she feels for him,' said John, 'how can she be happy in the sort of life he can give her? Cut off for ever from her family? Unless they forgive her and we both know they never will.'

'She must realise that. She'll be all right, John. She's with the man she loves.'

He shook his head. 'Oh Pansy, I feel responsible. Those Saturday mornings she crept out so early – she must have been meeting him. Oh, how I wish I'd stopped her.'

'John, love, she'd never have listened to you. There was nothing you could have done. Don't you dare go saying that to anyone else. It won't be an easy time ahead . . .' The Blythe family had been smashed to pieces and it was impossible to hope that the servants would go unscathed.

'I could have spoken to her. I should have taken more of an interest. I was too busy being a footman to be a friend.'

'But you *weren't* her friend. You were never going to be. Don't blame yourself – *she's* done this, all by herself. Well, her and him.'

But his eyes were full of tears. 'Why couldn't it have been me?' he whispered. 'I could have borne it if she married some mighty Pooh-Bah or nobleman but since she's thrown everything away anyway . . . it could have been me. Why didn't he love her enough to leave her in her natural world, where she belonged?'

'I don't know, John. Not everyone's as good as you.'

From the corner of her eye, Pansy glimpsed a Blythe approaching. It was no more than a shadow, but she'd developed a sixth sense about when they were coming. It gave her time to dart away from John and whip a rag from her pocket. She started dusting the urns and busts that dotted the hall.

It was Mr Blythe. 'Henry. Come with me, please. We are interviewing staff, one by one, to see if any light can be shed on recent occurrences within the house.'

'Yes, sir.' John followed his master and, unable to resist, Pansy silently followed them both. Mr Blythe didn't notice. Pansy noted the high, hard set of his shoulders, the urgency of his walk. He led John to the library where he slammed the door behind them and Pansy startled. This was not a house of slamming doors. He used such force that the door sprang open again, drifting to stand ajar by an inch. Obviously Mr Blythe was beside himself. Pansy sidled closer, poised with rag to pretend to be dusting the windowsills. A feeble sunbeam drooped onto the landing.

'My daughter is missing,' began Malvern Blythe. The gap in the door was too narrow to see so Pansy listened hard.

'Yes, sir. I'm sorry, sir.'

'Do you know anything about it? Anything at all?'

'No, sir.'

'You did not help her, make suggestions, supply her with provisions for her flight?'

'By no means, sir. I would never do that. I hold Miss Blythe, and this family, in the highest esteem.'

'We believe you, Henry.' It was Mrs Blythe's voice. 'Is there anything at all you can tell us that might help us work out where she has gone?'

'You plan to look for her, ma'am?' The hope in John's voice was unmistakeable. Pansy winced.

'No.' Malvern Blythe's voice fell like an axe. 'She is dead to us now for the shame she has brought on our family. We merely wish to understand what happened. If we find that anyone here had anything to do with her ill-considered course, they will be punished.'

Silence. Pansy imagined John lowering his eyes and prayed that, good and honest though he was, he'd be smart enough not to mention Rowena's early morning excursions. The fact that he'd never told her parents about them would have him out of the door before he could whisk his wig off. The silence lengthened. Pansy relaxed. He wasn't going to tell them. Then she heard him speak.

'Please, sir, please go after her.'

Pansy dropped her rag. She hastily bent to pick it up. *Oh no.*

'I beg your pardon?' Oh Lord. Mr Blythe's voice was like a pestle grinding against a mortar.

'Please bring her home. She will regret this, I know she will.'

'How *dare* you? How dare you tell me what to do? Interfere in the affairs of this family? Presume to know my daughter's mind? What is she to you?'

'Nothing, sir. She is nothing to me but the young mistress. Only I care about her, as I care about all of you. I would be . . . distressed to think of her alone and afraid.' Pansy closed her eyes. His every word was redolent with love. His tone of voice sang of it. This was bad.

'I never heard such bare-faced gall. You harbour some sort of misplaced tenderness for my daughter!'

'Sir, I just don't want to see her come to harm.'

'Out of my house. And never come back. Your employment here is at an end, do you hear? Fetch your things and leave within the next ten minutes. You will receive no reference and if you breathe one word of my daughter's actions to anyone, I will blacken your name all over town. You will never work again, do you hear?'

Pansy knew she should get herself away but she was rooted to the spot.

'Sir, I beg you, I've worked here for sixteen years. This family is my life. I would never disrespect it in any way . . .'

Then Pansy did rip her feet from the floor and hurried away. She wouldn't stay to listen to John beg. She knew exactly how successful his efforts would be. In the kitchen, she bumped into Mrs Clarendon still struggling to regain control. 'Where've you been, girl?' she demanded, grabbing Pansy by the arm. 'We need some order back here. Where were you all this time?'

'I'm sorry, Mrs Clarendon, but Mr Blythe just dismissed John.'

'John Hobbs? Never! Why?'

Pansy sighed. 'For speaking up for Miss Rowena. I heard it, Mrs Clarendon, that's all he did.'

The housekeeper let her go and shook her head. 'What *is* the world coming to? That man's been here longest of anyone after me and a better servant I never saw. What was he thinking, talking out of place like that? Go and clean Master Crispin's room, Tilney. The sooner we go back to some sort of normality, the better for all of us.'

'Yes, Mrs Clarendon.'

On her way upstairs, Pansy saw John, dragging his feet like

a man in a daze. 'John, I heard everything! What possessed you?'

He looked at her and shrugged. 'I don't know, Pansy. I couldn't help myself. She has no one to defend her and they're so unforgiving . . .'

'Presumably now she has her new fiancé to defend her! John, you're a fool. All these years in service and no reference? After how well you've served them. What will you do?'

'I'll go to my sister Hetty in Hampstead for now. That's all I can think of. I have to go, Pansy. He said if I didn't go right away, he'd beat me.'

Pansy snorted. 'John, you're six foot two and half his age.'

'Yes, but I can't fight Malvern Blythe. He'd go straight to the police. My reputation is ruined already, but I can't afford for folk to think me violent as well.'

Pansy sighed again. The rich and powerful had everything their own way, no matter the rights and wrongs of it. 'Go, John. Go to Hetty. I'll come and see you on Thursday.'

Pansy made her way to Crispin's room, chastened and deeply reflective. After all those years of stagnation, everything had finally changed. Rowena had made her choice. John was released from Garrowgate Hall. And with his departure, Pansy had no more reason to stay. The sequence was exactly as she had imagined it so often. But oh, the details were so very different! If someone had told her two months ago that this would happen, well, she would never have believed it. And she probably would have exulted in the idea of Rowena's downfall. But ideas and reality are two very different things, she was learning. That stupid, beautiful woman! What on earth would become of her out there in the real world?

Twenty-five

Rowena

It isn't all plain sailing. (Ha, I am even a little witty in my new life! Rowena Blythe was always a beauty, never a wit.) The physical deprivations continue to trouble me, and Bartek and I have had some fearsome rows. I still weep at night for all that I have lost and the severance from my loved ones. But I feel a little better than I did a week ago and my relief at that knows no bounds. I was starting to fear I would never acclimatise at all.

No doubt the weather helps. It is unusually consistent for late April. Blue skies canopy our way, trees brim with lime green and birdsong and it has felt pleasant to sit up on deck, feeling the tug of progress, feeling the soft breezes upon my face.

The *Supreme Monarch* is growing on me. It possesses ingenious hidden cupboards tucked away under the seats and in the walls of the boat to save space. Rather than having handles, the doors open when they are pressed in just the right spot. I have stowed my bag in one of them for the pleasure of the novelty. There is no running water on our floating home; we must fill up large cans from taps along the wayside. Bartek or Mr Flack nip onto the bank when we pass one and return with straining muscles. Then the cans are stored on the roof of the boat. At first, I found this an immense privation. Not to have an unlimited supply of *water*, of all things! And yet at night, once or twice, I have lain awake listening to the drumming of rain on those cans and to my surprise it is a pleasant music.

Our little cabin is painted cream, though there is a strange brown texturing upon the paintwork. The cupboards are decorated with lots of frills and lace. I can only imagine Mother's horror. 'Heathenish!' she would declare. Yet, together with the brasses that cover the walls and the brightly painted cupboard doors, they make me feel gypsyish and, yes, bohemian. I am a different Rowena here.

I love Bartek – and that is another very great relief. In those last days before I ran away, I wasn't certain, thinking that surely I would feel happier if I did. Now, I realise that if one is under undue strain, if one is exhausted and confused, it's hard to see anything clearly at all. All becomes tangled and fogged. Now that the thing is done, irrevocable, I see him as I saw him in the early days of our acquaintance: handsome, vital, magnetic. A romantic hero that no girl could resist. And I cling to him for he is my sole reason for being here, my only family, now, in this world of water and stars.

Sometimes, though, he does not feel familiar at all. Sometimes he looks at me with blank eyes and shouts at my many mistakes and failings. Then I feel cross and let down for what else could he expect? He knew the greenhouse from which he plucked me; he understood the soil in which I grew. An example. Two or three days ago Mr Flack mumbled and grumbled into his beard and Bartek translated for me – funny that I should need this service when Mr Flack speaks my first language, not Bartek's. The gist of this particular pronouncement was I am expected to take turns leading the horse. I said in no uncertain terms that I would not.

Bartek slammed his hand on the deck – he was sitting on the floor at the time, legs outstretched, leaning back on his elbows – and shouted at me. 'Always you are complain. Always there is problem. No this, no that. What is matter with you? You are here now, in this life. You must take part, yes? You are not queen.'

Immediately my eyes smarted. 'Well, there was my mistake,' I sniffed. 'I thought I *was* a queen to you. Do you not wish to ask me *why* I cannot lead the horse? You have no interest in my reasons, only rush to condemn me.'

'What reason can there be? You are queen in my heart – yes, yes – but in this real world . . . you are woman. Able body, pair of hands, much to be done.'

'Well, *you* don't seem to do much except laze about smoking and drinking,' I commented, and I did not exaggerate. Our days are indolent in the extreme. Funny how Bartek never smelled of either tobacco or intoxicating drink when he came to Garrowgate Hall but now, if I awake after him, it is to the smell of smoke and I go to bed with the aroma of red wine in my nostrils. He exhibits such deep pleasure and satisfaction in these two activities and looks so hedonistic and beautiful, half closing his green eyes as he savours the glowing wine or the wreath of smoke, that he seems the very epitome of his bohemian heroes. And I am the barefoot, beautiful, tangle-haired girl with whom he has chosen to share his life. For yes, he encouraged me to leave off my shoes when I am on the boat and after a couple of splinters early on, and ensuing fits of sobbing, I have come to like the ease of it. I like feeling the deck cool underfoot first thing in the morning, then warming as the day goes on. If my mother saw me now, shoeless, corset-less, in the company of two men, she would die. I am not always comfortable but I *am* glad to experience this. I never knew life could be so . . . varied.

Anyway, Bartek slammed the deck again and got up in disgust
at my accusation of sloth. True, he has taken a turn every day
at leading the horse. And he has fetched the water a time or
two. And when we pass through a tunnel, he and Mr Flack lie
on their backs on the roof of the boat, wedged between water
canisters, and move us along with the strength of their legs!
But that is all! It is Mr Flack who mops the deck (ineffectively
– how I long for a Blythe servant or two now, even that ill-
tempered, chestnut-haired one), prepares our rough meals,
tidies around when the chaos becomes hazardous. He leads
the horse, tends to the horse and negotiates the locks. This is
how canal folk live. I never imagined, not for a moment.

Bartek never did ask why I don't want to lead the horse.
Doubtless he assumes I'm just spoiled and lazy. I may well be
but also, I am afraid of horses. The Blythes were never riders.
My father first went into banking, following in the footsteps
of his own father, then he ran away to sea. When he went back
to moving money around, it was hard to remember that he
had ever been a seafaring man. He looks and sounds like one
born to sit in cool marble halls and count his money.

The point is, he did not ride, my mother did not ride. The
only horses we kept were carriage horses and I never went
near them. My brothers were offered lessons, which they
turned down; I was not. I was even nervous climbing in and
out of the carriage. Even with our groom – Johnson? Jennings?
– holding them in the traces, I did not trust those tall, stamping
creatures with their wild, liquid eyes. The very thought of *me*
alone with this hairy beast on the towpath fills me with a cold
terror. It is at least as tall as our horses at home and far greater
in bulk. I will tell Bartek this when he is in one of his more
yielding moods. They usually come at night when we are alone
in our tiny cabin. We have repeated the fateful act several

times now and I must admit, I did not imagine the passion between us. Then, in the throes of pleasure, he swears that he loves me truly. My only fear is that he will run out of patience with me before I have toughened up and learned all the many lessons I need to learn. For I cannot rush change. I hope Bartek understands that. My body and mind are still astonished.

Today, we are amiable. We sit on the rough bench, side by side, our dirty feet resting on an old crate that Bartek dragged over from the far end of the boat. Bartek is drinking wine, his arm slung around my shoulders. I have tried to drink with him but it is rough compared with the wines I am used to at London dinner parties and I never had much of a liking for that. I even tried smoking at his suggestion but I coughed so violently I was physically sick. I was mortified. How he could find me attractive after that I have no idea. He rolled his eyes and commented that I must overreact with that as with everything, but soon after he chuckled, and kissed my cheek and that night all was as usual between us.

'I hope you know, Bartek, that I am trying,' I say now, taking advantage of his sunnier mood and the fact that we are alone. 'I love you. If I seem to complain, it is not that I am sour at our circumstances. It is merely that it's all *so* very new for me, and I have given up so much to be here. Some days I don't know which way is up and which way down. Please be patient with me, my darling. I do not mean to be foolish and irritate you.'

He grins, a flash of white teeth against golden skin and winking green eyes beneath a yellow fall of hair. Green and gold, the colours of the canal, the colours of my love. Perhaps they can be the theme colours for our wedding. Then I remember that ours will not be the sort of wedding that I am used to. He bends to kiss me and I melt against him.

'This I know. I too am in new world. To have you at my side – a woman!' He makes a face of exaggerated horror and I laugh. 'I am not used to this. I never thought to fall in love. Or anyway, not for long, long time. I am young and stupid. I am used to many women but never for long. I am not skilled at gentle words and kindness that you need to feel at home. For this I apologise. We must both forebear with the other.'

The traitorous thought flits across my mind that he was skilled enough at gentle words and kindness when he was seducing me away from my home but I push it aside. Adoring someone from afar is one thing whilst living day to day together is another. He is trying. I appreciate that. I kiss his cheek.

'Bartek?' I want to explain to him about the horse but he has already tilted his head back, face to the sun, eyes closed. He loves nothing more than to sit like this. No wonder he is so permanently gilded. I wish we could enjoy a little more conversation, since I have read the one book I brought with me twice already, but I do not wish to nag.

'Mmm.'

He looks so relaxed I don't like to bring up my fears so I pick a new topic. 'Shall you paint while we are on the boat, do you think?'

'No. When we are in Cumbria, then I paint. Whole journey for to paint. While on boat, I enjoy life, and ready myself. And of course, I have muse with me!' He smiles joyously and squeezes my shoulders. I smile and snuggle into him. I am a muse, a traveller, a bold adventurer! What would Olive Westallen make of me now? I am a little sad to think that she will never know about any of this.

Twenty-six

Olive

We are edging towards May and I'm enjoying a warm Saturday afternoon in the garden. Clover and Angeline are playing in the lavender. Firmly persuaded as they are that fairies dwell there – and who is to say that they are wrong? – they are happily occupied, allowing me peace to drowse and dream. It is much needed; I am busier than ever these days. Besides the foundation, the old Hampstead Heath preservation campaigners have regrouped just in these last few weeks, this time naming themselves the Hampstead Heath Protection Society. It's high time. The London County Council has been making unsavoury efforts to civilise the heath, as if to turn it into some sort of ordinary parkland, if you will! They've been trimming the gorse and hedgerows, destroying their vibrant colonies of every kind of life, and replacing the natural path-ways with roads. Of course I was invited to their inaugural meeting and of course I went. Our heath is a treasure, one that must not be plundered.

I'm musing on the meeting and what I might do to help when Jenny comes to inform me I have a visitor. Imagine my disappointment when I hear it is Charlotte Bradcott. Charlotte is someone who used to style herself a friend – I always thought of her as more of an acquaintance, one of several who haven't spoken to me since I adopted Clover. Charlotte and her cronies didn't want a child of uncertain origin playing with their own little treasures and they considered my behaviour too eccentric to tolerate. I did not waste tears on *that* – but what can have brought about this unexpected call now?

Fifteen minutes later, I know. It was the only force mighty enough to bring someone like Charlotte to the door of someone like me: gossip. I was polite, of course; I offered her refreshment and made reserved conversation. I showed interest, but not too much, for I do not forget her true colours. As soon as I politely could, I showed her out. Then I called Jenny to watch the girls and ran to the Vale of Health to visit Julia! For despite the only mild interest I displayed to Charlotte, this is indeed an inconceivable story – one best chewed over with a real friend.

Jem answers the door to my urgent knocking and yells up the stairs. 'It's Miss Westallen, Mrs M.'

Julia hurries down, wearing a pretty pink day dress and an expression of alarm. 'Is everything all right, Olive? I thought the cavalry had come on a matter of national importance.'

'I'm perfectly well, thanks, only I bear gossip such as you have *never* heard. I need your listening ear – and cake if you have it.'

'How intriguing. Jem, is any of the lemon shortbread left or did you eat it all?'

'Me, Mrs M?' Jem looks injured. 'I left six bits!'

'I made forty,' Julia murmurs in an aside to me. 'Would you bring them out to the garden, please, and some of the ginger cake too?'

'I'll boil up some tea an' all and bring it through, then I'll leave yer to it. Yer'll want to talk like ladies, *I* know.' Dear Jem.

In the garden we sit beneath a fulsome evergreen. Its fragrance is fresh and bright. I sigh with pleasure, already feeling calmer. Julia narrows her eyes at me. 'Tell me, Olive. You're positively brimming with news – I've never seen you fidget so!'

'No, no,' I insist. 'We must wait for Jem and the tea, Julia, for once I start telling you, I promise you'll want no interruption.'

'Gracious!' she murmurs.

When Jem has been and gone. I sigh with relief. 'Julia, my dear. I have heard gossip of the most enormous kind. I don't suppose you've already heard?'

'Me? I never go anywhere. I rely on you to tell me everything. What's happened, Olive?'

'I have heard the strangest possible news. That Rowena Blythe is disgraced. That she has run away. That she is *penniless*. And *pregnant*!'

Julia just laughs and I do not blame her. The very thought of it is preposterous. Julia only met Rowena once at the foundation ball last summer – but one meeting is sufficient to divine everything one needs to know about Rowena. 'Olive, you tease. Who on earth has been spreading such fiddle-faddle? If Rowena has fallen from grace, I am an ostrich.'

'Then, my dear, prepare to preen your feathers and stick your head in any convenient sand. I do not know the facts of it, but there are rumours spreading like wildfire through Highgate, across the heath and now they are licking at eager ears here in Hampstead. She has fallen.'

Hastily I supply the facts, that Charlotte Bradcott came to see me – *me!* – so ruffled was she by the news. 'It seems that Rowena has usurped my role as Person-Beyond-the-Pale. She has run off with a man, no one knows who, but everyone seems agreed that he is nobody suitable. Apparently the Blythes are putting it about that Rowena has gone abroad very suddenly to study Italian, but no one believes it. There are whispers of a pregnancy but surely people are just putting two and two together to make seven, for how could anyone possibly know *that*? She's only been gone a couple of days! Even Charlotte admitted there didn't seem to be any very firm basis for that part of the story. Anyway, I hastened directly to see you, but on my way out I heard two of our maids muttering and I definitely heard the name Rowena Blythe. Julia, if the rumour is in Highgate and Hampstead, above stairs and below, there must be *something* in it. I shan't indulge the likes of Charlotte Bradcott by talking about it but you are one of my dearest friends. What do you make of it?'

Julia shakes her head as if to dislodge water from her ears. 'But . . . she *can't* have. I mean, it's *Rowena Blythe*! Of all people she is bound to follow the established pattern until her dying day!'

'I have always said so. Yet now there is this.'

Julia lifts a piece of ginger cake to her lips, then pauses, holding it aloft. 'Truly, Olive, you might as well tell me Mabs has sprouted wings or your father has become a pirate. Oh, I hope Pansy comes to see me soon. I told you about her, didn't I? The young woman who helped Jem recently. She is a maid at Garrowgate Hall and she promised to call again. Surely she will know something about it.'

'When you talk to her, I beg you to tell me everything. Immediately.' I frown into my teacup. 'I've always disliked Rowena, as you know. We've only met a handful of times in adulthood and on each occasion I have found her to be vapid, unoriginal, catty and vain. But if this is true, even a part of it, then I find I like her rather more. Am I very contrary?'

Julia smiles. 'Human nature is a capricious thing. It certainly renders her more interesting, I'll give you that. But Olive, how on earth will she *fare* out there in the world? Who is the man? Will he be good to her? Where can they have gone?' She takes a large bite of cake at last.

I shake my head, experiencing a prickling of concern for the girl. 'I can't imagine. I really can't imagine.'

Twenty-seven

Rowena

I am starting to make myself useful in small ways. As we glide ever onwards, Guy Flack teaches me to fish off the stern for eels. I sit with my legs dangling over the water and I rather enjoy it – the fishing, that is. I do not enjoy actually *catching* eels; they are slimy, writhing, altogether unpleasant creatures before they are cut up and jellied, which is the only way *I* have ever seen them before. I fling them onto the deck and let Guy or Bartek deal with them. Urgh. I cannot bear to handle them.

Sometimes I scramble onto the towpath and collect fruit and vegetables from the hedgerows and the edges of fields we pass. I have pulled spring cabbages and rhubarb to swell our meals. I have plucked glowing, succulent cherries to enjoy as I sit and dream. I also picked a quantity of small fruits and berries which Guy flung back onto the wayside with a gesture of disgust, garbling loudly at me. I gather (ha, I am witty again) that I had proudly brought poisonous fare for us to eat. Well, how do *I* know?

I am even learning to heat water in an old teapot, a hideous brown thing. Measham pottery, I read on its base. I have never heard of it before. I'm rather in awe of myself. I cannot believe I have such accomplishments to add to my existing list: pianoforte, embroidery, flower-arranging, dancing and the like. In what drawing room could I ever discuss catching eels?

Guy says very little, and what he does say is incomprehensible, so I still have no sense of him except that his plodding, dour figure has become familiar and therefore reassuring to me. He wears brown trousers of a thick woollen cloth with a short pile to it that I have never seen before. Bartek says it is moleskin and good for weathering the elements. He also wears a canvas shirt, a rainbow-coloured waistcoat and a gaudy neckerchief, all topped off with a white felt hat.

He is a lifelong canal man. On this journey he carries bales of raw cotton to the mills of the North. As we travel, the landscape changes; the fields and orchards of the South increasingly replaced by enormous brick buildings that gaze broodingly over the water, with tall, black chimneys and smoke. On some days, in the wrong weather, it's easy to imagine we're travelling into hell, but Bartek assures me that beyond all this, Cumbria is a land as beautiful as a fairy realm.

Bartek has begun sketching me, which feels reassuring, like a return to our beginnings when everything was so fascinating between us. I am glad of it since he remains surly with me much of the time, intolerant of my many failings. I can see that I'm not the obvious mate for a worldly man like him, yet I made no secret of what I was. It is only these last few days that he began the sketching and, at my suggestion, we have started reading *Scènes de la vie bohème* together. We are sharing something he loves and I am improving my French, even feeling a little clever for the first time in my life. And so I become giddy with hope that all will be well after all, that Bartek and I can still make the beautiful life that he promised me when he implored me to go with him.

Until Guy tells me it's my turn with the horse. I protest,

I explain my fear of horses, I beg to be excused this most terrifying of duties. I would empty both their chamber pots before I would approach that dreadful creature. But Bartek has just finished a long shift at the horse's head and Guy has things to do. I couldn't tell what, from his mumbling. It's my turn.

'Can't he walk alone?' I plead. 'Other horses do it. Why not ours?' I have seen them passing us, and it is so.

"Ee don't backer, Prince,' grunts Guy, impassive of face and bushy of beard.

I look to Bartek in confusion. 'He mean the horse cannot do that,' says Bartek, impatient. 'Is special training Prince has not had. Without one of us, he stop. Rowena, please, do not embarrass me.'

In all my life I have never been called an embarrassment. In my old society, there were just a handful of girls whose breeding, comportment and beauty were so impeccable as to be unassailable in our world – a world that is intolerant to fault in women. Verity was one, then there were Cassandra Carmichael and Sophia Parsons – and I was the most perfect of them all. Nothing less would do for my mother. I took pride in it. I understood the rules, I knew what was expected of me and I could deliver it. *Everyone* wanted to know me, I was the exemplar to which other mothers pointed. And now I am an *embarrassment*? Tears prick my eyes.

Oddly, of all the harsh words Bartek has thrown at me since we ran away together, this has hurt me the most, which surely says something about the values that have been instilled within me. But there is also a sort of fury inside me that makes me rise to my feet. I stalk to the edge of the boat and climb over the side, knocking my shin in my haste. I'm not familiar with fury, it is not one of the permitted states for young ladies like me. I hardly know what I am doing when I march over to Prince and stand at his head. He does not move.

I look at his long, wild fringes and great stamping hooves, I observe his brown and white patches – I never saw a horse that was two colours before. His massive jaw drips hair like stalactites, dust and grime coat his massive neck and dirty long mane. I imagine him stamping on me, barging me, sinking his long yellow teeth into my shoulder and crushing the very bone. So fearsome does he appear to me that if he turned and breathed fire, I would not be surprised. My legs start to shake. I want the fury to win over the fear. I want to take hold of his collar as I have seen the men do and encourage him to walk on. But the fear is winning and the whole world tilts and turns black.

When I wake up I am back on deck. Guy is at Prince's head. Bartek watches over me with a look more annoyed than tender. 'Oh goodness,' I say in a wisp of a voice. 'I fainted. How long have I been unconscious? I'm sorry, Bartek.'

'Two minute only,' Bartek tells me and offers me a glass of water. He holds his hand out, that I can pull myself up to sitting, and I gulp the water gratefully. I rub my head. There is a small bump.

'You are better now?' he asks. I nod, though I am not sure. 'Sit, stay to sit,' he instructs. 'Make sure you are better.' I nod and finish the water. He stands and watches the water slide by. Then he brings me a heel of bread and a pot of jam to dip it into. We dispense with unnecessary cutlery here. The sweetness and solidity of the offering bring me back to myself.

'I'm sorry,' I say again.

'I did not know was so bad for you. I am sorry too.' He paces about a bit then comes back to me. 'Better? You can stand?' I scramble to my feet and hold on to the side of the boat for a minute. The world has stopped swirling; the deck remains beneath my feet and the sky above me. My legs feel stronger.

'I am better,' I announce with relief. 'Please, Bartek. I'll do anything but lead the horse. Please don't make me try again.'

'No, you must not try again. Not with fear like that. Come, my Rowena, darling.' His arms enfold me and I melt with relief. At last he understands. At last he feels like my protector again.

'Is Mr Flack very angry?' I ask when he releases me. 'He's leading Prince again and he had other things to do.'

Bartek shrugs with supreme disregard, this man of mine who not so long ago insisted I must do my share. 'He was to go to shop in village a little way ahead,' he said. 'For supplies we do not have. Bread, we have little. I thought, some chocolate, some fancy cake perhaps, for treat for you. Wine, for me. Some extra, perhaps ham, butter. Now I will go. Or perhaps . . . you would like? Stretch the legs, get away from boat for a while, and from Prince.'

'With you?' A walk on solid land with Bartek at my side, his hand in mine, is a pleasing prospect.

'Chamber pots they also need to be clean. I can go to shop, if you prefer to do that?'

I consider. I do not much fancy walking into a strange village alone, going among civilised people attired as I am. Floating along with only Bartek and Guy, I have almost forgotten there are other humans in the world. I wish that he would come. Holding his hand, I could brave any upturned noses. Then again, I wish to prove my willingness after the debacle with the horse. I must do *something* useful and the chamber pots do not call to me. And I *do* like the thought of chocolate.

'I shall go. Where is the village?'

Bartek points and sure enough I see a path leading away from the canal bank and, a little further, a cluster of roofs. 'Five minutes only to walk, Guy he says. I ask him to stop boat while you go and we can be busy with chores. Hurry back, my darling.'

'I will.' I press open secret cupboards to find my shoes; I'm not going barefoot into town. Then I realise I need stockings and run to the cabin to roll some on. Once shod, I fish out the bag I packed the night I ran away.

'Why bag? You leave me?' asks Bartek, looking worried.

'I'm looking for a bonnet. I can't go with my head uncovered.'

'Ah, my princess. Always lady. Here, give bag, I give money.' He takes my large bag from me and fishes out the smaller reticule that lies on top. He brings a few coins from his pocket and thrusts them inside. 'Now you look respectable. Shoes, hat, bag. But please to become again my barefoot muse when you return.'

'I shall.' I kiss him and he climbs off the boat with me, asks Guy to stop a while, sees me on my way.

As I walk I realise I have become somewhat confined on the boat. I ventured onto land to forage, but always remained within sight of the boat, with Guy and Bartek signalling to me where to look. But this is the first time I've walked truly alone since that horrible, fateful flit in the depths of night. The path bends and when I look back the boat is out of sight. I feel anxious, but I kick myself. When Bartek and I are settled this is exactly what will be expected of me as his wife. He will paint and I will keep house – how to do that I've no idea but I hope to make friends and learn from them. I will need to make the journey to the village shop and carry our goods home. Today will be good practice. In our new home I shall become part of the community. People will greet me when they see me, and it won't be the deferential reverence that has always been shown to Rowena Blythe. It will simply be the greeting of one neighbour to another. Perhaps I shall like that. Perhaps I shall enquire after babies, husbands and the progress of roses.

The walk is considerably longer than the five minutes Bartek promised but soon enough I arrive at the village store. I have visited shops aplenty, of course, with Verity, but only ever high-class establishments where we were offered seats and sherbets and treated like royalty. The surroundings were always plush and airy. Here I see a mass of shelves crowded with every kind of edible and practical item. Tins of polish, dusters, boot black and other things I cannot identify are massed together, next to edible provisions in tins and boxes. Fresh produce is displayed at one end of the shop. I'm not sure of how to proceed. Do I wander round gathering what I need or do I ask the shopkeeper for assistance?

The question is answered when the plump woman behind the counter, apron straining around her ample form, speaks up. 'Can I help you, pet?'

Goodness! I have never been called 'pet' before. In my mind's eye Mother has another fit.

'Yes, I need several things . . .'

'My, aren't you a pretty thing, and so well spoken. Like a princess, you are. Come on up here then, pet, and I'll get what you need.'

I sidle up to the counter, hardly knowing whether to be comforted or affronted by her familiar manner. Bartek sent me off without a list; I try to remember what he said. 'We need cake, and chocolate and red wine . . .' It sounds a terribly indulgent list, I realise. Surely I was to buy something more substantial. I wrack my brains. 'Butter!' I exclaim in triumph. 'And bread. Ham!'

'Well, now, you hold your horses. Give me a little minute to keep up with you. Nice white bread from our bakery.' She dumps a loaf on the counter. 'Chocolate . . . large or small?'

'Oh, large.' That's easy. The question of which wine to buy for Bartek is not so easy but considering the dreadful stuff he's been happily drinking, I cannot think it will make much difference. I pick two bottles at random. The ham is sold in slices and when she asks how much I want I struggle. Three of us, two hungry men, a long journey still ahead . . . I hazard at twenty slices and she looks taken aback. 'Having a party, are we? Now, where's your basket, dearie? Let me pack all this up for you.'

Of course, I have no basket. I had given no thought to how I would carry everything back to the boat. 'Oh, how silly of me. I left in such a hurry I forgot it. Whatever shall I do?' I've never owned a basket in my life.

'Oh dear, dear. Let me see now . . .' She rummages under the counter for a long time and eventually stands up, purple-faced and puffing. She clutches an old sack of some kind and her sleeves are covered in white dust. 'An old flour sack, will that do you? Not the most elegant way to carry your things, I grant you, but better than carrying them in your arms, wouldn't you say?'

'I would, yes. Thank you, you're most kind.'

She chuckles. '*Most* kind, am I? Well, it's my pleasure. The amount to pay is . . .' She tots up some numbers on a piece of paper, sucking the pencil like a cigarette as she performs the arithmetic. She names her price and I find that Bartek has given me far more money than I need. He must have overestimated – perhaps things are much cheaper here. The shopkeeper packs my sack and I grip the neck as there is no way to fasten it. I thank her again and we bid each other good day.

I feel better as I retrace my steps out of the village. I have carried out my commission successfully. I hope this will redeem me a little in their eyes after my failure with Prince. The sack is heavy with the bottles of wine and I shift it from hand to hand as I go. It occurs to me that they will not last him very long and he may have wished me to buy more.

I return to the towpath, ready to smile and wave. But the smile dies on my lips and terror leaps into my heart. The boat is gone.

Twenty-eight

Pansy

The Thursday after Rowena's vanishing, Pansy's day off was cancelled again. Besides John, two maids had been dismissed for trivial reasons – the Blythes were like touchpaper these days, the slightest thing could set them off. Mrs Clarendon didn't dare ask Mrs Blythe about hiring someone new so she was scratching about to reorder things. Pansy didn't mind too much; she even felt a little sorry for Mrs Clarendon and she couldn't think clearly about her future at a time like this. Everything felt unreal.

By the following Thursday, nothing had changed; Garrowgate Hall was still rocked by the news and the servants were under the strictest orders not to breathe a word of it to anyone, on pain of instant dismissal. Pansy's first order of business was to run over to Hampstead and see how John was faring – surely even her mother would understand why she couldn't attend to her own destiny today.

After a late breakfast she hurried over the heath. The ponds shone silver in the early light, cormorants standing guard in the reeds, ducks and coots dabbling at the surface. Trees were bursting into summer fullness but Pansy paid scant attention to the joys of nature in her preoccupation.

The Blythes were putting it about that Rowena had gone

abroad. A marvellous opportunity to study Italian had arisen quite unexpectedly, according to the official story. She wouldn't be back within the year. As if anyone would believe that. What interest had *Rowena Blythe* in intellectual or cultural pursuits? And just after her birthday when everyone knew she was expected to marry? Nonsense. What the Blythes would say at the end of the year, no one could imagine, but they were buying themselves some time. Their greatest concern, thought Pansy in disgust, was how they could emerge from this with the smallest stain, dignity and position preserved. It would not be easy.

Serve them right, throwing out John like that. If they only knew that they had ousted their most loyal servant, who would have served them faithfully until his dying day. But what concept could a Blythe ever have of the worth of a working man? *Stupid, narrow, vain folk*. The words echoed through Pansy's head as she strode across the wooded tangles and open, tussocky spaces of the heath.

Hetty's pretty little whitewashed house in Hampstead was in a small, cobbled terrace off the high street. Pansy tapped on the door and it flew open almost at once.

'He said you'd come,' said Hetty, beckoning Pansy in. The door opened directly into the front room, which was cosy and simply furnished. At the back of the room was a narrow passageway and a staircase to the upper floor. 'I was hoping you would. I'm trying to be gentle with John – he's got enough to contend with – but I need to vent my feelings to *someone*, if you don't mind.' Hetty was some years older than John – close to forty perhaps. She was widowed and this had been her marital home. Her married name was Hetty Simon, but Pansy forever thought of her as Hetty Hobbs because she was John's sister.

'By all means,' said Pansy, closing the door behind her and taking in Hetty's appearance. Her brown hair was stringy and her face looked drained. 'Have you slept much lately?'

'Hardly at all since John came.'

'That's nearly two weeks, Hetty. This won't do. Let me make you tea and you can talk to your heart's content.' Her gaze drifted to the stairs. 'Where is he?'

Hetty shrugged. 'Either snatching some blessed sleep, or simply sitting in his room brooding. That's the worst of it, Pansy, his lovely sunny temperament destroyed by those blasted people.' She swayed a little and put a hand to her head.

Pansy frowned. 'Have you had breakfast?' When Hetty shook her head, Pansy put an arm around her and guided her into the tiny kitchen where she set water to boiling and found a few things to make a simple breakfast. There was only a small window and the room was dim, but it was clean and warm.

'I should be doing all this for you.' Hetty sighed, sitting at the table with her head in her hands.

'It's fine,' said Pansy. 'You look done in. Let me help.'

'Some day off for you.' Hetty smiled. 'I'm grateful, Pansy. It's been . . .' She trailed off as if it was impossible to know where to start.

'I'm surprised it's still this bad,' said Pansy, adding a pinch of salt to the porridge and giving it a stir. 'I know it's a huge shock, but it didn't happen yesterday. Is he not coming to terms with it even a little?'

'Pansy, he hasn't even started. He's lost his livelihood, his prospects – a young man like him with so many working years ahead. Money's tight for me, non-existent for him . . . But none of that seems to feature on John's list of things to worry about. All he can think about is *Rowena*.' Hetty made a sour face as she spoke the name. '*Is she all right? Have they married yet? Will she be happy if her family never softens towards her?* I swear, he worries about her more than about himself – *or* me.

'To begin with, I had some compassion for the girl – it can't be easy, what she's done. But now I'm sick of the very name. Money's tight here, Pansy, has been for a while. I'm eking out my Brian's pension and John used to help with a few coins here and there. They made a difference, they really did. Now that's finished, and I'm providing for two. We can't go on like this for ever. And is he looking for work? No. Is he even *thinking* about it? No. All he's doing is moping about her ladyship. God! I love my brother but sometimes I could just . . .'

Pansy put a bowl of porridge in front of her and noted Hetty's hands, clenching as if she wanted to strangle someone. She had some sympathy with that. She sat down opposite Hetty and squeezed her hand across the table. 'Trust me, I know. I've been wanting to do violence to Rowena Blythe for the longest time. And . . . I love John too. Well, perhaps I shouldn't have said that but you must have guessed, for all that he's oblivious. But even I get frustrated with him. His blind devotion, his head in the clouds. Trust me. I know.'

Hetty ate the porridge grimly, as if it she had some grievance with it. Then she took a long swallow of tea and looked at Pansy. 'I'm sorry my brother is such a fool. Nothing would please me more, Pansy, than for you to become my sister. I wish his infatuation would vanish once and for all and that he'd start to think of you that way . . . But it isn't worth hoping. You know that, don't you? He speaks of you often but he cares for you the way he cares for me.'

'He'll never think of me that way. I know that.' It was a lie. Because who *knew*, really? If the Rowena disaster had taught them anything, it was that even the impossible could happen. 'And I've come to terms with it, really.' Another lie. Hope had burned down to an ember but it was still there, stubbornly glowing. 'It's tragic the way John had to leave the house, but it's better for both of us that we're not all under the same roof any more, me, him and Rowena. I'm looking for new work, trying to make a good life for myself.'

'Good for you. You'll make an excellent life, Pansy. I wish I could be as sure about my brother. Hush! I can hear the creak on the seventh stair. He's coming.'

Sure enough, a moment later, John appeared at the kitchen door. Pansy tried not to let her face betray her shock. His hair was unwashed and sticking up everywhere. He didn't look as though he'd shaved since she'd last seen him. His eyes were dark and haunted, his shirt was barely buttoned and his trousers were loose. The pristine, shapely footman was gone.

'John.' She stood, unsure of how to greet this wreck of a man, but he strode towards her and threw his arms around her, cradling her tightly for the longest time. He wasn't as clean as he had been. Pansy could smell his hair, his sweat, his despair. Even so, she closed her eyes, soaking up his warmth. It was so sweet to be held by him like this. He needed her; surely that could turn to something?

Eventually they let go. From the corner of her eye, Pansy could see Hetty watching them, lips pressed in a thin line. 'Pansy,' said John. 'You came. Is there news?'

'Is there . . . ?' As quickly as his embrace had lit a spark of joy in her, his question quenched it. She'd known he would ask, but she'd thought that first he might ask how *she* was. But if he cared about Rowena more than his own sister, why would he have any interest in her?

'John!' said Hetty sharply. 'For the love of God. Your friend has come to see you – on her precious day off – and you can't even ask how *she* is? What's the matter with you? Did Rowena Blythe take your manners with her when she fled?'

He ran his hand through his hair and looked wretched. 'I'm sorry, Pansy. Hetty's right. Thank you for coming. How are *you*?'

Pansy had been looking forward to seeing him for twelve long days. Missing him. She had been sure that she could rise above her own feelings and comfort him. But now she was stung. 'Oh, never mind that, John. I'll tell you what you really want to know, which is about Rowena. No, there's no news. Rumours aplenty, flying all over the neighbourhood, but no one's seen or heard from her. We still don't know where they've gone and the Blythes are still furious and not bending one inch. Sorry not to have better news for you.'

He sank down at the table beside Hetty. There was a long silence. Hetty looked at Pansy, Pansy looked at John and John gazed down at his hands. Then he looked up and spoke. 'Do you think she's all right, Pansy?'

At that, Hetty stood abruptly and flung her spoon into the sink with a loud clatter.

'John!' cried Pansy. 'I don't *care*! Do you hear me? I don't *care* how she is. She's made her bed. I care about you, I care about Hetty. Not her. You care enough for all of us. But it's not me you want to see, so I'm off. I'll leave you to your wallowing. I never thought you were so selfish. You should pull yourself together for your sister's sake. As for me, I'm done with you. Goodbye, Hetty.'

And she turned on her heel. She stormed out, slamming the door behind her harder than she meant to, leaving John behind with his weary sister, the pot of cooling porridge and his thoughts of Rowena.

For a long time, Pansy wandered around on the heath. She stayed on the Hampstead side. Part of her *still* longed to go back to John and make things right between them. But the amends weren't hers to make. She wondered if she should go and apologise to Hetty for her abrupt exit, but Hetty would understand. It wasn't that neither of them could sympathise with a broken heart but John's love was *ridiculous*, always had been. Hetty needed him to help her and Pansy needed him to be her friend. John had no right to this. Rowena had never been his to mourn.

Pansy knew what Mums would say, that a man so obsessed with someone else was not worth one jot of Pansy's heart. Pansy knew it was so but it didn't mean that all her love had gone away, just like that. Still, she'd be damned if she'd be like him and let her world come to an end because of it. She found a deserted clutch of trees where she sat on a log and indulged in a noisy, private cry, then she got up, brushed herself down and thought about what she could do with her day. She decided to call at the Vale of Health.

Julia and Jem gave her a warm welcome. After a short while, Julia suggested that Jem make a start on some chores – some upstairs doors needed fixing, apparently.

'I understand,' said Jem, springing to his feet. 'Women's talk again, is it, Mrs M?'

'Women's talk indeed, Jem,' Julia agreed. Jem vanished and Julia smiled at Pansy. 'You look as if the weight of the world lies on your shoulders, my dear. You and Jem are already fast friends but I thought you might need a little adult conversation. If I'm wrong, I'll call him back.'

'No, you're right. I've had quite a morning before I came here and I'm a bit . . . despondent.'

'I've heard rumours about Rowena Blythe. Is it anything to

do with that? I don't wish to pry, but I hope it hasn't affected you?'

Pansy laughed. 'You must be the only person who doesn't. Want to pry, that is. The whole world is ravenously curious. We're all sworn to secrecy but I don't care a whit about Rowena or any of them. Does that make you think very badly of me?'

Julia smiled gently. 'I imagine they're not the easiest of employers.'

'That's an understatement.' Pansy fumed silently in a rush of remembered slights: Maude Blythe's indifferent eyes; Rowena Blythe's icy indifference as Pansy dressed and undressed her, passing hours in her company without acknowledging her with a single word; Verity Blythe's narrowed gaze following her about the room like a cat watching a bird; those dreadful Sunday bonnets . . . She told Julia everything. How Rowena had fallen for an artist's assistant and run away, how the fabric of life at Garrowgate Hall had been rent, how the Blythes had frozen in fury, weaving a web of lies and secrecy to protect themselves from the scandal. Then she explained about her feelings for John and John's for Rowena, John's dismissal and Pansy's disappointing visit to him that morning.

'So to answer your question,' she concluded, 'I'm not affected in any of the obvious ways – I still have my position, my work goes on the same – but John is gone and my heart has been ripped out along with him. I want to be gone from there more than ever but how can I think about my happiness when I miss him so? But I'm furious with him too! What's disgusting is that the Blythes are already blackening his name in Highgate, saying he used to look at Rowena in inappropriate ways before she left. He never did!'

'That's very wrong,' sighed Julia. 'I'm sorry, Pansy, it must be hard. And it's quite an extraordinary story, impossible to believe. I met Rowena once – well, I didn't *meet* her, she'd never converse with a divorcee – but I *saw* her, at a ball last year. She was quite something to see. How will the Blythes recover from this, with their famous pride, the store they put on everything being done just so?'

'Rowena's put them in an impossible position,' Pansy agreed. 'When this gets out properly – which it will – it will reflect on them. People of their type will condemn them just as they've always condemned others whose lives took an unfortunate turn. It's poetic justice really. But it certainly doesn't make the house a pleasant place to be. The atmosphere's awful, Julia, like a dark sky waiting to burst into a thunderstorm.'

'What will you do, Pansy? It can't be good for you, being there. I think you should talk to Olive at the very least. Shall I see if she'll call on us today? And in the meantime, how can I help you feel better? I have a marvellous cinnamon loaf cooling.'

'You're a wonderful friend, Julia, and I hardly know you. Yes please, cinnamon loaf always helps. And I'd love to meet Miss Westallen. Thank you. Perhaps by the time she gets here, if she comes, I'll be able to think of something else besides stupid John.'

Julia opened the door and the sound of banging could be heard from above. 'Jem!' she called. 'Before you see to the doors, would you mind running over to Polaris House and seeing if Olive will come and meet Pansy?'

Jem came clattering down the stairs, red-faced, hammer in hand. 'What's that, Mrs M? Go and fetch Miss Westallen, was it?'

'Yes, and then we must have luncheon on the lawn,' Julia decided. 'Jem, tell her to bring Clover and Angeline, if she'd like. The doors can wait till tomorrow.'

Jem's eyes lit up. 'Right ho, Mrs M!' He dropped the hammer

on the stairs and ran from the house with an exuberant slam of the door. Julia smiled fondly. 'Clover is Olive's little daughter,' she explained. 'Jem adores her. She's only five years old, but quite the ruler of my boy's heart already. Angeline is her young companion, and Jem's sister.'

Not forty minutes later, Jem racketed into the sitting room, cap askew, hand in hand with a cherubic little girl with flowing honey-coloured curls and petal-pink cheeks. Next to her was a second child, equally delightful, with shining black ringlets and a round, smiling face. 'I fetched 'em, Mrs M!' Jem cried. 'They're all 'ere and ready for grub!'

The children were followed by a tall lady in a navy-blue costume and a navy hat trimmed with white. She had a lustrous mass of nut-brown hair tied up at her neck, bright, enquiring brown eyes and a determined jaw. Pansy had, she remembered now, heard Verity and Rowena make fun of that jaw a number of times. But she thought Olive was graceful and handsome; she had presence, Pansy thought. She couldn't wait to tell Mums about her.

Pansy smoothed back her hair nervously. The Blythes might be rich and proud and influential but the Westallens were all those things and respected besides. Pansy felt nothing but scorn for the Blythes, but Olive Westallen was someone she wanted to impress.

'Welcome, all!' called Julia, hugging the girls. Then Julia and Olive embraced. 'Olive, please meet my new friend, Miss Pansy Tilney. Pansy, this is Olive Westallen, my dearest friend.'

Olive shook Pansy's hand with a strong grip and looked deep into her eyes. 'A pleasure to meet you, Miss Tilney. Julia has told me only a little about you but I understand you're searching out your destiny and for that I admire you.'

'Thank you, Miss Westallen. I've heard a great deal about

you and it's an honour to meet you. Julia mentioned you might
be so kind as to talk to me about possibilities for me. If it's no
trouble, I'd be very much obliged.'

'Faddle, no trouble at all. It's my delight to help enterprising
young women. The role of the female in today's society . . .
well, don't get me started on it, that's all. Not if we want to
enjoy a pleasant lunch and digest our food!'

Pansy laughed. 'I agree. It was only when my mother urged
me to think about what I might want to do that I realised how
few choices there are. If I'm honest, I'm not getting very far
at present. But I do want to try to live better.'

'And what more could anyone ask of you? Shall I call you
Pansy?'

'Oh, please do.'

'And I am Olive, as you know. I gather you're only free on
Thursdays. I'm not usually at the office on a Thursday but if
I arrange next week differently, would it suit you to call in the
morning and we can talk about your prospects?'

'I'd like nothing more.' Pansy cast a delighted glance at Julia
who was smiling broadly. Jem had disappeared into the garden
with Clover and Angeline. Olive sat down. Such was the force
of her presence that the others followed suit.

'Marvellous. Come at ten. Meanwhile, let us be sociable.
While the children are otherwise engaged, please tell me
everything there is to know about Rowena Blythe and this
scoundrel she's run off with, otherwise the curiosity might
strangle me.'

'Olive!' cried Julia. 'You're shameless.'

'Yes indeed, but I dislike to beat around the bush. I do not
usually gossip, Pansy, but in this case I cannot retain my moral
high ground. Do you think me disgraceful?'

Pansy shook her head, needing no encouragement to tell it

all again. Olive listened carefully and looked troubled. 'Gracious.' She looked at Julia. 'I never thought to feel any great sympathy or care for Rowena Blythe but . . .'

'I know.' Julia nodded. 'The poor, foolish girl. It might seem very romantic on the face of things but I can't believe this will end well for her.'

'And when it doesn't,' mused Olive, 'she will need to be strong and resilient and clever . . .'

The three of them sat in silence, the sounds of the children's laughter drifting in to them from the garden, and reflected uneasily that these were the last adjectives anyone would ever apply to Rowena.

Twenty-nine

Rowena

Frantic. I look all around me in terror. Where have they gone? It strikes me that I must have come the wrong way, taken a wrong turn somewhere. I'm in the wrong spot. I run back to correct the error – I must be quick, Bartek will be worried – when my legs falter. They realise it before I do – there was no wrong turn; it is a straight path.

Fear and confusion fogging my mind, I return to the canal, dully wishing for a different prospect this time. But there's only the same, straight stretch of murky green water, full of shadows. I look to right and left, right and left, like a spectator at a tennis match. Perhaps they moved on to a water tap just ahead? But the canal is straight for some distance and there's nothing in sight.

My legs buckle. I find myself sitting on the grass verge at the edge of the towpath while my brain still casts about for an explanation. They've hidden the boat to play a joke on me. When they appear, we will all laugh. Or, Guy has taken the boat on but Bartek is waiting here for me so that we can walk together to catch it up and have some precious time alone. 'Bartek!' I cry, a wavering ladylike drawing-room cry. Then louder. I shout as I have never shouted before. 'Bartek! Bartek!' I roar. He must be asleep. I must rouse him so that he can emerge from the trees, tousle-haired and smiling, and take me in his arms. I scramble to my feet and run around in aimless circles, as if searching from this or that spot will reveal him to me.

I abandon the stupid sack of stupid provisions and run alongside the canal into the distance. It seems safe to assume they will not have gone backwards. I stumble a ridiculous number of times. I am not usually clumsy; it seems my legs are yet again trying to tell me something. I grow warm, then hot, wiping my eyes as perspiration blooms into my hair and pours down my face.

I run and run, until I am weak and trembling. Finally, when I look back, I cannot see where I started. I have rounded the distant bend. Ahead of me lies another long, straight stretch of canal – there is not a boat to be seen. I stand for the longest time, staring at the horizon, as if wishing might make them appear.

I don't know how long it is before I start to walk back the way I have come. I have some vague idea that I must return to the appointed spot. If they return – *when*, please God, *when* they return – how will they find me if I am not there? My hair hangs in rats' tails about my face, as if I've been caught in rain; the fabric of my dress is damp. I am footsore after my mad dash in shoes that were created for gliding along marbled corridors. A pain in my side makes me struggle to breathe. I hobble around and beyond the bend, back to the place where I said farewell to Bartek.

The sack of provisions still lies on the grass. Fancy, it has not been stolen away; this is a very quiet spot. There is not a single passing barge I might hail to ask for information or advice. The *Supreme Monarch*, it seems, has abdicated.

Eventually I collapse onto the grass again. I clutch the sack because it is something solid to hold on to. I have no idea of the time but the sun is high and quite strong. Cloud shadow scuds over me at intervals and I watch the washes of dark and light with no thought or feeling. Time passes. More time still. And then the strangest imaginable thing happens, impossible, and yet I swear it: I hear Olive Westallen's voice! Clear as a bell, as if she were right beside me; Olive, whom I barely know. I crane my neck but, of course, she is nowhere. Perhaps my mind only conjured it, because she of all people would surely laugh to see my predicament. Yet in my imagination, her voice did not sound mocking.

She said, 'Rowena. You must be strong, resilient and clever.'

Once I have amply assured myself that she is not actually here, I ponder her words with a bitter little laugh. Those are qualities for which I have never been famed. I dismiss the odd little occurrence. But then I think of the pleasure I have taken in improving my French, experiencing a different way of life, learning new skills. My intelligence, such as it is, asserts itself. 'I am not non-existent,' it declares. 'Use me now!'

I huff. Between my own inner voice and an imaginary Olive Westallen, I feel quite badgered. Don't they understand it's quite hopeless?

But at last, I start to think. I don't know how to read the time from the signs in the sky but even I can recognise that the afternoon is no longer in its fullness. Darkness will fall at some point and I had better not be alone outside when it comes. I am close to a village; certainly there will be somewhere to spend the night. I do not even know the name of the village, I realise, nor what part of England I am in. Accommodation will cost money, I realise with a shock, then remember that I have some. I count the money that Bartek pushed inside my bag when he sent me to the shop. And then I wake up.

The truth: Bartek didn't overestimate the amount of money

I would need for the errand. This is guilt money. I relive recent events in rapid time. The horse, my fainting. It was the last straw for Bartek, wasn't it? He had grown sick of me days earlier. He told me he was used to lots of women, that it wasn't like him to fall in love with just one. And when that one proved to be fragile, easily daunted, petulant . . . well, that was not the remote, flawless beauty who inspired him. At close quarters I was obviously a grave disappointment. So Bartek found a way to be rid of me.

I close my eyes, sick at my own stupidity. So anxious to prove myself, to keep his approval. And all the while he was nothing but a selfish, beautiful rogue, carried away by a vision. Unworthy of me. Or, perhaps he was exactly what I deserved.

He coaxed me into leaving the boat, made a theatre of asking Guy to wait. No doubt they set off the moment he was sure I'd gone. With my *things*! My bag is on that boat! I have no change of clothes, and the two or three pieces of jewellery I'd packed, to sell as a nest egg when we were settled, they have sailed away with Bartek too.

I'm numb. I don't want to move but the thought of spending the night here at the waterside hauls me to my feet. I trudge back to the shop with the kindly shopkeeper and I try not to think – I cannot afford to examine things too closely at present. I have done more thinking today than is quite usual for me and I cannot say I found the experience rewarding.

I tell the shopkeeper that I was due to meet friends but my party has been unavoidably detained and I need a room for the night. She recommends the local inn, The Red Lion, just across the street. I ask her where I am and she tells me that this is Liscombe in Lancashire and I ask her the date and it is apparently the sixth of May. I have been travelling two weeks. A short space of time in which to be stripped of everything!

I hesitate outside The Red Lion. I've never been inside a public house before; it was one of those invisible boundaries in my old world. Crossing the threshold of a tavern would take me beyond the pale, place me in unspeakable danger – so I have always believed. Well, I am already beyond the pale *and* endangered. Clutching my sack of odd provisions, I take a deep breath and go inside. My eyes adjust to a dim room, large, yet somehow cramped in design, with dark corners and low beams and wooden tables at which bearded men stare into large glasses. A barkeep in an apron asks my business. I enquire about a room, heart rattling in my mouth, and he slopes off to fetch the landlord, who shows me to a small bedroom under thatched eaves. Compared with Garrowgate Hall it is cramped and rough. Compared with the boat it is a palace.

He asks if I will take dinner, or some ale, but all I want is to be alone. I think to ask for drinking water, but my thoughts are too disordered for anything more. I just want to be rid of everyone.

Once the water is brought, by a waif-like maid who bobs a curtsey, reminding me of home, I bolt the door. Alone with my shame and my new predicament, I throw myself on the bed and cry and cry.

Gales of emotion sweep through me. I'm reminded of a storm I once saw at sea from the coast of Brittany. All is dark, dangerous and plunging, and I am tossed every which way. Like that other storm, this one takes an age to blow itself out; when I sit up and look about me, pushing my dank, dirty hair off my face, it is dark outside. I clamber off the bed and look out. The street is quiet and the clock tower shows that it is past midnight. I pull the drape and take off my clothes. I find a washbasin and a bar of strange-smelling soap and wash my body, do the best I can with my hair, slop a great quantity of water all over the floor and mop it up with the thin towel when I am done. I plunge my undergarments in the water and hang them up to dry over the back of a chair. Then I crawl into bed and, despite every likelihood, I sleep.

The morning brings nothing but further torments. When I wake it takes me a long time to remember where I am – my very soul is resistant to the truth. The man I fell in love with, to whom I gave myself as if in a dream, for whom I have cut all ties with friends and family, has tired of me and abandoned me on the side of a canal, miles from home. It doesn't make pleasant remembering.

What will become of me now? The question sounds plaintive even in the silence of my head. The night's deep sleep and the warmth of the bed recede; I feel exposed and alone. I start to quiver. Where can I go? What shall I do? My life is utterly destroyed – both my old life in Highgate *and* the new life towards which I was sailing. I am disgraced, close to penniless, entirely friendless and possibly with child. I am destroyed. My dark reflections are interrupted by a knock at the door. I startle, heart racing, and stare around the room wildly. I slept naked, my undergarments still draped over the chair.

A female voice calls through the door. 'It's the maid, ma'am. I wondered if you needed anything.'

'Just a minute, please,' I call, flying out of bed. I pull on my dress, dispensing with the underthings, then wrench open the door. The same slender girl who spoke to me last night stands there, an absurdly over-large cap covering her head and half her brow, a giant apron wrapped around her one and a half times.

'Can I bring you water? Or breakfast?' she asks, staring at me with great curiosity. I wonder how I must look, long hair tousled and halfway down my back, my dress fine but filthy.

It is also patently unfastened, I realise as it slides down over one shoulder. I snatch it back up. I don't know what to say. How much is breakfast? I have food, in that flour sack from yesterday. Should I eat that and conserve my money? How much money will I need when I do not even know where I am going? The only place I can go is home, surely, and yet . . . it is the last place on earth I can go.

'Some water, please, and may I ask you some questions?'

'Yes, ma'am.' The maid bobs another curtsey. A gentleman walks past us along the corridor and throws me an interested glance. Mortification!

'Come in, please,' I mutter hastily, stepping backwards out of sight and slamming the door behind her. She looks a little startled.

'Forgive me, I have only just woken,' I explain. 'I do not yet know what I need. Please, take a seat.' I pull out the ladder-back chair, snatching away my underclothes, leaving a wisp of stocking still dangling from one of the rungs. Cheeks burning, I toss it on the bed with the rest. The maid eyes it in amazement. Despite myself I glance down at her wrinkled grey woollen stockings and realise why.

She sits very straight on the chair, as if taking a test in school. I sit on the bed. I take a deep breath and try to compose myself. What do I need to know? 'First of all, I should have asked last night and I did not: how much is a night here at The Red Lion?'

She names me a price that is well within the amount I carry. So far so good. 'And . . . where are we? I mean, where am I? What is this place?' I've already forgotten the name of the village.

'Liscombe, ma'am.' She has the air of a schoolgirl answering questions on a test and looks relieved to have passed so far.

'That's right, yes. And . . . where *is* Liscombe? What part of the world? What county?'

'Liscombe, ma'am? It's in Lancashire.'

'Yes, so it is.' I nod wisely but in truth, Verity and I paid scant attention in geography; anything beyond London and Hertfordshire is very hazy to me. 'Is that . . . the north of England?'

'Yes, ma'am.'

'Very north?'

She wrinkles her brow and looks a little worried. 'I'm not sure, ma'am. How'd you mean?'

How far am I from home? How close did I come to reaching Cumbria and earning a place in Bartek's new life? 'I mean . . . how close to Cumbria are we?'

She shrugs mightily. 'I'm sorry, ma'am, I don't know. Born and bred here in Liscombe, me.'

'No matter. Then can you tell me, what is the nearest city or large town?'

'Oh, that'd be Blackburn.'

Another name that means little to me. Actually, it means nothing at all. 'And if I wanted to travel from here to, say, London, how would I go about it?'

Another shrug. 'I never been anywhere, ma'am.'

'I see. So you don't know if I can catch a coach from here, or a railway, or . . .' In truth, my ideas about travel are probably as vague as hers. I've always been ferried from A to B in the greatest of luxury and never made my own arrangements. Lack of funds has presumably constrained her. An excess of them has always sheltered me.

She looks doubtful. 'There's a railway station over in Blackburn. You'd best be askin' the landlord, ma'am. He can tell you such things better 'un me.' I'm not sure I can face the landlord. Talking to him would involve going downstairs for I cannot entertain him in my room as I'm doing with the helpful maid. I am still a dither of indecision. 'If you come down for breakfast, ma'am, you could ask him all you need to know.'

But I'm not ready. I don't *know* what I need to know. 'Is this room available tonight if I decide to stay a day longer?'

'I believe so, ma'am. I can check if you'd like.'

'Very well, please do. And bring me some water and tea with lemon.'

She jumps to her feet, no doubt relieved that her strange interrogation is over, bobs me another curtsey, and then vanishes. I hastily throw on my undergarments and put my dress on properly this time. Then I realise I have no hairbrush or comb. They too are on the boat with Bartek.

The room is available; I stay the extra night. I know I should be conserving my money but first I need some idea of what I'm conserving it *for*. My emotions are clamorous. I need to be alone to come to terms with all that has happened, and my fears for the future. All the small crises of my pampered, protected life before now have been shared with Verity. As well as I know her, I cannot imagine what she would say to this.

I'm drenched with grief, I'm hot with rage. Loss tosses me every way like the ocean and I cannot make anything of it. I simply cannot imagine what future lies in store for me now and the fear that our lovemaking has created a child strikes me cold in the heart. I open my window and stare down at the cobbles below. The simplest thing would be to jump. But I do not have the physical courage for that.

The tea, when it comes, is strong, unpleasant and small comfort. I spend the rest of the day crying, going round in endless circles of thought. Where can I go? Home. The word chimes in my heart like a bell but I have a horrid feeling that home as I've always known it is gone for good, as if a chasm in the earth has opened up behind me and swallowed it whole.

There is a small part of me that wants to go on to Cumbria, to hunt Bartek out and confront him, shout, shame him and demand reparation. For a woman in my position in our society to be used thus . . . it is despicable! He has condemned me to a dreadful life as a pariah and he will go blithely on his way. *How dare he?* There is an even smaller part, a sliver, that wants to throw myself on his mercy and beg him to love me. Goodness, I had not known there were so many parts of me! I never imagined so many conflicting voices could rage inside my head.

Cumbria is not truly an option. Even I have pride enough not to beg for his favour. And although a furious tirade would be satisfying, I do not think I have it in me. More to the point, what would it achieve? There I would be among the fairy-tale lakes and mountains of Cumbria, my anger and my money all spent . . . then what?

I could start somewhere new entirely. London and Cumbria are not the only places in the world. Here, even, in Liscombe. But I shrink from taking root where *he* left me, as if I'm a seed blown in by a random wind. What fresh start could I possibly make? I am bred for one thing and one thing only: to be a society bride. Beyond that, there is nothing. I think again of Olive Westallen – no society bride yet full of purpose nonetheless; I really do not know how she does it.

My only hope is to go home, try to win over my parents, and start again in whatever way I can. If I am with child, they will send me away to give up the child then I'll return and live a life based on a lie. They will dictate my life from hereon, even more strictly than before. I will surrender my brief autonomy, and something in me resists that. But I was never bred for autonomy.

I pace and fret, sleep fitfully throughout the day, go to the window and lean out several times, wishing for an end to all this. I let myself tilt forwards, my feet lifting off the floor but I tilt back again each time. I grow hungry and eat some of the bread, some of the chocolate, and think and think and *think* . . .

I wake the following morning to the acceptance that, of course, I must go back. Maude and Malvern Blythe are not the sort of parents to welcome me back with open arms, weeping and thanking God. I shall suffer, I know that. But eventually some sort of peace will be restored, maybe, one day. They'll find me a suitable husband. He won't be the catch we were expecting, since he will have to be prepared to over-look the rumours that will inevitably circulate. But they'll do their best to repair the damage I have caused, because they have invested *so* much in me. Perhaps even because I am their daughter and they love me.

Thirty

Olive

On Friday I am invited to a luncheon by Mr Harper. Lionel. It takes place at his home, a fine red-brick house on the lower slopes of Parliament Hill. It has a large, blue front door surrounded by unusual blue tiles and bordered again by squares of thick glass, also blue. The small, neat front garden, divided into two by the front path, is a mass of glossy green leaves and a rainbow of azaleas: red, peach, yellow and purple.

I expect another gathering of business people discussing their trade – again I am confounded. This time, the company is purely social: Lionel's sister Ida plus her husband; his closest friend Edward Burrows plus his wife. The atmosphere is light, the matters under discussion are family concerns, mutual friends and personal projects such as watercolour painting and garden design. All *my* time has been taken up by the foundation and the girls lately, so I have no artistic endeavours to describe, nor any works underway at home – but Ida, who's expecting her second child, asks me all about Clover and Angeline and everyone is always very interested in the foundation. In general, I am never short of a remark or two.

Time flies in Lionel's airy dining room with its high ceiling and long picture windows that look onto the back garden. Everything is immaculate, tasteful, from the gleaming mahogany table and chairs to the snowy mantel graced with glinting yellow-silver candlesticks, to the sweep of butter-gold drapes. A brown globe, similar to the one in my father's study, stands in a corner and around its base are several interesting-looking objects – from Lionel's travels, I assume. There is an ebony statuette of a woman clad in a knotted cloth, a basket on her head; it is intricately worked. There is a large, curled shell, obviously from foreign shores. There is a string of beads that, if I'm not mistaken, are ceremonial beads from New Zealand. I am not the daughter of a sea captain for nothing. I make a note to ask Lionel about them later.

After lunch we disperse naturally, Ida to pick at the drawing room piano and her husband Max to admire her, the Burrows to play cards and sip sherry in a corner of the same room. Lionel offers to show me the garden and, since it is a fair May day with sunshine dancing on the pathways and lighting up the flowers, it's an irresistible prospect. We stroll side by side, close but not touching, through an outdoor world as beautifully kempt as his home. Our feet crunch on paths of tiny white gravel and we pass a sundial on a tall grey column, surrounded by clouds of roses and peonies.

A small pagoda stands at one end of the lawn, a charming white clematis clambering about its edges. Thence Lionel leads me. There is a cushioned seat within, scattered with fallen leaves from the trellised roof above. He brushes it with his hand and we sit. The garden and rear of the house from here make a pleasing prospect.

Lionel clears his throat. I wonder if he is about to kiss me. In the three weeks or so since the evening at Micklethwaite's Chop House, I have seen him several times – he calls into the Euston office more often these days. I know Mabs has observed, for she shoots me frequent knowing glances from those hazel eyes of hers, but I haven't confided in her about our evening out – the kiss on my hand and the appellation of 'beautiful'. I don't know why. Perhaps because questions would naturally follow and I still don't have answers; something about all this doesn't feel quite real to me. This is the first time we've been alone together since our riverside walk.

'Olive,' he says, in a momentous tone. Then he appears to change his mind for he says next, 'this garden is not so extensive as those at Polaris House.' I do not believe the relative size of our gardens accounts for his serious, almost anxious expression. No one's garden is as big as those at Polaris House.

'Nevertheless, they are delightful. So beautifully designed, everything pleasing to the eye. I have very much enjoyed the luncheon, Lionel.'

'You have?' I assure him of it again. 'And you liked Ida, and Edward?'

'I like everyone very much. You have a most congenial inner circle, Lionel.'

'I'm pleased you think so. My house is not so large as Polaris, but it is large enough, I think?'

I laugh. 'Large enough for what? Lionel, you live alone. This house is gracious and well appointed – impressive, I should say. Polaris is far too big for us Westallens, even with the girls, but we love it, of course, and I cannot imagine living anywhere else.'

'Is that true?'

'Well, yes.'

He gazes into a stand of nearby acanthus, looking troubled. I have the feeling I've said something wrong though I can't think what. 'Lionel? Are you well?'

He turns to look at me again. 'I wanted to ask you something, Olive, but now I'm not sure . . .'

'Well, you can't say that and leave me dangling! That's entirely unfair. You had better say it now.'

'Yes. Yes, I had better. Olive, the thing is . . . the question at hand is this. Will you marry me?'

I can feel my face stretch with astonishment. I had not been expecting *that*! The moment draws on between us, Lionel with his hope, I with my amazement. At last it dawns on me that I had better say something.

'Why, Lionel, my goodness! I'm flattered, of course, and . . . and *gratified*. But this is very sudden!'

'Yes,' he acknowledges, nodding his head gravely. 'Yes.' He falls silent with an air of resignation. 'And then again, no!' he bursts out. 'In one way, I concede, we have not been courting very long and I am being hasty. But in another, Olive, dear Olive . . .' – here he clasps both my hands – 'we have known each other a sensible amount of time – almost a year – and I have admired you from the first. We know that we work well together as partners, for we have done much together for the foundation during that time, and I should like to collaborate on another important venture with you – life itself! I know you do not wish to leave Polaris House but this place has many charms. I wish to welcome you as its mistress. And the girls, naturally, would come too.'

I open my mouth to answer him but nothing comes out.

'And I love you,' he hastens on. 'The thought of you in my life as my friend, my colleague, someone I can turn to, brightens my days! I imagine how it would be to have you as my wife, beside me in all things . . . it would give me great joy,' he ends humbly.

I am genuinely touched. Still rather confounded, but touched. I had not imagined his thoughts had run on this rapidly. Still, it seems they have and I must respond. 'Lionel, I truly am moved and flattered. I was not expecting this, certainly not for a very long time, and you have taken me quite by surprise. May I have some time to think about it? I don't want to prolong your uncertainty but I cannot say yes right away . . .'

'And I had rather you didn't say *no* right away.' He smiles. 'Of course, you may have all the time you need. May I ask, what is the nature of your hesitation? Is it that my position is inferior to yours? Or that your feelings about me are ambivalent? Or . . . some other concern that I might perhaps allay?'

I take a deep breath. It is understandable that he should want to know. 'You see, for the longest time I have not thought of marriage at all,' I tell him. 'When I was younger, of course I had romantic dreams like any young girl. But as I grew older, the desire fell away. Not through resignation, you understand, but because I am unsure how the condition would actually benefit my life. Perhaps that sounds cold or overly pragmatic but I may as well be honest with you. There are many reasons people marry – for security, for status, for companionship . . . I lack none of those. My life is vastly pleasing to me as it is. To make so great a change with no real imperative . . . feels both intriguing and frightening.'

'I understand.' He is listening carefully, I can tell. A breeze blows through the pagoda and lands a petal on his head. I would reach up and remove it except the gesture would feel too intimate and tender, when I am setting out a list of reasons to marry and dismantling it one item at a time. 'And what of love, Olive? Would that constitute a real imperative? What of one special person, all of your own, to take care of you in all the intangible ways that life demands?'

'I didn't know you were such a romantic, Lionel.'

'I am. I do not see why such a quality cannot exist beside a head for business. Are you *not* a romantic, Olive?'

I frown. I'm not entirely sure. I'm passionate, certainly, in the broad sense. I have a great fever about life, a determination to make it the best it can be. Lionel Harper would doubtless be an excellent person to help me in those respects. But romance has seemed to me, for a long time, a whimsical kind of thing, dangerous when untampered by reality. Just look at Rowena Blythe! Now is not the time to mention *her*. 'I'm not *against* the idea of romance,' I say slowly, 'but I should not like it to rule my world. But Lionel, I want you to know that I like you very much indeed. I admire you. And I'm considering no other offer – I'm sure you realise that. You would make an excellent husband, of that I have no doubt and we are an excellent match, I do see that . . .'

'But perhaps your feelings for me aren't strong enough yet to propel you into a new arrangement?' I nod with some relief. 'That's all right, Olive. I hope they will grow in time but if they do not, I shan't try to talk you into it. My proposal stands, but shall we continue getting to know each other and see where time takes us?'

'I should be very pleased to do so.'

'Good.' He stands and bows. 'Shall we return to the house? The others will wonder where we are.'

'By all means,' I say in a low voice, rising to my feet and following him.

I feel strange. I have not had so many proposals in my life that it can feel anything other than momentous. I feel a little . . . *chastened*, I don't know why. Something about not giving the answer that would have made him unequivocally happy. Something about knowing that marriage is the ultimate goal for most women. Something about being given a rare chance to take a step that one cannot take alone, that could, in theory, bring all sorts of blessings into my life . . . and not jumping at it. I sigh as we enter the house. Ida casts us a quick glance that makes me think she knew what her brother was about, but with no announcement ensuing, she makes small talk with energy and skill so that Lionel and I are both absorbed back into the everyday.

I leave soon afterwards, craving solitude. Recent days have thrown up one shocking thing after another. Rowena Blythe making a controversial choice while Olive Westallen receives a proposal of marriage from a wealthy, eligible man? This is a reversal of the natural order of things.

Thirty-one

Rowena

I arrive back in London as dusk settles over the city. I'm exhausted and even more frightened coming home than I was leaving it. Over the hours-long train journey, which I loathed, my sense of optimism has diminished further. How *can* my parents still love me after all I have done?

It seems a lifetime since I was last at Garrowgate Hall. I feel like the heroine in a fairy tale, vanishing to a magical realm for a hundred years then returning home to discover that no time has passed. It seems half a lifetime even since this morning. I took breakfast at the inn and made enquiries of the landlord; he offered me passage to Blackburn on an ale float for sixpence. The indignities keep mounting. It was uncomfortable, cramped and pungent, but it got me there. I took with me the remainder of the bread, chocolate and cake but left the rest with the maid. The ham was starting to look unappetising and I had no desire to lug two bottles of red wine about. Useless to me and an astringent reminder of Bartek.

The station at Blackburn was in the midst of some great development which apparently began last year. I wondered the trains could find their way in or out for the almighty confusion. I could make no sense of anything. I had to ask several people where to go, what to do, and some were very impatient with me. It then transpired that I was sixpence short for even the cheapest ticket. How I rued that ale float then. I burst into tears. The ticket seller took pity on me and sold me a ticket anyway; I will always think of him with gratitude, even though it was third class. Even after I took my seat, crammed in with all sorts of folk who would never normally have crossed my path, I was afraid I had somehow boarded the wrong train, and would end up in Scotland or Liverpool.

How I craved to be alone, instead of being subjected to the over-friendly enquiries of the fat, moustachioed gentleman opposite, instead of avoiding everybody's eyes, instead of tolerating the excited chatter of a boy to his father. I honestly thought it would never end. But end it did and here I am, back on home ground, supposedly. As I stumble from the station on weak legs I realise my obstacles are not over; this does not feel like home at all. London it may be, but when was I ever unchaperoned on the streets, far from the gracious homes of Highgate?

I have no money for a cab so I must walk. There are rough crowds and the streets are an enigma. I ask for directions, again and again. I'm sick of speaking to strangers who stare at me, unable to puzzle me out.

After walking for about thirty minutes, I ask the way once more and the moment the man turns, I regret it. He is no gentleman, that is immediately clear; his clothes are rough and his narrow face is pocked and malevolent. His eyes gleam when he looks at me, sending a stab of fear through me, but he sends me on my way with a tug of his cap and an appraising glance. I walk away and realise very soon that he has sent me wrong. I find myself in a narrow alley that surely can lead nowhere good. I turn back towards the main thoroughfare when I see him again, approaching me with two friends.

My parents have told me no specific fates that may befall a well-born young lady among the poor of London, only that they are a bad and dangerous lot. Even without detailed warnings, my blood runs cold; I know I am in very grave danger.

"Ullo again,' says Narrow-Face. 'Fancy seein' you again. Must be fate. But yer goin' the wrong way, miss. Di'n't I tell you it's that way? Come on.' He catches my arm and tries to turn me. I yank myself from his grasp.

'Thank you so much for your assistance. But I remembered I'm to meet a friend on that road first,' I say, pointing to the main road. 'Silly of me. Good day.' My thought was to be polite and respectful in the hope that he would respond in kind, but I have miscalculated. My fear is evident in my voice, which is high and wavering.

'We'll be yer friends,' says a second man, even thinner than the first. He looks like a wooden walking stick that's achieved human form. 'Bet yer a lovely friend to 'ave. Bet yer proper friendly.' The brick walls of the alley press in on me; they almost appear another living being, wishing me ill.

'No really, I must go. She'll be expecting me, I don't like to keep her waiting.'

'Oh, she'll be all right, won't she, boys?' says the first man and the others chorus agreement. They are all about me, jostling, and they are walking further, further away from the crowd, taking me, in a reluctant shuffle, with them.

'No, *please!*' I cry. 'I don't want to go with you.'

One of them gives me a rough shove in the back and I stagger forwards quite a way before I can regain my balance. 'Don't look that way to me. Looks to me like yer very keen. Can't get there fast enough, I'd say!'

The others laugh and my imagination runs riot at the fates that await me. I start to scream. A hand clamps over my mouth and two hands grip my arms, pinning them at my sides, fingers digging in, and I am manhandled forwards so my feet hardly touch the ground. I struggle, but it's useless. There's no way my strength can best these monsters. I do, however, succeed in jerking my head away and managing another mighty scream before somebody hits me hard across the face – it's not a slap, it's a hard, solid knock – and I'm too dazed to scream again. I think my head might have fallen off. We turn a corner and I see a dead end. I close my eyes and feel the wall hard against my back and hands scrabbling at my skirts and I understand that the thing that happened with Bartek, that has already ruined my life, is about to happen again, but with no tenderness, no passion and no lilacs. I want to die.

Then suddenly, a shout. The hands fall away. The body that was pressing me against the wall turns and is gone. Released, I slither to the floor for my legs cannot support me. I can't bear to open my eyes but I hear a great number of thumps and cracks; there is a mighty fight taking place. I open one eye and see a fourth man, well dressed, beating away my assailants with a silver-topped cane. He is extremely vigorous and, though outnumbered, he is nimble on his feet and manages to evade all their blows. He has, too, an air of authority that soon chases the three men off, fast as fury, down the alley.

'And don't come back or I'll call the constable!' my rescuer roars after them. 'Vile, pigeon-livered filth! Despicable to use a female thus!' He turns to me and gently lifts my chin with a finger. 'Are you all right, miss? Do you need a doctor?'

'I . . . I . . .' I can't speak. Relief, gratitude and a sudden surge of all the grief and privation of the last weeks have overwhelmed me. I dissolve into tears, except that crying means screwing up my face and that hurts too much because of the blow they dealt me so I stop crying as fast as I can. I fix plaintive eyes on my hero, unable to prevent a sobbing wail from leaving my throat. I sound like a baby owl.

'Poor creature.' He pats my shoulder gently. 'You've had quite a fright. There's no excuse for their behaviour, no matter what you are. I've no time for mafficking of that sort.'

Through my haze of despair I catch the words 'no matter what you are' and feel confused, but he is still speaking. 'Do you have a place to sleep tonight? You should not be on the streets after a shock like that. Here, let me give you some money so you can be safe. I expect nothing for it. Although . . . if you think you might feel recovered shortly, I would be very gentle, a better client than many, I'll wager. You're a fetching little thing underneath the grime and the bruises.'

I am confounded. He is a hero. He saw off three men single-handedly, he came to my aid, an upholder of compassion and morality. But now he seems to be saying . . . No. I have misunderstood.

'Sir,' I mumble, in a voice not my own; my mouth is sore and my lips feel strange. 'I thank you with all my heart for rescuing me. I dread what surely would have befallen me had you not come along. I owe you my gratitude for ever.'

'Well, aren't you a pretty-spoken girl? As pleasing to the ear as to the eye. Here's an idea. I keep two rooms in Holborn for business when I'm in the city. Why don't you spend the night there with me? You would have food and water to wash your injuries. A night to recover. And if you should wish to show your gratitude . . .' He trails his finger down my arm and there is no mistaking the light in his eye. I can hardly believe it.

'Sir, I am not what you think me. I have suffered some ill luck recently – tis a very long story – but I'm on my way home to Highgate, to my home and family. I am not . . . I would never . . .'

'Good heavens! I beg your pardon. I assumed, seeing you with those men, your appearance . . . I had guessed you for a wagtail. Are you sure you are not?' I nod. Yes, yes, I am quite sure – though I have never heard the term wagtail before in my life, I am certainly not one! 'Then I shall call you a cab to take you home. Can you stand? Here, lean on me.'

I'm a little reluctant to touch him, given that just a moment ago he was propositioning me, but my legs are still very weak and the pain in my head is making me dizzy. I concentrate on putting one foot before the other and getting out of this cursed alleyway. We reach the main road without further misadventure where he keeps his word and hails a cab. It rumbles to a halt before us; I eye the snorting, sweating London cab-horse with fear. The stranger hands me a coin. 'To Highgate, this will be ample. You're *quite* sure you have a home to go to? If you came to Holborn with me, I would not force—'

'I assure you, sir, I have a family and home. I thank you again, with all my heart, for your assistance. I have had some terrible adventures but thanks to you, they are over now.'

In fact, I'm not at all sure that I have a family and a home any more. But I am not about to complicate matters further. The ease with which a person of my own class could make such assumptions about me, all because of a succession of unfortunate events, has made me realise more than ever how fragile my vaulted position in society always was. I have been walking a tightrope these three-and-twenty years and I never even knew it.

'Where in Highgate do you go?' He is going to instruct the driver for me. Now that he accepts I am what I say I am, the social dance I know so well has begun again – he will respect me now. Properly speaking, I should ask his name. He would give me his card and I would use it to pen a note of thanks . . .

But I don't want to. He thought that I would exchange my body for a night under his roof. Because he didn't know who I am, he did not have to veil lust with pleasantries and conventions. Is every man I have ever danced with the same?

I name a road a little way from Garrowgate Hall. The last thing I need is for all of London to hear that Rowena Blythe was found in such a predicament. He closes the door on me and the carriage rattles off.

Within minutes I recognise dear old Highgate and stumble from the carriage to walk the last streets to my home. I am as scared of this homecoming as of any other thing that has befallen me. What manner of welcome will I receive?

Thirty-two

Olive

Jenny shows her sister into the parlour and I gasp. The exact person I wanted to see. 'Oh Mabs, I couldn't be happier to see you!' I cry, and throw my arms around her. Jenny withdraws tactfully. Mabs hugs me back before wriggling free and squinting at me.

'You all right, Olive?' she asks. 'It's nice to be popular but I only saw you a couple of days ago!'

'Well, the fact is, something happened today.' I wave at the two wingback chairs by the fire and we sit. Even though the weather is steady and warm, the fire unlit, there's always something comforting about an arrangement of chairs around a fireplace. 'It's extremely fortuitous that you should call this evening because I've been going around and around in my thoughts for the last two or three hours . . . Why *have* you come, by the way? Let me not run on so much that you forget the reason for your call.'

'Only that Peg's been invited to a dance tomorrow and she's got a lovely new frock. I wondered if you might lend her that burgundy stole of yours with the gold edging? It'd look ever so fine with it.'

'Oh certainly, I'm happy to lend it. Dear Peg. I'll ask Jenny to fetch it when she . . . ah, there she is! Thank you, Jenny.

Welcome refreshments. Would you be a dear and fetch my burgundy stole when you have a minute? Then leave it by your sister's coat. She's borrowing it for Peg.' Peg is yet another Daley sibling. They are all over Hampstead like a smattering of cheerful freckles.

'Right you are, Olive. So long for now, Mabs.' Jenny has brought plum cake, always an excellent choice and, instead of the usual tea, there is sherry. She clearly sensed it was an occasion for something with a little kick to it.

'What's happened, Olive?' demands Mabs when Jenny has gone.

'It's nothing bad, just . . . extremely unexpected. It's this, Mabs. Mr Harper has *proposed* to me!'

'Ah, I see.' Mabs is disappointingly sanguine. 'I could see that one coming.'

'*Could* you? Then you might have given me a little warning!'

'But could you *not*, Olive? Surely you must have.'

'Well, only in the very, very distance.' I make a flapping gesture with my hand to demonstrate just how far off a possibility it had seemed. 'Far away, not even visible, lost in the haze of the wide blue yonder . . .'

'What I want to know is, what did you say?'

'I said I needed time.'

Mabs nods. 'Sensible. Very sensible. And how do you feel about it?'

I sigh, a great deep sigh that drags itself up from my very slippers. 'That's what I've been asking myself ever since. I don't know, Mabs. You know how I feel about marriage. Especially now that there's Clover to consider. Angeline too. To hand over my power like that to a man . . . to place our fates in his hands . . . Why? Why would I do that?'

'Because you trust him? Because you love him – if you do.

Because you want something for you? Otherwise . . . you would say no, wouldn't you?'

I nod slowly and stretch my feet out, rotating my ankles thoughtfully. It reminds me of what Lionel said: *One special person, all of your own.* 'Here is my chance, Mabs,' I say softly. 'All those things we're told we must want, as a woman. All those things that, even two years ago, I wanted so badly. How I used to envy Rowena, with her proposal after proposal. I used to worry about what would happen to me after my parents' day . . .'

Mabs reaches out and takes my hand. 'Oh Olive, I never knew that.'

'Yes, yes, I did. I knew I'd be provided for, of course – amply. But I feared I'd be swallowed up by grief without them to light my days. I feared the loneliness. And I wanted a child, Mabs, so badly. A husband was the key to everything.' Mabs nods. 'If I had met Mr Harper then, and he had wanted to marry me . . . my goodness, I'd have been overjoyed.'

'But now?'

'But now, I *have* a child. I have Clover. I did that for myself. I still dread losing Mama and Papa – *horribly* – but I have the foundation and the girls and wonderful friends I did not know then – you and Abigail. And Abigail's story . . . well, a cautionary tale if ever there was one, don't you agree?'

Abigail is another friend of ours. Her husband was a cruel and controlling man, the sort who twisted her mind, kept her to her room, prevented her from seeing her parents and brother. Mabs nods. 'Of course I agree. But Olive, not every man is a Lucius Finch. Look at your pa. Look at Mr Miles. Look at Kip.' Mr Miles is a quaker elder known to us both, the most excellent of men, and Kip is her beau, a handsome, wholesome, ambitious lad who makes her happy.

I gaze around the familiar, beautiful room. The red velvet curtains, the India rugs, the glorious paintings on the walls. '*Is* Lionel Harper a James Westallen or an Arnold Miles or a Kip Miller?' I muse. I'm not asking Mabs, of course, since that is a question I must answer for myself.

'Until you know the answer to that, you can't even think about marrying him,' Mabs decrees. 'It's like you've always said, Olive, you've too much to lose. I still say you deserve love – you know, *that* kind of love – with the right fellow. It's a . . . well, it's an adventure all by itself, is what it is. But you have to *know*, Olive, without a flicker or a shadow of a doubt.'

I sit forward and gulp my sherry. 'You're right. That's exactly it. On paper, Mabs, he's a first-rate match. Wealthy, intelligent, cultured, enterprising, respected . . .'

'But those are all just words, aren't they?'

'Indeed. Well, thank you, Mabs. You've done me good, clarified matters a little. I'm sorry to run on at you like that over something so insoluble.'

Mabs speaks firmly. 'Don't apologise. Don't you remember last year? All the troubles I had? Who was there for me then, Olive? You, that's who. And it's not insoluble. It's just that it won't be you or me that solves it.'

Bless the girl. I smile weakly. 'Then who will?' I ask.

'Only time, Olive. That's what'll sort it for you. Give it time and you'll learn what you need to know. He's a good man, Olive. But the important question, and the one you need to answer, is whether he's good enough for *you*.'

Thirty-three

Rowena

I don't know what to do. I cannot go to the front door looking the way I must; my rescuer's assumptions about me speak volumes. It would be even more absurd to go to the servants' entrance. And neither will admit me without running the gauntlet of one servant or more. I could try the terrace doors and perhaps slip in unseen if they are unlocked. Were I to run into the footman I sometimes saw there, it would not be so bad. If anyone might be charitable towards foolish, wayward me, it would be him.

I let myself into the grounds, through heavy gates of black iron. I walk up the straight, sweeping approach, lined on either side with fragrant, fronded cedars. Shadows gather beneath. The white steps to the front door gleam in the dimpsy and I lose my nerve at the sight. I duck around to the side of the house and try the terrace doors but they are shut fast.

I return to the main entrance, climb the steps and realise that I have never opened this door myself before. Always, I am expected. Always, a footman knew when I was due to return from an outing, opening the door before I could so much as lift a hand.

I will not knock. It is my own house, still. Though think of the fright I shall cause! Incredible how difficult something as simple as going home becomes, when all habit and ritual has been stripped away.

The handle is large and heavy in my hands – black bronze shaped as a leaping dolphin. The dark green door is heavy, the barrier to a fortress, but I push it and it slowly opens to reveal an ever-widening slice of familiarity. The black and white marble-floored hall dotted with classical statuary. The great spherical urns of cream-coloured china, brimming with white flowers according to the season. At present there are roses, anemones and – oh God – some late white lilacs. The irony floors me: lilacs, signifying love. How they misled me. Their scent seems cloying and deceptive to me now.

Enormous family portraits hang on the walls – there are Mother and Father side by side with Garrowgate Hall behind them. They are formally dressed and proud. There are the boys grouped together and one of Felix alone, since he's the eldest. And there is the fateful portrait of me, wearing the silver gown, the coveted Lethbridge signature dashed at the bottom in burgundy paint. I falter. In the painting, I am so glittering, so proud. My face is aglow, I fancy I can see the light of love in my eyes. Can I really face them after all I have done?

The footman on duty – *not* the one who practises his calisthenics on the terrace – leaps towards me with an expression of outrage. 'I say, young woman, who the devil are *you*? You can't just waltz in here as if you own the place! Out with you, out!'

He grabs my arm and turns me about and just like that I've had enough of being manhandled by men who think they know something about me. 'Excuse *me*, Henry! It is Miss Blythe and I wish to see my parents. Tell me where they are at once.'

He drops my arm and stares. Astonishment is writ large on

his face. I must look worse than I'd thought if even our own servants do not know me, but as he stares carefully into my face, a creeping recognition dawns. He stands back and bows. 'Pardon me, Miss Blythe. They are in the card room. Please follow me and I . . . I'll announce you.'

What an impossible dilemma I have placed him in. He would never normally escort me from room to room like a visitor, yet clearly he feels the need to forewarn my parents. I follow him, feeling the awkwardness acutely. At the door of the card room he turns to me, his face anguished. 'Please stay here just one moment, Miss Blythe. I had better tell them you have come. I apologise.'

'It's all right, Henry. But please make haste.' I incline my head graciously.

He raps the door. I hear my father's voice. Henry disappears within and closes the door behind him. I stand and wait. And wait. I hear a longcase clock in the corridor tick lugubriously. I don't think I ever noticed that tick before. My heart feels very high up in my body, pressing towards my throat. It drums a warning. Then quietly and without drama, the door opens. I hear Henry. 'Yes, sir. Very well.'

He comes out, does not even look at me and hurries off. Then my father appears and looks me up and down. 'Good God, Rowena,' he says, then turns and steps back within. For want of any other instruction I follow. I look about for my brothers but Mother and Father are alone. Father closes the door behind me and for the first time in my life, I see my mother trembling. It seems I have interrupted a game of Hearts.

'Mother, Father,' I begin, before any recriminations can pour forth. 'I am so sorry. I am so deeply, deeply sorry. I've missed you so much, and the boys, and home. I should never have run away. I don't know what I was thinking. I was in love, but he has used me. I have been so stupid, and no one could reproach me more than I do. Please, please forgive me!'

The silence stretches on like the creak of a slowly drifting door on a dry hinge. Interminable. Excruciating.

When my father speaks, his voice is low. 'You are beyond the pale. After all we have taught you, all we have impressed upon you. You have thrown your privileged upbringing away; you have thrown it back in our faces.'

'I know!' I burst out, covering my face with my hands. 'Oh Father, I know. If you only knew what I'd been through, what I have suffered . . .'

'No amount of suffering can cancel out what you have done. All your beauty, accomplishments, polish, were nothing but a veneer. Now we know your true nature and we are sick to the core. To think that *our* daughter should prove to be such a creature. Weak. Hedonistic. Licentious. No lady at all.'

I was prepared for rage and censure but even so, these words are unbearable. I can hardly speak but speak I must, for my survival. 'Please don't say so, Father. I have been truly what you thought me all along. Only I made a mistake – one mistake! It was a big one, true, and a bad one, but I was confused, deceived. I thought . . . I listened to my heart and it was wrong. *I* was wrong, Father. Only say you'll forgive me and I swear I'll be good for ever. I'll be everything I ever was and more . . . if you'll only give me a second chance. Please, Father, please!'

As I speak, my father recedes from me. Physically he has not moved from the spot, but he has withdrawn inside himself to such a degree that he seems to be gliding away into the distance. I can see that he is unmoved and I fall to my knees, sobbing, heartbreak at last overpowering me. I have worked miracles to get myself back to this house despite my lack of worldly skills. Through my tears I see the gleaming polished mahogany of the floorboards, the silken red and gold weave of the rug, its glossy cream border. Oh, to see and touch luxury once again, for riches mean I am safe, I am where I belong.

My parents stand without moving all the while I cry. At last, I look up at them incredulously. What manner of person can witness another in tears and never move to comfort them or soften their pain?

'Are you finished?' asks Mother. 'Listen to me, Rowena, and take heed of every word I say.' I nod. 'You deserve no pity; you chose your own path and when you set out upon it you left this life behind. You savagely destroyed everything we had built for you, to pursue pleasure and lust. You are no daughter of ours any more. You are not welcome at Garrowgate Hall and you never will be. It is too late to repent now.'

'But Mother, I love you. I have always been obedient, always done everything you've asked. It was one stupid misjudgement. I was in love, Mother. Surely you understand that?'

She snorts. 'Love. Don't be stupid. I cannot bear to look at you. You're like a smut on the carpet.'

'But where will I go? How will I live? I have nothing! No money, no clothes besides these I'm wearing. I cannot make a living and no man will marry me now. Would you have me end up in the poorhouse, all because of one wrong choice?'

She snorts again, her scorn searing. 'You understand nothing. Go where you will, we do not care. Go on, get out.' She turns her back on me and stalks to the window.

'Father! It's dark. I'm frightened. Please, may I at least stay the night?' If he will only relent to that, I might wake to find them softened towards me in the morning.

'In fact, Maude, she will have to.' Despite the fact that he's addressing my mother and ignoring me, I feel a little hope. Oh, I long for my own bed like a lover.

'*What?*' Mother turns, looking at him askance.

'Think, Maude, you let your feelings drown out common sense. If we send her from here, she will be at large in the neighbourhood, giving the lie to the story we have told. Her appearance, her demeanour . . . think of the disgrace! We cannot have our daughter running around London telling her tales of woe. We must remove her, at first light. Let us confine her to her room and I'll make all the necessary arrangements tonight.'

Confine me? I scramble to my feet, my heart beating so hard I fear it must explode. I could die from the sheer horror of what is unfolding. He wants to send me away? I am to spend the night in my dear familiar room only to leave it again in the morning? My legs quake like aspens, I can hardly breathe. I run to my mother, who was ever at my side, always guiding, correcting, criticising, explaining . . . My actions must have hurt her most of all for they reflect on her the most. I throw my arms around her from behind, feel her unyielding body flinch.

'I'm sorry, Mother. You have always been the best mother any girl could want. You've done so much for me and I'm so grateful. I love you so much! I want to make it all up to you . . . *Please* let me stay here, Mother, *please*! I have been through too much change already and I truly do not think I can survive another.'

'For God's *sake*!' she spits, turning and pushing me away.

'We'll send her to Aunt Althea in France,' my father continues as if I never spoke. 'I'll send a letter on ahead, this very evening, and take her to the steamer myself in the morning. No one must see her. I'll send money for Althea to set her up somewhere – it had best be Italy. That way, the world can continue to think her there and it will not be a lie. Then in a few months, when we have had a chance to think, and providing there is no child, well . ... I do not know, perhaps we can tell of an Italian husband, though it's hard to think how to make that sound respectable. But this must be our next step, you do see?'

Mother buries her face in her hands for a moment, then looks up and nods. 'Come with me, Rowena. Come with me.'

She grabs my arm and hauls me from the room. We are halfway up the stairs before I come to my senses, even a little. I start to struggle and she grunts in annoyance. 'Rowena! Come!'

Perhaps it would even be the sensible thing, to go along with their plan. There will be money for my keep and, in the short term, a family member to arrange things, albeit Great-Aunt Althea, who loathes me. I've already realised for myself that the future is a blank for me now. Why not let them fill it in for me? But now I have seen – and there is no unseeing it – that they do not love me at all. They want to bundle me up and dispatch me like a parcel. Already they've concocted a story about me and now they are organising reality to match it. I will never be free of their machinations, never! Tomorrow, if these cold, unfeeling people have their way, I will be aboard a steamer – when I have not yet begun to recover from the train, or the assault. I will find myself in France and then Italy . . . when I long only for the comfort of familiarity. But they are not the only people I can turn to. There is still a shred of hope, if I can only free myself.

Possessed of a strange energy that comes from I know not where, I snatch my arm from her grasp and turn to run. She comes after me and seizes me again but I shove her, hanging on to the banister so that I don't fall. Positioned a couple of steps above me as she is, I can only push at her thighs, and not with any force, but the surprise of it is enough to make her stumble so that she sits down hard on the stairs above me. I run.

I pound down the stairs, clutching my skirts; I must not trip. I reach the hall – no footman to be seen. At the front door I turn and look back. Mother has risen and is running after me. 'Malvern!' she shrieks. 'Malvern!' I have no choice. I run from my home and leave it for ever.

Thirty-four

Pansy

S ome sort of drama was going on upstairs. Clem Clearwell, the senior footman now that John had gone, came hurtling into the kitchen and told everyone they must all stay where they were, master's orders. No one was to so much as peep above stairs until they were told otherwise. He darted off again to fetch any servants at work in the upper rooms, herding them to the basement like a sheepdog bringing in stragglers. At this time most of them were already in the kitchen or scullery – polishing shoes, mending clothes, preparing food – so it wasn't long before they were all gathered in one place.

'What on earth is going on?' asked Pansy.

'I'm not to talk about it,' said Clem. 'Master said he'll ring when he's ready and then I'm to go and get further instructions. I'm sure it won't be long and there's plenty of work down here to keep us all busy meanwhile.'

Grumbling, the staff returned to their jobs. Pansy was rolling pastry, not part of her official duties but one of the maids who'd been dismissed was a kitchen maid. Pansy's mother had taught her enough of the arts of the kitchen that she could help Mrs Andrews now and then. *This place gets stranger all the time*, she mused as she pressed the rolling pin back and forth across the doughy circle. *I wonder what's up there that they don't want us to see.* A thought struck her and she laid the rolling pin on the table. *Or who!* Could it be Rowena? Had she come home? Surely not. Rowena was gone. Pansy shook her head and carried on working. With the Blythes, you never knew. She didn't care.

Fifteen minutes later they heard Mrs Blythe calling her husband's name, screaming like a banshee. Then they heard the front door slam and looked at each other with wondering eyes but said nothing. After another fifteen, the bell rang for Clem. He came back with the news that they could all resume normal duties.

'Before you go,' said Mrs Clarendon, 'I'll take this opportunity to tell you that the Blythes are having visitors this weekend. Mr Blythe's cousin Martin Waverley and his wife and children arrive from Taunton tomorrow afternoon. Mrs Blythe told me earlier. They leave on Monday.'

A ripple ran around the room and Mrs Clarendon nodded. 'I was as surprised as you, things being as they are. Perhaps we can see it as a sign that everything is getting back to normal.'

Pansy glanced at Clem, who looked as if he very much doubted such a thing. What – or who – had he seen this evening? Then she looked at Lou, who gave her a meaningful look. There would be speculation in the attic that night.

'I want you all to chip in, you know what's expected when there are guests. It won't do us any harm to be reminded what it's like to entertain. As for specific duties, I'll talk to you individually in the morning. There's a lot to do but we've done it before and it's only a small party. Very well, carry on.'

The staff dispersed, curiosity buzzing on their lips. Excitement too; it was good to have something to think about other than the fall of their young mistress and the foul tempers of the remaining Blythes. Mrs Clarendon watched Pansy for a moment as she pressed the pastry into a pie dish.

'Is everything all right, Mrs Clarendon?' asked Pansy. It was unnerving, having an audience.

'You've been most helpful since Henley and Brewer were dismissed,' said Mrs Clarendon. 'Two maids down is a horrible position to be in, but your efforts have been noted. Thank you, Tilney.'

Pansy looked up in surprise. 'You're welcome. It's something I know how to do, so it eases the load for Mrs Andrews a bit.'

'She appreciates it. It's what we need at a time like this, all hands on deck, working together to keep things smooth until we're through this . . . this strange time.' The housekeeper sighed and Pansy could see how rattled she was by recent events. Without Rowena, this wasn't the household any of them were used to.

'It is strange, no doubt about it,' said Pansy, thinking how curious it was that she was finally seeing a more human side to Mrs Clarendon, just when she was so close to leaving. To her further amazement, Mrs Clarendon sat down beside her, looking troubled. 'Can I get you some water, ma'am?'

'No, I'm fine. I just wanted you to know . . .' She paused and Pansy thought she saw an inner battle going on behind her stern, practical expression. Pansy waited quietly. 'You were friendly with John Hobbs, were you not?' asked the housekeeper. Pansy hadn't expected that. Was she going to be in trouble for it? But she wouldn't disown John, just because he was out of favour.

'Yes. I was.'

'Have you seen him since his dismissal? I wondered how he was faring.'

Pansy had a quick, painful memory of John's diminished frame, his hunched shoulders and unwashed hair. As much as he had annoyed her yesterday, she still hated to think of him suffering. 'I saw him just yesterday. He's not doing well, Mrs Clarendon. This job, this family, was everything to him.'

'I thought as much. Please tell him that if he needs a reference for future employment, I'll happily provide one. And please tell no one else. Mrs Blythe would be furious. I'd probably lose my place too and at my age . . . well. But it's not right what they've done. None of what's happened was John's fault and I know what kind of servant he was.'

Pansy looked at her in wonder. She'd never liked the woman but what a lesson this was that everyone has more to them than they show. 'Thank you, Mrs Clarendon. He'll be so grateful. He feels hopeless, you see, without a reference. But you, as housekeeper here . . . yes, that's a wonderful idea. And there's no reason Mrs Blythe should ever find out, is there?'

'I sincerely hope not. Anyway, you'll pass the message on? And keep it quiet? Good. Now, Tilney, will you do the shopping first thing in the morning? No dawdling over it, mind.' She handed over a piece of paper written in smudged ink and stained in two or three places with grease. 'I've talked to Mrs Andrews about the menu for the visitors and we've made a list . . .'

Thirty-five

Rowena

What was I thinking, throwing myself on the mercy of my parents? Imagine, only this morning I was sitting in my room in The Red Lion in Liscombe, reassuring myself that they would – maybe – take me back because they love me. I am a fool, over and over again. There is only one place I can go now. In fact, why I didn't go there first?

I'm whimpering as I run. I can hear myself but I can't stop the sounds coming out. I run up the hill a little way, then I turn right. Up a little more and I arrive at a row of smart red townhouses with white balconies. The front doors – black, green, blue – stand above tall steps in steep flights and, to separate each frontage from the next, black railings mark out neat squares, crowded with glossy evergreen shrubs. The seventh of these is where my brother lives. My brother and my best friend.

I stumble as I climb the steps and fall, hitting my knees hard. I scramble up and make it to the top, hammer on the door, hang on to the handrail to stop myself tumbling down, for my legs are as precarious as they were at Garrowgate Hall. A maid answers the door. She takes one look at me and says, 'Wait there, miss.' Does *she* know who I am? A moment later, Verity is there. She stands before me wearing a fine silk gown the colour of weak tea and trimmed with snowy lace. Her pretty brown hair is gathered in bunches of ringlets in an old-fashioned style that becomes her. Around her, it has grown quite dark.

It is so good to feast my eyes on her tasteful attire and flawless femininity. In the familiar lines of her face and the fashions she has chosen, I see sentences written in a language I used to speak. I see the life we have shared. Everything about who she and I have always been is encapsulated in her perfect, pretty appearance. People do not realise what an art form it is, to look this way. I have missed it all so much. Everything will be all right now that Verity is here.

'Oh Verity! Such a sight for sore eyes. Oh, my dear friend, have pity on your foolish sister who has done everything wrong and paid for it a hundred times over. Mother and Father will not know me. I cannot go home – they want to send me away! Verity, I have lost everything. What shall I do?'

In hindsight I should not have said so soon that my parents had disowned me for the Blythes have always been the yardstick by which Verity measures herself. She looks at me now with that narrow-eyed gaze with which I am so familiar. In the past she has directed it at sloppy servants, at friends of ours who have comported themselves ill, at Olive Westallen and her many eccentricities. Never at me. Never at me.

'Verity? Will you and Felix not help me?'

'Rowena, what have you done? What were you thinking? There is simply no excuse.' She looks at me as if she is a housekeeper and I am an inexplicable smear of mud on a carpet. I am so very, very tired and worn, yet I cling on to the handrail still while I try to find words to reach her.

'Verity, my darling. I thought I loved him. It was so strong it blew me away. Remember when the wind snatched your green hat that day in Waterlow Park last summer? It was just like that. When I landed, I found myself far away and I hastened back to make reparation to the people I truly love, the people I should *never* have left. Oh Verity, if you knew how unhappy I am!'

In contrast to my wild words and breathless speech, Verity is cool and composed. She raises one perfectly arched brow. 'Just like that? You wish to pick up the threads just like that, after ruining us all?'

'I have not done so! Please don't say I have. I know it will be awkward. I know there will be questions. But we can face them down together. Please, Verity, talk to Mother for me. She may listen to you. And eventually, perhaps, relent. All I want in the world is my old life back and I know it won't be easy but I'll do anything, Verity, anything. Please let me in. I think I may collapse. I have been travelling all day.'

'But my dear, that has nothing to do with me. *I* have not done anything so foolish. You can't come in here, Rowena. Your behaviour has cast a shadow over all of us, whether you like to think it or not. I, your parents, your brothers . . . we must all be beyond reproach now, to stand any chance of coming back from this. Your parents will not admit the truth, of course. They have put it about that you've gone to Italy. I'm sure *I* could have thought of a more convincing tale but still, that is what they have said and we must all go along with it. I cannot be seen to sympathise with you. Go away, Rowena. You are not the friend I thought you were.'

'What friend did you think me? One who could never err? One who did not have feelings? Verity, I tell you this, if you came to me in need, in despair, I would *never* turn you away. Surely that is the measure of a friend.'

'If you like, dear. But we shall never *be* in that position, for

I am too sensible. All my life I wanted to be a Blythe and now that I finally am, you've gone and spoiled it. How much of a friend can I consider you? I'm going in now. It's late. Please don't call again.'

'Let me see Felix! Let me speak to him, even for a minute. *Please*, Verity!'

She looks at me pityingly. 'Oh my dear, he is not here. But even if he was, he would not wish to see you. He has been hit by your . . . *departure* worse than any of us. You have destroyed him. Even this morning when he left for a few days' business on the south coast, he said to me, "Verity, my love, I pray I never see my sister again, for she is like gristle in my throat, a burr on my skin." So don't think about coming back another day. He is my husband, dear. It is my duty to honour his wishes, to love and protect him.' And she shuts the door in my face.

I crumple in a heap on the top step. I wrap my hands around my head and rock, too wrung out now for tears. I wait for the dread to pass, but it doesn't. Then the door opens again and I spring up in wild hope but it is only the maid. 'Missus says please get off her steps or she will send for the constable.'

Thirty-six

Pansy

O n Saturday morning, Pansy went shopping before the shops were even open. She went to The Garden of Eden first because she knew Mr Ollander would serve her before hours. That way she could be back at the house nice and early and impress Mrs Clarendon even more. After all, Pansy would need a reference soon. It also meant she could chat without feeling guilty about not being in the other shops.

Mr Ollander was bursting with curiosity about Rowena. 'Every other customer who comes in here is talking about her,' he marvelled. 'The news is spreading like wildfire, even when it contradicts the other news. I've heard that she's expecting a child, I've heard that she's given birth to twins . . .'

'That was fast!' snorted Pansy.

'. . . I've heard that she's married a circus performer. I've heard that she ran off with a groom who promised to marry her . . .'

Pansy felt an unexpected twinge of sympathy for Rowena. Even if she wanted to come back, how could she ever hold her head up here again? 'Everything but the official story, then, which is that she's gone abroad to study Italian.'

'Has she?'

'No.' Pansy filled him in on the little she knew. It was unfair, she reflected, that John had been dismissed when he was loyal as the day is long, while she, who still had her job, was being far from discreet. On the other hand, she'd only told Julia, Olive and Mr Ollander, hardly people who would spread rumours. Not like Mr Ollander's wealthy customers, who claimed to be friends of the Blythes but talked about them avidly, hoping for worse and greater scandals.

Hipólito helped Mr Ollander compile Pansy's order and offered to drive it to the house to save Pansy carrying it. When she saw it all massed up on the counter, it did look an awful lot. 'Take it straight round to Mrs Andrews in the kitchen,' she suggested. 'She'll be civil.'

She hurried through her errands and hastened back to the house, her two baskets pulling at her arms. She'd be glad to get this lot into the kitchen. She cut along a narrow path between the rhododendrons because it was a minute or two quicker than the main driveway. She must be carrying ten tons of meat and cheese.

From the depths of the greenery, she heard a noise that was out of place in the Blythe gardens – a whimper. She looked round suspiciously. Nothing to be seen, only the tall, thick stands of glossy trees. She took another few steps but then heard a groan and paused again. Probably she should quicken her pace and get out of there. If it was an intruder, she could be in trouble. Then again, she could always wallop him with a ham bone.

It was a relief to put down the baskets. She pushed her way between close-growing trees, leaves brushing her face. At the heart of the shrubbery was a tiny clearing and there, curled up on the ground, was a filthy, bedraggled woman. How on earth would some anonymous beggar have found her way here? Pansy had a feeling: a very bad feeling. She of all people didn't want to get involved, but she couldn't just walk away. Filled with dread, she bent over the pitiful figure.

'Miss Blythe?' she said. 'Rowena?' The woman scrambled to her feet, wild and confused. Her dress was dirty, her hair loose and full of leaves; her face was swollen almost beyond recognition, red and purple and painful looking. Pansy swallowed. What had *happened* to her? Because despite her shocking appearance, there was no doubt that it was, indeed, Rowena Blythe, the last person in the world Pansy would ever want to help.

Her head spun with questions while the proudest person she'd ever known stared at her with terror in her eyes. 'What . . . what's happened?' Pansy asked at last.

'Help me! Please, you *must* help me!' Rowena suddenly came to life and grabbed her wrist imploringly. 'I have nowhere to go and no money. If you don't help me, I will die.'

Pansy couldn't help it. Rage and resentment bubbled from a deep wellspring inside her. She closed her fingers around Rowena's hand, hard, and removed it. She'd been told by this woman that she *must* do one thing or another too many times.

'I don't *have* to do anything for you any more,' she said, her voice hard and angry. 'I *might* help you, if you ask politely. But you can't order me about.' It wasn't what she had meant to say.

Rowena's eyes clouded. She shrank back, looking crushed, and Pansy was flooded with guilt. She didn't *want* to be this heartless person. But oh, the timing of it. She'd reached the limit of her tolerance for Rowena's imperious ways a long time ago. She lifted her chin, an involuntary movement that declared she was no one's inferior and certainly not *this* woman's. Yet how she behaved now, in her enemy's hour of defeat, would define who she was. What would her mother do? What would

Olive Westallen say? A battle was raging inside her. This was the person who had made her feel that she was less than nothing for seven long years, the reason why John could never be hers . . . But today, she was just a young woman in desperate need.

'Damn it,' said Pansy. 'Why me? Why did it have to be me who found you?'

'I'm sorry,' said Rowena. 'It wasn't an order. It was . . . a plea. My parents want to send me away – for ever – and my brother and Verity have cast me out. I've nowhere to go and no one to turn to . . . I've travelled a long way and it's taken everything I have. I'm so afraid.'

Pansy sighed. 'So that *was* you last night. You came to the house?'

Rowena nodded. 'I had hoped . . . that despite everything . . . but no.'

Pansy bit her lip. Confronted with Rowena's absolute dejection, she felt a surge of pity despite herself. Imagine Mum *ever* turning Pansy away like that! She tried to think of a wrongdoing that would make her mother disown her and she couldn't. She remembered too her warm, laughing father. She was the fortunate one, she realised, not Rowena. 'And Verity too,' she murmured. Those two were thick as thieves, always had been. She was surprised at Felix, though. There was no goodness about him after all if he could be so unrelenting towards his only sister.

Rowena pressed her lips together and shook her head, tears welling.

'And you slept here last night? Outside?'

'I wanted to be hidden. I know I have no reason to expect pity from you and no right to ask for help. But what else can I do?'

Pansy took a deep breath. 'I'll help you,' she said. 'I don't know what to do with you, mind, but I won't let you come to harm.'

'Thank you.'

They fell silent, Pansy thinking furiously. Her first idea was to send her to Elstree. Mr Ollander would drive her there, Pansy could get back to work, and who better to nurse body and soul than Laura Tilney? But it would be asking a lot of her mother, who knew how unhappy Rowena had made her daughter. Besides, it was unlikely to be a short-term arrangement, because where could Rowena possibly move on to? And Pansy couldn't bear the thought of Rowena being in her home while she lived in Rowena's, of having her there when she went back to visit, polluting the very best thing in her life. She wasn't that unselfish.

Then an idea occurred to her. She would take her to Julia. Julia had a big house and she grew vegetables in her garden, baked wonderful cakes . . . Pansy was sure she'd help. The thing was to get Rowena away from Garrowgate Hall as soon as possible. If the Blythes even dreamed she was helping Rowena, she'd be out on her ear.

'Can you walk?'

'It's painful, but yes.'

'When did you last eat?'

'Yesterday morning.'

'Wait here. I have to go and see Mrs Clarendon or I'll be in scads of trouble. But I'll be back and I'll bring you something to eat if I can. Don't move, you hear me? You're well hidden here at least.'

Rowena nodded. 'Thank you. Thank you for helping me.'

Pansy hurried off without a word. She grabbed the laden baskets and ran to the house, hardly feeling her arms now; she had bigger problems. She found Mrs Clarendon in her office, frowning over an array of lists.

Pansy knocked and slipped inside. 'Mrs Clarendon, I'm sorry to have to ask but please, I need to go out for an hour.'

'Good heavens, child, what are you thinking? You've remembered we have visitors today?'

'I remember. And I've just brought all the food to Mrs Andrews. I've been ever so quick. But something's happened. I'm sorry, I can't explain. I just need to go and sort it out. An hour at the most, I promise.' She held her breath. A month ago she wouldn't even have bothered asking but everything was different now.

'Very well. You've been faster than I expected this morning, I must say. Off you go but hurry back. I want you to help Grimes prepare the Waverley daughter's bedroom when you're back.'

'I will. I promise. Thank you, Mrs Clarendon.' Pansy fled before she could change her mind.

Thirty-seven

Rowena

Of all the servants who could have found me, why did it have to be this one? The surly, pretty chestnut-haired girl with the lovely figure and the flare of resentment in her green eyes. She hates me; I always suspected it. I still don't know why, but it was there, written all over her face. She said she'd be back, but will she? Or will she bring someone to drag me off to the poorhouse? I wouldn't put anything past a scowl like that.

I suppose, if I am honest, she has little reason to like me. Because I've started to think so differently about everything, I can see it now.

I stumbled back here after my dreadful encounter with Verity last night because I needed to be on familiar ground, no matter the dangers, no matter how unwelcome I may be. I didn't come straight away, though. I had passed some foxgloves growing at the edge of the cemetery, near Verity's house, and after she turned me away, I went to find them. I reached through the railings to pluck as many as I could, then returned to my former friend's house with my armful of brilliant blooms. I knocked again and gave them to the alarmed-looking maid to present to her mistress. Foxgloves for insincerity. Verity will understand me.

Then I came here, crawled into the shrubbery. The meaning of rhododendrons, when given as a gift, is *Beware*! These trees have been at Garrowgate Hall longer than I have. Their message was always before me, but I was oblivious to the many dangers of life and love. I hear it loud and clear now.

I passed most of the night in terror. I must have fallen asleep at some point for I was roused by that maid, bending over me. Oh, the look on her face!

I push at my hair. It's long and thick – having it unbound like this makes me feel more of a slattern than any other aspect of my appearance. My face is sore and fiery. It needs tending to, no doubt. The morning is already warm and a robin hops from branch to branch chirping at me. 'Hello, pretty Mr Redbreast,' I whisper. It cocks a curious eye at me. The wait grows intolerable. Surely she has abandoned me?

At last I hear someone pushing through the foliage towards me and swallow nervously. Will I see my father again, or a constable? But it is the girl – and she is alone. 'We have to go,' she says without nicety. 'I don't have much time. I brought you this. We can't let anyone recognise you.'

'This' is a hat with a veil attached. Utterly inappropriate for the weather and time of day but she is right, for my sake and hers. I bundle my hair up inside it and fasten the ribbons firmly, though my chin is sore. 'Better?' I ask. She nods.

'I brought you something to eat and drink too but we'd better get away from here first.'

Sustenance and a disguise! She has already shown me more sympathy than I had hoped for. 'Thank you,' I say, 'truly.'

But she turns without a smile or a word and weaves ahead of me through the trees. We stay amongst their shelter for as long as possible before we have to break cover, then we hurry to the gate. I stumble after her, my feet afire with blisters, my

legs stiff after my night on the hard ground, but fear of being
spotted by my family outweighs the pain. I dread the very
thought of them now. If they saw me, would they seize me
and send me away by force? They were prepared to 'confine'
me to my room after all. We hasten a short way down the hill
then cut onto the heath at the very spot where I used to meet
Bartek – I shudder at the thought. Then we climb Parliament
Hill, striking out across open heath. Her back is stiff and hostile;
she does not *want* to be helping me.

'Please,' I call, 'may we slow a little?'

'No,' she calls back over her shoulder. Perhaps it was necess-
ity, not sympathy, that made her think of the hat and food. I'm
tripping with every other step now as my shoes rub harder
and my feet swell in protest. I think of Hans Christian
Andersen's Little Mermaid, trading her tail for legs that made
her feel she was walking on blades of fire. 'Where are we going,
anyway?' I hope that conversation may slow her down a little.

'To a friend of mine, Julia Morrow,' says the maid, not slowing
at all. 'She lives over the heath and I'm sure she'll take you in
for a while. You'll be safe.'

But I scarcely hear her reassurance, for the name clangs
alarm bells in my head. 'Wait, Julia Morrow? Is she . . . is she
a divorcee?'

She looks back at me scathingly. 'Surely you're not worried
about the effect she'll have on your reputation?'

Oh, if that was all it was. 'No, but I recognise the name.
She's a friend of Olive Westallen, I believe.'

'That's right.'

'Then I can't go there.'

She stops dead and fixes me with a disbelieving stare. 'You're
desperate, if I'm not mistaken. Now is not the time to be
choosy about the company you keep, Miss Blythe.'

I sway, the disappointment of knowing that, after all, there is nowhere I can go overwhelms me. I stumble again and this time I fall. I look up at her. 'It's not that. I'm so very grateful to you for thinking of it. It's just, you see . . .' I tell her a little of how it's always been between Olive and me, about the mysterious feud between our fathers.

'But I'm taking you to Julia, not Olive.'

'But if Julia is to Olive as Verity was to me . . .' I imagine the reception we might have given Olive, had she come to us in similar circumstances . . . The thought is a terrible one. I remember Verity's cold-hearted handling of me last night. Me, her former best friend! If Olive or Julia had thrown themselves on our mercy . . . Well, Verity would have led the way but would I have stepped in? Or simply followed her lead? I cannot tell. I am a different person from before. 'Please, please, can you not think of something else? To go to a friend of Olive's now, after everything that has befallen me . . . I know I deserve no compassion. I'm filled to the brim with shame and self-loathing for I've mishandled *everything*. But she has never liked me . . . Please don't take me there.'

She stares down at me, confounded. 'Well, you're as easy to please as you ever were,' she says tartly. 'Come on. You're making people stare, wallowing in the grass like that. Let's go to those trees, sit down a minute. You can eat something and I'll think . . .'

I follow her gratefully but slowly, for my feet are now ablaze. She reaches the copse and watches me hobble painfully towards her. I collapse onto a tree stump and she kneels, picks up one of my feet. I glance down and then away; there is blood. She gives a little tug at my shoe and I gasp. 'It's worn through,' she says, brandishing it at me. So it is. She tosses it away then reaches for the other and does likewise.

'I suppose you're too fine to be shoeless, but these are giving you more problems than protection.'

'As a matter of fact, I'm accustomed to being barefoot,' I say, defiant. 'On the boat at least.'

Her eyes widen. 'You were on a boat?'

'I travelled on a canal boat for two weeks.'

Her mouth starts to twitch. 'Rowena Blythe on a barge.' Then she frowns, as if determined not to show any interest. 'Here.' She hands me a small stoppered bottle from one pocket and a bag from the other. It contains bread, cheese and a cream puff. 'It's not very exciting. It was all I could grab without attracting notice. The drink is apple juice.'

'I don't think a meal has ever appealed to me more,' I tell her. I wolf it down. She sits on a fallen trunk, facing away from me. She rests her elbows on her knees and her chin in her hands. I daren't say a word. I concentrate on eating and drinking and gathering strength while I can. A breeze blows soft into the little stand of trees; the other walkers on the heath pay us no mind. It is a moment of impossible simplicity in the midst of a ruined life.

At last she turns to face me. 'I've thought of another place,' she says with the air of someone approaching the gallows. It's clear that, wherever it is, it is the very last place she would wish to take me if she had a choice. She laughs, bitterly. 'It's somewhere where you'll always be welcome, always be looked after, no matter what you may do.'

I look at her in horror. 'A nunnery?'

The maid gives me a very sarcastic look. 'Yes, plenty of those around here. No. I'm not talking about charity. I'm talking about somewhere that *you*, Rowena Blythe, will always be greeted with open arms, always protected, always treasured.'

I look at her incredulously. 'Can there be such a place?'

'Hard to imagine, I know. Come on, let's go. I'm already

taking longer than I'm meant to. I don't want to get in trouble for you.'

'No, no, you mustn't.' I get to my battered feet and already, in the cool grass, they feel better than they did in those hard, chafing shoes.

'I didn't know they were that bad,' she says, looking a little overwhelmed. 'My friend has a cart. I could have asked him to take us. What will we do when we get to the streets? I didn't think to bring any money so I can't call a cab.'

'Then I'll go barefoot on the pavements,' I declare bravely. 'I can do it.'

We set off again, making up time on the grassy slopes that we will no doubt lose on the hard streets. When we reach Hampstead, I grit my teeth and try to walk normally. I don't want anyone to look down and notice my bare feet. The maid lends me an arm so I may lean on her and not appear so unsteady.

'I don't know your name,' I say.

'In Garrowgate Hall I'm known as Tilney,' she replies without taking her eyes off the street ahead.

Tilney. Yes, I've heard that name, without ever knowing who it belonged to. 'What's your given name?'

'Pansy. It means thought.'

'Yes. That's pretty. Might I call you Pansy, or would you prefer Miss Tilney?'

She gives me a swift glance then. 'Pansy will do.'

I recognise the high street of Hampstead. We're passing shops and tea rooms I have visited in my old life. She takes me to a cobbled side street of whitewashed cottages and knocks on a door. I still cannot imagine who might live here, who would be pleased to see me, as she said. I've never known anyone who might live in a place like this.

The door opens. A plain-looking woman of middle age stands in the entryway. Her hair is brown and lifeless, her face careworn. Why should she welcome *me*?

'Hetty, I'm so sorry to do this,' Pansy bursts out. 'I know it's a terrible imposition but she has nowhere else to go. Nowhere. Her family have shown her no mercy, she's injured . . . I found her this morning. I didn't know where else to take her. It won't be for long. We'll think of something. I'll help any way I can . . .'

The tumbling explanation makes me aware that I have put her in quite a predicament. Not as great a predicament as *I* am in, but still. She'll be gone in a minute, back to my old home. I shall be alone here with strangers and the thought makes me cling to her.

The woman raises her hand stemming her flow of words. 'Of course. You couldn't leave her on the streets. She'd better come in.' Although the words are reassuring, her tone is not. She looks at me with the same familiar dislike as Pansy has always shown, though surely I have never seen her before in my life! Where is the treasuring, the protection that Pansy promised?

'I know it's the very last thing you need,' mutters Pansy as we step inside, 'in more ways than one.' The sour-faced stranger doesn't disagree. I *would* flounce off telling them they needn't bother if I had any choice at all. But I do not. 'This is Hetty Simon,' Pansy says to me.

I take a deep breath and greet this Hetty Simon with civility. I hold out my hand. 'Miss Simon, I'm deeply grateful to you. My name is Ro—'

'I know exactly who you are,' she cuts in. 'You are the woman with whom my brother has been in love for almost a decade.'

I am thrown. Who on earth can her brother be? I think of all the men with whom I have danced and flirted. There's a movement in the dim passage behind her and a second figure appears, ducking because he is taller than the door. 'Good God!' he murmurs. 'Can this be? Am I dreaming? Pansy?'

'I was desperate, John. Or more to the point, *she* is. I have to go. I'll come back on Thursday. Good luck.'

Without so much as a goodbye to me, she hurries away. I think the luck was wished entirely to them. I am speechless to find myself alone with strangers, in a small house in the heart of Hampstead. But the man bows to me and says, 'Good day, Miss Blythe.' He is as respectful as if I were all gleaming and perfect as I always used to be. He looks unkempt, unshaven, yet I realise I do know him after all.

'Henry!' I exclaim.

Next to us his sister makes a strangled noise and I remember that Henry is not his real name. For the first time it strikes me how outlandish it is that we called three different men by the same name for the sake of our own ease.

'Miss Blythe, my name is John. John Hobbs. You are welcome in our home. We'll take care of you. My sister will make you comfortable and you're not to worry about a thing. You're safe now.'

Thirty-eight

Pansy

Pansy ran most of the way back to Garrowgate Hall to compensate for her slow walk to Hampstead. She desperately wanted to stay on Mrs Clarendon's good side for her own sake and John's. *Land sakes!* She'd forgotten to tell him about the reference! Well, who could blame her with that damned Rowena Blythe hanging off her? The morning had been so surprising she would need a good long think about it tonight. But for now, there was no time to think about anything, only getting back as fast as she could.

Entering the kitchen was like plunging into a whirlpool. Maids scurrying, pots bubbling, Pansy could hardly tell which way was up and which was down in the fevered swirl. She found Mrs Clarendon in the hall, talking to Maude Blythe, and hovered out of sight on the basement stairs. She leaned against the wall, panting after her mad dash, until she heard the housekeeper's footsteps clipping her way.

'I'm here, Mrs Clarendon, I'm back,' said Pansy, pushing herself off the wall. 'Thank you again and what do you want me to do first?'

'Lord,' said the housekeeper, looking somewhat breathless herself. 'The mistress has just told me we're to host a jubilee ball! As if just getting through this weekend isn't enough on my plate!'

'When?'

Mrs Clarendon shrugged. 'Sometime in June, she said, or maybe July so it'll stand out after all the other celebrations. The high and the mighty coming from far and wide. It seems they want to show the world it's business as usual here at Garrowgate Hall. You can bet your last penny she'll be breathing fire down our necks every step of the way. They have to be flawless, now, don't they? Lordy, I'm getting old for all this.'

'Think about it on Monday, after the guests have gone,' Pansy advised. 'What can I do to help?'

'For now? Go and prepare Tertia Waverley's room. We're putting her in the green bedroom. Make it perfect – flowers, lavender on the pillow, a tray of bon-bons . . . every nice touch you can think of. She's eighteen; such things will please her. And it must be spotless, of course. Grimes is up there now. Then straight back to the kitchen once you've finished. Mrs Andrews wants you for a few things.'

'Yes, Mrs Clarendon.'

'And Tilney, I take it there'll be no more mysterious errands? Your business is all taken care of?'

'Yes, Mrs Clarendon. Nothing more, I promise.'

'Good. And one more promise from you, if you please. If you've ever thought of leaving Garrowgate Hall and working elsewhere, don't do it before the jubilee ball.' Mrs Clarendon was full of surprises today! 'I'm not asking, I don't want to know,' the housekeeper went on, 'only the next couple of months will be harder than ever and I need all the experienced staff I can get. You know the ropes, Tilney, you're steady. If you want to stay here, well and good. You've a bright future ahead of you, upper housemaid within the year, I should think. But if you're dreaming of pastures new, put them off until after the ball, I beg you.'

She was in deadly earnest, Pansy could see that from her set face. She was also blocking Pansy's way up the stairs. Pansy hesitated. She'd wanted to get out of this place more than anything for the longest time. But it was May now. Another month or two wouldn't hurt; she may not have found anything by then anyway. 'You can count on me,' she promised, feeling uneasy. 'I won't let you down.'

Mrs Clarendon stood aside and Pansy ran up the stairs. Even more to think about and still no time! When she burst into the beautiful, airy green bedroom, Lou looked up and grinned. 'Pansy Tilney! Where've you been, dark horse?'

'Can't tell you yet, Lou. But I will, I promise.'

'Dark horse,' muttered Lou again, tossing a duster at Pansy. 'Do the picture frames, will yer? You're taller than me.'

Pansy started dusting, glad that Lou hadn't pestered her. She was bursting to tell her, but she daren't share the secret with anyone at Garrowgate Hall. If the Blythes found out she'd helped Rowena, she'd be mincemeat. She trusted Lou, but this was too big to share. *Had* she got away with it? What if a Blythe had spotted them leaving from an upstairs window? But surely then they would have been hard on their heels? Still, Pansy wouldn't breathe easily until the guests were gone on Monday. If no furious Blythe summons had come by then, she could probably relax.

The Waverleys arrived at four and the house was perfect, as Mrs Clarendon had insisted, though at five to four the servants were still sprinting from room to room, topping up decanters and tweaking flower arrangements. As the Waverleys swept in, staff were scurrying to the hidden regions of the house, fanning themselves and collapsing on steps or at the kitchen table. Pansy lurked at the top of the basement stairs again, with Lou and Mrs Clarendon, to watch them arrive. It was the only part of working here that could possibly be described as fun – seeing the grand folk with their airs and their lovely clothes. Clem Clearwell was on duty to greet them since John wasn't there any more.

The Waverleys were indeed very fine, but Pansy thought they looked nicer than their Blythe relatives. Mr and Mrs Waverley were very civil to Clem and they smiled a lot more than old Maude and Malvern. They had three children of their own and two were with them now. Their son, Tristan, was about twenty-five and striking-looking with a riot of curls that looked like sunlight dappling a hazel hedge.

'Jam *tart!*' breathed Lou appreciatively, earning a disapproving scowl from Mrs Clarendon.

His sister Tertia, eighteen, was pretty, slender and cheerful. You could see the family resemblance to Rowena in her dainty nose and golden hair, but her manner was as fluid and eager as Rowena's had been rigid and remote. Even so, it was strange to see another lovely young woman here, as if things were *almost* the same – but not quite.

The ill-starred portrait of Rowena gazed remotely over them all. Pansy had noticed the Blythes couldn't even bear to look at it, after spending all that money on it. They probably wished they could get rid of it, but if they were to keep up the pretence that Rowena was abroad and all was well, it had to stay.

It was midnight before the servants finished their work. The Waverleys had to be settled in, refreshments sent. Then there was all the unpacking to do since no rich person, however amiable, can travel with a sensible amount of luggage. They had to be dressed for dinner, after which there was dinner itself. Then drinks and entertainments and eventually, when at last the family retired, clearing up.

Pansy tumbled into bed, certain she'd be off to a deep sleep in an instant, but her brain demanded its chance to ruminate on the day. So she lay awake for two hours or more, thoughts racing, while Lou and Maisie whistled through their dreams in their beds nearby.

Pansy tossed and turned, tried to drift off and failed. She lay on her back, staring up at the ceiling in the dark, and tucked her hands behind her head, arms akimbo. Rowena Blythe's escapade had come to a sticky end, as anyone could have predicted. And her parents had proved to be as unrelenting as anyone could ever have guessed. Pansy wondered what on earth had happened. Not that she cared. They weren't ever going to be friends.

Part of Pansy wanted to stay well away. But she'd have to go and see Hetty for one thing, to see if she was all right. Poor woman, this was the last thing she needed. *And* she couldn't resist seeing John again; she was desperate to know how he was now that Rowena Blythe was under his very roof. Pansy sighed. Imagine, not only had she helped the damn woman, she'd taken her to the very person Pansy loved, delivering her into his waiting arms! Well, it wasn't as if keeping them apart meant that John would marry *her*, so why not? One of them may as well be happy. Because there was no doubt in Pansy's mind that Rowena would marry John now. It was the greatest respectability she was ever likely to achieve and she wasn't designed for independent living; she needed someone to take care of her, pave the way, make everything easy and pleasant and wonderful. Pansy would like all that too, but it didn't seem as if life had that in store for her.

She flumped over onto her front, buried her face in her pillow. Did she really want to see Rowena and John together, his look of disbelieving delight, her stupid, coy smiles . . . ? Urgh!

She flailed onto her side. She was *not* going to let Rowena and John take over her thoughts and feelings. She had done that for far too long. That had changed lately, and everything had felt so much better. Now she was being pulled off track again, preoccupied by other people's lives instead of her own. She wasn't going to race over there first thing on Thursday. No. She'd promised Olive Westallen that she would call into her office at ten that morning. And she would make the most of that meeting if it was the last thing she did. She'd gobble up every pearl of wisdom, be grateful for every moment Olive could spare her. And only when she was all done there would she make her way to Hampstead to find out what was happening in Hetty's house. For she would, inevitably. Morbid curiosity would have its way.

Thirty-nine

Rowena

I awaken from a deep slumber to find myself in a warm bed; for a moment I can't think where I am. I open my eyes with difficulty – exhaustion has invaded every fibre of my being. I see a pitched ceiling above me, a gauzy white curtain fluttering at a small casement window, ajar just a little way, a plain square of wooden floor, a white china ewer atop a little table. Until just over two weeks ago, I slept every single night of my life, barring our family trips to the continent, in my beautiful gold and peach bedroom at Garrowgate Hall. Since then, I have slept on a boat, in an inn and in a shrubbery, each circumstance more preposterous than the last, according to Blythe family standards. Now I find myself in the cottage of our footman and his sister. This could be the most outlandish situation of them all.

I struggle to a sitting position. I am clean, truly clean for the first time in ages. Bits and pieces of yesterday return to me slowly as sleep falls away. Hetty filling a tub in the kitchen with hot water – I was mystified until she explained that I was to bathe in it. I was a little alarmed that there was no lock on the kitchen door but she assured me, somewhat wryly, that she and her brother would be able to restrain themselves and respect my modesty. The water felt good. I scrubbed my skin and worked soap through my hair. (Now, freshly washed but without the influence of curlpapers or tongs, it has expanded around my face and shoulders like a rising loaf.) Hetty had laid out a rough but clean towel for me, and a clean dress. It fits pretty well; Hetty is scrawny but I am very slender. I never wore brown before.

Then my reluctant hostess threw away my bathwater and made breakfast for the three of us. Conversation did not flow and we ate swiftly. I should have offered to help clear up afterwards but I did not think of it at the time; I was too stunned. Henry – no, he is not Henry, he is John Hobbs, I *must* remember! – kept gazing at me across the table with a look of wonder on his face. But every time I caught his eye, he looked away. No doubt he is astonished to have me here – no more than I!

Then Hetty saw to my injuries. There was no warmth in her manner but her touch was gentle. She dabbed arnica onto my face and feet, as well as a few bruises on my arms that I hadn't noticed but that were very black and tender nonetheless. I wanted to break the silence between us but I couldn't think of anything to say.

The headboard behind me is hard. I turn a pillow on its narrow end and rest against it, drawing up my knees. What will become of me? I'm safe now and I am grateful; this is a most unexpected reprieve. But my problems will not go away. And I cannot stay here for ever; it is clearly not a wealthy household and I doubt they can afford me. What to do? Where to go? If I can only stay here long enough to gather my wits, to think of *something* . . .

The rest of yesterday passed in a blur. John and his sister, who is a widow I gather, mostly left me alone as if I were a gazelle grazing in the garden or a peacock in the rafters. I could think of no conversation as the events of the last days all caught up with me in a rush and condemned me to dumbness. I sat and stared into space in their tiny front room, which seems to serve as sitting room, drawing room and parlour all rolled into one, whilst they busied themselves in other parts of the house.

The sounds of their industry reached me and time passed. Hetty announced an early supper and John reappeared, looking more like his old self, whiskers shaved, hair combed, shirt neat and clean. I gather he no longer works at my old home. I wonder why. I couldn't eat again – my stomach was knotted and sick – so I begged to go to bed and I think Hetty was relieved to see me go. I have slept like the dead.

I don't know what time it is. It's light, but then it's summer so it may yet be early. The house is quiet. I get up and dress, so that if they should call for me, they will at least find me presentable. Then I return to my perch on the bed, trying and failing to order my thoughts.

Bits and pieces of conversation from yesterday creep into my head like latecomers to a party. Hetty's words: *I know exactly who you are. You are the woman with whom my brother has been in love for almost a decade.* Pansy's words: *Somewhere that you, Rowena Blythe, will always be greeted with open arms, always protected, always treasured.* Is it possible that Henry . . . that *John* . . . carries a flame for me? The very thought is . . . well, I don't know what it is.

Mother would say it's disgraceful, Verity would laugh and say it's too, too tragic. Even my brothers would say, 'That's a bit out of order, Ro, fellow like that!' I don't know what *I* think about it. I remember the first morning we spoke, when I came upon him flushed and sweating on the terrace. He was covered in confusion – I had simply assumed he was flustered at being caught in such a state by one of the family. I would notice him around the house after that, cravat arranged just so, collar starched and erect, livery neatly buttoned. The very image of self-containment. It always made me feel easier in my skin when I saw him on duty in the hall. He was always cordial, always solicitous and had such a gentle smile. I do not think it a horrific presumption if he loved me a little – I'm sure he cannot now.

At last I go to the window and look out. The room overlooks the street, which is also quiet. Brown cobbles glisten in the sunshine; a road-sweep leans on his broom, taking a philosophical moment perhaps. Small white cottages like this one run along the opposite side of the street too. A flash of memory visits me, sudden, dramatic: the view from my old bedroom window. The gardens at Garrowgate Hall. A long lawn, elaborate flower beds, pathways of snowy gravel, a sweeping cypress, a willow beside a pond . . . I have lost so much.

I think of waking up there. Stretching like a cat, luxuriating in bed for hours, ringing for a maid when I wanted tea or breakfast. Reading, giggling, dreaming and eventually rising. Deciding on a dress, standing rather sulkily while it was fastened around me. Suddenly I can't stay in this room any longer.

I long for the sweeping stairs and airy corridors of home. But this door opens onto a cramped landing with another door right in front of my nose, and the stairs are narrow and steep. I go down them, meaning to be quiet – I am once again barefoot. I had not bargained for how they creak.

The downstairs room is in darkness but a shape stirs in the shadows and makes me shriek.

'Miss Blythe,' says a voice. 'Don't be afraid, it's only me, John Hobbs. Wait a moment and I'll make you tea.' Another memory flash: the tall, fair-haired maid, Smithson I think, entering my room in the morning carrying a steaming pot of fragrant Earl Grey. Anything I wanted for the asking and all I had to do was extend my fingertips.

The dark shape of John Hobbs reaches for the shutters and opens them, letting light flood in. He has been sleeping on the sofa, I observe from the heap of blankets. Fortunately he is quite decent. He runs his hands through his hair and rubs sleep from his eyes – then he makes me a little bow. A bow! 'Please follow me, Miss Blythe,' he says.

There isn't far to go, only a few steps into the kitchen. There, he pulls out a chair for me and sets water to boiling. I am too shy to speak. He wears a shirt, trousers and braces that hang loose. He makes the tea swiftly and sets a pretty china cup and saucer before me.

'Thank you, Mr Hobbs.'

'You're welcome.'

'Will you not take one yourself?'

He hesitates. 'Very well.' He sits opposite me. 'How did you sleep, Miss Blythe?'

'Very well, thank you. A long, deep sleep. A blissful escape, in fact . . .' I am saying too much. I flush and change the subject. 'You slept on the sofa, Mr Hobbs. Do you not have a room here?'

He smiles. 'I do, Miss Blythe. You slept in it.'

'Oh!' I am aghast. I have ousted the man from his bed! He mistakes my horror.

'It's quite all right, Miss Blythe. We put clean linen on it and gave it a thorough sweeping, prepared it like a guest room.'

'Thank you again! But that's not why I exclaimed. I have horribly inconvenienced you. Mr Hobbs, please let me take the sofa tonight.' A memory flash: the cramped cabin bed I shared with Bartek. Me pinned against the wall, his body wedging me in. John Hobbs probably still thinks of me as a princess in a castle but that sofa would be a more comfortable bed than some I have used lately.

'Certainly not,' he says briefly. 'Now, are you hungry, Miss Blythe? Would you like some breakfast? Or is it too early for you? The housemaids knew your daily habits. The footmen did not.'

This reference to the old days rouses me. 'But Mr Hobbs, you are not footman here and I am not the mistress. I am a very grateful guest. Please don't think otherwise. Although, I *am* hungry, as a matter of fact.' Of course, I had missed supper. 'Should we wait for your sister? What time is it anyway?'

'It's just before eight, and Hetty's already eaten and gone out, Miss Blythe. I can offer you toast, porridge, eggs, kippers . . .'

'Toast, please. And more tea if it's no trouble.'

'It's none.' He stands. 'And with the toast? Butter, honey, cheese?' I dither like a child and he smiles again. 'All of them, why not?' he suggests. 'Though perhaps not on the same slice.'

I smile too. 'May I help?'

He looks around, perhaps assessing the damage I might do. 'You could refill your tea, Miss Blythe, and mine too if you please.'

A simple task one might give to a child, but I do it carefully, proud to return the pot to the stove without having spilled a drop. We devour the toast in companionable silence. A memory flash: Verity and I eating cheese on toast late at night after a party, licking our fingers and stuffing ourselves silly. She often used to stay with me after social events. We would giggle and gossip to our hearts' content. 'You're the best friend a girl could have, Ro,' she often said. I'm glad I took those foxgloves to her door.

I'm glad too that Hetty is not here – the atmosphere is easier without her. So much so that it barely flickers through my mind how inappropriate this is. 'I'm afraid I'm a dreadful imposition, Mr Hobbs,' I say at last. 'I think your sister is a little . . . nonplussed by my appearance here. I hope she will give me the chance to explain.'

'I'm sure she will. But you don't have to explain anything to us, Miss Blythe. We are simply a refuge for as long as you may need it.'

'Please know that I don't intend to abuse your hospitality for longer than I must. Although, I don't know where else I can go. I shall think and think until I come up with something. I was so surprised to see you yesterday. When Pansy brought me here, I had no idea . . .'

'I'm very glad she did. I do not wish to pry into your business, Miss Blythe, but I hope that as the days pass you may come to think of me as a friend. Sometimes it can help to talk things through with someone, no matter how hard they may be. I would promise you my absolute discretion.'

'I can see that you would,' I say, looking at him. 'You are very kind to me, Mr Hobbs, and I've done nothing to deserve it, I'm sure. I don't even know where to start. What . . . what do you know?'

Before he can answer, the front door opens and closes. A second later Hetty is with us, her thin cheeks red as if she has been for a long walk. My heart sinks to see her unhappy face.

'Good morning, Mrs Simon.' I'm determined to win her over. 'Can I get you some tea?'

She looks at me in surprise then nods. I scramble to my feet again but realise I don't know where the crockery is kept. John passes me a cup and saucer and I pour her tea, this time slopping a little in my anxiety to please. 'Oh, I'm sorry, is there something to wipe it?'

'It's fine,' she says gruffly and holds her hand out. I pass her the cup. She takes a sip then looks up. 'I heard you talking when I came in. Answer her, John, we may as well get everything out in the open now.'

'It can wait,' said John. 'It's her first morning here. You needn't discuss things with us until you feel comfortable to do so, Miss Blythe.'

His sister disagrees. 'No, John, there's no time for softly, softly. She's here among us, it's a problem, we have to know the facts and see what can be done.'

'But Hetty . . .'

'Actually, I agree with Mrs Simon,' I say in a small voice. *Actually*, I'd feel much more comfortable discussing everything alone with gentle John but I cannot possibly say that. I take a breath. 'I was too stunned to talk or make sense of anything yesterday. I'm more grateful than I can express that you took me in. Mrs Simon, I said to your brother earlier that I shall not presume upon your hospitality longer than necessary and that is so. However, the truth is, I have no idea where else I can go. I need a solution, and if you think that discussing everything openly is the place to start, I am willing.'

I think it's the bravest thing I've ever said in my life. Hetty watches me, inscrutable. I wonder what she's thinking. Then John begins.

'We know, of course, that you ran away,' he says painfully. 'We also know . . . that you went with the artist's apprentice.'

'You do?' I shrink. But then again what difference do specifics make to my overall disgrace? I cannot afford to be precious and private among these people who are all I have now.

He nods. 'Your parents were very angry, very shocked. They questioned everyone. I hoped they wanted to find you but it seems they wanted someone to blame. They were determined that if any servant had helped you, they should not stay.'

'And my brother lost his livelihood,' Hetty cut in. 'My brother who worked for your family for sixteen years, who was loyal and steady, has nothing now. He's staying with me because, like you, he has nowhere else to go. My means are slight. Too slight to look after a grown man, much less a society beauty to boot. They cut him off without a reference, all because of your folly.'

Her tone is viperish. But I understand her resentment towards me better now. John frowns at her. 'Enough, Hetty, that is not her fault.'

A memory flash. John on the terrace. Me hurrying out, a light in my heart, on my way to see Bartek! I hear my own voice, blithely lying. *I'm going to meet a friend, Henry, I mustn't keep her waiting.* I shudder. 'Oh Mr Hobbs. Were you dismissed because you saw me leaving those several mornings? You kept my secret and lost your job because of it.'

He shakes his head. 'I didn't tell them I'd seen you go. I'm not so stupid.'

'Then why?'

He looks reluctant so Hetty tells me. 'Because he spoke up for you, that's why. They'd nearly finished with him, he was just about to go back to work, when he asked your parents to forgive you. He asked your father to search for you and make sure you were happy.'

'Oh.' I am more touched than I can say. Can any man be so caring?

'Yes, *oh*!' sneers Hetty and we all fall silent. I contemplate *my father* receiving advice from a servant and marvel that John has lived to tell the tale! My goodness, he is brave.

'Thank you,' I say, 'for urging kindness and leniency for me, even though I didn't deserve it. But you shouldn't have done it. It would never have made any difference.'

'I know that now, Miss Blythe. And why didn't you deserve leniency? All you did was fall in love, isn't that right?'

Hetty snorts. I bury my face in my hands then snatch them away – my face is still tender. 'I did.' I don't know where to look. 'And yet it was all so complicated. I thought, or hoped, that I had found . . . something greater than the society match my parents wanted for me. In view of how things turned out, I feel ashamed of my stupidity.'

'As well you might,' snaps Hetty.

'Hetty!' shouts John furiously.

'No,' I say, 'she is right again. Mrs Simon, I feel terrible being here, adding to your burden. If I were a truly unselfish person, I would go away. But because I don't wish to die on the streets, I shall stay until I can fathom something better – if you'll have me.'

'Of course I will. I've no reason to favour you but I won't see you hurt further. Still, you can't stay for ever. We couldn't accommodate that, you hear? We've problems enough.'

Forty

Olive

Pansy Tilney interests me, not only because she's a friend of Julia's, but because she is such a complicated mix of traits. She is striving to have a better life and be a better person. She's appreciative, warm and intelligent. She's also sad and bitter and irritable; I saw it that day at Julia's when she spoke of Rowena. She's like a rope made of two different threads, her better nature and her less admirable habits woven tightly together.

She presents herself at my office at ten o'clock sharp, wearing a most becoming straw hat and a pretty summer dress of green poplin. As she said, she is not a desperate person, and therefore very different from most we help. She isn't penniless, her looks and speech are more than averagely pleasing – she just needs a nudge in the right direction to achieve, perhaps, great things. I am the woman for the job!

I suggest we go to a coffee house since I want to hear her story and here she may feel constrained. Mr Gladstone and Mabs would overhear every word, and others will rattle in and out – those we are helping and, of course, Mr Harper, who calls in almost every day that I'm here. He's been as good as his word and not mentioned his proposal again. I greatly appreciate that as I need considerable time and breathing room to understand what I feel.

I show Pansy around, introduce her to my erstwhile colleagues, watch her taking everything in keenly. Her green eyes are watchful – I fancy I can see despair and hope battling it out in them. She looks more pinched than when I met her at Julia's; I wonder what has happened since I saw her last.

When we're ensconced in my favourite coffee house hereabouts, she looks around appreciatively at the maroon and cream decor, the gleaming glassware and towering cake stands. 'This is a nice place,' she says. 'My mother would like it. Thank you, Olive.'

I beam. 'Pleasant surroundings are always conducive to a good heart-to-heart, I think, and I want to learn all about you. But first, what will you have? It's my treat. Well, the foundation's.'

'Really? How kind. In that case I'll have coffee with cream and some of that violet-coloured cake over there. I've no idea what it is but it's pretty.'

'It's lavender and buttercream – as you see I'm a regular here.' We order and Pansy begins to explain everything to me.

Hers is a tale of ordinary joy and tragedy. A happy family, the death of a dear father bringing heartbreak and a change of fortune. A speedy departure from the family home to try her luck as a maid in one of the finest houses around. Some luck, to be caught up with the Blythes! She tries to explain how her seven years there have eroded her spirit but makes an inelegant account. These things are subtle and hard to put into words. But I can imagine. I know the Blythes. She appears to dislike Rowena especially – well, who can blame her? – and mentions a footman named John, who was her chief inducement for staying there. He is gone now, dismissed in the wake of the Rowena debacle. Apparently he pleaded Rowena's case before her parents! Good, brave, doomed fellow.

'I knew it wasn't good living there, feeling as I did,' she concludes, 'but I knew that just going into service elsewhere wouldn't be worth the upheaval. It was my mother who said I had to search for something that would make me happy. She said I had a bright future in store and I deserve better.'

'And do you agree with your mother?' It's an important question because if she's merely carrying out her mother's instructions, the chances are she won't get very far. If, however, her mother's words have lit a spark inside her and the quest has become her own, then anything is possible.

Pansy looks thoughtful. 'It's not easy to say,' she says and I appreciate her honesty. 'Because I'd do anything for Mum, and she's always right. But since I started thinking about it, I've begun seeing things differently. Like meeting Julia – and you. It's made me consider I might have . . . potential, I suppose. Mrs Clarendon – she's the housekeeper at the hall – said the other day that I'm a good worker and might be promoted soon. Even though I've no intention of staying there, it made me feel good about myself.'

'Of course it did.'

'I've been trying out different things, like working in a deli-catessen and a hat shop. Both the storekeepers said they'd have me back again. It was . . . gratifying.'

'How very enterprising,' I murmur. Too few women have the spirit to be experimental; it is bred out of them. 'And did you enjoy those trials?'

'No. I dislike shop work on the whole. It bores me and the customers were insufferable – Blythes all over again. But – and I know this might sound strange, Olive – even finding things I *don't* want to do was interesting. It made me realise that if I could say no to something, I must value myself more than I'd thought. And that made me think more about what I might *want* to do.'

She tells me about her love of hats, how even in her bleakest,
Blythe-blighted days, a trip to the hat shop window could
brighten her mood. She modestly acknowledges her own good
taste and suggests that although she does not want to sell hats,
she *might* like to make them. But she doesn't know and appren-
ticeships are expensive . . .

'That's something I wondered if you could help me with,'
she says, looking worried. 'I know you've much more deserving
cases than me . . . I don't expect you to use your charity's
money on me, but if you knew of somewhere I could try out
the work before I pay for an apprenticeship . . . It's a lot to
spend if you're not sure it's the right thing.'

The poor girl. She is trying so hard! It's thrilling to see
someone try to puzzle out their own way forward. 'I'd be happy
to help, Pansy. I could even ask my own hatter if he'd let you
spend a week or two learning the ropes. Mr Bailey Endicott,
he's a decent fellow. But you won't be able to work with Mr
Endicott or anyone else while you're still at Garrowgate Hall,
will you? So what should our plan be?'

'I can't leave yet anyway.' Pansy looks miserable. 'I promised
Mrs Clarendon. She's been decent to me lately, and she's all
in a flutter because Mrs Blythe wants to throw a jubilee ball . . .
She made me promise to stay till it's over. It's only a month or
two, I suppose.'

'Let me see what I can arrange for you, Pansy. You're clearly
a very bright young woman. Unusually so, I would say. You
deserve a helping hand.'

Her green eyes sparkle. 'Thank you, Olive. I'm so grateful.
And if you have any other ideas, I'm willing to try anything.'

'That's excellent. I'll put my thinking hat on.' I grin at the
millinery-related pun and consider her. Something tells me
that there's more to Pansy than hats. There's nothing wrong

with hatting as a career, but her love of attractive headwear is
not what is most interesting about this young woman. As for
what it *might* be, well, I don't know her well enough to say.
But I'm not done with her yet.

I signal for more coffee and when our cups are filled, I ask
her whether there is any news of Rowena.

Her shoulders slump and she is at once an altogether
different Pansy. 'As a matter of fact, there is. I seem to have
got . . . embroiled.'

Forty-one

Rowena

On Thursday, Pansy comes, as she promised she would. She doesn't come early, however, and the morning drags on as we listen for the door. Hetty is eager to see her; John longs to thank her for bringing me here. I have mixed feelings. I too am grateful but I dread her spiky manner spoiling the hard-won equilibrium of my days. This is my sixth day in the little house in Hampstead and I have learned my lesson from my time on the boat. I must pull my weight. And since I received no practical upbringing whatsoever, I need help and training to do that.

I've demanded that Hetty and John show me how things are done here and now I can make beds, launder clothes in the tub in the backyard, hang them to dry and sweep floors. I can cook porridge and a simple vegetable soup. It is a great deal to learn in less than a week but this is how I want it; I am no longer a decoration. Lessons with Hetty are actually easier than those that John gives me, because John is so deeply offended by the thought of me embarking on mortal toil that he hesitates to instruct me and apologises every five minutes. It's excruciating. He's every bit as keen on my place in the social order as my parents ever were, which is ironic.

Hetty on the other hand expects my help and gets on with

it. She is not the warmest teacher in the world, but there is a certain harmony to our interactions now, since we are working towards a common goal, that of making me less of a parasite.

We've talked a great deal too, the three of us, about my adventures. Whilst I know she thinks I'm utterly idiotic for getting myself into such a mess, she did also say that I've suffered enough for one lifetime. I was glad to hear her say so. Hetty is the only one of us blunt enough to raise the question that troubles me at night: am I with child? How would I know? She watches me like a hawk, but she and her husband never had children so I'm not sure she knows the signs any better than I.

When the knock comes at the door, my stomach plunges. I'm vastly nervous of hearing news from Garrowgate Hall. Pansy comes in looking very pretty in a green dress and a rather sweet straw boater. I've never seen her in her own clothes before; she has some taste. I greet her with a compliment and an offer of tea. She looks extremely surprised.

I busy myself with the tea while the other three sit around the kitchen table. John offers his thanks and I add mine. Pansy apologises to Hetty again.

'But it's all right,' says John. 'I'm looking for work and I'll be earning again before you know it. I've moped around long enough. That will help things considerably.'

'Without a reference?' asks Hetty acidly. 'Good luck.'

'But that reminds me,' says Pansy. 'The most important thing I needed to tell you. Mrs Clarendon will give you one, John. She feels bad for how they treated you so she said you're to give her name so they contact her directly, and she'll deal with it.'

'Oh!' The relief in John's voice is enormous. I suppose for a man in his position, to be out of work is a terrible thing. And he has such dignity. 'That's very good of her. Please thank her for me, Pansy, tell her how much I appreciate it. See, there's nothing stopping me now, Hetty. I'll get something in no time.'

'Well,' says Hetty. 'Good.' It makes me feel better too, since my actions led indirectly to his dismissal. I set a tray prettily with the tea things and carry it to the table.

'There's a turnout,' says Pansy, meaning, I suppose, my waiting on them.

I try not to bristle. 'Everything is different now,' I comment and start to pour. 'How are you, Pansy? Have you had a pleasant morning?'

She looks taken aback. 'I'm well enough. And yes, it was a good morning.'

'We thought you might come sooner,' John remarks.

She hesitates. 'I had a meeting.' Her tone suggests that she doesn't want to discuss it further.

Hetty remarks that rain clouds are gathering and asks me to fetch in the washing – so they can talk about me, I presume. Well, so be it. They have been friends all along. I am the interloper. In the moment before the door closes behind me, I hear Pansy say, 'Ruination seems to be the making of her!'

I take down the clothes slowly, to give them time, then go back indoors and ask the question I dread, but must. 'How is life at Garrowgate Hall?'

She looks troubled and I know the news is nothing good. 'It's . . . strange. And I need to tell you something, Rowena. They're looking for you.'

Something inside me flutters. 'They've forgiven me?' Even as I ask it, I know that is not the reason.

Pansy's brow furrows further and her green eyes darken. 'No. They haven't confided in *me*, of course, but it's pretty obvious that you being in the area isn't a good thing for them.

I suppose they're afraid you might turn up again when they
have company or even just the fact of you, after everything,
could be . . .'

'An embarrassment,' I supply.

'Yes.' Pansy has the grace to look apologetic. 'So they want
to find you, and pay for you to go far away and stay there.'

'That's what they said that night. So nothing has changed.'

'No. Did they tell you they want you to go to France, to
your great-aunt?'

'Yes, they said as much. But Great-Aunt Althea has always
detested me. I can't bear the thought of it. And exile? Having
to travel again after all my trials? Oh, no, no, no.' Then a heavy
thought drops upon me. I *should* go. For Hetty and John's
sake, I should go to France, lighten their load. My parents will
fund it and they will be free of me. But I can't bring myself
to say the selfless thing right away. 'How do you know all this?'

Pansy flushes a little. 'Sometimes the servants listen at doors.
Sometimes it's the only way to know our own fate, especially
lately,' she adds, defensive.

I could not care less about servant morality at this point.
'Did *you* hear it, yourself?' Her flush deepens and she nods.
'My parents – did they sound . . . *concerned* about me? At
all?' Her discomfort visibly grows and she shifts in her seat. 'I
take it that's a no.'

'In all honesty,' she bursts out, 'your parents are vile people.
We heard the whole thing, me and Lou, and it didn't sound
as if they care for you a bit. All they care about is not being
shamed. I can't lie, you've never been my favourite person,
but *this* . . .' She breaks off, biting her lip and shaking her
head.

I take a shaky breath. 'I see. Well, it doesn't surprise me. I
have no choice after all but to go, do I? So, go I must. I said

I wouldn't impose on you longer than necessary and this will mean I can keep my word. May I walk back with you, Pansy? I've no money for a cab and no doubt I'll get lost on the heath on my own.'

Pansy is mute. Is the thought of my company on a walk *that* bad? I feel my eyes glowing with tears and look down at the table. I don't want them to think that I'm playing for sympathy. But the silence goes on for so long I have to look up. John is stony-faced, his jaw working as if to contain some sort of outburst. Hetty and Pansy are exchanging looks in a rapid unspoken dialogue that I cannot interpret.

'You can walk back with me, of course,' Pansy says at last. 'But . . . you don't *want* to go. To France.'

All three regard me seriously. I shake my head. 'I don't. You think my parents are vile? Well, Great-Aunt Althea is a hag. She *hates* me! She used to call me a prissy little bore and never showed me the slightest kindness. But it's not just that – there are other reasons I barely even understand. I wanted . . . well, I did not *want* any of this but, given recent events, I wanted to find some way of my own, rather than live a life *allowed* to me, by people who despise me. But I have no idea how I would have done it. I would probably have failed and it is you, Hetty, who would pay the price of that experiment. So I must take what is offered to me.'

'You don't have to go.' It is John, of course. He likes having me here, that is clear. His sister is a different matter.

'What if she is with child? Did they say anything about that?' Hetty looks at Pansy again. 'Will they provide for that eventuality? We still don't know, you see.'

Pansy hunches her shoulders. 'They didn't mention it.'

Hetty sighs. Now we are all looking at *her*, as if she carries my fate in her hands. It is too much to ask of her. I get to my feet. 'There is no choice to be made. It's not as though I can honestly promise I'll find employment next week. I'm not unwilling but . . .' I spread my hands to express my general uselessness. I'm about to say that I'll fetch my things, then I remember that I have none so I sit down again. 'I'll leave whenever you're ready, Pansy.'

'You'd be a long way from home,' John points out.

'But where is home for me, now?' I whisper.

Hetty reaches across the table, grasps my wrist and stares into my eyes. 'You're not unwilling?' she demands. 'To work, to pay your way?'

'Certainly. But I can't ask you to put any store by that. Who would have me?'

She shakes her head and lets go of me. 'I have no idea. Really. But if you want to stay here, Rowena Blythe, you may. Keep away from your parents and find this way of your own that you wish to seek.'

Warmth kindles and spreads within me. 'Can you mean it?' I whisper.

'I don't like it,' she states. 'Parents sending their child away because she slipped up. Slipped up badly, yes. Embarrassment, for rich folk like that . . . yes, it's hard to bear. But there isn't one of us around this table who hasn't made mistakes. Not as spectacularly as *you*, perhaps, but still . . .'

'What if I can't do it and you're stuck with me? I have no useful skills. And I'll be . . . notorious, I suppose. I can't imagine what place I might find.'

'That doesn't mean there isn't one, though,' says Pansy. 'I . . . I know something of trying to find a way that isn't clear. I haven't done it yet. But some people, clever people, think I can do it. I never thought *you* could but perhaps . . . Anyway, it's up to you. I don't care.'

But I think she does. I have the oddest feeling that I can't understand. My parents cast me down and I fell. But I was caught in a safety net woven of people who do not really know me and did not much like me, apart from John. But they were unwilling to see a fellow being suffer. Somehow, these people are willing to take a chance on me, to allow me to make a life. From nothing. A blank canvas.

I take a deep breath. 'Very well. Thank you. I wish to stay.' John's face is radiant, Hetty's approving, Pansy's resigned.

I hope I don't let them down.

Forty-two

Olive

I do not like uncertainty. It is a cloud that hovers, shielding the sunlight and giving a certain weight to the days. Worse than sorrow or fear, it's an insidious enemy that saps one's vital strength.

I like to be clear-sighted, full of purpose and vigour. I like to surge forward as if carried on a sparkling wave. But there are times when we get caught in some strange undertow and are dragged from our course, tumbled about in confusion. It is part of life, I understand, yet I would avoid it if I could.

These last days I have grown more and more tired. My activities are the same: I work at the foundation; I enjoy my parents and children; I see my friends. Nothing has changed, no onerous burden has been added. And yet I go about slightly fuddled – a condition I resent greatly. It's as if a net has been cast about me. It does not strangle me – but it's there, I feel its touch. The touch of uncertainty. And it's there because of Mr Harper's proposal.

I spend long, solitary hours considering it. He has been true to his word and not bothered me with it again – which is a mark of true character, I think. He is excellent company. Gratifyingly intelligent. He and I work together on behalf of the foundation so we already have a shared goal and common purpose. He is good-looking, I have always thought so. There is nothing in the match that would shock society, though I care little about that.

He's offering me all that anyone could desire: a beautiful home in the neighbourhood I love; companionship; a mutually supportive partnership in life; someone to be at my side and put an end to this solitary figure that Olive Westallen has ever cut hitherto. Most of all, he offers me a chance to strike out on something new. To take a bold step in life, and change my condition, to imagine myself anew. I remember determining, a short while ago, that my life should continue to improve even further. Perhaps this is my chance to bring that about? Instead of the eternal spinster, playing by her own rules, making her own choices because there is no one else to make them, I would become a married woman, perhaps even give birth to a child and have a different experience of motherhood. I would be one half of a team, I sigh. *Would* I?

Would it really be like that? I try hard to imagine married life, day after day. Not only the good, happy days, but the days when one of us comes home in a foul humour. The days when we disagree over some small matter. Would his wishes take precedence then, as the man of the house? As a younger woman I craved this opportunity for my heart to find a home and have my own special person to share my days. But have I been alone too long to grasp it now? Would I be placing my shoulders in a yoke? The world is full of stories of unhappy marriages and it is rarely the man who suffers. Not never, but rarely.

I do feel a great deal for Lionel. I love him, yes. But is love enough to make me upend my world, which is a perfectly good world to begin with? There is much to gain. But there is so much to lose. I am at an impasse. The matter grows no clearer with the passing days and I grow weary and lacklustre as the question nags at me. I need to take my mind off it for a while – that is the point of Lionel giving me time after all – but it's almost impossible to relinquish the search for the right way forward. People's hearts and lives are at stake. It may be the biggest question I've ever asked myself: is love enough?

I've spent this Friday morning at home with my girls, occupying ourselves in joyous nonsense. I remember how Lionel was originally put off by the fact that I'd adopted Clover – he was shocked by her background and shocked that I had taken such an odd step. It's all in the past now. Now, he embraces Clover as a welcome part of me, as he should. So I should forget about it, shouldn't I? Everyone has weaknesses and blind spots. He has changed and what more can I ask? There is no such thing as a paragon and I am certainly not one.

But Clover, my darling child, that sweet, innocent soul . . . the memory of him taking offence at her, without ever having met her, does prick me sometimes. And that unconventional step I took is entirely illustrative of me. I am not a maverick for the sake of it but if there is something I really need to do, then I do it and consequences be damned. How does *that* sit within a marriage?

I *must* think of something besides Lionel. These thoughts of actions and consequences bring to mind the perfect distraction: Rowena. I have never liked that family but my goodness! This is something even I had not expected of them. Their precious figurine of a daughter, threatened with exile, forced to run away to any despicable fate. Why, if not for Pansy, *anything* might have befallen her.

We have never been friends so, in her disgrace, I'm probably the last person she will wish to see. But she is my neighbour now, down the hill in Peregrine Lane. She's staying in a household with no income and her life is in ruins. Likely she does not want *my* help. But does that mean I should not offer it? At once, I know the answer. I must call on her. It is so good to be certain of something again.

There is one small obstacle, though, in the form of the longstanding feud between our two fathers. I go in search of my parents and find them in Papa's study discussing some business or other. The children are with them, playing make-believe with Papa's large tobacco-coloured globe. After greeting me enthusiastically and warming my heart most thoroughly, they return to their imaginations and I know they will not take notice of our conversation.

'Papa, there's something I wish to ask you and you must be entirely honest with me, for this is your home as well as mine.'

'Why, thank you for acknowledging it, my dear,' says Papa with twinkling irony. 'What is it?'

'I know your feelings about Malvern Blythe, Papa . . .' I watch Papa's face close over as it always does when that name is mentioned; the hard darkness in his eyes is quite unlike my darling father. Nevertheless, I persevere. 'But would you object if I invited Rowena Blythe here to visit? Perhaps just to sit in the garden with me? I wouldn't ask if I didn't think it import-ant. You see, Rowena has found herself in some trouble lately and . . .'

'Rowena?' exclaims Mama. 'Do you know something of her, Olive? Gracious, the *rumours* I've heard! Kindly tell me all you know at once, if only to set my mind at rest. I've been worried about the poor girl. *What*, James? I have! She is not her father, you know.'

Her interjection was in response to the flames kindling in my father's eyes at the very thought of a Blythe eliciting my mother's compassion. In all other matters he is the fairest of men – just, compassionate and wise. A beacon amongst living beings! But mention a Blythe and my father becomes a brooding madman. Mama and I do not know the cause of it and in my estimation we never will.

'That's true,' says Papa, 'but why must Olive be the one to help her?'

'The answer to that is plain,' I reply breezily. 'I must always be the one to help *anyone*, because I am a great meddler and cannot keep myself out of things. But in all seriousness, Papa, listen to the story and you will understand.'

I tell them what Pansy told me. That Rowena arrived back at her home a week ago, dirty, dishevelled and penniless. That she had a swollen, pulpy face from some violent incident. That her parents showed her no compassion but planned to pack her off to foreign climes *on the next steamer* – yes, I had to repeat that bit twice for neither Mama nor Papa could credit it – following which she called on that sickly-sweet viper in ringlets Verity Crawford-Blythe, her supposed best friend and sister-in-law, only to receive the same treatment. That Pansy found her in the rhododendrons the next day and took her to the home of her friends, who cannot afford a third person in the house, but took her in nonetheless.

'The poor, poor girl!' cries Mama. 'James! Can you credit it?'

Papa shakes his head with a troubled expression. 'Even for Malvern Blythe . . .' he murmurs. 'But then again . . .'

'So you see, Papa, I need to talk to her. My first loyalty is to you, always. But Rowena will need a great deal of support in the weeks ahead. The reason I want to invite her here is because I don't know these people she's staying with and by all accounts their place is very small. If Rowena *will* talk to me, I'm sure they won't appreciate their unfortunate guest and a complete stranger taking up space in their home ad infinitum.

Perhaps she won't wish to see me at all, but in conscience I must try.'

'Of course you must!' So says Mama.

Papa nods. 'I see that. Yes, Olive, you may bring her to our garden. I wish . . . I wish I could say she may stay here, I hope you know. But I cannot. It is not the girl herself, you understand. But if Malvern were to hear that I was sheltering his runaway daughter . . . my dear, you may be sure the heavens would fall. It's best to keep her away from me for everybody's sake.'

'Thank you, Papa, you are good.' I pause, poised to ask for the hundredth time what went wrong between those two former friends.

But Papa can see what I'm about and throws up his hands. 'Lord, but my study has grown crowded! May I claim it back, for I have accounts to settle and shipping inventory to check?'

Mama and I take the hint and rustle out. 'I'm glad you're helping her,' says Mama. 'If I were in direst need, I would want a friend like you.'

'There's never been any love lost between us, as you know, Mama. But I'll call on her tomorrow, rest assured.'

Forty-three

Rowena

John and I are sitting in the tiny backyard, which for once is free of laundry drying and rugs airing. He has carried out two chairs from the kitchen and placed them at a respectful distance from one another. The day is beautiful – bright and sunny but not oppressively hot. He did ask if I wanted to take a turn on the heath but I'm too afraid. In the old days, I couldn't walk two minutes without acquaintances and neighbours – even complete strangers – wishing me a reverential, 'Good day, Miss Blythe!' I cannot face the curious gazes, the shocked recognition. And there is the small matter that my parents are hunting for me. I presume they cannot bundle me up and *force* me to go to France now that I have friends here – but I had rather not take the risk.

I have seen only the inside of Hetty and John's house since I arrived a week ago and John says it isn't healthy. Even Hetty agreed to this sunny interlude, though I feel uncomfortable idling while she rolls pastry in the kitchen. But Hetty takes a brisk walk each day for her health; I'm not sure she approves of my wish to hide away. I can hear people in the yards on either side of us, beating mats or scrubbing clothes; I keep my voice low as we talk. It is pleasant out here, listening to the leaves of shrubs and vines rustle, feeling the sun on my face at last.

I remember sitting on the deck of the boat with Bartek and how I was at all times nervous, excited and full of trepidation for the future. This is very different; John is an excellent person with whom to sit quietly, to rest in the moment at hand. I am not among the finest folk of the area, nor am I escaping from reality with a colourful rogue. I am simply with good, decent people living an ordinary life. Hetty is sharp, yes, but I understand her better now. John is not sharp. John is the gentlest, most harmonious soul I have ever known.

'This is pleasant, John,' I murmur with my eyes half closed. My face is getting better, the swelling going down and the cuts healing. The ache is now only slight.

'Yes,' he says and we lapse into silence again, but it is not the silence of two people withdrawing into their separate mental worlds, it is the silence of two friends wordlessly sharing the same experience. I never considered such differences before. A butterfly flutters past, light and soft as a scrap of old patchwork.

'Rowena,' says John. The three of us have, some days since, settled into using Christian names, though John found it difficult to address me differently at first. I was 'Miss Bly-Rowena' for a while but he has the hang of it now. 'Rowena, I want you to know that Hetty and I, we're pleased that you've decided to stay.'

'I appreciate that.'

'And I will continue to do all I can to protect you. I want you to find your way. I do not want you to worry about your parents, or fear being homeless. Your life is yours, now, to forge as you wish.'

I turn to face him. Goodness but such a warm light gleams in his blue eyes. How can someone so attractive be so humble? I'm not sure he realises what a great gift his words are. For a woman, having been brought up to serve other people's designs, to have decisions and plans made *for* her . . . to think of being in charge is terrifying! But also, it makes a gentle tug inside me like wind plucking at a kite. As if, in a moment, there will be a lift . . . then soaring.

'I have an interview for a position next week,' John continues.

'John, that's wonderful. Where is it?'

'A big old house down in Chelsea. Senior footman. I was amazed to see the listing, there are so few these days.'

'Yes, I know the fashion is changing. And is that what you want, to continue as a footman?'

'I hardly know. It's all I've ever done. I wouldn't mind trying something new but honestly, I'll take the first post I find. I need to earn money. I've imposed on my sister long enough and now there is you to think of.'

'But John, I am not your responsibility!'

'Nevertheless, I wish to have means. As I am now, I'm no help to anyone.' He stares into the pots of herbs, looking very determined.

A breeze lays a lock of hair across my face and I push it clear. 'That's not true. You have helped me vastly this past week. Just your kindness has transformed me.'

He smiles. 'I'm glad to hear it, but I want to offer more than that.'

His words hang on the air, an echo of declarations many men have made, in an entirely different context. Surely he does not mean that he . . .

Just then Hetty's frowning face and screwed-up topknot of hair poke through the door. 'Caller for you, Rowena,' she barks.

I startle. 'For *me*?' I had not heard the front door. Only Pansy knows I am here; surely she hasn't given me away? 'Not someone from Garrowgate Hall?'

'No. Go through. I haven't got time to entertain.'

'But who is it?' But Hetty has gone. I look at John in alarm.

'I'll come,' he says, rising. I stand reluctantly. I don't want anyone to call on me here. Who on earth can it be?

John stands back to let me go ahead of him. 'Go on, go on,' flaps Hetty as I pass through the kitchen into the small front room. And there, dressed in a fine navy costume and a jaunty hat, is Olive Westallen.

Dear God. Not the *last* person I would wish to see, but close! 'How did you know I was here?' I blurt out, all my social graces deserting me.

'Miss Blythe, how good to see you,' she says, all *her* social graces in place and impeccable. She comes towards me, hand extended and I shake it numbly. 'I do apologise for calling unannounced but I wanted to welcome you to the neighbour-hood with my very best wishes. I can call again if now is inconvenient.'

As if it is perfectly ordinary to find me here! As if we are friends! As cordial and charming as if . . . Oh! I do not know how to talk to her. 'How did you find me?' I ask again.

'Our mutual acquaintance, Miss Tilney, told me of your arrival in Hampstead. I wanted to ask if I might do anything to help you settle in.'

Pansy! That traitor. Why is Olive here? To air her superiority, now that I have fallen? Curiosity? Charity? Oh yes, Olive is a remarkable do-gooder, is she not? I do not need her charity. I do not have to answer her questions! 'She should not have told you,' I retort, turning away, aware of John hovering protect-ively behind me.

But then I remember something. I remember collapsing on the grass on the bank of the canal, the barge gone, my fate stolen . . . In the midst of that despair it was Olive's voice I heard.

Rowena. You must be strong, resilient and clever, it said then. I thought I must surely fail if that were the case, but I have proved to possess more of those qualities than I ever imagined.

I hesitate. The idea of me and Olive at loggerheads with each other comes from another world, the world of our families, the world of Verity and I talking nonsense about every person we know. The idea of Olive as superior or condescending originates from our old rivalry – her intelligence pitted against my beauty. Her unconventional life against my exemplary one. Her worthiness against my empty-headedness. How can such ideas hold substance now? I am not as stupid as I thought, certainly I am no longer exemplary and where has my beauty got me, other than into fiery pits of trouble? I hesitate and look at Olive again.

She regards me steadily and I do not see spite or condescension in her gaze. I compose myself. 'I'm sorry. I was not expecting a guest, you caught me off guard, Miss Westallen. I'm pleased to see you. How are you faring?'

'Very well, thank you. And yourself?'

And then I laugh. There is only so far parlour talk can take us. 'I have been better, Miss Westallen. I have also been worse, if you can believe that. Have you met my friends, John Hobbs and Hetty Simon?'

Olive smiles and shakes hands with John. 'I met Mrs Simon just now at the door. Mr Hobbs, a pleasure.'

In a trice, it is John and Hetty who sit in the yard while Olive and I take tea in the humble front room. If Verity could see me now!

Olive sips her tea, perfectly composed, and clears her throat. 'Rowena, I've heard of your misfortunes, of course. All the wild rumours worried me – then Pansy told me what really happened, the little she knows of it. Pray do not be angry with her – she told me knowing that I was concerned. You and I have not always been friends but you have a true friend in me now, if you need one.'

I see that she means it. I can imagine Olive and me being bosom friends as easily as I can imagine a secure, independent future for myself, which is to say not at all. And yet, I have to start believing in impossible things or I will stay here, for ever. This is not a new life. It is a hiatus.

I take a deep breath. 'Olive, I thank you, truly. I have great need of a friend. Well, I have John and Hetty, but they have troubles enough. I don't want to add to their load. I can only stay here so long. I've no idea where to go next or what I shall do . . .' My voice has risen with each sentence. I sound frantic even to my own ears.

'Of course, my dear,' says Olive, calm as ever. 'These are very great decisions to make and you are at a low ebb. Commendable as it is that you wish to spare your friends, you mustn't rush yourself now or you will hurtle straight from one dreadful situation to another. This complete break from your old life . . . I can only imagine how difficult it is. Don't go through that suffering for nothing. Go through it to get to something better than you ever imagined.'

'That's exactly it – that's what I want. Only . . .' I spread my hands and look at her in bewilderment. 'I still can hardly believe any of this has happened . . . that I did any of the things I did. I still have trouble making sense of it. And I can't *think* what lies ahead for me.'

Olive's mouth twitches. 'I hear you ran away with an artist.'

I flush hot with shame but jut out my chin. 'I did. And if you ask me now, I have no idea how or why it happened. But there it is. I did it, and he abandoned me. And now I am the very definition of a disgraced woman.'

'Oh, as to that,' says Olive, flapping a hand. 'I don't care a fig for those sorts of ideas. They will make it harder for you, of course, since there'll be plenty who will judge you accordingly. They'll obstruct you or simply delight in telling you all the ways in which you are dreadful. My advice is to ignore them and find instead the company who will *not*. You have had an adventure. Men have them all the time. Why should we not?'

I smile a small, sad smile. 'It was *quite* an adventure,' I concede. 'I only wish that the consequences had not been *quite* so catastrophic.'

'I would dearly love to hear the tale but I don't wish to presume upon Mrs Simon for long. I came to invite you to Polaris House, that we might talk for longer. As for now, I understand you are all at sea – but have you any ideas at all about what you might want? Or what you don't want?'

I almost adore her for her absolute focus upon what is ahead of me, not what lies behind. No wonder she gets things done! I have no idea what I might want but I have some answers to what I *don't* want.

'My parents are hunting for me,' I begin. 'They want to send me to France and set me up there with a dreadful relative, so that I'm out of the way and can't embarrass them. I don't want that. I don't want to be beholden to my parents, not after they turned me away. I don't want charity; I do *not* want to be sent to an accommodation for those with nowhere to go. I want to stay here and I want to make my own way; I want to contribute to something. But I possess few skills of practical value. I was raised, as you know, to be purely ornamental. But I've been through terrible trials, and they did not finish me. I must believe I have some worth and I want to use it. Somehow.' I bite my lip. 'It is vague, I know.'

Olive beams. 'Rowena, you are a strikingly beautiful woman. In the past I have envied you, often. But I have never *admired* you more than I do now.'

I cannot deny it, her admiration means the world to me. I crinkle my brow at her. 'You have? You do?'

'Of course. You've been used most grievously. Not only by the artist but by everyone else who should have cared for you. You've been stripped from the life you've always known and have no visible prospects. It would have finished a good many people. But not you! You're back on your feet and looking for the next possibility. I take my hat off to you.'

I press my lips together and hold back tears. I have done something right! Not everyone outside these four walls disdains me. There's something about Olive that makes me feel anything might be possible.

'No respectable man will ever want to marry me,' I reflect with a sigh.

'Likely not. Men are conservative creatures, even the best of them.' She sighs and I wonder if she knows this through personal experience. Verity and I never considered Olive's love life, beyond laughing at our greater popularity with the male sex. Much good that did me! 'But consider, dear, do you *need* to marry?' Olive goes on. 'If you can support yourself and if you have friends to cheer your days . . . There are many spinsters in our world and they do not die of it. You make an unlikely looking spinster, tis true, but then the world is full of unlikely things. Your life might become more interesting than it ever was before.'

It's an outlandish idea, yet isn't it just what I was thinking months ago at Garrowgate Hall when Mother pressed me to choose a husband? I wished then that, like Olive, I could stay at home for ever. Olive's delight is quite infectious. She looks about, sees the world, with all its chaos and oddities, and is charmed. I could never see things like that before. But now . . . *I* am one of those oddities! And despite all that has happened, I *am* still standing – barely.

'I wish, my dear,' she continues, setting down her empty teacup, 'that I could invite you to stay with me at Polaris House. Then you could take the time you need without the worry of troubling your friends. But because of our fathers . . .'

'I know. I do understand.'

'I would happily offer Mrs Simon some money for your keep . . .'

'But I would not allow it,' I say firmly. 'I cannot be beholden, Olive.'

'But as a loan? If we are saying – and I believe we are – that we have faith in your future, that you will find a way forward, then would it not do?'

I hesitate. I don't *want* to say yes, but I know the worries Hetty has. Even if John finds work soon, it is not up to him to support me. It's not up to Olive either, of course . . .

'Think of this, Rowena. Your parents should have helped you. Failing that, Verity or your brothers should have helped, but none of them did. But if they had, you would have accepted, would you not? Can you not think of me the same way? A few shillings only.'

I imagine what it would be like to know that Hetty can afford her weekly shopping. I imagine how light I would feel, staying here where I feel safe, relieved of the guilt of draining her scant resources. Olive is as rich as I once was. I know how little a few shillings will figure with her. And she knows the difference they will make to me.

'I would like more than I can express to help out Hetty while I'm here,' I admit. 'But Olive, if you call it a loan, you're showing more faith in my future than I have myself. What if I can never pay you back?'

'Then my family and I shall starve and be out on the streets,' she says gravely.

I cannot help but laugh. 'Very well. Thank you. For Hetty.'

'Very good,' she says unemotionally, passing me a small purse from her pocket. 'Here, and a shilling or two for yourself. No, don't protest,' she adds, raising her hand. 'A woman cannot walk the streets without a single coin, Rowena. It is not safe, you know that. Now, will you call on me next week? I am at home on Tuesday and Friday. I have cleared it with Papa. We can take tea in the garden and talk as long as we wish and solve *all* your problems. Will you?'

My problems are too legion even for Olive Westallen to fix in a single afternoon. But to call on a friend. A simple pleasure. I dither, tempted.

'There will be cake,' she wheedles. 'We can sit amongst the lavender and if you like, I'll show you my divination cards. They are my secret pleasure; I tell very few people about them.'

'Do they help you see the future?' I'm astonished that the mighty Olive Westallen, bastion of academia and intellect, might dabble in something so intangible.

She considers. 'Sometimes I think so. Most likely they simply help focus my mind. I shall show you and you can see what you think, if you are interested.'

I am, very. And who can resist cake? 'Thank you, Olive. I shall come.'

'Good, then I'll take my leave. Mrs Simon no doubt has much to do. Remember, dear, *We know what we are, but know not what we may be*. Ophelia, in *Hamlet*,' she explains, seeing my blank expression. I never cared for Shakespeare. 'Let us discover what you may be.'

And she is gone. A whirlwind of energy suddenly departed, allowing the dust to settle around me. I am bemused. Olive Westallen admires my strength of character! She is now my friend. Oh, and she indulges in divination! How intrigued Verity would be, but I'll never tell her now, not under any circumstances. I do miss my old flower dictionary. Holding that book always soothed me. Funny that of all my dresses, diamonds and treasures, this is the possession I miss.

I'm holding Olive's money in my hand. I shake my head in wonder and count it out. I keep two shillings for myself, because Olive is right that it is unsafe to have nothing, then take the rest to Hetty in the kitchen. Her eyes bulge at the sight of the coins. 'I have taken out a loan,' I explain. 'Now I am a paying boarder while I work things out. Might I have some paper and a pencil?' Hetty fishes them out of a drawer.

I take one sheet and write down the total. I shall not forget this, and I shall pay Olive back as soon as ever I can. I take another sheet and write a note to Pansy. John is still outside, now weeding the wooden kitchen planter. I go to the kitchen door.

'John, might I ask a favour?'

'Of course! Anything!' He stands up, looking so eager to help that my heart melts a little. It is rare to have such a friend as this – rare and to be treasured.

'Would you take this note to Garrowgate Hall for me? It's for Pansy. I was hoping she might read it before her next day off.'

'I'll go now,' he says, laying down his little trowel and brushing the soil from his hands.

'You're not at her beck and call any longer!' points out Hetty from within. 'That weeding must be finished.'

'I'll go now,' he repeats and disappears inside.

'I'll finish the weeding,' I say to no one in particular and kneel before the planter, hoping I won't uproot our summer's vegetables by mistake.

Forty-four

Pansy

Bloody Rowena Blythe! Still causing difficulties, even when she wasn't there. *Why can't I just ignore her?* wondered Pansy, stomping along the landing towards Rowena's room. *I would if I had any sense.* But somehow, despite all her indignation and knowing it was a foolish thing to do, Pansy was going to do Rowena a favour.

The request had come on Saturday, in a note, delivered by none other than John, who had borne it faithfully across the heath. That had been a pleasant surprise, to see him once again at Garrowgate Hall. Mrs Andrews had ushered him into the kitchen for a cup of tea and all the staff had been pleased to see him. There was no danger that a Blythe would see him, not down there in the kitchen. When no one was looking, he'd given Pansy a note and *even then* she'd hoped it would be from him, saying . . . well, she hardly knew any more. It was a habitual, limp little leap of hope, a silly thing. Anyway, it had been from Rowena.

Dear Pansy, she'd written.

I hope you're well and that your work isn't too demanding this week. And I hope you will visit us on Thursday for we all look forward to seeing you. I am starting to make plans, like you. Perhaps I can tell you

*a little of them when you come. Meanwhile I need to
ask you just one more favour. Please do not do it if it's
inconvenient. But if you are able and willing, please
would you take one thing from my bedroom and bring
it to me? My old flower dictionary – perhaps you have
seen it? A compact book bound in green leather that I
always kept on the bureau in my room. Who knows,
perhaps they will have burned all my belongings by
now, but if it's still there, I would dearly love to see it
again. Foolish perhaps, but it would be a comfort.*

*In either event, I send you my most cordial regards and
appreciation.*

R

When Pansy had read it, she'd rolled her eyes, and had done
so several times since. For the love of God – a *flower dictionary*?
Her first reaction was that she certainly would not. It might
only be an old book, not money or jewellery, but if a Blythe
caught her taking anything from this house, she wouldn't just
be dismissed; she'd be arrested.

Yet here she was, approaching Rowena's old room, the door
of which had remained firmly closed since her departure, save
for some light dusting now and then. It was Pansy's day off
tomorrow and yes, she would visit the little house in Hampstead.
If John had fared well in his interview, this might be her last
chance to see him for a long time. She didn't *have* to take the
book – Rowena had said she didn't. Well, of *course* she didn't!
Yet here she was, pushing open the door, stepping into that silent
chamber filled with the ghosts of a bygone time, of a foolish
young woman with nothing but beauty to recommend her.

Pansy closed the door behind her and looked about, assailed

by memories: Rowena being fastened into a shimmering gown; Rowena's hair being swept up from her neck and secured with gems; Rowena lounging in bed, eating buttery toast and giggling over *Punch*; Rowena and Verity, discussing the relative merits of two hats with the gravity of two barristers discussing a case. Unbelievably, she couldn't help feeling sorry for Rowena. To have lost so much! Well, if she was going to do this, she'd better be quick. She couldn't be found in here.

A glance showed that everything was untouched. The book was where it had always been kept. Pansy remembered Rowena consulting it each time she received a bouquet. *Lilies for majesty, Verity. And camelias say that his destiny is in my hands.* A silly giggle. *A sweet message, is it not?* And Verity would usually say something pragmatic like, *It's an impressive arrangement, and he has the money for it. Will you marry him, do you think?*

Pansy shook her head and grabbed the book. It was perhaps a sense of injustice that had moved her to do this for Rowena, a sense of horror that her family could treat her so shoddily. That Rowena had to weather her trials with none of her small, silly comforts . . . it felt cruel and Pansy couldn't abide that. She ran her hand over the dark green cover, then shoved it into her apron pocket and opened the door a crack. The corridor was empty. She stepped outside, closed the door softly behind her and hurried towards the stairs.

Her heart was pounding; having something of Rowena's in her possession was making her as nervy as a cat. She wouldn't sleep a wink that night. When a figure stepped out of a room just ahead and blocked her way, she jumped out of her skin.

It was Felix Blythe. What was *he* doing here at such an hour? Pansy had hardly caught sight of him since he married Verity and moved into their townhouse up the hill. Pansy looked up into his weary face and laid a hand over her heart. 'Oh, I beg your pardon, sir, you startled me.'

'Did I just see you coming out of my sister's room?' he demanded. Pansy shook her head; no words would come. 'I did. I'm certain I did. What were you doing in there? Answer me!'

'Nothing, sir, nothing. I only went to look around. It's strange with her gone and I just wanted to . . . I was in there a lot with her when she was at home, sir. I wanted to remember.'

He narrowed his eyes, as blue as Rowena's, and looked at her closely. Pansy wanted to die, horribly aware of the bulky little volume in her apron pocket. If he only glanced down, he would see it, a square shape that was clearly a book. And if he seized it, he would recognise his sister's favourite at once. Pansy remembered now the first time Felix had courted a young lady. He asked Rowena's advice about which flowers to send to woo her and Pansy had wished for a moment that she could be the lucky girl who'd caught his eye. But Felix didn't look down. He continued to stare into Pansy's eyes, searching out the truth. She tried her best to return his gaze unwaveringly but feared she was blushing; her skin felt hot and fevered.

She had always liked the Blythe boys better than the rest of the family. Felix in particular had a warmth and amiability to him. She had always thought him decent. But now that the brothers had apparently turned their backs on Rowena too, she wasn't so sure. One thing was certain – they had loved their sister before she fell from grace. If he thought she was snooping or stealing, he'd be furious.

'I meant no disrespect, sir, I promise,' she breathed, wilting under his scrutiny. She had never seen him at quite such close quarters before and she was a little overwhelmed. Then he turned away and rubbed his hands over his face. He looked terrible, she noticed. He had shadows beneath his eyes and a tortured expression on a face that used to wear only smiles. You didn't notice it at first, with the beautiful suit he wore and the elegant way he carried himself. He had that air, that Blythe air, as if none of them could ever be toppled. But they could.

'No. I don't believe you did.' He looked her up and down. 'It's Tilney, isn't it?'

'Yes, sir.' She blushed again, that he knew her name.

'I miss my sister, Tilney. You don't know anything of her whereabouts, do you?'

'No, sir,' she replied at once. The worst thing was that she half wanted to tell him. She couldn't shake the thought that it was Verity who had sent Rowena away, not Felix. Although Verity had sworn that she was acting on behalf of her husband, how could they know if that was so? Pansy for one wouldn't put it past her to lie. But if Verity *had* told the truth, Pansy must never tell Felix where Rowena was; he would lead his parents straight to her. No, she had promised to keep the secret and she would.

He didn't move aside. It was as if a thousand cogs were grinding in his head, as if he'd forgotten all about her. Pansy ran her eyes over his face again and bit her lip. She wanted to comfort him. But that was absurd – and wrong. 'It's very sad, sir. May I be excused?'

At last he stepped back. Pansy ran up the stairs to the attic, the book bumping against her legs with every step. She ran inside and slammed the door, stuffed the book, wrapped in the apron, beneath her pillow. Then she threw herself on the bed and waited for her breath to steady. And she tried not to think that when Felix had let her go, it was with the air of one who had learned all that he needed.

Forty-five

Rowena

On Friday afternoon I make myself ready to leave the house to call upon Olive Westallen. Heavy rain prevented me on Tuesday, and I cannot say I wasn't relieved. I fear becoming one of those persons who, following hardship and confinement, cannot walk about the world and shrink behind familiar walls. Olive said I would find her at home on Tuesday and Friday, so after Tuesday reached its grey and dreary close, I had to wait until today. This morning I lingered still, claiming that the afternoon is the proper time for a social call. It was mere procrastination; Olive is so unconventional I could turn up at midnight or six in the morning and she'd scarcely turn a hair! But despite my desire to hide from the world, I do *want* to visit Olive.

If John were here, he would have walked me through the village and his presence would have given me courage. But John was offered the job in Chelsea. Well, they could hardly do better. He set off early this morning with a cloth bag containing his clothes, a few books and some personal items. He is to have Sundays off but not this first Sunday, so it will be more than a week before we see him. How empty the house feels without him. Strange to miss someone so much, when we have only shared a house for a few weeks.

I did venture out this morning, just to the end of this street; the others had spoken of a flower seller who has her stand there and I wanted to take Olive a bouquet. The language of flowers is *my* language, although Verity scorns it as passé. Pansy brought my flower dictionary to me on Thursday, the dear girl. She did it with a scowl on her face and a reminder of the very great risk she had run on my behalf. She assured me it would not happen again – but there is nothing else I want.

The dictionary is a great comfort. I have absorbed so much of its lore over the years, but there are always nuggets of information about the lesser-known plants to be discovered and the feel of it in my hands is dear to me, the illustrations soothing when I turn the pages before bed. Last night the book fell open on the page for lilacs and I noticed a pertinent thing: lilacs do not simply represent *love* as I had remembered but, more specifically, the first flush of love. Would I have succumbed so readily to their magic had I been aware that they spoke of those heady, early feelings when all is madness? I have my dictionary with me today to show Olive, should she be interested.

The bouquet I have compiled for her is a pretty thing, I think, though modest. For the sake of a few pennies I bought some stems of pink lisianthus to symbolise my gratitude, of deep purple heliotrope for devoted affection and of violet pelargonium, a token of true friendship. Small and delicate lily of the valley dot the arrangement with white. These simple flowers stand for a return to happiness, and Olive helps me feel such a thing is possible. Even without any of the grand satin ribbons I used at home, it is pleasing to the eye, though small. So small that I added three stems of peppermint leaves from Hetty's herb box to swell the offering; peppermint means warm feeling. It was fun to see what I could make with limited means.

It's a more uplifting nosegay than those I have mentally compiled for Verity over the last days. Whenever I remember her hard words, her disdainful gaze that terrible night, my thoughts have run, without regard for the season, on thistle for misanthropy, marigolds for grief . . . even basil, for hatred.

At three o'clock, I smooth down Hetty's frock, fetch my veiled bonnet and ensure my shillings are in my pocket. I tuck more cotton inside the shoes I have borrowed from Hetty; they are slightly too big. Hetty watches my fussing with scathing eyes.

'They will not set dogs upon you,' she calls after me as I hesitate on the threshold. 'I'll see you for dinner.'

I walk to the flower stall and turn left up the hill through a bustling village with tempting shop windows and strutting crowds. It reminds me very much of Highgate. I should like to linger and gaze, but I walk steadily, trying to be as unobtrusive as possible. High up the hill, there's a lane called Holly Hill that winds still higher. I start my way along it, then turn right along a raised stone walkway, railed in black iron, and weave my way up into the very heights of Hampstead, according to John's directions. He was so specific that I asked if he'd ever been there. He hadn't, but said that everyone in Hampstead knows Polaris House.

I'm distracted a moment by a flowering rosebush brimming over the garden fence of some medium-sized house. The roses are beautiful – pale pink, which symbolises grace. Olive has true grace of character, I think, and my fingers itch for my small silver garden scissors. I narrow my eyes at the bush and notice a bud on a slim stem. Glancing about to see that I'm alone, I twist and snap the flower. The stem is resilient and a guarding thorn bites my finger. I tug harder and it yields; I tuck it triumphantly into the kitchen twine with which I tied the flowers. A dog within starts barking at the strange rustling at his perimeter and I scuttle off. I can see the headlines now: *Rowena Blythe steals flowers from garden: How did she fall so low?*

Soon I find the Westallen home, hidden behind a high brick wall, bounded by a tall black gate. *Polaris* is etched on one stone gatepost, *House* on the other. The place is staggering. As big as Garrowgate Hall at least, yet so different. My old home was stately, square and white. Polaris is rambling and angled with sloping roofs and pitched eaves and even a turret! It is built of stone of a rather outlandish burnt-orange colour and, in the distance, I think I can see a tennis court. Good heavens.

A slender maid with round eye-glasses opens the door. At Garrowgate Hall we would never have employed someone who wore spectacles. When I tell her that Rowena Blythe is come to pay Miss Westallen a promised visit, the maid shows me most courteously to a bench in a delightful ornamental garden brimming with lavender and bees. Then she fetches her mistress, bearing off the bouquet I created for Olive to put the flowers in water before they droop. I see at once that this is a very different household from my old one in Highgate. I can tell just from the way she carries herself.

Soon, Olive comes hurrying out. The two children are tripping in her wake, a delightful surprise. Their skirts are too long and their little hands make a poor job of gathering up the voluminous layers. When they reach me they both make grand curtseys and I gather them to me for a hug. Beautiful creatures. I remember meeting them last year at the ball, Olive's daughter Clover as fair and slender as a wood sprite, her companion, Angeline, as dark-haired and dimpled as a little Christmas pudding. I could eat them both.

'They've been wearing their best occasion frocks all day

because I told them you might visit,' laughs Olive. 'Hardly the proper garb for a sunny day in the garden, but what do I know? I'm only an adult.'

'Quite right,' I say gravely, releasing the girls. 'These children clearly have the right sort of ideas. I feel terribly underdressed. I do apologise, Miss Westallen, Miss Daley. I had not realised it was a formal occasion.'

'That's all right,' decrees Angeline, the bolder of the two, while Clover regards me from huge hazel eyes. 'You're allowed to wear whatever you want when you come to P'laris House. But *we* must be fine because we're *princesses*.'

'Of course you are. I beg your pardon, your highnesses, for addressing you both as miss.'

They burst into giggles and run into a nearby apple orchard. Olive shakes her head, smiling, and sits beside me. 'I'm so pleased you've come. I'll show you the grounds by and by but Jenny will be out with tea and the promised cake in a moment so shall we chat for a while first?'

'That sounds a most agreeable plan.' I sigh. I already feel very glad I came.

'And thank you for the beautiful flowers. Jenny showed them to me before going to look out our very best vase. It was thoughtful of you.'

The afternoon passes swiftly and the golden light deepens. We begin by talking about my situation. Olive is a good listener; a tilt to her glossy head, a look of sympathy in her brown eyes. I have talked to Hetty and John and Pansy . . . but this is different. With John I have to be careful what I say because John is a man and I don't wish to be improper. With Hetty I worry that she'll throw me out if I say the wrong thing and with Pansy there is always the fear that her hard green eyes might turn me to stone. Olive's intelligence, so often and so bitterly resented by me, is emotional as well as intellectual; it flows from her, making me feel I can say anything.

So I start at the beginning, with Father's decree, one dismal day in February, that I must have my portrait painted by lecherous Lethbridge. 'I have heard the tales, my dear,' Olive comments with a shudder. Then, once we are furnished with Earl Grey tea and divine chocolate cake, I describe the altogether happy surprise of Bartek arriving in his place. I talk of falling in love and how happy he made me for that short time. I tell her about the day in the lilac grove and our decision to run away on a barge. And I tell her how *that* turned out . . .

Olive listens carefully to it all and when I finally fall quiet, we sit for a while listening to the drone of the bees and the squeals of the children out of sight among the trees. Olive sighs. 'I don't think it was love that made you happy then, you know,' she says, 'or only in part.' I am attentive. What then, if not love?

'I think it was what he represented,' she goes on. 'He opened up new horizons for you, offered you new ideas, new possibilities, new areas for reflection . . . nothing is more seductive than *that*, my dear. There is so much nonsense spoken about women, as if all we crave is a fat diamond ring, as if we are one-dimensional creatures wanting nothing more than to preen and be admired and eventually secure the great prize that is a man.' I swallow. That is *exactly* what I was.

'And we start to believe it of ourselves, because that is what we are told, by *everyone*!' Olive sounds indignant. 'You, Rowena, have lived the most constrained life imaginable. Dos and don'ts, rules and restrictions, all there to guide you to the only conceivable outcome – a society marriage. But what of your brain? Your imagination? Your *soul*, my dear?'

I give a little shrug, out of my depth. Verity and I certainly never discussed my soul. Mother and Father were more concerned with my *hairstyle* than my soul! 'But those are the things that made you susceptible to the romance that Bartek offered, don't you see? Only, you don't need him for *any* of those things. Your brain and your soul are your own! The world is a huge and fascinating place and it is waiting for you.'

I cast about for something to say. She is so articulate, so passionate, and I'd like to respond in kind, but these are new ideas to me. She *is* perceptive. I always knew Bartek wasn't the husband my parents wanted for me. That exhilaration I felt in his company was because of his beauty, yes, but only in part. It came from hearing about Poland, reading about Bohemia, beginning to consider life itself as a blank canvas. I try to express some of this to Olive, haltingly, imperfectly and she nods encouragingly. 'But he really was very beautiful,' I confess sheepishly.

'And who does not enjoy a handsome face and a manly form?' She chuckles. 'They only made him all the more irresistible. I understand that the thought of romantic love is powerful. Who knows, you may yet experience it for you're so beautiful and men will overlook many a reservation for beauty. But I don't think you want to be loved for that.'

'I don't, not any more. In fact, I'm not sure I want to be loved *at all* if it upends one's life so thoroughly. I just want to . . . live a life I can feel proud of. I still wish I knew where to start, though.'

Olive laughs gently. 'Yes, a beginning is always a good thing.'

We go on to talk of other things. She shows me her divination cards and explains to me more about how she uses them. I'm fascinated. She offers to read them for me and I dither then decline. There is too much uncertainty at present; I had rather not know. Then I show her my flower dictionary and there is none of the taunting impishness that showed on Verity's face whenever I tried to talk to her about it.

'So does the bouquet you brought me carry a message, in addition to being so very pretty?' asks Olive, looking intrigued.

'It does indeed, several.'

'What a *beautiful* thing! Please explain it to me,' she begs.

Rather bashfully, I do, and I can see that she is genuinely touched. 'Rowena Blythe,' she murmurs in amusement. 'I never knew you had such hidden depths.'

I have hidden depths? Well, that is a relief.

Forty-six

Olive

Over the weekend I ponder Rowena's plight at some length. I am astonished how much I enjoyed her company as we sat in the garden and talked. The sweet, diffident way she showed me her flower dictionary, like a child eager to share. Her honesty about her misadventures. And her wish to do better, *live* better. I'm impressed. And my heart goes out to her. It's obvious that the rift with her family, the way they have tossed her aside like a piece of meat gone bad, has gashed her deeply. Hardly surprising. Thank God for John Hobbs and Mrs Simon. John clearly worships her; she hasn't said so but it's obvious. Such unconditional regard is a beautiful thing and John is very good-looking, I noticed last week. I think Rowena has noticed too; she blushes like a petal whenever she says his name.

Her current situation is no permanent solution – when Mrs Simon answered the door to me last week, I saw a woman at the end of her tether – and I can't keep giving her handouts. Well, I *can*, but she would not be happy to accept them. I've arranged an appointment for her at the foundation. She is to see Mabs. I think we're already too close for me to be objective or for her to feel comfortable about me dispensing charitable aid.

Unofficially, though, I can meddle, and during lunch on Sunday I have a brainwave. Once I've swallowed the last of my game pie, I fling on my hat and stride with purpose to Belsize Park. We Westallens are all great walkers so we no longer keep a carriage. Besides, the weather is so fine, as we ease towards June, that a couple of miles there and back is a delight. In Belsize Park resides my friend Mrs Lake, and if she agrees to my plan, it will help her as much as Rowena, I am convinced.

Mrs Lake (first name Zenobia, and this is not the only thing about her that delights me!) is an elderly widow, once rich as Croesus, now considerably reduced. Her husband died sixteen years ago and she lives all alone, save for her one remaining servant, Bertha. They are no company for each other. Mrs Lake is formal and old-fashioned and intimacy with a maid would be a step too far for her.

If she allowed Rowena to stay in one of those echoing, empty rooms, Rowena would have somewhere to live with no urgency to move on. She and Mrs Lake would be company for each other. Hetty would have her small cottage to herself again. And Bertha would have another soul in the house, someone young and different. It would be a boon to all concerned.

Five-and-twenty minutes later I am walking home again – seething. She said no! Categorically and unequivocally no. If there is one thing I love, it's an elegant solution and if there's one thing I loathe, it's an elegant solution gone to waste. I said my farewells, I confess, in a more heated manner than usual.

I return to Hampstead still in high dudgeon. I don't want the girls to see me cross so I decide to call upon Lionel.

'Olive, my dearest,' he greets me, opening the door himself since his manservant has the day off. I like that about him.

There are men in Hampstead who would not open a door. 'What a pleasant surprise. Will you come in?'

Amiable greeting! I feel soothed already by his welcome and allow him to escort me to a comfortable chair by the open French doors. A warm breeze and the scent of roses drift shyly in to set me at ease. Lionel rings for a maid to bring tea and 'something delightful'. She soon appears with fluted glass dishes of brown bread ice cream. My favourite! And just the thing to appease my ruffled feelings. I pick up the silver spoon and dive in. When all that is left is a smear of vanilla ice cream and a few rogue caramelised breadcrumbs, I set the dish aside and turn to my tea, which Lionel has already poured. He is solicitous; I like that too.

'Thank you,' I say. 'It's good to see you, Lionel. I hope you've had a pleasant day?'

'Remarkably pleasant, and it's improving yet. But from your agitated demeanour and urgent consumption of brown bread ice cream, I suspect yours has been less satisfactory?'

'I've been disappointed this afternoon, Lionel. I had a first-class idea that would have helped two friends greatly, had the one of them agreed, but she did not – and now I'm at a loss as to how to help either of them. It's extremely vexing.'

I see him suppress a smile but it's there in the twitch of his lips. 'My fair crusader,' he soothes. 'I know how you like to order the world to your highest standards. Would it help to tell me the matter?'

'You know, Lionel, I think it might, but it must be in the strictest confidence. I can trust you with someone else's secret, can I not?'

'Of course you can. You know you can.'

I know it. With all his faults, Lionel is not one to carry gossip. So I tell him about Rowena. It all comes out in a big burst, so aggravated am I by her suffering, the injustice of her family's actions. And then I recount the part of the story concerning Mrs Lake.

When I have finished I draw breath, a big one. My goodness, what a monologue! Lionel is very quiet and I wonder if I have rattled on too fast for him to follow. I look at his handsome, grave face and I can see that he is thinking many things. I wait for him to order them and sip at my tea, now considerably cooled.

'I . . . I am sorry that you have been foiled, my dear, in your exertions to help . . .' he says cautiously, adjusting the drape at the window, which is perfectly fine.

'But?' I prompt.

'But . . . well, you can understand Mrs Lake's reservations, surely? And really, are you certain that Miss Blythe's is a cause in which you want to be entangled?'

I'm at a loss. Entangled? I'm concerned for the girl. And how can he guess at Mrs Lake's reservations when he has never met her once? 'I'm not sure I understand you, Lionel. Might you elaborate?'

Lionel frowns and sits more squarely. 'I admire your compassion, Olive, you know that. But really, Mrs Lake is an old lady of very fine background, I understand, and really, to expect her to take in a . . . a . . .'

'Yes?' I enquire, somewhat icily.

'Well, a *fallen woman* – to put it politely – was without doubt a step too far.'

'What a ridiculous phrase that is – *fallen woman*. Have you never thought it? Fallen from *what*, for goodness' sake?'

'Well, from her pedestal.'

'Her *pedestal*? Lionel, she is a living, breathing human being, not a statuette! Women are not meant to perch motionless on pedestals, we are meant to be free to walk the earth, to live, to err, even! That is why we have feet.'

'But Olive, such a *grievous* error she has made. Run off with an artist? Seduced? Spoiled? *Rowena Blythe?* She should be better than that. It's the scandal of the century. I daresay she is sorry now and, of course, I wish her no harm, but this mess . . . well, it's of her own doing, is it not?'

I squint at him. He is in deadly earnest. And really it should not surprise me. This is how the majority of people would think about the matter. But I had expected better from this intelligent, considered man I have come to think of as my friend and more. However, he is looking at me a little sternly, as if to correct *my* mistaken views, when I myself long to persuade *him*. I have a horrible feeling I will not succeed; even so, I shall try.

So I swallow down my indignation, which burns inside; I wonder if it's sending up coils of smoke, dragonlike, to escape through my nostrils. 'Lionel, dearest, I agree that it's all very surprising, but if you think about it, there were *two* people in the making of this situation, Rowena *and* the man in question.' I speak in a very even tone and I'm proud of myself. This is how married couples communicate, I believe; there is hope for me yet! 'In fact, there were many more than two,' I go on, warming to my theme. 'There were her parents, who groomed her for an utterly unfulfilling life, and failed to teach her any real wisdom to prepare her for affairs of the heart. And society at large for placing such preposterously high expectations on women to be—'

'Olive! Please. You surely cannot blame Maude and Malvern Blythe for the fact that their daughter gave herself to a rogue with a paintbrush? And *society at large*? Is the prime minister to be blamed for her lewd conduct?'

'Lewd? Lionel, she *loved* him! And I do not believe I mentioned the Marquis of Salisbury.'

'But Olive, a young lady cannot behave like a common slattern and expect others to take the blame. She has misjudged most grievously and must expect consequences.'

'Why, she is living the consequences daily! She has lost *everything* and received the most hard-hearted treatment from her own parents. Is no one to help her? For your information, Lionel, Rowena does *not* blame anyone else. She shoulders responsibility for the debacle in what I consider to be a most admirable manner. It is I who make the point, because I wish you to consider her more sympathetically. She was unprepared when the heat of love swept over her. She made a mistake in an ill-advised moment and now what? Is she to accept consignment to the gutter hereafter? No, Lionel. *I* say that she must stand and walk tall!'

'I said nothing of the gutter. I'm sure there is *somewhere* for women in her situation. But Olive, what place can there be now for a woman like that in polite society? Do you expect her to mingle among us, that everyone may overlook her experiences? Who will marry her now?'

Oh, I am boiling. And if he 'but Olive's me once more . . . 'Ah, there we have it. It all comes down to marriage, doesn't it? That great prize each woman is supposed to long for.'

'That is not what I meant. I simply mean . . . well, *you* are a product of this same society, *you* had a similar upbringing. Yet *you* have never simply run off and had . . . inappropriate relations with anyone. Have you?'

I snort. 'Of course not. But then . . .' I stumble, for I was about to say that I'd never felt such an overwhelming passion as Rowena has described for her Bartek, but I feel that is not a tactful thing to say to the man who wishes to marry me. 'But then, our upbringing wasn't really similar at all, you know. Yes, we are both wealthy and advantaged, but Lionel, you know my parents. They allowed me choice, freedom, a fine education. I have true friends, Clover, my life's work in the foundation. My life is . . . my God, I am blessed beyond expression. Rowena's upbringing was rigid, cold. And her best friend was *Verity*! Can you not see that she must have been crying out for something to make her come alive?' By now I have tears in my eyes, whether of frustration or heartache for poor Rowena I do not know.

Lionel looks puzzled. 'Olive, what do you want of me? I merely said I was unsurprised that Mrs Lake didn't want to take in a woman with a stain on her virtue and reputation.'

Stained. Spoiled. Fallen. I shake my head to clear it for it is clouded with injustice. '*You* were taken enough with her once upon a time,' I seethe. I have never asked Lionel about that brief interlude when he was infatuated by Rowena and perhaps this is not the time, but honestly! The memory of his visibly ardent admiration then makes this clear-cut judgement of her now much harder to bear.

He looks affronted. 'I don't know what you mean.'

'Yes, you do. You met her at the foundation ball. We were talking, then Rowena walked in and you followed her around all night. I did not see or hear from you for weeks. I know you called upon her several times – you know how news travels – then she turned you away, I assume, for some months later you returned your attentions to me.'

He has gone quite pale. 'I did not realise you had remembered . . . that you were aware . . . I'm sorry, Olive, if this has upset you. It's true that I was briefly distracted by her, but we never had anything in common – I quickly came to realise it. She had no interest in me and her parents had their sights set higher for her – which is ironic, now. My regard for you was unwavering throughout. You are the most admirable woman I know. I wanted to resume our . . . friendship at once, but I didn't want to seem fickle or disrespectful, so I waited. But my feelings continued to grow and in the end I could stay away from you no more.'

'I remember our history,' I reply peevishly. 'That is not why I brought it up. It's just that . . . she *captivated* you – and many other men besides, all because of how she looks, which is not of her doing – and now you simply *judge* her.'

He slumps a little, nods. 'Yes. I can see it does not reflect my better nature.' There follows a long silence, filled by a blackbird trilling outside and a fat fly buzzing into the room and landing in the ice cream dish where it sets about getting drunk on the dregs.

'What happened to Rowena has happened,' I say softly. 'I still want to help her. I still think she deserves to make a good life. Do you not?'

'Honestly I do not,' says Lionel, for he is always honest – one of his good qualities. 'Or more saliently, I simply cannot see, the way our world is arranged, how she could have a place among people like us.'

'People like us.' I sigh. I do not even know what that means any more. 'I had better go, Lionel. Mama will be wondering where I have got to.'

'I'm sorry.' He stands too, hands at his sides. 'You came here to feel better and I have made things worse, I think. But I cannot pretend to a view I do not have, simply to please you.'

'I would not wish you to, Lionel. At all times, the important thing is that you should be you and I should be me. Thank you for the ice cream and the tea.'

He nods, clasps my hands briefly and sees me to the door.

There, he kisses my cheek. A moment follows when I think he might ask me something, then comes a moment when I think I might say something, but somehow these moments pass and I set off home, deep in thought.

A realisation dawns. Lionel's admirable qualities are not enough for me. This is the second time that I have come up against his rigid morality. Even if Rowena *has* behaved atrociously – and I cannot bring myself to feel that she did – even then there is a case for compassion, *I* believe. She has hurt no one but herself. Rowena has *behaved like a common slattern*, so she can have no place among *people like us*. His phrases haunt me as I hurry along and I cannot wait to get home and scoop the girls up in my arms.

I can *understand* Lionel's thinking, for it is common enough, but I do not feel comfortable with it. A lady must be beyond reproach, spotless of virtue, a shining angel of goodness, in order to be acceptable to a man. Men make the rules and we must live up to them – or fail. I do not want any part of it.

I will not marry Lionel Harper, I realise. It is no wild thought formed in the heat of the moment; it is a deep shift inside me. I cannot marry a man who sees women that way – and most men do. In fact, I cannot marry at all, that is suddenly clear. I have far too much to lose. My fortune would be forfeit, my freedom curtailed. What was I thinking even to consider it? Why did I ever think my life needed to improve still further when it is already so plentifully blessed? Lionel is a dear man – even his views about Rowena were mildly phrased compared with what many men would say – but I cannot be his wife. Brown bread ice cream is wonderful, but it is simply not enough.

Forty-seven

Rowena

On Monday I walk to Euston for my appointment with Mabel Daley. Mabs. The assistant manager of the Westallen Foundation is a woman; how extraordinary Olive is. Yet how wonderful. Imagine if she weren't the only one. Imagine if women, like men, could use their intelligence to make a living in the world – the world in general, not just Olive's eccentric little corner of it. This is wild thinking; Olive is rubbing off on me.

The distance is some three miles according to Hetty and I am unaccustomed to walking so far. Also, the memory of that Friday night when I returned from the North and was accosted in an alley is strong in my mind. But I refuse to use any of my limited funds on a cab. My tattered feet are healed and it is broad daylight, the sun is shining. Olive strides about all over London. Pansy too. Why then should I not?

Hetty has given me detailed directions – written them down no less! I am nervous the whole way, startling at every noise, sometimes crossing wide roads to avoid dubious-looking men. I keep imagining that I'm being followed but whenever I whirl around I see nothing but the bustling crowd and arrive without incident at the address Olive gave me.

The foundation makes its base in the upper floor of a

warehouse owned by a Mr Harper; Olive says I know him. She says we met at the foundation ball and that he called on me thereafter. I have no memory of him. So many men called after that night and they have all blurred into one. Verity deemed it a great triumph and I agreed with her at the time. Now, when I look back, the vast number of men who fell at my feet all because of my face, figure and golden hair, seems to me to be . . . obscene. I climb the stairs as directed.

Mabs is slight and sweet-faced and looks younger than me. She wears a simple but tasteful costume in deep blue; her fair hair is caught in a sensible coil at the nape of her neck. I cannot help but stare – I have simply never seen a woman in such a setting before. In truth, I have never *been* in such a setting before. The office is a large space, all one room, with windows that overlook bustling streets. It boasts three desks at which sit Mabs, Olive and an older gentleman; he is all whiskers and cravat. He tips his black hat to me then carries on making notes in a ledger. Olive greets me with a raised hand but is busy with a young man sitting before her desk. He is filthy, I cannot help but notice, and dressed in rags. He speaks in an agitated manner, waving his hands around. Olive listens with her habitual respectful calm.

'Olive says you're looking for work but you don't know what to do – that you wish to help others and make some money while you're at it.' Mabs drags my attention back to why I'm here for I cannot stop staring around, mouth open like a goldfish.

'Yes, sorry. That's about the size of it,' I tell her. The phrase is one of Hetty's; I don't believe I've ever used it before.

'Tell me more,' she says and I hesitate; I'm not sure what she wants to know. 'I don't mean what's brought you here,' she adds warmly. 'You don't need to tell me your story. But I'd like

to know what interests you, what you're good at, your education, things of that nature. Anything you feel like telling me,
really. Sometimes another person can judge better what you
have to offer than you can yourself. We always say that here.'

'I sincerely hope that's the case,' I sigh. 'You know of my
background, of course. I've never worked a day in my life and
have acquired no practical skills whatsoever until the last few
weeks. I fear that I'm completely useless.'

'I doubt that very much,' says this surprising young woman.

'How old are you?' I ask impulsively. 'I beg your pardon; I
don't mean to be rude. It's just . . . what an impressive position
you hold. And it's so unusual to see a woman being paid to do
anything other than cook or clean or . . .'

'I know. I'm the luckiest girl in the world and it's all thanks
to Olive, of course. To answer your question, I'm nineteen. I
had no education beyond a bit of the alphabet and some
counting until last year. Then I learned to read, and write, and
now Mr Gladstone there is training me in business and
accounting and the like and I go to evening classes to learn
other things.'

'What kind of things?' I know we are here to talk about me,
not her, but I'm intrigued.

'I'm learning French and Italian. A little history and geography. And I'm taking a literature class because I love it – *and*
because my beau wishes to be an author and I want to be able
to talk to him about that.' She blushes petal-pink at the mention
of her beau and I feel a pang in my heart. I hope she will be
better treated than I was.

'That's . . . incredible,' I breathe.

'Oh yes, that's the beauty of life, y'see, Miss Blythe. Anything
you need to learn, anything you're lacking, you can just go out
and learn it! Well,' she corrects herself, her face clouding,

'provided you've the means, that is. The people who come to us here very often don't have a brass farthing. I was like that for most of my life. Things changed for me and now anything's possible. So we must change things for other people, whenever we can. Including you, Miss Blythe.'

The dear girl. She is as earnest and impassioned as Olive herself . . . What a pair they make! I compose myself and take a deep breath. I tell Mabs everything I can think of that might help her change things for me.

'Completely useless?' she crows when I stop talking. 'I should think *not*, Miss Blythe! Why, you have plenty to offer and that's a fact.'

'I do? Please enlighten me, Miss Daley.'

'There are a number of things that occur to me so it depends how you feel, of course, but the most obvious solution is that we could employ you here. We have the funds to pay a tutor – only modestly, of course, but it's a start.'

'A tutor? In what?' True, I learned rudimentary Latin and so on in the schoolroom but that's long gone from my memory now. I can read and write, of course, but I'm no Olive!

'In all kinds of things. Forgive me, Miss Blythe, you say you have no skills but that's because you've been brought up so privileged. You don't know how many people would kill to be like you. Most of the people who come to us can barely clothe and feed themselves. They can't go to school, it's all about just getting by. Survival. They scratch a living any way they can – scrubbing, laundering, labouring. They don't have the luxury to think about *anything* else. For them, to be able to *speak* as you do is a skill.' A wistful expression crosses her face and I suspect she is remembering something from her own life. She speaks very well, in fact, but no one from my old world would mistake her for one of them. There's the odd slip in her accent, the occasional turn of phrase, that suggests this way of speaking isn't natural for her. She expresses herself clearly and confidently, and I think the slips are rather charming, but I can imagine that the progress has been hard won. I never thought before of something as basic as *speaking* as something to aspire to.

'Reading and writing, of course,' she goes on, 'but I'm thinking more about how to dress respectably, how to carry yourself, and all the skills a lady's maid might need. So many of our girls would love to work in service, you see. Live in a clean house, a safe roof over their heads. But they aren't able to dress hair or fasten a corset – they wouldn't even know where to start. And employers won't consider them because they look so . . . disgraceful. I used to look that way. You could teach them all that, couldn't you?'

'Oh my goodness. You put me to shame. I never put any thought into the skill of the servants at my old home, I took it all for granted. Yes, Miss Daley. I could teach them all the skills they might need to please even the most demanding mistress. For I was one.'

'How about it, then, Miss Blythe? Would you like to join our little organisation? We badly need someone to teach such things.'

'Are you sure? It seems so . . . so easy. Has Olive asked you to make up a post for me? Because I couldn't bear to be a drain on the charity's resources. I want a job, a real job. Even if it's scrubbing,' I finish with aplomb, though I very much hope it won't be scrubbing.

'She said nothing of the sort, I swear it. For all that we'd love every one of our girls to be managers or economists or . . . or *queens*, the world's just not made like that. Service is the biggest, most practical area they can hope to work in and better their lives. There's so many of them, and for all I'm coming up in the world, *I* can't teach them things like that. Mr Gladstone can't . . .' Here she grins and I laugh at the thought of the grave, bewhiskered gentleman demonstrating how to create barley curls or wield a crimping iron. 'Olive could, but she's far too busy. If we had *you*, you could hold classes, teach five or six at once. What do you say?'

I swallow, a little nervous at the thought of facing young women from so deprived a background. I have seen such people on the streets; they may be rough, rude and aggressive. What if my students eat me alive? Then again, I wanted to help and here, help is needed. The prospect of becoming a colleague of Olive and Mabel gives me a sense of pride that I feel blossoming in my chest. It spreads outwards, warm as bathwater. Who would have thought there'd be a way to turn my spoiled, gilded youth into something useful?

'I say yes, Miss Daley. I say yes with a little trepidation and a wealth of gratitude.'

'Well, that's good, Miss Blythe!' Mabs's narrow face is alight. 'That's more than good, it's wonderful. When should you like to start? Next week? Don't worry, we won't throw you in all at once. You can meet the girls one at a time first, give them some individual lessons and get used to it a bit. Does that sound all right?'

I tell her it sounds perfect. I can't deny that my head is spinning and I'll be glad of that week to adjust my mind. Once I begin a paid position, my time for thinking and adjusting will be well and truly over. Garrowgate Hall feels several lifetimes ago now.

We tell Olive of the arrangement and she shakes my hand most heartily. She thanks me, as if I am not the one who has been saved from the workhouse. On the way home I imagine no footsteps close behind me, I have no sense of being watched. I wish I could tell John. I am seized with the impulse to jump in a cab and surprise him in Chelsea, just to tell him my news. He would be so proud of me, I think, and I would love to see the delighted expression on his dear, lovely face. But that would be wholly inappropriate behaviour. I wend my way to Hampstead, amazed, bewildered and . . . happy. I shall tell Hetty instead.

Forty-eight

Olive

W ell, that's Rowena in a better situation. I couldn't be happier as I watch her go, a new buoyancy in her step. I needed some good news today. When I leave here this afternoon I shall go to see Lionel to tell him I cannot marry him. The old wisdom, when faced with an important decision, is to sleep on it. I did, and it wrought no change in my heart. Having taken that precaution, I cannot delay telling Lionel; it would not be right.

I still do not know where Rowena is to live but really, now that she has employment, that is her business. It will be perfectly possible to live on her wage, modest though it is. She will be all right. Mabs is a genius at finding clever solutions – almost as much as I. The women and girls who come here will gain so much from meeting Rowena. They will be put at ease by her gentle manner, her honesty. I feel sure that she will be a patient, intuitive instructress.

If only I could feel a similar sense of fit for Pansy. Mr Endicott is a good man and the finest hatter around. I should know – I cannot resist a jaunty hat. He will treat Pansy well but she and millinery do not sit together in my mind the way Rowena and teaching do. Just as I am thinking this, Julia and Jem appear.

'What a delight!' I cry as they bustle in. Jem goes to nose

into whatever his sister is doing and Julia sits down with me for a chat, pretty in primrose yellow. I am still preoccupied by Pansy. 'Julia, when I first met Pansy at your house, we were full of talk of Rowena Blythe, were we not? And Pansy's wish to leave Garrowgate Hall.'

'That's right,' says Julia, untying her bonnet. 'How is Rowena?'

'Very well indeed. In fact, you just missed her. But I'll tell you of that later. I have a line of thought brewing and my fearsome intellect must not be derailed.'

Julia snorts with laughter. 'Very well. What, then?'

'You said that when you first met Pansy she had been of service to young Jeremiah. But did you ever tell me the circum-stances? If you did, I've completely forgotten and am losing my mind.'

'I'm sure you're not, Olive. I may not have told you. Did I tell you about the theft of the lilac bonnet?'

'Vaguely. It sounds like the title of a penny dreadful.'

Julia arranges herself more comfortably in the hard chair and thinks back. Really we should acquire more welcoming chairs for visitors, but when faced every day with people in the direst circumstances, it's hard to justify spending our funds on furniture. 'Well, Jem had gone to Highgate to collect for me a particular lilac bonnet I had fancied in a window. On the way back, he was set upon and it was stolen from him.'

'I remember that bit. At least, you said that he'd been robbed and Pansy helped him.'

'Yes, but before Pansy, a gentleman came to his aid. Did I tell you about Mr Cruz?'

I shake my head. 'No, and that is an unusual name so I would certainly remember.'

'Well, Hipólito Cruz is a gentleman from Dominica who works for Mr Ollander over in Highgate.'

'Ollander . . . the delicatessen?'

'That's it. A very good soul. It transpires that Pansy knows them both. Mr Cruz picked up Jem and dusted him off, offered to see him home safely, but Jem's yelling had attracted two policemen who arrested Mr Cruz on sight, despite Jem telling them over and over again that he was not the assailant.'

'Let me guess. Mr Cruz. Dominica. He looks different, he is an outsider, so he necessarily had to be the villain of the piece?'

Julia sighs. 'Precisely that. Anyway, it transpires that Pansy saw his cart outside the constabulary and went in to enquire. She discovered her friend in wrist-irons and Jem squawking his head off with indignation. According to Jem, she laid into the policemen rather fiercely and brought about Hipólito's release!'

I raise my eyebrows. 'Good grief. That was plucky.' Something is brewing in my mind. Laid into them fiercely, did she? I want to hear more. I shall ask Jem to tell me everything that was said. I look up and open my mouth. Mr Gladstone smiles and nods before I have even asked the question.

'No, Olive, it is not too early for luncheon. Yes, I shall watch the office so that you and Mabs can go to the coffee house with Mrs Morrow and Jem.'

I close my mouth again. Am I that predictable? 'Excellent. Thank you, Mr Gladstone. Jem, my lad, I have questions for you.'

Forty-nine

Rowena

T he closer I draw to Hetty's little white house, the higher my spirits rise. I picture myself setting off to work in the mornings, spending my days with people who have never had one scrap of the privilege I always enjoyed. I cannot imagine their lives, but I shall learn from them and they will learn from me. I need not only help girls. I think of John, of all the Henrys at Garrowgate Hall. I remember all the afternoons spent with Mother as she hired and dismissed them. I cannot teach the skills of a footman, a gardener or a groom but I can tell them what to expect. Perhaps I *am* a little useful after all. I daydream as I walk and my nerves fall away. Walking is a wonderful thing for settling the mind.

As I turn into Hetty's quiet little street, I hear a man's voice, very close behind me. 'Rowena.'

I jump out of my skin, my peace of mind immediately fleeing. Slowly I turn and there stands my brother Felix.

My jaw drops. I cannot speak. I cast an anxious glance over my shoulder. How close is the safety of Hetty's front door, if he made a grab for me? It is *Felix*, my adored older brother, but I remember Verity's words – they have burned into my mind like a brand. *You have destroyed him . . . He said, 'I pray I never see my sister again, for she is like gristle in my throat, a burr on my skin.'* I cannot move.

'Rowena, oh dear God, it *is* you! I could not be sure; you have been walking so fast and that dress . . . oh my darling sister. Will you not embrace me?'

So Verity was lying. Here is my brother with his arms outstretched in the middle of the little cobbled street, his face as open and dear as it ever was. I don't know how he found me but this is all I have wanted since our parents cast me out. 'Oh *Felix*!' I fly into his arms with a sob and I nestle there, held, belonging.

At last we let go and look at each other, clutching hands. I drink in the sight of him like a draft of cold water on the hottest day. He is scrutinising me for damage, I can see. 'I am well, brother,' I reassure him. 'Oh Felix, I have so much to ask you.'

'*You* have? Rowena, I feel as if I shall burst with questions. Will you invite me in so that we can talk? You are staying just there, are you not?'

'How do you know that? Never mind, tell me when we are settled. Felix, I want to talk to you too, but I'm staying with a friend who is . . . not grand, but very proud. Already Olive Westallen has called upon me and Hetty, my friend, was quite disarranged by having such a fine caller in her little home. She is very kind to have me there, Felix, and I have put her to quite some inconvenience. I don't want to take you there and make her uncomfortable all over again.'

'Then let me take you to lunch. There's a coffee house just round the corner, a tea room down the road . . .'

I dither. I do *long* to talk to Felix, of course. But my bruises are gone now and I cannot wear a veiled hat indoors. Anyone might recognise me. 'I'm afraid to be seen,' I whisper. 'If word should reach Mother and Father that I am in Hampstead . . . they wish to . . .'

'Pack you off to France. I know. But Rowena, I shan't let them do anything of the sort unless it's what *you* want.'

'It's not. It's not one bit. But Felix, do you know what I have done? Can you really love me still? Should you not hear the tale before you promise me your protection, in case you change your mind?'

He laughs. 'I know the bones of it, for you told Mother and Father. As to the details, they cannot be worse than the rumours I have heard. Rowena, you are my *sister*. If you work in the most scurrilous brothel in town, if you are living with ten sailors, I care not. I love you still.'

My eyes fill with tears and I start crying openly, out in the street. I cannot help it. I have been strong for so long. I received salvation from Pansy, friendship from John and Hetty and inspiration from Olive – nothing will ever make me forget those things. But I had given up hope of a similar bounty from my family. My brother still loves me. 'Our parents did not. Verity did not,' I sob with my face in my hands.

'Ah, Verity,' he says, his cheerful voice suddenly like acid. 'I should not trouble yourself about *her*, sister, or indeed any of them.'

'What of Crispin and Ignatius? Do they detest me?'

'In no measure. They love you, Rowena, just as I do. But living in Garrowgate Hall as they do, they are more constrained than I. Come. Dry your tears and come with me to eat and we shall talk about everything.' He pulls me to him again and strokes my hair with one hand, wipes my tears with his opposite sleeve.

'I walked past that tea room this morning,' I mumble. 'It did look ever so pretty.' Goodness, what a long time it is since

I was treated to such luxury. And I am suddenly ravenous, perhaps a side effect of the two pieces of good fortune today has offered me so far.

'Then the tea room it shall be.'

I consider. Soon I shall go to work, several days a week. Soon enough it will be known that I have started a new life here, that I have not gone to Italy or France, or set up with sailors or anything else that my parents might want, or dread. My time to hide is over, whether I'm ready or not.

'Let me just run in and tell Hetty where I'm going. I don't want her to worry.' I go inside and tell Hetty in two minutes that I have a job and a salary, that my brother is pacing outside and that he loves me.

'Life isn't dull with you around, Rowena Blythe,' she comments.

I run back out, wiping disbelieving tears from my eyes, and take my brother's arm. Soon we are sitting in Astrid's, a rather gorgeous tea room with mullioned bay windows and decor of pink and gold. I have no hankering at all for most elements of my old life. But beautiful surroundings and delicious edible treats hold their charm – eternally I should think!

We order soup and a great array of cakes and tea and Felix even insists on champagne. 'If ever there was a day to celebrate, this is it,' he says. 'I truly thought I'd lost you. Verity swore she hadn't seen you but I knew she was lying. I knew you'd go to your best friend and I knew she would not have the love in her heart to look beyond the scandal.'

'She told me that I had destroyed you, that you never wanted to see me again.'

'And you believed her? I'm disappointed in you, sister.'

I laugh. 'For *that* you're disappointed in me, not all the rest?' He grins. 'Felix, my parents turned their back on me. So did my best friend. If Pansy hadn't helped me . . .'

'Pansy? That's Tilney, the maid. The pretty one with the striking eyes?'

'Yes. She had no reason to like me, I see that now, yet she wouldn't leave me to my fate. A *servant*, Felix, whose name I had never taken the trouble to learn, whom I had always treated with disdain, did more for me than my own family.'

'Then God bless her a hundred times over and I shall give her a reward. Yes, a fine, fat reward. She is how I found you. I saw her coming out of your room on Wednesday evening. She said she'd been looking around, feeling nostalgic, or some such.' I scoff at the thought of Pansy experiencing any such emotion with regards to me. 'I knew she was up to something else. She looked as guilty as sin and her face was bright pink. But instinct told me that she wasn't stealing, that she had some other purpose in being there. So I asked Mrs Clarendon when her day off was. It turned out to be the very next day so I returned to Garrowgate at first light and I followed her here.'

'I admire your instincts,' I tell him, tucking into a steaming bowl of delicious crab bisque. 'She found me in the shrubbery at Garrowgate the morning after those *horrible* encounters with Mother and Father and Verity. I had spent the night there, I had nowhere to go. Pansy took me to Hetty's, and she is the sister of John, one of our footmen. Well, he *was*. Mother and Father dismissed him for standing up for me.'

'Is he very tall, light brown hair? I thought I hadn't seen him for a while on my visits to the old place.' I nod and explain how good John and Hetty have been to me, and how Olive has given me money and other things more valuable. I tell him that just this morning I have found employment and he grabs my hand across the table.

'Rowena, you don't need to work now! I shall take care of you. I'll set you up in a household of your own, provide you with an annual sum. Verity will hate for you to receive one penny of the fortune that she married but that will only increase my pleasure in doing it . . . and I'm sorry if it makes me a bad husband for saying so.'

I smile and lay my other hand over his. 'My dearest Felix, you're so kind, but there is no need for all that. I *want* to work, you see.' I tell him all about my job and how I want to contribute to the marvellous work of the Westallen Foundation. To his credit he listens and does not say one thing to dissuade me, though I can see in his eyes that it's not easy for him to think of his sheltered sister encountering the harsher truths of the world.

'Can it be true,' he asks, bewildered, 'that this is what you want? That this is what you choose? My delicate sister?'

'It is. I promise you. For I am very changed, now. Besides,' I finish, 'the days when I could play the lady are gone now, Felix, even if you did try to make me respectable again. Everyone knows what I did. I have to forge a new path, one that is true to my whole self, including the part of me that ran away with a man and brought disgrace to my family.'

Felix nods, considering. 'I admire you very much,' he says and I want to cry all over again.

'Felix, I'm the talk of the town. How can you be so . . . do you not judge me at *all*?'

He looks down at our entwined hands, then takes his back so he can continue with his soup. After a few more sips he clears his throat. 'It's very arbitrary, isn't it?' he reflects. 'What's allowed and what's not, I mean. I never thought of it before I married. And happiness . . . well, we don't talk about that much, do we, our sort of people?' I listen quietly for I can see that my brother is struggling with his thoughts. 'You were set to marry well and live the life that was always mapped out for you. You failed most spectacularly and now that life is ended.' I nod. That's about the size of it! 'I, on the other hand, married the perfect girl, someone so suitable she was practically family already. No one had a word to say against it, not even Mother and Father. Our union is sanctified, sanctioned. My life, as I have always known it, will carry on.' I nod again.

'And I am unhappy.' He looks at me beseechingly. 'I am so desperately unhappy, Rowena, that I can hardly find the words to tell you. It needn't have ended up like this, not if Verity had more to recommend her than good breeding and a pretty face, but she does not, and by following the rules I find myself shackled to a woman who is shallow and selfish and cruel. Her casual disregard for others shocks me on a daily basis. Our most interesting conversations revolve around who said what about whom in Highgate, or the price of lace. There is no way I can free myself without destroying her, for there would be no future that Verity would want if she were divorced. For all that she makes my life a misery, I could not do that to her.'

'Oh Felix.' I don't know what to say so I clasp his hands again. The soup can wait. 'I always wanted to ask you, but it didn't seem appropriate in the old days – why *did* you marry her? It seemed to happen very suddenly and I always . . . wondered.'

He sighs, squeezing my hands very tightly. 'I have often asked myself the same question and I'm afraid I haven't come up with any satisfactory answer. I believe the short answer is, that Verity decided it, and I was swept up in her course. You know how we were, you and I? We didn't question the rules, did we? I knew I needed to marry well and there was no one, highborn or low, who had captured my heart. When it became clear that Verity was setting her cap at me – or her bonnet perhaps – I was flattered. I thought, why not? It seemed to make sense.'

'I believe many people make their choices in the same way, Felix. You were not so foolish. And neither of us could have imagined back then that she would prove so . . . so very . . .'

'No. Indeed. But a match that looks well on the outside but that has no balm or lightness to it within the home is . . . an oppressive thing. I would not want that for you, Rowena. And that is why I do not offer to hunt down this Bartek rogue, drag him back here and force him to marry you. A year ago I would have done exactly that but now I would not condemn you to an unhappy marriage for the sake of respectability. So although I know you have been to hell and back these last weeks, if you can make a better life than mine, I would have you do it.'

Fifty

Pansy

Pansy's first Thursday with Mr Bailey Endicott, hatter, could not roll around fast enough. With barely a month until the diamond jubilee ball, Mrs Clarendon was run ragged and pulled the staff along in her determined undertow. Maude Blythe was in high feather all day every day.

'Find out what colours and motifs are to be used in the jubilee parade!'

'Order one hundred crates of Mr Ollander's finest champagne!'

'Procure me artificial flowers for the ballroom – I want it swathed, Mrs Clarendon, do you hear me? *Swathed!*'

Her instructions were endless, her vision grandiose. Pansy, who had never been particularly interested in the jubilee, was now obliged to spend her evenings poring over the reports in *The Times*. When she learned that the officiating clergy would wear specially designed copes to harmonise with the architecture of St Paul's, she laughed. Would Mrs Blythe dress up as a cathedral? Would she wear a dome on her head? Nevertheless, she passed the titbit along to Mrs Clarendon.

Mrs Clarendon dutifully told Mrs Blythe that Tilney, housemaid, was being vastly helpful, because she still wanted Pansy to become upper housemaid by Christmas – but Mrs Blythe couldn't care less. Pansy had no such desire and was happy to be overlooked.

To her, this was all so much nonsense: the extravagance, the pomp and glory, all designed to mark one solitary day in a life. Yes, it had been an extraordinary life but the queen was, after all, just a woman. She had done many noteworthy things, but Pansy survived the Blythes every day. No one was celebrating *that*!

So it was with relief, as much as anticipation, that Pansy presented herself at Mr Endicott's sizeable and splendid Hampstead shop on Thursday. Mr Endicott took her straight to his workshop at the back, leaving the store in the care of a young woman called Miss Bentley. The workshop was even bigger and immaculately arranged. The workbenches were completely bare, ready for the day's activities. Tools and fabrics were ranged neatly on shelves. Hat blocks rested on stands around the room and she spotted two spirit lamps tidied away in a corner. On the top shelves were hats of every style, not a cobweb to be seen, even that high up. Mrs Clarendon would be impressed.

'All obsolete,' said Mr Endicott, noticing the direction of her gaze. 'Fashions have changed more rapidly this decade than I've ever known before. You see? The jutting brim that was so popular in 1891 and 1892. The witch-crown that we saw *everywhere* in the middle years of the decade. The yeoman, that was all the rage *last* year . . .'

'Goodness,' said Pansy politely. She did love hats, but mostly she just picked one she liked the look of and stuck it on to see if it suited her!

Mr Endicott's knowledge was encyclopaedic and he continued to account for the superfluous hats, like a schoolmaster pointing at a map. 'The high-crowned toque, the three- or four-pointed toque . . . well, we still sell those, of course, but these samples have small flaws. I had an apprentice at the start of the year who was quite ham-fisted. I hope *you* will not prove ham-fisted.'

'I hope so too,' said Pansy.

'There, t'was not her fault. It is an exacting skill and one must have the right sort of hands for it, as well as the right sort of eye and the right sort of brain . . .'

'Goodness,' said Pansy again. So *many* parts of her anatomy that might prove lacking!

'You'll find nowadays that the toque is growing larger. We're moving towards a soft, full crown with a turned-back brim, very wide.' He sketched the shapes in the air with his hands as he spoke. 'I'm working on just such a one at present. See here.' Mr Endicott moved to a nearby shelf on which sat a number of shapes in velvet, tarlatan and felt. 'The next time you come, I shall begin a hat from scratch so that you can watch and learn. However, this morning I shall describe the process and what is required from a dedicated hatter. It is important to have a clear idea of whether this profession is the right one for you or rather,' he paused reverently, 'if *you* are right for *it*!'

'I see.' Pansy had a feeling that the morning would be rather dry; Mr Endicott's manner of delivery was quite overwhelming. 'Thank you, Mr Endicott. I appreciate you taking the time to teach me.'

'It's my pleasure. Now, the first step is to select your millinery supplies and tools. In order to do that, you must be thoroughly acquainted with the materials at your disposal, so I shall explain the properties of each . . .'

After almost an hour, Mr Endicott's account still hadn't reached the part where you actually started making a hat! But at last he paused, frowned and nodded. 'Now I shall describe the process of constructing a buckram hat. I shall endeavour to impress upon you that it is a complicated process . . .'

He succeeded! Soon, Pansy's head was so full of the application of millinery wire and the formation of crowns that the words poured over her like rain. She wished she could sit down and started to feel thirsty.

'High trimming on these larger toques,' he droned. 'Chiffon, net and lace on summer styles. Flowers, of course. They continue to be popular, though currants have had their day, thank goodness. On other styles a single distinctive ornament, an aigrette of ribbon, perhaps, or a cock's feather on the crown . . .'

When lunchtime arrived, Pansy ate with Miss Bentley in the workshop, while Mr Endicott tended the shop. 'Doesn't he eat?' she asked. It wouldn't surprise her if Mr Endicott was a special being who could live on hats alone.

'He will once we're finished,' Miss Bentley replied, pouring Pansy some more elderflower cordial. She'd slugged down her first glass in a single draft, she was so thirsty. 'How are you finding him?'

'Oh, very nice, very informative,' said Pansy, blushing.

Her companion laughed. 'He's a dry old stick, but a good employer and the best there is if you really want to learn.'

'As you do?'

'Oh yes, all I've dreamed about my whole life is making hats.'

Pansy nodded. She hadn't. Would her enthusiasm for a pretty accessory and a mild interest in the process be sufficient to inure her to Mr Endicott's dense tutelage?

She was inordinately relieved when, after lunch, he told her that he'd arranged for her to visit a flower-making factory in Cricklewood. 'Flowers, flowers, flowers,' he sighed. 'Hats aren't gardens, that's what people don't seem to realise.' He put her in a cab, paying the fare up front. Pansy realised what an effort he'd made to give her an educational day, then felt guilty at having been bored at all. But there was no doubt that her spirits lifted as the cab rolled away. Well, if a flower factory couldn't kindle a so-far dormant passion in her for hat-making, nothing would.

Four hours later, another cab arrived to take her back to Highgate. Pansy stared unseeingly out of the window all the way back. The visit to the factory had kindled a passion in her all right. But not for millinery. Perhaps it was not so much a passion as a fierce blaze of horror at the miserable lives she saw there. Then and there she forgave Rowena Blythe for being so selfish and blinkered for she realised that she had been just the same. Yes, Pansy had suffered indignities and hardships of which Rowena had been utterly ignorant. But the same could be said about her. She had always been clean, warm and safe. She had a steady income and the choice to better herself when she finally stopped resenting her lot. But *these* people – the poor souls crowded into the workrooms of the factories – Pansy had never imagined such lives.

She'd been greeted by Mr Gilling, the factory manager, a proud, florid man with a springing profusion of whitish whiskers and a gleaming top hat, then shown around by Mrs Murton, an employee who had worked there for seventeen years. When Pansy shook her hand, the woman's grasp was awkward, her fingers curled over like a claw. Probably a condition she'd been born with, thought Pansy, careful not to stare.

Mrs Murton took her into a badly lit room where five men sat at one table and five at another. She gestured to one group. 'These are the stampers,' she said in a soft voice, so that Pansy had to duck to hear her over the din of metal being struck.

The men were stamping out fabric flower shapes, using mallets to strike the cutting tools. They merely glanced at Pansy then continued work with a glazed sort of focus. One paused to rub a shoulder, a grimace on his face, then he carried on too.

'And here's where they dye the fabric,' murmured Mrs Murton. On the other table the men were laying out coloured flower shapes on large sheets of paper. A young fellow around Pansy's own age looked up and smiled. 'Wotcha, miss. Afternoon.'

'Good afternoon,' said Pansy. 'Are you drying the flowers?'

'That we are. This paper's porous, see, protects the table, but if we run out, we just use newspaper. Can't send 'em through till they're good and dry.'

'Of course. And do you have other jobs to do besides?'

'No, this is pretty much it. Sometimes we put the veins on the leaves too, but nothin' that ain't stampin' or colourin'. It's the women as makes up all the flowers, you never get a chap doing that.'

'In some factories, women do the stamping too,' put in Mrs Murton anxiously. 'It's quite hard work so Mr Gilling is very good to employ men here.'

'Oh yeah, he's all heart,' grinned the chatty fellow with discernible irony.

'Albie, hush,' said Mrs Murton. 'It's not right to speak of him like that.' She glanced around as if the walls really might have ears. 'Come along, Miss Tilney, there's plenty more to see.'

But Pansy didn't want to be hurried. *Now* she was fascinated. What a strange, unseen world this was. What very specific, repetitive work. Cleaning for the Blythes wasn't the only form of drudgery the world had to offer, it seemed. 'Some are black,' she said with a frown. They looked out of place amid the peaches and greens of the summer season.

'Mourning flowers,' volunteered the helpful Albie. 'Only two places make 'em – here in London and up in Manchester.'

Pansy thanked him as mouse-like Mrs Murton ushered her from the room and he gave her a cheery wave with blue-fingered hands.

The next room was set up along the same principle, with different tables for different activities and women and girls grouped around them, intent on their labour. Pansy was amazed by how young some of them were. There were girls who couldn't have been more than ten, working with the same grim-faced concentration as the older women. All were hunched forwards, heads protruding like tortoises. They were squinting, too; this room was just as badly lit as the first, with only small, dirty windows high up. Inadequate gas lamps supplemented the trickle of natural light.

'Goodness, it's not very bright,' observed Pansy.

'Oh, you mustn't say that!' cautioned her guide. 'Mr Gilling, he's brought in twice as many lamps as there were before, just this year.' Pansy could hardly imagine. She submitted to the official tour, watching as the flower makers heated the metal ends of tools over spirit lamps. What a difference between Mr Endicott's workshop and here. Plain, utilitarian lamps instead of decorative ones. Dingy surroundings instead of bright and tidy. And instead of Mr Endicott, alight with enthusiasm for his trade, women who worked in a daze, all light gone from their eyes.

'There are around four thousand flower makers in London,' Mrs Murton told her. 'A hundred or so of them work here. Mr Gilling is one of the leading providers of artificial flowers in London. We make flowers for ladies' hats and bonnets, of course, as well as mourning flowers, as you've seen, and large sprays for theatres too. Stage sets, you know.'

'How very impressive,' said Pansy, because questions seemed to make her guide so nervous. It occurred to her that here Mrs Blythe could source all the flowers she needed for her ball, but she couldn't imagine what a large order like that would mean for these poor hardworking souls.

'Heating the fabric shapes the petals, because flowers don't have flat petals, of course. Here we pride ourselves on making the most realistic flowers to be found in our great city.'

'Wonderful,' murmured Pansy.

'Here, the ladies are winding millinery wire around the petals to bind them to the stalks. As you will see, it's painstaking work. Each petal is secured with a separate loop so they hold fast with wear. In the case of many-petalled flowers like roses, care must be taken lest the stems look too bulbous when they are covered. Minnie, that's a little bulky there. Tighter and flatter, if you please.' She plucked a flower from the grasp of one of the workers, tossing it onto a pile of rejects. 'We have very stringent quality control here,' she added.

'So I see!' Pansy narrowed her eyes at the despondent Minnie, who was flexing her hands and rubbing her palms. The girl's fingers were bright red, not from dye, but because they were shredded and sore. The others kept working; it looked depressingly fiddly.

'Here, the beginners are being trained,' Mrs Murton continued, towing her on. Even younger girls – children – sat with older girls or women. 'Millicent there instructs her younger sister and Maggie is showing her youngest daughter . . . It's quite a family-oriented business, which is rather lovely.'

Pansy didn't think *lovely* was the word she would use. The door opened behind them and Mrs Murton jumped. Mr Gilling walked in. 'How are you finding everything, Miss Tilney?' he asked in a jovial voice.

Pansy could sense Mrs Murton quaking beside her. 'It's absolutely fascinating, Mr Gilling,' she said politely. 'I'm very impressed. I had no idea that you operated on such a grand scale.'

'Hah, splendid!' He rubbed his hands together in glee. 'Well done, Mrs Murton. Now, I'm sorry to interrupt, but I must borrow you for ten minutes. Miss Tilney, would you excuse us briefly?'

'Of course.' Pansy tried not to sound too eager. Was she really to be left alone here with all the workers and her many questions? Mrs Murton hurried after him, casting worried looks over her shoulder. 'No chatting, ladies!' she called in her faint voice. 'Let Miss Tilney look around in peace. I'll be back *very* soon.'

Alone, Pansy looked around: tables and tables of industry, rows and rows of stooped shoulders and peering eyes. Dust lay thick upon the tables and the sound of coughing filled the place. At one table the youngest children were clutching bound roses and pliers in their small hands. 'What's going on here?' Pansy asked.

'We's openin' the cuts, miss,' said one little girl, holding up the rose to show her. Using the pliers, she pulled open one petal at a time until it formed a lifelike shape.

'Mr Gilling says we're like God, because we open the flowers,' said another, looking quite awed.

'It do get ever so dusty, though,' said the first.

'You're doing a wonderful job,' said Pansy. 'What are your names? I'm Pansy.'

'Oh, we do pansies too!' exclaimed one of the children, pointing to another table where cascades of purple and yellow pansies were massing. 'I'm Beryl.'

'And I'm Annie.' So they went around the table.

'How old are you?' They were eight. When Pansy was eight, she'd been walking to school along the leafy lanes of Elstree and returning to the farm each mid-afternoon to one of her mother's homemade scones and a glass of milk, then she'd be out to play with Matthew and Eveline, or to brush the cows. Her heart was filled with pity and she rued her bitter complaints about her own lot in life.

She wandered back to the table where the flowers were being bound with wire. 'Would you like a seat, miss?' asked a young woman of eighteen or so, getting to her feet.

'Oh, no thank you! You're very kind but I like to stand and look around. How long have you been working here?'

'Five years now, miss.'

'Please call me Pansy. And do you like it?'

'Not much, if I'm honest. I'm Tabby Gates. It's hard on the eyes, see, because the light ain't very good. You get awful headaches.'

'I can see that. I can imagine.'

"Ard on the 'ands, too,' said another, older, woman. 'I'm Pauline Jackson, Miss Pansy. Been here twelve years now and me hands are startin' to go like old Claw Murton there.' She held up her hands pitifully. Pansy could see that they couldn't flex fully and the fingers were slightly curled. So Mrs Murton's hands weren't a birth condition? They were a hazard of the job? Pansy could hardly believe it.

'Hard on your lungs, too, with all this dust,' said a third. 'Lily Branner. Never 'ad a cough in me life till I came here. Now I'm lucky if me lungs stay in all week!' She cackled at the colourful image and Pansy smiled.

'How long is your working day?' she asked, wanting to know everything before Mrs Murton came back.

'Too long!' said Tabby. 'Fourteen or fifteen hours, mostly.

Twelve if we're lucky but that don't happen often.' The other women shook their heads in agreement.

'And sometimes more,' added Pauline. 'Especially in spring – that's boom time. Eighteen hours then.'

'Eighteen!' screeched Pansy. She didn't want to stir them up in case Mrs Murton returned to mutiny, but really. She herself often put in a fourteen-hour day at Garrowgate Hall but never longer, and at least she was moving around, with plenty of light, fresh air when she ran errands and Lou to make her laugh with her irreverent ways.

'It's the colours that play hell with you,' said Tabby. 'These carmine and blue, they're so bright. Try staring at those two all day. Makes you feel sick!' It certainly was a combination to dazzle the eyes.

'But white's the worst,' sighed Pauline. 'It's the contrast . . . Ooh, it's terrible, is white.'

Pansy couldn't help thinking that it wasn't the colours that were the problem but the darkness. She moved to another table where three women were decorating the flowers with tiny beads. They were squinting even worse than the others. Dark paper was spread over the table so the beads would show up better; they glinted softly in the gaslight.

'Ah, you've found our embellishers.' The quiet voice at her shoulder made her jump; she hadn't heard Mrs Murton coming in. 'Now, let me show you where we box up the flowers for delivery . . .'

Pansy had followed her in a daze, unsettled and yearning to *do* something . . . but she didn't know what.

Fifty-one

Rowena

On Sunday, Hetty and I rise early in a flurry of excitement for John is coming home today. We don't know what time he will arrive, but Hetty says he will come as soon as he can. I think she is right. She bustles around the kitchen preparing a welcome breakfast for him, her normally sallow cheeks pink with joy. I sip at my weak tea, rather listless, relieved when my offers to help are waved away.

My own eagerness to see John is no less than hers, but is tempered by dread of my future. My excitement about working with Olive and making a difference was short-lived. On Friday, a doctor called, sent by my brother. Felix and I talked long into the afternoon on Monday. I am heartbroken that his marriage is so unhappy. He deserves so much better. He's right: what makes someone a good match has nothing to do with birth and fortune. We have both been unlucky in love, in very different ways. And no, it did not escape my notice that he thinks that Pansy is pretty.

I told him the whole story of Bartek. Felix asked the obvious question, very apologetically, and I had to admit that I didn't know whether or not I was with child. 'I shall send a doctor, Ro. Someone very discreet. You need to know, either way.'

He was entirely right but even so, my heart sank when Dr Barrow arrived. He carried, besides his medical bag, a large wooden box and a ladies' hatbox, which I thought was curious.

He was, as Felix promised, a perfect gentleman. Hetty made herself scarce yet again, sweeping and dusting upstairs while he asked me questions and examined me gently. Answering him was excruciating, talking of my experiences with a man, a stranger. Yet his kindly and matter-of-fact manner made it possible, at least. He informed me that I am, indeed, expecting a child.

I stare into my clear brown tea. Of late I have been unable to stomach milk in it; apparently altered appetite is one of the symptoms. Why do women never talk about such things? At least, women like the Blythes and the Crawfords do not.

A baby. That will put an end to my grand aspiration to work and help others and be independent like Olive. Although Olive has two children, she never had a baby. Clover and Angeline arrived fully formed in her life, and she has her parents and a raft of servants to help her with them. I cannot expect Hetty to keep us both here and conveniently mind my child whilst I am at work. I have told her, of course. As soon as she heard the front door shut behind Dr Barrow she was down the stairs, almost as anxious as I, it seemed. Almost.

She hasn't said much. I dare to hope her silence is sympathetic and I'm grateful to digest the news before I am showered with *hows* and *whats* to which I have no answer. The only thing I know is that my baby is due in January. According to the doctor, it must have happened that very first time with Bartek, back in the lilac grove in April.

A baby. I am stunned. Even though it was an entirely probable outcome, it is somehow astonishing to think that this rite

of passage should happen to *me*. I suppose I shall have to let
Felix help me now. To have my chance at independence
snatched away before it ever began is galling, unendurable,
and yet I am not *wholly* dismayed. I do love children. Olive's
little girls enchant me. Despite the circumstances, I want this
child.

The front door rattles, plucking me from my reverie. It is
John, come home. Hetty flies to the door and I hear her excited
cries and his deep laughter. I stay where I am to give them a
moment alone but when I hear his footsteps I stand to greet
him.

'Rowena!' His face when he sees me is pure joy. My heart
flutters in response; it cannot resist such a smile. 'Good grief!
I see you are Miss Blythe again! Should I bow?'

When Dr Barrow took his leave on Friday, he left the box
and the hatbox; Felix had sent them over for me. Apparently
he told our parents he must have some of my things for a
young woman in need. Well, it was not a lie. In the hatbox
was a cream bonnet with a low brim and ribbons to draw it in
at the sides. I cannot wear that veiled hat for ever.

Inside the other were some of my old costumes, my silver-
backed hairbrush and mirror, some hair ornaments and several
old volumes of *Punch*. There were also affectionate notes from
my other brothers. Crispin and Ignatius are yet dependent on
our parents. They promise to meet with me, but it will be
harder for them than for Felix. Those notes meant more to
me than anything else.

So this morning I am dressed in a sea-green day dress, with
cream ribbons in my hair, and John has not seen me dressed
like this since the old days. I laugh and go to him, hands
outstretched. 'I shall never be that again, John. I am, now and
always, your true friend, Rowena.'

'I'm glad to hear it. I've fetched and carried for sufficient wealthy folk for one week.' He tumbles into a chair, resting his elbows on the table, and beams up at us. 'You two are a sight for sore eyes. I have so looked forward to today.'

'As have we, John, as have we,' says Hetty, bustling past and setting out the special breakfast. I pour more tea for the three of us – that, at least, I am allowed to do. We eat our fill whilst listening to John's stories of his new position in Chelsea. It sounds all too familiar: a grand house, a proud family, a dwindling staff. The last footman retired, and there was some debate before they decided to replace him. *After all, a footman does make a hall look so decorative*, was their reason. John's role, apparently, involves a lot of standing around.

'It's dull,' he admits, 'and hard on the back – I moved about a lot more at Garrowgate Hall – but it's a good wage and the family are not dreadful. The staff are friendly. It could all be a lot worse.'

That doesn't sound good enough for John, to me. 'You'll have to keep up your calisthenics,' I tell him. A memory flash: John in his loose trousers and shirt, sweating, muscles bracing, as he did his exercises on the terrace in the early morning sunlight. That was the first time I ever spoke to him.

It's the happiest day, despite my worries. We talk and talk, then take a stroll around the village, all three of us. We go home to make luncheon, late, since our breakfast was large. Then John asks if I'll take a stroll on the heath with him. He fixes his sister with a meaningful glance and she bids me go without any acerbic comment.

I cannot easily shed the concern that people will see me out walking alone with a man, that gossip will spring up like spreading flame. I tie on my cream bonnet again, fixing the ribbons so tight that the sides pinch my face and the brim draws down low. John takes a look at me and chuckles. 'I think you need not hide away *quite* that much,' he says, reaching out to loosen the ribbons. 'You'll choke yourself.' The hat eases about my head and he carefully ties a new, less restrictive, bow. The brush of his hands against my face both soothes and tingles; a wholly inappropriate reaction from a woman who is carrying someone else's child.

We set off into the evening sunshine and make for the heath, which teems with walkers. Families, courting couples, pairs of friends promenading. I'm assailed by memories of Verity, then push them away. I shall think of Olive instead, though she does not so much promenade as *march*. Indeed, I shall think only of John for we are chatting like old friends and he is fascinated to hear about my visit to the Westallen Foundation. I tell him about my offer of employment and all the ways in which it made me feel proud and hopeful.

'But you speak as if it's in the past,' he observes. 'Did you turn down the offer?'

'No, I accepted it. I am due to start tomorrow. I have been nervous and delighted and awed and ecstatic all week long.'

'But that's marvellous! Rowena, you said you wanted to forge your own way and you're doing just that. Such an achievement! You should be proud. Or are you worried that Hetty will expect you to leave once you start earning money? I do not think she will. I know her manner can be sharp but she's told me she's growing fond of you, and you're company for her now that I'm in Chelsea.'

'It's not that . . .'

'In fact, now that I mention my new position, I want to ask you something, Rowena.'

I want to tell him about the baby but he looks agitated and

suddenly I have a feeling that I know what he's about to say. We have reached a beautiful spot – a spreading oak at the top of a rise, a sweep of heath below us and to either side. Wildflowers scatter the expanse, and the scent of summer grass rises, beguiling. I need to tell him *now*, but the words dry in my throat at the sight of his earnest, determined face.

'Rowena,' he says, turning to face me, taking my hands. 'I don't know if you ever realised but I have always loved you. Your great beauty was not the reason – though you are, of course, so very beautiful. I always sensed that there was something about you . . . something *other*. Something special. I knew it was hopeless, but now I wonder . . . I should like to ask you . . . would you do me the extraordinary honour of becoming my wife?'

I am utterly tongue-tied. Is this my tenth proposal? My eleventh? Yet all the others left me unmoved. This one stirs more feelings in me than I am ready to name. I gaze into his dear, handsome face.

'I don't mean to imply that now, because your circumstances are changed, you're bound to accept me,' John hastens to explain. My heart melts at his humility. 'I'm as undeserving of you now as I ever was. But everything *is* different now, and I have something to offer you at last. I know I'm not the sort of husband you expected but I earn a good wage and you know that I am steady. I would love you and provide for you and honour you. I don't expect you to love me too, but if you feel even friendship for me, which I believe you do, I think I could make your life better. I can offer you a haven. I can offer you protection. I offer you my heart.'

He drops to his knee in the grass and draws out a ring from his pocket. I, who have worn the famous Blythe tiara, who have dripped in emeralds and used to own a ring with a sapphire the size of a hen's egg (currently somewhere in the North with Bartek), stare down at a thin gold band with a tiny diamond chip set upon it. It glints in the sunshine, a cheerful gleam for such a serious moment, and I honestly think I have never seen anything so beautiful.

Fifty-two

Olive

On Sunday afternoon I'm surprised by a visit from Pansy. She's been granted a short break because she's been working so hard in the run-up to dreadful Maude Blythe's pretentious ball. Apparently the housekeeper is compensating the extra hours where she can, sensible woman.

'I needed to speak to you,' Pansy says with some urgency, 'and I didn't know when I'd see you otherwise. I hope you don't mind me calling on you at home.'

I tell her I'm delighted to see her and in sore need of a distraction, though I don't trouble her with the reason why. It's been several days now since I told Lionel there could be no future for us. His hurt and indignation were vast and it is painful to think that I was the cause of it.

'I have been respectful, have I not?' he demanded. 'I have been patient and understanding. I thought we were fine friends and I *promised* you a good life! But it seems all this is not enough for Olive Westallen.'

That cut. As if I were ending our relationship because I wanted more than he could offer – unreasonable riches perhaps, or simply impossible things! And a good life is not in his keeping to bestow upon me or withhold! I already have one. But I did not want to anger him more, so I humbly told him again that, dearly fond of him as I am, I had realised that I could never marry. Anyone. He did not believe me. He demanded to know if someone else had captivated my interest, made me an offer. I had to quell rising annoyance; I dislike having my honesty questioned. My word is good, everyone knows that. *Lionel* should know that. I am not Rowena Blythe – as she *was* – to play with a man's affections that way. Besides, how on earth would I have the time or energy for wooing a second man in addition to pursuing a relationship with Lionel, running the foundation and looking after two children?

The conversation went on far longer than I wished it to, simply because he *couldn't* believe that my word was final, that there was no more to my decision than I had shared with him. He said many other things that have rankled throughout the week; they have got under my skin, as was no doubt his intention. Close friends tell me that men do not handle rejection well. All *I* know is that I do not like it. Perhaps I am unrealistic but it seems to me that casting aspersions and being unpleasant, even in disappointment, is not a sign of true regard and caring. Our relationship has changed form, yes, but I am still me. It was I who made the decision but that doesn't mean it was easy. I miss him, but how could I have yoked my life to a man who is petulant and sour when things don't go as he wants them to? I have been out of sorts all week.

'Olive? Are you all right?' Pansy's voice rouses me from my gloomy reverie. Goodness, it is very easy to sink back into it. I wonder when I shall start to feel like myself again.

'I'm fine, dear. I've had a difficult week and I'm rather preoccupied, but I'm glad you've come. Let me ring for tea, then you shall have my full attention.'

I seat her in the drawing room – my family are elsewhere about – and request tea and shortbread. It is a day for shortbread. I remember that Lionel was very fond of Mrs Brody's shortbread and my heart gives another disappointed lurch that sweeps through my whole body and leaves me weak, but I must push these memories to a special place in my mind now else I shall never get anything done again.

'Tell me!' I command, seating myself with Pansy.

And then she begins quite a tale. She looks very awkward and apologetic as she describes her morning with Mr Endicott; it is clear she did not enjoy her time there and feels bad about it.

'But Pansy, dear, that is what experiments are *for*,' I point out gently. 'If we had known in advance that you were to love or hate it, there would have been no need for the trial.'

'But you went to all that trouble to arrange it for me and Mr Endicott *poured* himself into teaching me. I'm so very grateful . . .'

'I shall go to the trouble of arranging ten more experiments for you if necessary. As for Mr Endicott, why not send him a small token of thanks and a note to explain? He will understand. He will not want a reluctant apprentice, any more than you want work you cannot feel passionate about.'

'Thank you, Olive, truly. And there were all these *hats* . . .' She frowns at some memory of the day.

'Pansy, it's a milliner's. Naturally there were hats. I should hope it was positively *brimming* with hats!' I chuckle, congratulating myself on my hat-related pun, but Pansy is lost in thought and does not fully appreciate my brilliance.

'No, I mean *spare* hats. In the workshop. Just sitting there, going to waste, Olive, all because they were the fashion of 1895 or 1896 instead of 1897. Shelves and shelves of them. I thought of the poor folk who don't even have *one* hat and can't make themselves presentable for an interview – well, *they* wouldn't care if it was a cloven crown or a witch-crown or, or . . . and that wasn't even the worst of it, Olive. The worst was the *flowers*!'

'Flowers, dear?' Then she tells me all about the factory: the dim light; the thick dust; the shredded fingers and the children, as young as eight, working in that unwholesome environment. Why, that is not much older than Clover and Angeline! Pansy minutely describes the process of flower-making; and she describes the workers, their lacklustre faces, hunched shoulders and peering eyes.

'I had never imagined,' I murmur, though really, there are so *many* injustices and hardships in the world, how *could* we imagine all of them? I question my fervent friend at length about all she has learned and we lapse into a satisfying philosophical discussion about the human condition which results in Pansy asking one salient question: 'But what shall we *do*?' She is a girl after my own heart.

For the time being at least, Lionel is driven from my mind as I reflect on the lack that drives people to do such wretched work. All to make something as pretty as flowers! Certainly the Westallen Foundation must help. But it also makes me reflect on Pansy – her future, her talents. I continue my line of thought from last Monday when I heard all about her defence of Mr Cruz. What would be her most fitting avenue? A thought occurs to me and I give a little gasp.

'Olive?' asks Pansy.

I have had an idea. But it's audacious – even for me. I sit up straighter and scrutinise her; her bright green eyes are still blazing with indignation. This idea will take some investigation before I suggest it to her, otherwise it is merely words.

'I am well,' I reassure her. 'I think it's fair to say that millinery is not where your future lies, Pansy, but never fear. We shall think of something.'

Fifty-three

Rowena

I sink into the grass at John's side for my legs are quite weak. Of course I must say no, that much is clear; what surprises me is how reluctant I am to say it.

'Dear John,' I say and his face is filled with hope. I must disabuse him of it at once! But oh, how I dread it. London is littered with hearts that have broken because of me but I do not want to break John's. Hetty will hate me again now.

'I cannot marry you, John,' I say at once, 'though I am honoured and appreciate your offer more than I can say.'

'You don't love me,' he surmises dully, sinking to the grass beside me, the hope dimmed in his eyes, as it must be.

'I am with child,' I tell him. It is no answer, but he needs to know and I cannot answer the question of whether I love him for I have never considered it before; I have been too caught up in trying to survive to think of romance. Yet when I think of our growing closeness, the deeply honourable man that I know him to be, it seems not impossible that I might, in time.

He grasps my hands. 'Let that not stop you! I knew it was a possibility, you know I did. Surely it is all the more reason for you to marry? I will love your child, Rowena, as my own. I'll protect it, I'll give it my name.'

I gasp. Can he mean it? I try to imagine any man of my old circle reacting with such equanimity to the thought of taking on another man's child. It's impossible. I would think him too good to be true if I didn't already know him so well. For John *is* this good and he loves me this much. It makes his offer even more tempting and yet even more out of reach. I must never take advantage of him.

My eyes grow warm and prickly. 'John, it's not the reason. My life is so complicated and it is so neat a solution. You're the best man I know – any woman would be lucky to be your wife. But you deserve the very best of everything, and you deserve *love*. I don't want to marry you to solve all *my* troubles, when you have loved me so faithfully for so long and I knew nothing of it, breezing about the world all caught up in my own empty head.'

He frowns. 'So, you don't love me,' he says again, but it is almost a question this time.

'I've never thought of you that way. Our friendship has grown to be the most important in my life. I admire you and appreciate you, in a way that I didn't . . . all those years! John, here is the real issue. *I* do not deserve *you!*'

We fall quiet and two white butterflies dance a lively polka before our faces. I realise that I am clutching his hands just as he clutches mine; I should probably pull away.

'Might you come to love me in time? If we married soon, we could pretend the baby is mine, come a little early.'

I shake my head, stifling a hysterical laugh. 'John! Do you know what you're offering? You can't have thought this through. What if the child resembles . . . Bartek?' I hesitate to say his name. 'What if there is a striking resemblance and every time you look at him – or her . . .' I add but instinct tells me it will be a boy. 'What if every time you're reminded that your wife threw herself away on another man before she married you? What would happen to this child if we had our own children? By law the eldest son has first entitlement – to whatever little we may have. If we have our own boy, what then? You are a dear, good man and I know you have a heart the size of London but you can't have thought this through and I cannot put you in such an invidious position.'

He frowns and takes a deep breath. 'Rowena, we must always be honest with one another. And so I tell you truly that yes, I have thought it all through. The moment you appeared on our doorstep I knew I needed to have something to offer, to marry you. When my sister first raised the possibility of a child it gave me a shock – in my rush of love it hadn't occurred to me. And yes, it gave me pause for thought. I considered all the things you mention now and I was not immediately overjoyed. But Rowena, it did not take five minutes before those doubts dissolved. The most important thing in the world to me is family. Hetty and I have lost our parents, you know that. My sister has saved me. And to have you as my wife . . . that would mean everything to me. It makes those considerations you mention insignificant. The child is part of you. Therefore he or she will be part of me, whether or not you accept, so I ask you again, might you one day love me?'

I sit quietly, fearful to give him false hope and yet he said we must be honest, and that holds true for friendship or matrimony. 'Yes, I might come to love you, John,' I admit at last. 'If I'm honest, I believe I'm already halfway there. My feelings for you are . . . very warm. But I cannot marry you on the assumption that I might, one day, feel certain of it. You deserve a whole-hearted wife, not one who is broken and used and who thought your name was Henry for more than a decade!'

More silence. Then he takes back his hands, squares his

shoulders. 'You are not broken,' he declares. 'You are stronger than you have ever been. You say you don't deserve me, but I disagree. You say you were empty and selfish. Well, I loved you then and I love you more now. You say that you are used but you're no one's *tool* for them to use! You made a choice that went wrong. That is all, it's part of life. You are *magnificent*. I shall *wait* for you to love me,' he concludes, getting to his feet. 'For if you realise that you truly love me, then there would be no obstacle, would there? I shall wait, Rowena Blythe.' So saying, he strides away, leaving me among the meadow grasses and the cornflowers.

I sit a long while alone on the heath, bonnet pulled close around my face. I hardly know how to order my thoughts. John has always loved me. Well, Pansy had hinted as much, or was it Hetty? At this point I can hardly remember. He has proposed marriage. Imagine, the chance of a life with a man who knows the real me, not Rowena Blythe the society queen. He knows my worst secrets, and still he wishes me to be his wife. I enjoy his company so much. I know he would always be kind. My baby would be a little Hobbs and the scandal would be far less than if I carry on alone. I know all this.

But what I said was true. I don't *want* to marry him for my own gain. It seems quite likely that I *will* love him, one day. But I must wait until then, even though, as he walked away, I had the strangest sensation of letting an uncommon treasure slip through my fingers. And there's another reason besides. I don't quite understand it but it is all mixed up with Olive's Athena-like self-sufficiency, with Mabs's stalwart example. Women forging their own way. Women who hold a position in the world without reference to any man. I probably shan't be able to work for very long now and Felix will aid me materially –

perhaps all independence is only relative. But I want a taste of it, at the very least.

I rise and make for home. The summer air is soft and balmy in the early evening, the sky still bright; the month of May is nearly at an end. At the door I hesitate. Will John still be there? Will Hetty accuse me of toying with her brother? Or will she understand that I'm trying to do right by him? I sigh and step inside.

'Rowena? Is that you?' Hetty appears before me as I untie my bonnet. 'Thank goodness! You look like a shepherdess with your hat tied like that.'

'I've been sitting on the heath and trying to work things out. Is John here?'

'He's gone. I gather he asked you to marry him.'

'Yes. And I said no. But I wasn't being cruel, Hetty. I care about him so very much.'

She jerks her head towards the kitchen. 'I know. I'll make you some cocoa.' I'm startled. Cocoa is very much reserved for high days and holidays in Hetty Simon's house. 'Come! Sit! You look like a dying duck in a thunderstorm.'

A curious image. But it wouldn't surprise me if I did. I pull out a chair and slump at the table. In the recesses of my mind Mother's voice scolds me. *Posture, Rowena!*

'Why did you refuse?' asks Hetty as she spoons cocoa from her special blue tin into two cups.

I try to explain my reasons and she is a more sympathetic listener than I would have expected. She comes to sit when the cocoa is ready and cups her hands around the drink, nodding along as I talk.

'Well,' she says when I fall quiet and sip my cocoa, 'regarding the matter of whether or not you deserve my brother, I think that's for him to decide, don't you?'

'Perhaps.' The cocoa is deliciously sweet.

'And regarding the matter of you wanting to work, well, I suppose I could look after your baby for you if you like. Not *every* day, mind you, but perhaps Miss Westallen would employ you only for two or three days a week.' She shrugs as if it doesn't matter to her. 'If it would help.'

'It *would*, Hetty. It would help marvellously! But I couldn't ask that of you. It's too big an imposition! It's too much to—'

'*That's* for me to decide,' she interrupts. 'The only thing that is for *you* to decide, Rowena Blythe, is whether or not you come to love my brother. If you don't, then I agree that you shouldn't marry him, no matter how tempting a solution he offers. I care about you, girl, but my brother deserves better than that. But if you do . . . If you *were* to come to care . . .'

She fixes me with her sharp gaze and I swallow nervously. 'Yes?'

'Well, for what it's worth, you would have my blessing.' I'm so surprised I gulp my drink and burn my mouth. Hetty Simon's blessing. A valuable commodity indeed.

Fifty-four

Pansy

'Olive Westallen doesn't hang around,' Pansy muttered, thrusting the note into her apron pocket. Only two days after Pansy's visit to Polaris House, she'd received a message whilst she was sweeping out the ballroom. Her dusters awaited their turn – the chandeliers were to be dust-free, cobweb-free and sparkling by the end of the day. It was a bit soon if you asked Pansy. There were still three weeks until the ball – plenty of time for the dust to settle and for the spiders to spin. But Maude Blythe's word was law, so here was Pansy, tackling the vast space all alone. At least it meant she could take a minute to read Olive's note. It was written on cream card, embossed at the bottom with the initials OW in olive green.

Dear Pansy,

I realise you are at work and terribly busy. However, if you can beg leave to escape for a short time tomorrow (Wednesday) at noon, you must come to the address overleaf. I shall exert no pressure save to say that it is the opportunity of a lifetime, you will regret it if you do not and I have done wonders to arrange it.

Warm regards,
Olive Westallen

On the back of the card an address in Holborn had been carefully written. Pansy had no idea whose it might be. She would finish the ballroom as quickly as humanly possible, she decided, applying herself with verve, then speak to Mrs Clarendon.

'Tomorrow?' cried the housekeeper when she did. 'Oh Pansy, today's the first of June. It's the month of the jubilee. The month of the *ball*!'

'I'm aware,' said Pansy drily. As if anyone could forget the infernal jubilee! 'I'm sorry, Mrs Clarendon. I'm not asking to vex you. But look!' She proffered Olive's note which Mrs Clarendon scanned with a resigned expression.

'A summons from Olive Westallen. You're leaving us, aren't you?'

'Yes, but I don't know when. And not before the ball – I promised you and I'll stick to it. But I do want something other than this, and Miss Westallen is helping me, and—'

'Go,' said Mrs Clarendon. 'If you're leaving anyway, I can't stop you, and I wouldn't want to. You deserve better. Better even than upper housemaid.' She smiled grimly.

'Thank you, Mrs Clarendon. I'll be back as soon as I can.'

'I appreciate that. After the ball I'll see if I can get you an extra day off. You could stay the night with your mother. You'd like that, wouldn't you?'

'More than anything!' Impulsively, Pansy gave Mrs Clarendon a kiss on the cheek. If someone had told her four months ago that she would *ever* do that, she'd have laughed in their face.

The next morning, Pansy was up early to donkey-stone the steps. A wide sweep of white steps led up to the front door of Garrowgate Hall and they must always be gleaming. She and Lou scrubbed together, one at either edge, working inwards to meet in the middle, then moving up to the next step. It was

one of the most physically demanding tasks of her job. When
that was done, she helped Mrs Andrews organise the larder
to make room for all the extra delicacies on order for the ball.
Then she and one of the Sarahs started cleaning the dining
room but when the clock struck eleven, she stopped. The
donkey-stoning had left her dishevelled, grimy and perspiring.
She needed to wash and tidy herself. She didn't change; if
Maude Blythe caught her leaving the house in her own clothes
at this hour, Mrs Clarendon would be in trouble as well as
Pansy. At least in her uniform she could say she'd been sent
on an errand, though it was a shame to meet the opportunity
of a lifetime dressed as a servant of the Blythes.

She couldn't imagine whom Olive had arranged for her to
meet; she supposed there must be *someone*, not just Olive
herself, else why not simply meet at Olive's office? Pansy had
been very good about not dipping into her savings, but Holborn
was five miles away and she'd promised Mrs Clarendon she'd
be quick, so she took a cab. Besides, it was a warm day and
she'd be sweaty all over again if she walked.

When the cab dropped her off, Pansy was bewildered. She
found herself standing before some sort of fine-looking estate,
here in the heart of the city. Cloistered white buildings glinted
peaceably in the summer sun and from the street she could
glimpse a manicured lawn. Was it a college? Quite a number
of people hurried in and out; it seemed to be a place of some
importance. As she waited she noticed that many of them were
men in black robes and curled white wigs. Was Olive bringing
a *lawsuit* against someone?

'Ah, there you are!' said Olive's voice behind her. She was
wearing a jade-green costume trimmed in black, with a smart
black hat finished with a peacock feather. 'I'm so pleased you've
come. There's someone terribly interesting and impressive I

want you to meet. This is the only time she has free for some time and I didn't want to delay. I may have got a little carried away,' she conceded, setting off apace.

'Who is she? What's this place?' Pansy's curiosity got the better of her as she hurried to keep up.

'This is one of the Inns of Court, Pansy, and we're meeting a lady called Eliza Orme.' Pansy was none the wiser. The only famous people whose name she might recognise were music hall actresses. She'd enjoyed a show or two when she was younger and her sister, who loved music, often talked about performers she admired. She didn't think this Eliza Orme would be a music hall singer. 'Oh, I must tell you,' bubbled Olive, 'I can't wait. She's the first woman in England ever to gain a degree in law!'

Pansy grew ever more baffled. She hadn't known women could do that. It *was* very impressive but what did it have to do with her?

'I may have made rather a leap,' Olive went on, 'but Julia and Jem told me the other day how you helped your friend from the delicatessen that day you met Jem. You stood up to the police and made them let him go. Then you came to me on Sunday in a flutter about the flower makers. You're not passionate about hats, you're passionate about *justice*!' She paused triumphantly to gauge Pansy's reaction.

Pansy stood stock-still. 'No, I . . . Well, yes, things do make my blood boil. But what does that have to . . . ?'

'It struck me that if you were a man coming to the foundation for help, I would suggest a career in the law. I was slow to think of it for you because I didn't think women *could* work in the legal profession. In fact, I was right.' Olive stopped before a door of dark wood set into a small stone building and knocked flamboyantly. 'Women *aren't* allowed to work as solicitors or barristers, so my dream of seeing you striding around a court-room in a wig has flown,' she said with a regretful look at Pansy. 'But then I remembered meeting Miss Orme some years ago at a function – her father and mine both attended and we were the clever daughters they took along. I tracked her down and we talked. It persuaded me it was worth your while meeting her.'

'I don't know what to say,' said Pansy, smoothing escaped wisps of hair back from her face. She was rather flattered that Olive had ever had such a dream for her, even if it was impossible. 'I never dreamed of such a thing, Olive. You have too much faith in me, I think. I'm not that bright. I fear Miss Orme will be very disappointed in me.'

'Pfff,' responded Olive scathingly as the door opened and a thin, pale clerk showed them in.

Miss Orme welcomed them into a small office. She was a stout woman of around fifty, with dark hair pulled back from a tranquil oval-shaped face. A shaft of dusty sunlight fell through a casement window across a desk heaped high with papers. 'Good to see you again, Olive. And you must be Miss Tilney.'

Pansy shook her hand, slightly awed to think that this woman had a degree in *law*; that she was the very first woman in Britain to do so. How did one go about breaking ground like that?

'Thank you for seeing me, Miss Orme. Olive has told me of your wonderful achievement. I know you must be very busy.'

'Particularly so at the moment. I've taken on a great deal of work and I'm giving several presentations on parliamentary franchise this month so I'm preparing in every spare minute. Next month will be quieter but time, who waits for no man, must wait for Miss Westallen.'

'Indeed it must,' said Olive comfortably, taking a seat at the window where leaves danced around the casement, sending dappled shadow into the room. 'Pansy, ask Miss Orme questions, if you please. I shall stay well out of it.'

Miss Orme pulled up a chair for Pansy and sat near her by the desk, looking at her expectantly. Really, thought Pansy, Olive might have prepared her a little. What on earth did one say to such a person? So she asked the only question she could think of. 'How did you come to do such a thing as gain a law degree when no woman had done it before? How does anyone come to hold such expectations for themselves?'

'That's a good question,' Miss Orme responded, glancing at Olive as if reminded of an earlier conversation between them. 'My whole family was always interested in women's education. Like Miss Westallen's, my parents were very encouraging. I became a student at University College in 1871 when women were first allowed to attend lectures.' Her lip curled impressively at the word *allowed*. 'But we weren't *allowed* to receive degrees until 1878. I completed mine some years later.'

'What she hasn't said,' put in Olive from her seat by the window, 'is that some years *before* that, she wrote for *The Examiner* arguing for degrees for women in that very university!'

'Who knows if that made a difference?' said Miss Orme modestly. 'It may have done.'

'Of course it did!' cried Olive, apparently forgetting her resolve to stay out of it. 'And she received scholarships, Pansy, scholarships!'

Suddenly Pansy did feel a tingle at the thought of following in the footsteps of this grave, learned woman, at the thought of attending lectures and learning about the law. The law! The very fabric from which society was fashioned. *That's what I want to learn*, she thought, feeling suddenly breathless. Not how to make a brim and a crown, but how to make laws and policies. But it was all too ambitious! And Pansy needed an income. She couldn't just study for interest's sake.

'Olive said that women still can't practise law.' She turned back to Miss Orme. 'What is your work?'

'Oh, she's right. The restrictions upon us are still intolerable – but we must tackle this with a two-pronged approach.'

'Like a toasting fork!' said Olive excitedly, abandoning her detached demeanour and leaning forward urgently.

'Quite so,' nodded Miss Orme, making a little skewering motion with her hand. 'We must concentrate on making a way for ourselves where we can within the existing system *and* make time to work on changing that system. We cannot qualify as a barrister or a solicitor but I have been devilling for years now together with my colleague Miss Lawrence and—'

'Devilling?' asked Pansy.

'It's the term used for training and junior work in the legal profession. It means drafting legal documents for the most part. It is interesting work, Pansy, and I make a good living from it.'

So you *could* make a living with a law degree, thought Pansy, feeling as though her eyes had been opened. Whoever thought of such a job for women? Yet here was the living proof. And she wasn't the only one because her colleague was a woman too.

'And do tell Pansy about your friend in India, Miss Orme,' said Olive. 'I want her to understand that there are other ways she might use such an education.'

'Ah, yes. I told Miss Westallen about a friend of mine, Cornelia Sorabji, who was the first woman to study law at Oxford. She's Indian, so she had even more to contend with than I and I had plenty, you may believe. Cornelia lives in India now where she too cannot practise law. But she undertakes advisory work for women who do not have a voice at all within their society and helps them in all manner of ways.'

'Advisory work,' murmured Pansy. Her head was spinning. She remembered when her mother had first charged her with finding something better to do than cleaning for the Blythes. All she could think of then was shop work or hats! Now she was sitting in a legal office with two women who were mighty presences. They genuinely believed that anything was possible and weren't especially willing to wait for the world to catch up. Like a snake shedding her skin, Pansy was eager for transformation, to do something big. Suddenly she had a million questions for Miss Orme, instead of just one.

Fifty-five

Rowena

Life is changing unfairly fast – too fast for me to keep up with it. For three-and-twenty years I was a cosseted society darling with no idea that that might ever change. Then, in the space of less than two months, I fell in love, was abandoned on a towpath, have been attacked, propositioned, disinherited and rescued. I am estranged from my best friend but friends with my former rival. As if all that is not enough, I am a working woman and I am to become a mother. Oh yes, and then there's John . . . whom I miss more every day. Why should that be? It is not as if I have nothing to distract me. My poor pretty head is awhirl and not, any more, with slippers and trimmings.

I step out of the office at the end of my third day at work. Olive was unperturbed by the news of my pregnancy. 'We knew it was likely, did we not?' she said, as John had said on Sunday. 'Carry on as we discussed for now and when the baby comes, we shall reassess. You're a boon to the foundation, Rowena. Even if we can only have you one or two days each week, then that is what we shall do.' I cried a little in relief and gratitude and she gave me a cheery pat on the shoulder.

June is at its best and brightest and the streets are busy

around me but the rushing crowds are nothing compared with my teeming mind. My job is wonderful! I have a desk in the corner of the foundation's large office where I must keep meticulous records of the students who come to me: of whom I see on which days, what I teach them, which interviews they attend, what money or clothing they receive to help them make a good impression. I, who was never an avid student, enjoy the feeling of studiousness as I scratch away at my ledger. I keep it as neatly as I can – Verity would laugh; she used to call my handwritten notes spider scrawl and it's true that I dashed them off with little care. The pen and I were not well acquainted! But I must present my notes to Mabs at the end of each month and after that Mr Gladstone will see them, so I take a pride.

I'm astonished that I enjoy the administrative work, but my favourite part of the job by far is helping the girls. Already I have met nine who wish to go into service. I've talked to them at length about what they can expect if they succeed, and have given them every bit of advice I can think of to do so. Only one of them, Maria, seems uninspired but Olive says she is a particularly sad case; Olive says her mother and father are people one would never wish to meet. Maria is a thin and wan creature, with huge, staring eyes and nothing to say. I felt like a failure at first that I could not kindle a little enthusiasm in her but Olive says it will take time with someone like that. 'We can do something about poverty and lack of opportunity, but we can do nothing about someone's home environment, their families and past experiences,' she said, quite rightly.

The other girls are all more or less promising; two or three are gratifyingly excited to think that they might reach such exalted heights as lady's maid one day. Imagine, a position that

I used to consider beneath my notice is a high aspiration for some. I wish for my charges a more respectful mistress than I was. On Friday, I shall see all nine together and give them a practical lesson in dressing hair. I was always on the receiving end of such attentions, but idly watching someone in a mirror every day of my life does mean that I've picked up a few things. I shall be instructress and also model; they will practise on my own plentiful tresses. It's liable to be painful – with a hot flush of shame I remember dismissing an inexperienced maid who once attempted a chignon for me because she tugged my hair – but I don't mind if it helps them.

I stand in the doorway, letting the experiences of the day settle for a moment. Margie White, one of my students, comes barrelling out and bumps into me. 'Oof, sorry, miss.' She gasps and ducks when my arm shoots out to steady her. The poor girl actually thought I might hit her.

'Please don't worry, Margie. It's my fault for standing just where people want to come in and out.'

'Thank you, miss,' she says, looking relieved. 'Miss, can I say something?'

'Of course!'

'Thank you. For talkin' to me. Makin' me feel like I can do it. I never 'ad that before.'

'Oh Margie, I'm so pleased you find it useful. Are you coming on Friday?'

'Oh yes, miss. I'm that excited about it.' Then her face falls. 'Unless me ma says I 'ave to stay 'ome. Sometimes she takes in extra laundry on a Friday. The rich folks, they want it clean for the weekends. Sometimes she won't let me out because she needs the help.'

'Don't worry. If you miss it, I'll give you the same lesson another day. Any day you like.'

'Really, miss? That's proper kind. That's a relief, that is. So long, miss!'

'So long, Margie.' I stand and watch her go. She cuts a dreadful figure, with her overlarge dress sagging and stained. A hand-me-down from her older sister apparently. She has no bonnet and her hair is a stack of mousey strands escaping from an inadequate pair of pins. Her gait is graceless. As she is, she will make a terrible impression on any housekeeper who might interview her. I understand now why Mabs wanted my help. Until I met Margie and Maria and the rest, I still thought perhaps she was humouring me. When Margie's time comes, I'll have her spick and span so that any family would count themselves lucky to employ her.

I set off walking, enjoying the summer sun and full of plans. I have so much before me. My own tiny boy or girl. Work that I can love – a means of supporting myself, even if only partially. I have my brothers, good friends and choices. No, my life will never be extravagant again. I shall struggle often, especially when the baby comes. But I am still so very blessed. Meeting Margie and the rest has taught me that. And my life is my *own*. All mine! I can choose who and what I have in it and who can go to the gallows (Verity Crawford!). I can choose where I live, how I work, how to bring up my child . . . I feel my chest swell with the joy and pride of it. As I ponder these questions, wherever my thoughts wander, one face keeps bobbing in my mind: John.

John is unquestionably someone I want to keep in my life. So are Olive, Hetty and Mabs . . . even Pansy . . . but John is different. I want my child to have a father, to know what it is to be dangled by strong hands or carried aloft on broad shoulders – clearly my own childhood is not the model for *this* daydream. And John is the person I imagine when I see that

picture in my mind's eye. And it is not *just* for my child. I too
wish to have him always nearby. Memories rush upon me
repeatedly – my brain trying to make sense of all the changes
no doubt: John standing tall and silent in Garrowgate Hall,
immaculate and proud in his livery. John taking me in without
a moment's hesitation when Pansy took me to him that terrible
day. The strength and gentleness in his eyes when he said,
We'll take care of you . . . You're safe now. John sitting near
me in the courtyard, while butterflies danced. John dropping
to one knee on the heath, offering me a small diamond and
his stout heart.

With every new experience I have had at work these last
days, I have longed to tell John. I've stored up every detail
to share with him and a light dances in my heart because of
it. I told him I needed to wait to be sure that my feelings
for him were true. I thought it would take a little longer
than this! But I needn't wait any longer. If this is not love
– this thorough admiration, the joy I take in his conversation
and presence, this eternal turning to him that my mind
makes, this devotion I feel – then what is? I *cannot* wait any
longer!

I shall hail a cab. After all, I am earning a little money now!
I am filled with wild excitement. But no.

I hesitate. A flood of feeling has led me wrong before. I do
not want to go to John on an impulse. If I mistake myself
again, it is John who would lose out this time, not me, and I
would never, ever want to hurt him. I force myself to walk
instead in the direction of home. I must wait. I *must* wait.

But oh, I am sure! I have never been surer of anything.
From the very first, from even before that, he has been my
truest friend. And it is not only friendship that I feel, it is a
feeling akin to the glow of sunshine. It has been brimming

awhile on the horizon, though I did not notice it at first. Now, it has burst into full daylight. What is the point of learning to trust myself if I do not do so on this most important and precious matter? This debate takes me halfway home before I pass a stand of cabs, stop and climb into one.

I direct the driver to Chelsea. I do not know the exact address but I know it overlooks the embankment and I know the name of his employers: Prentiss. When we arrive, the rushing river is pewter-blue and choppy from all the pleasure boats and cargo boats sailing up and down.

I leap from the cab and the very first person I ask is acquainted with Mr Prentiss. He directs me to a tall red-brick townhouse with a black door not far away. I'm flummoxed that there is no door knocker – am I meant to pound the door with my fists? Then I observe a small sign that reads *Please Ring* above a brass rosette. In the centre of the rosette is a white button. An electric doorbell – how very modern! Father would have forty fits before he'd have such a thing at Garrowgate Hall.

Nervously I press the button and startle nearly out of my skin when a loud *brrrriing!* sounds within. As soon as I have done it, I slap my hand over my mouth. I should have gone to the servants' entrance! What a dreadful faux-pas. But where *is* the servants' entrance in a townhouse? I cannot see one for only the front face of the house is accessible, joined as it is to its neighbours. What if John gets into trouble because of me? Again? Appalled at the thought, I turn to run but the door behind me opens. And of course, it is John.

'Rowena!' His eyes open wide. He glances behind him then steps outside. 'Are you all right? Is anything wrong?'

'No, no, I'm quite all right. I'm sorry to come to you at work. Only I wanted to tell you . . . well . . .' I falter. I must either be far more abrupt than I'd hoped or sound very mysterious. I opt for the former. 'John, I have come to tell you that I love you and if your offer of marriage still stands, I wish nothing more than to say yes.'

He laughs in sheer disbelief. 'Truly?'

'Yes.'

'Already?'

'Yes.'

'And you couldn't wait until Sunday to tell me?' he teases, his face breaking into smile after smile. Now he hangs on to the door handle as if his life depends upon it.

'No, I couldn't. It came over me, John, in the middle of the street. All doubt washed away, only clarity in its place. And clarity made it . . . urgent. I'm sorry, I should have waited. I should have gone to the servants' entrance. Only, where is it, John? I can't see one!'

'It's there.' He points down to a basement surrounded by black railings. I see now a tiny gate and narrow steps descending beneath the street. 'And no, you shouldn't have waited. Clarity is good. Urgency is good. Only, Rowena, dinner guests will arrive any minute, and I've no time to talk.'

'I'll go. I just wanted you to know.'

He catches my hand. 'Thank you, Rowena. You've made me the happiest man alive.' I can see it; it's dancing in his blue eyes. 'Until Sunday then.'

I nod happily, tears of joy blurring his face before me. I turn to go but he tugs my hand, pulling me back. 'Wait, you forgot something.' He reaches his free hand inside his handsome burgundy coat (his uniform was black and white at Garrowgate Hall) and withdraws a tiny box that I have seen before.

'You carry it with you?'

'Next to my heart. Always in hope.' He snaps it open and

takes out the beautiful ring. He places it on my finger and, with another swift backward glance, softly kisses my cheek.

I cannot help myself. I stretch out my hand and turn it this way and that to catch the light. The dainty ring looks well on my slender finger. I beam up at him before turning and hurrying down the steps, a betrothed woman.

Fifty-six

Pansy

'You're quiet today, Pansy,' observed Hipólito, as Steed jogged along the road to Elstree.

Pansy turned to smile at him, the June sunlight warm upon her face, even at this early hour. Birdsong tumbled through the air and she felt utterly relaxed, for the first time in a long while. 'I'm enjoying the ride. It's so long since I've been home and it's such a lovely day.'

He nodded. 'Last time you were riding beside me, it was dark and cold.'

'I've missed it. The rides with you, seeing Mum. I've missed Elstree.' It was, Pansy reflected, new experiences and new people that had carried her through the last few months, compensating for the drudgery of working at Garrowgate Hall and accepting that John would never be hers. Novelty, and a sense of new horizons opening up, had soothed and stirred her spirit. But a person needed familiarity too: family, and the places where things went on just as they always had. Home.

Pansy had slept poorly after meeting Miss Orme. Everything she'd learned had swirled around in her head through the night and kept her simmering with possibility. She'd woken for the sixth or seventh time when Lou and Maisie did, and sat up with a groan, wondering what to do with her Thursday. Only then did it strike her that she could go home. She'd already written to Mr Endicott thanking him for his tutelage and explaining that millinery wasn't for her. She would go and see him in person too, but it didn't have to be today. She was awake early and hadn't seen her mother for aeons, so she got dressed with the others, slipped out early and waited under a fading sky until she saw Mr Ollander moving about inside the store. What luxury to have a whole day just for pleasure.

'I'll come back to pick you up this evening,' Hipólito said when he left her at the end of the lane. 'Mr Ollander has a big delivery coming for Mrs Blythe's ball. I'll have a long day in the storeroom and I'll be ready to get out again by then.'

'Thanks, Hipólito. You can come in and have a slice of Mum's fruitcake, she'd love to see you.' Hipólito could never resist her mother's fruitcake. Pansy waved as he drove away then ran all the way to the cottage, her tiredness forgotten.

She barrelled through the door, calling, 'Mums! Mums! It's me!' and Laura came into the flagged hall, wiping her hands on her apron.

'Pansy? Good grief, how wonderful to see you! Oh my darling, come here!' Pansy flew into her arms and they hugged tightly, laughing and jigging up and down with excitement. 'You're here for the day? The whole day?'

'Yes! And Mrs Clarendon said that after the ball I can have an extra day off because of all the work I've been doing, so I'll come again then and stay the night!'

'I would love that. Let me get you some breakfast, then I want to hear all your news.'

Pansy followed her into the dear, familiar kitchen. Summer sun lay across the floor and the table, the warmth releasing the scent of the dried herbs in the rafters and two loaves of freshly baked bread cooling on the range. 'Oh home! Home!'

she cried luxuriously, stretching her arms above her head and waving them joyfully. 'Can I help? How are you, Mums? Are you well? I don't suppose Ev's here, is she? Oh, it's been so *long!*'

'It has felt a very long time,' Laura agreed. 'I was about to write to you and tell you to suspend your quest and come and see your mother immediately. I'm fine, Pansy, absolutely fine. No, Eveline's not here. She loves her job and living in Camden. The plan is for her to come on a Sunday every other week. The alternate Sunday she'll go out with her friends in Camden. She'll write to you soon, I'm sure. Nothing's really changed here. If you go and see Matthew this afternoon, he'll be over the moon – he talks about you often. He calls in almost every evening and I see the neighbours a lot so I'm not lonely. I have missed you, though. Let me look at you.' She stopped in her preparation of tea and bacon and gave Pansy the sort of exacting scrutiny only a mother could manage.

'You look better,' she announced. 'That pinched look has gone from your face and your eyes are sparkling again. Don't tell me anything important for five minutes. Let me get your breakfast in front of you so I can sit and listen properly. You haven't already eaten, have you?'

'No.' Pansy grinned. 'I'm starving. I was at Mr Ollander's by six o'clock and he offered me breakfast but I saved myself for yours, of course.'

'Good!' Laura rustled up bacon, sausages, scrambled eggs, mushrooms, bread and butter and tea, then sat opposite Pansy expectantly. Through huge mouthfuls of her mother's delicious home cooking, Pansy told her about Jem and Julia. About Olive Westallen. About Rowena and Hetty and John. About the hat shops and the factory. And about Miss Orme. She talked for ages as the morning grew high and wide around them. The green fields beyond the window were dotted with sheep. Without asking, Laura refilled her mug then sat down again.

'Mum,' said Pansy at last. 'I know this sounds rather mad. It's a very new idea and I'll need to look into it a great deal – but I think I want to study law. I think I want to try for a university degree.'

She looked at her mother anxiously. Saying it aloud felt outrageous. You could think such things in the privacy of your own head, or in the company of such women as Olive and Eliza, but anywhere else, it sounded like lunacy. Yet her mother was beaming.

'Pansy, you clever girl. You're right, I could never have imagined this. But it's wonderful! I always thought you could do better at school. You were so bright, but you couldn't wait to get out of there.'

'Nothing really interested me in those days. I just wanted to enjoy life and then, when Dad died, I wanted to earn money and help us all. But this is different. This interests me. It *fascinates* me. I could use it to earn a living *and* help people. Maybe people like Hipólito who don't get fair chances – he's coming for cake this evening by the way – or people like the girls in those factories.'

'I'm so proud of you, my daughter. Anyone would be lucky to have you on their side.'

'And Mum, what about . . . marriage? Family? When you told me I had to leave the Blythes, you said you wanted me to fall in love and be happy . . . I've accepted that I can't be with John now, but there's no one else . . .' Pansy broke off, flushing. It was true that she was at peace with the fact that John would never be hers – there was only so long you could fight the inevitable. It wasn't entirely true, however, that there was no one else. Unbidden, Felix Blythe's face had leapt into her mind when she said it. Ridiculous! Even if he were a bachelor, he was as far above her as the stars in the sky. The irony of this, after all the grief she'd given John about Rowena, was not lost on her. And he had a *wife*, for goodness' sake, and not just any wife but Verity Crawford! Pansy got up quickly to hide her inexplicably warm face and fetched two glasses of water. 'And if this works out, I'll be too busy studying to think about meeting men,' she continued when she returned to the table. 'I don't know if this is what you had in mind when you set me to looking for my happiness.'

'I had nothing in mind, other than that I wanted to see that hard, burdened look gone from your face – and it is. It was your happiness I wanted you to find, Pansy, not mine. Yes, I would love for you to have what I had with your father, but *my* ideas about it don't matter, only yours. This won't be an easy path you've chosen, but I expect you've thought about all that, haven't you?'

'Yes. I don't know *how* it's to be done yet, but Olive says that if I want to, we'll start looking into scholarships and . . . well, if it's right, there'll be a way to make it work, won't there?'

Laura smiled and squeezed her hand. 'There will. Pansy, I knew you'd find your way, and that it would be spectacular. I'm proud of you, darling daughter.'

Pansy flushed again, this time with gratitude, and gazed at her mother, thinking how lucky she was to know such love, the sort that would always sustain her and give her strength, that would never falter or fade. Not everyone had such a mother; just look at Rowena!

'Besides,' said Laura with a dreamy expression, 'there are bound to be all sorts of excellent and clever men at the university.'

Fifty-seven

Rowena

S unday is the happiest of days. John is with us bright and early and Hetty has prepared a fine breakfast once more. 'Let me, while a sister might still think herself foremost in his life,' Hetty says, 'for soon he will have a wife and it will be you who sees to his every happiness.'

When I returned home on Wednesday, brandishing my diamond ring, she was very pleased, after her own fashion. 'I never thought I'd say this,' she said wryly, 'but I couldn't be happier.' I kissed her cheek and she swatted me away.

'I'll gladly let you make breakfast,' I say now, 'but you'll always be his sister, Hetty.'

'More's the pity,' says John, nudging her mischievously. Hetty shoves him away from the stove. It occurs to me that she will be my sister too, very soon. I don't share the thought with her just yet, in case it does not please her, but it makes *me* happy. I had a clutch of brothers growing up, but no sister. Verity used to call herself my sister but she never was.

'His *treasured* sister,' I add, not at all sure that this is the time for joking.

'That is so,' agrees John, coming to sit beside me and taking my hand.

'Oh, please save that sort of behaviour till I'm out of the

way,' groans Hetty, dishing up kippers, boiled eggs and toast, and pouring small glasses of celebratory ale. We pass the whole of breakfast teasing and laughing thus, full of plans for the future. John is going to speak to his employers about married quarters and has already been promised a pay rise next spring. I am going to work as long as I am able and return as soon as I can. I mean to make myself so indispensable to the foundation that I too might hope for a pay rise one day. We shall save and save and eventually, perhaps, buy a tiny place of our own, like Hetty's. I have never been so happy.

'I'm glad you're not planning to come here,' she insists. 'There's no room anyway and I'm not sharing my home with a couple of lovebirds and a squalling babe.' John rolls his eyes. 'But don't go too far away either,' Hetty adds.

John says we must marry as soon as possible because of the baby. It will be a small ceremony in whichever church will accommodate us soonest. The three of us and John and Hetty's cousin Wesley. My brothers, or whichever of them can be there. Olive and Pansy.

We pack a picnic and take a long walk on the heath, lolling on a blanket in the shade when we grow tired, eventually eating a late luncheon carried by John on his strong back: ham and soft bread, cider and strawberries and apple cake. We roll home, too full for an evening meal, and I realise that I shan't see John for a whole week again. Yes, we must arrange married quarters! Thank goodness I have my work to keep me occupied and distract me from missing him.

Back at the cottage, two gentlemen are waiting by the door. The taller one is unmistakeably my brother Felix. When they see us, the smaller figure breaks into a run. It is my youngest brother, Ignatius.

'Nash!' I cry in delight as he hurls himself into my arms. 'Oh Nash, it's so good to see you.'

'I'm sorry, Ro,' he sobs into my collar. 'I never meant to leave you out in the cold. They didn't tell me and Crispin much, only that we mustn't know you any more or we'd be disinherited. We didn't care about that but we didn't know where you were *anyway*, and then Felix found you and said we mustn't tell Mother and Father, but I hate them to think I don't still love you because you ran away. I don't *care* about that—'

'Hush, now,' I soothe, stroking his hair. 'It's all right, darling. I'm so happy to see you. We'll work it all out, don't you worry.' He's only fifteen after all, a gangly creature somewhere between boy and man.

'It's all right for Crispin,' he grumbles. 'He'll be twenty-one at Christmas and then he can do as he likes. I'm stuck with them *for ever*.'

'It's not for ever. Six years goes faster than you could ever imagine and in the meantime we shall see each other sometimes, and write . . .'

I smile up at Felix, who's looking uncomfortably at Hetty and John, who are looking uncomfortably back at him. 'I beg your pardon,' says Felix. 'We didn't mean to interrupt your Sunday but I had some time and Ignatius wanted to see his sister . . .'

'And *I* wanted to see *him*.' I beam. 'Hetty, please meet my brothers. Felix, the eldest of all of us, and Ignatius, the youngest. John, you know them, of course . . .' It strikes me how strange it must be for John to see them here.

Hand-shaking all around and then Hetty says, 'You'd better come in then. We can't get to know each other in the street.'

'We don't wish to impose,' says Felix hastily, no doubt remembering what I said about Hetty's dignity. But if she's put out at having two ridiculously wealthy gentleman enter her modest home, she doesn't show it. We all crowd in and more cider is poured – much to Nash's delight – and I'm proud of her. I'm proud of my brothers too for they will never have visited a home so cramped and humble, yet they behave as if they were in Garrowgate Hall, formal, respectful and no staring about in amazement as I'm sure I did when I first arrived. But it really is no house for formality; the cider and the fact of the five of us crowded around the kitchen table soon sets us all at ease.

'They call me Nash because Ignatius is quite a mouthful,' Ignatius explains, draining his first glass swiftly and the colour rising in his smooth cheeks. 'But it could be worse because we all call Crispin Crisp when we're at home. I shouldn't like to be called Crisp.'

'Nash is a very dashing name,' says Hetty and Nash grins.

I can't help but laugh. He is so winning, so amiable. How was I so different from my brothers, so stiff and cool? Was it because I was a girl and the stakes were higher for me? Anyway, now is no time for pondering. Now is the time for sharing news, and there is a very great deal of it!

'I have news,' I announce, at the exact same time as Felix says the very same thing. I wonder what his could be but, ever the gentleman, he gestures for me to go first. Well, I am bursting to tell them. Some of it makes me a little nervous but I must begin to practise at saying it out loud. They are my brothers after all. 'I have a job,' I begin. 'I work for Olive Westallen at her foundation and I'm a tutor of sorts for the young women she helps. Also, I'm engaged to be married to John and . . . and I'm expecting a child.'

They look, as might be expected, thunderstruck. Nash beams because he can see that I am happy. Felix looks at John and his face is a brewing storm. 'The baby isn't John's,' I explain hastily. I don't want my brothers to think he has dishonoured me – or that I have slept with a second man out of wedlock. I am not *that* wanton!

'But to all intents and purposes, he or she will be mine,' says John. 'Its origins do not matter to me. I wish Rowena to be my wife and her child to be my child, under my care, bearing my name. We shall not tell anyone else the truth – as far as the world is concerned, I am the father. But we must tell you because you are . . .'

Colour floods into his face too. I'm surrounded by blushing men! I know he cannot finish that sentence, not after years of service, watching the pair of them dashing in and out of the polished hall in muddy boots or falling down the stairs after adolescent forays into Father's best port. But I am not afraid to say it. 'Because you are family,' I finish for him.

Felix looks relieved that he doesn't have to challenge John to a duel or whatever it is men do nowadays. 'You must be a man of exceptional character, Mr Hobbs, to accept Rowena's child as your own. I commend you.' He shakes John's hand across the table. 'Then, it is a match for practical reasons?' He frowns, no doubt worrying about my happiness.

'Only incidentally,' says John firmly. 'It is above all a love match.'

I nod and smile and then my brothers congratulate us. We tell them our plans and they ask about my role at the foundation and at last I remember that Felix also has news. 'What did you want to tell me, Felix?' I ask as Hetty cuts the last of the apple cake into five small pieces. 'You said you had news.'

'Yes! And the very best news imaginable,' he beams. Then he casts a clouded glance at John, as if he might not think so. 'At least, I *thought* it was until . . . Perhaps it can keep for another time.'

'No, it can't,' Nash argues. 'Mr Porter needs her to sign the papers, remember?'

'Ah, yes.' Felix looks even more agitated now that he's been cornered. I'm baffled. Mr Porter is our family solicitor. What can he want with my signature? 'Well, as I say, it's excellent news and it will somewhat alter your circumstances so it's probably best you know right away. It's Great-Aunt Althea. She's passed away.'

Hetty and John arrange their faces into sympathetic expressions as befitting the news of a death of someone they've never met. 'I'm so sorry to hear that,' I say. 'Well, our parents can't send me to stay with her now, can they? John and Hetty are stuck with me. Goodness, I haven't seen her since I was . . . ten? Eleven?'

'Eleven,' agrees Felix. 'Nash here can't remember her at all. The thing is, Ro, she's left you everything.'

I laugh. 'That's absurd. Great-Aunt Althea *detested* me. She wouldn't have left me so much as a brass ring. She was a cantankerous old lady,' I explain to John and Hetty. 'She loved my brothers because she said they had verve. She would visit when we were younger and praise them to the skies. But I was a prissy little thing in ringlets and the object of her scorn. She said she had no time for walking dolls with no spirit. I was terrified of her.' I remember it well, how her words hurt me. I was so used to being praised and adored. I avoided her when I could and fell silent when I couldn't and the two of us never learned to get along.'

'But our parents wrote to ask if she would have you to live with her, didn't they? They told her all about the . . . scandal.' Felix looks uncomfortable with the word but I have made my peace with it. 'Then they had to write again to say that after all you were nowhere to be found. I have here a copy of the letter she left for the solicitor, Rowena.' He fishes it out of his breast pocket and unfolds it. 'Here.' He points to the relevant paragraph. 'The rest is legal fandangle. This is the bit.' I read it. It is brief but my head is spinning so it takes me longer to digest than the few lines require.

I bequeath all my worldly goods – my fortune, my houses in London and Provence, all my possessions, et cetera – to my great-niece Rowena Blythe, whom I like better now she is disgraced than I ever did before. As she is finally showing a little grit, I trust she will make good use of it.

And there it is, my life changed entirely – again – in the space of one paragraph. I push it wordlessly towards John and Hetty who read it far more quickly than I did then look at me like dogs waiting for a snack. Hetty's eyes are gleaming. John has gone quite pale.

'How . . . how much does this fortune amount to?' he asks, looking at Felix, not me.

'Without the houses, almost twenty thousand.'

Hetty inhales some of her cider and starts coughing wildly. John reaches out to knock her on the back a few times, like a man in a trance. I feel somewhat unreal myself. He looks at me at last, his expression anguished. 'Then I release you from your obligation,' he says formally.

'What obligation?' I query inelegantly.

'Why, our engagement, of course. You're a woman of means again, Rowena. Independent means this time, and considerable. You do not need such meagre support as I can offer and as for protection, you will not need it. Your fortune will secure you friends and you need not fear the scandal any longer.'

Hetty is making strangled noises, trying to speak but unable to because of the coughing. Nash stands and picks up her mug, which he helpfully drains of cider then refills with water for her.

'John!' I cry, quite enraged. 'You think I want such friends as *those*? Are you forgetting that I agreed to marry you because I love you? I accepted your proposal for that and that alone. So don't talk any more nonsense of releasing me from my obligation. I do not release you from yours. You made me a promise.'

'One I beg to be excused from,' he says stiffly, getting to his feet. I watch in horror as he rises above me. 'You and I cannot be now, Rowena. I'm delighted for you – this is the answer you needed, the windfall you deserve. But you are – once again – a wealthy Blythe. And I am a footman.'

Hetty has recovered at last. 'John!' she shrieks. 'That is ridiculous! *Ridiculous!* She loves you, any fool can see that. And you are the worthiest of men. You have loved her for so long that I was sick of the sound of her name before I even met her. Do *not* spoil this chance of happiness now – for *both* your sakes!'

But John has a resolute look in his eyes. It fills me with dread. He shakes his head with a heavy air. 'I must go,' he says. 'I must get back to work. I'm sorry, Hetty. You surely can't imagine that I would agree to be a kept man. And why would Rowena live in married quarters in a townhouse when she has twenty thousand? She is fish and I am fowl. Or the other way around. Either way, there is nowhere we can make a nest. Rowena, I shall always love you and wish you every happiness. Goodbye.'

'John, no!' I wail, leaping to my feet, hanging on to his arm as if my life depends upon it. 'John, I *love* you. You will break

my heart if you continue with this. I know you're proud but
love is more important, surely? We shall *find* a nest. We shall
build our own. Nothing about us was conventional, even before
this news. Please be daring now and stand by me for richer as
well as poorer.'

He dashes a hand across his face and I can see that he is
crying. 'You understand, sirs, don't you?' he implores my
brothers.

'No I jolly well do not,' retorts Nash.

'I understand . . .' begins Felix, looking distressed.

'*Felix!*' I cry.

'Bad show, old chap!' Nash looks appalled.

'Let me finish!' Felix orders, with some authority. 'I understand, but I don't agree. John, I would feel the same if I were
in your position, truly. But I hope you will find a way to overcome your reservations. I know something about the love of
a good woman, if only through not having it. Making a proper
match does not ensure happiness. So why cannot an *un*equal
match bring it? And for heaven's sake, man, you're prepared
to accept a scoundrel's by-blow but not legitimate wealth? That
makes no sense.'

I look up into John's unhappy face with a little hope but he
shakes his head. 'I'm sorry. I cannot.' He removes me from
his arm, gently but firmly, as he would a ladybird, and walks
to the door. He pauses and looks back at us with a baffled
expression, as if wondering how three Blythes ever came to
be there in his sister's kitchen.

'At least say you'll think about it, John!' I beg in a faint voice.
'Please think it over – there's a different way to see it. Or I'll
refuse the inheritance! I don't want it if it costs me you.'

'No,' he says again. 'I'm sorry.' And he leaves.

Fifty-eight

Olive

It is Tuesday the twenty-second of June, the morning of Queen Victoria's diamond jubilee, an occasion of historical moment. Naturally, I have made some splendid plans. But surely nothing the day holds can be as extraordinary as recent events in my own little corner of the world? Rowena Blythe once again a wealthy woman. Rowena once again without any prospect of marriage – for now that she loves John she will certainly turn to no one else. He, more than two weeks after the news of her inheritance, still holds fast to his position and will not marry her. The poor girl is quite devastated. She was on the brink of refusing the fortune, hoping to persuade him they had a future together after all, but both Hetty and I had quite a bit to say about that!

'A man who needs you to be poor and dependent is no man that you should want,' I told a weeping Rowena in brisk tones last week. 'Sorry, Hetty,' I added – the three of us were in her kitchen at the time – 'I know he is your brother but all the various ways that men make us feel bad about having anything of our own is a theme guaranteed to make me hot under the collar.' But Hetty was in agreement.

'My brother is an idiot,' she said succinctly. 'A good, kindly, moral, misguided idiot.' She has an uncanny grasp of character.

Thankfully Rowena came to the same conclusion on her own, several days on. 'I look at the lives of Maria and Margie and all of them,' she told me at work one morning, 'then I look at yours and I know which *I* want. The difference is your wealth. I can do too much with it to give it back, help so many people, as you do. I only wish I could share all my plans with John but he will not talk to me. And I cannot do anything about what he chooses to do.'

I couldn't have said it better myself! I was impressed and I told her so. But oh, she did look dreadfully sad. I wonder what it's like to know whole-heartedly that you want someone beside you every step of the way through your life, to have no doubts whatsoever that you would be happier *with* that person than without. I cannot imagine ever being quite so unambivalent; I'm just so used to doing things alone. Is it only habit? Would meeting 'The Right Man' – whatever that means – make me feel differently? Or is it my character? Surely we cannot all be destined for the same path through life, otherwise why are we all made so different?

I've since heard that, following Will Brown's completion of his apprenticeship, Lionel was unable to keep him on within his own company but found a post with Mr Kemp's, for which Will could apply. He provided a glowing recommendation and Will was successful. Now the lad enjoys excellent prospects. It is like Lionel, neither to neglect the boy to spite me, nor to employ him when he was not truly needed to please me. So he goes on through life in his own way and I continue in mine.

The entire household, Westallens and staff, will be attending the jubilee parade. The queen is to make a magnificent progress from Buckingham Palace to St Paul's, with a great many stops on the way for the people to admire her. The event has been planned in meticulous detail since March by a committee chaired by the Prince of Wales. There is to be an opera gala, a meal for the destitute and an unprecedented amount of spectacle and expenditure; I don't know whether to feel cynical or excited. My girls, however, are unequivocal. They are going to see the queen, therefore this is the very best of days. They bounce around me as I fix my hat, a fine, royal purple specimen with a dashing hawk feather slashing the crown.

'Mama, Mama!' gasps Clover, almost fainting with excitement. 'We're going to London to see the queen! Will she have blackbirds in a pie? Will she eat bread and honey? Will the king be there?'

'Auntie Olive! Are we going to Buckingham Palace? Will we see the cat?' I turn and give Angeline a quizzical look. I don't know what nursery rhyme she's been reading. I tell them that there will be bread and honey and almost certainly a number of scavenging cats, but no king and no blackbird pie.

The queen is now seventy-eight years old. When she came to the throne she was a girl of eighteen. I wonder what I shall be like sixty years from now, should I be lucky to live so long. I wonder what I will have achieved, who I will have lost, who I will have met. Who I will have helped – that is always an important question for me. Certainly I think that setting Pansy upon her path towards the tangled maze that is the law may be my finest work to date! A diamond jubilee is certainly a pause for thought.

'Olive! Are you ready?' Papa is calling me from below. I look over the banister and see everybody gathered in the hall. Mama is just adjusting her green bonnet and frock. The servants look resigned as if they have been gathered ready for some time.

'I'm ready,' I call back. 'Come on, girls. No, Clover, you are not to slide down the banister. I wish you to attend the jubilee with your head intact. Use the stairs, if you please.'

We emerge into perfect sunshine, no doubt ordered by the royal secretary. Papa has arranged carriages for the friends who are to meet us there but we, the household of Polaris House, shall walk. Eccentric, perhaps, but it is not five miles and what better way to soak up the jubilant atmosphere? Our entire staff is somewhere in the distance, impatient not to miss a moment. I suspect in an hour or so we shall overtake them; we Westallens are built for stamina. We are somewhere in the vicinity of Chalk Farm when I stop dead in my tracks. A familiar figure, striding in the opposite direction, arrests my gaze.

Mama sees what I have seen, catches Angeline up in her arms and hurries on. Clover is already some way ahead, riding on her grandfather's shoulders.

I have not seen Lionel since that awful evening when I told him I would not marry him. He has taken to calling at the foundation on days that I am not there and all foundation-related communications have been conducted through Mabs. I wonder what his plans are for this day of days. Perhaps he has none; business will not stop for the queen.

He catches sight of me and startles. He falters in his stride, then tips his hat and hurries on with naught beyond an offhand 'Good day to you'. I stand and watch him go, a tall figure among the crowd. I feel a certain disbelief and sadness that we have come to this, no more than a casual greeting as if between strangers. But then I wonder, what else might I have expected of him? He has been disappointed, he was civil; to see each other now, to converse and learn news of one another, would keep both of our wounds open for longer than needs be. I think after all that there is wisdom in his distance. I watch him go and send a little prayer for his happiness travelling after him along the Euston Road.

Fifty-nine

Pansy

Probably the queen and all the people she had around her thought that her jubilee was a really big event, thought Pansy as she polished silver candlesticks, her fingers smeared and grimy. What they didn't realise was that it was all mere preamble, paling into insignificance really, before the *truly* important occasion, which was Maude Blythe's ball. Not a servant had the day off, nor even a part of it, to watch the celebrations.

'Good grief, I trust you are in jest, Mrs Clarendon,' the mistress had retorted when the housekeeper, who had been begged and badgered by the maids, put the request to her. 'There is far too much to do. The house won't run itself, you know.'

So here they all were at Garrowgate Hall, missing out on the festivities, like so many downtrodden Cinderellas. Some of the maids had sobbed when they heard the decree. Pansy laughed. If she had a penny for every time she'd heard that the house wouldn't run itself, she'd never need a scholarship, that was for sure! She had no interest in the jubilee, so she didn't care. And who would she spend it with? Rowena and John were both moping, Hetty was grim. When Pansy had heard that Rowena and John were engaged, she was surprised to find herself truly happy for them. They were both gentle souls and, though she'd never believed she might think this, they were a perfect match. She, Pansy, was too fierce for John, or rather, he wasn't fierce enough for her. And now they *weren't* engaged again! All because of Rowena's inheritance and John's stupid male pride. Pansy had often thought him a fool – loved him, but thought him a fool. Now she thought him a fool twice over. Still, that was his business; Pansy had her own to take care of.

In the two and a half weeks since Olive's Big Idea, letters had flown back and forth between Olive and Miss Orme, and Miss Orme and Pansy. Now, Pansy was equipped with a course of study to bridge the gap between her departure from school at sixteen and the dizzy horizons of a university degree. Once she caught up, Olive had told her there would be a reading list, a letter of application to copy and adapt for various scholarships and a great many more official papers. But for now she must concentrate on the work in hand. She had a couple of textbooks in her attic room – much to Maisie's horror – one at her mother's house and one at Olive's. From now until she finished at the Blythes', she would alternate her Thursdays between Elstree and Polaris House. That way she could study wherever she was, without having to carry heavy tomes with her every time. Even while she toiled at other subjects in which she needed a thorough grounding, she couldn't resist peeking ahead to the law. Torts and precedents and compromise agreements baffled her, yet trying to understand them excited her and reminded her of why she was studying at all.

Today Pansy was sitting in the scullery where she and John had sat back in February, one Sunday after church. They'd been polishing silver then too and he'd been droning on about Rowena. Pansy huffed. How had she borne it?

What had John said back then? *This life looks as if it should be right for her. But it's not.* How could he know her so well, love her so well, only to refuse her now because she was rich again? It seemed idiotic to Pansy. But then who could understand men? Pansy laid down the candlestick for a moment and smiled, glad and grateful to be cured of him. She took a deep breath and thought of all the things that used to make her yearn for him, as a test: his kind eyes, his broad shoulders, the easy way they had together, his solid values. No, still no pain. That part of her life was finally over.

'My mother doesn't pay you to sit here daydreaming, you know.' A stern voice, a footstep and a tall figure darkening the room.

Pansy was exasperated to have her brief moment of happy reflection jarred. 'She doesn't pay me much at all!' she retorted before clapping her hands over her mouth with a gasp of horror. 'Oh sir! I'm sorry,' she gasped. 'Forgive me, I was far away for a minute.'

It was Felix Blythe, laughing. 'I'm sorry, I couldn't resist. Please don't be alarmed, I shan't tell tales.'

'Oh sir!' Pansy was inarticulate for a minute and resorted to scrubbing the candlestick fiercely with the rag.

'Wait,' said Felix. 'Please stop a moment. Joking aside, I have something very important to say.'

'To me, sir?' Pansy did as she was bid and looked up at him, puzzled. She had a horrid feeling there might be black polish smeared over her face. Goodness, he really was handsome, wasn't he? Say what you like about Maude and Malvern Blythe, they produced good-looking children.

Felix nodded and pulled an envelope from his breast pocket. 'I wanted to thank you, sincerely, on behalf of myself and my brothers, for all you did for Rowena.' Of course. She'd helped his sister. It was thoughtful of him to come and say so. 'Miss Tilney, I love my sister. We all do. She might have died if not for you. I can't bear that I didn't know where she was, and so could do nothing to help her. But you did. I shall for ever be grateful.'

Pansy frowned, remembering how reluctant she had been to give that help. But give it she had, and Mums had said she was prouder of Pansy for that than for anything. 'Well, sir. I was brought up always to help, if help is needed and if I'm able. She was so wretched that day. I couldn't have left her there. No one could.'

'Well, my parents and my wife managed to remain screamingly indifferent to her suffering. Yet you, who ran a considerably greater risk by going to her aid, proved to be her guardian angel.'

Pansy felt all hot about the face. If he only knew that she used to picture Rowena's face whilst beating the rugs! 'I wouldn't go that far, sir. I've been cross enough with her on occasion, if I'm honest. I'm sure an angel would have been a lot less grumpy about it.'

He smiled. 'I don't care how grumpy you were. My sister is safe and well, thanks to you. Please accept this small token of my gratitude.' He handed the envelope to Pansy and she opened it. Inside was a cheque for five hundred pounds.

'Sir!' she squawked, dropping it like a hot coal onto the table, then pushing it back at him. 'I can't take that! I don't need payment for helping Rowena. She wasn't my favourite person back then but she's changed. She's my friend now. I'd do it again in a heartbeat.'

'You're getting polish on it.' Felix took the cheque, wiped a smear of polish off it with a handkerchief, then gave it back to her. 'You have a little on your face too, by the way. It's not payment, Miss Tilney. It's gratitude. You must allow me to express it. You must.'

Pansy rubbed her face with the back of her hand and looked at the cheque again. Five hundred pounds. She needn't work here one moment more once her promise to Mrs Clarendon was fulfilled. This put a law degree firmly within her reach, unless it was beyond the limitation of her own brains. She could leave after the ball and rent a room from Julia at a modest rate – Julia had said as much only the other day, when they were pie-in-the-skying. She could study night and day. And she would. There was no way she would let this chance slip through her fingers. She wasn't a fool. She wasn't *John*.

'Miss Tilney? Are you all right?'

'Oh, yes, sir. Thank you. I . . . I'm so grateful. This could do a lot for me. But I still don't feel *right* accepting it.'

'I say again, you must. Miss Tilney, there's a lot in life that I can't make right. This is something I can. It means a lot to me and, without wishing to sound arrogant, you must realise that I can easily spare it.'

Pansy took a deep breath. 'Very well. Thank you again. I accept.'

He beamed. 'I'm delighted. You said it would do a lot for you. Might I ask what? A trousseau? A new wardrobe?'

She snorted and looked at him scornfully. 'Sir, you've been spending too much time with the likes of your wife. Is that all you think women care for?' Immediately she blushed, realising how inappropriate she had been to reveal her private feelings about Verity.

'You're right, I have,' he said with a clouded face. Pansy was astonished. Was Felix Blythe not happy with Verity? Then again, who could be? For a surprising moment, he looked as if he might confide in her, then he shook himself. 'No indeed.

I realise women think about a great deal more than that, my sister has taught me as much. I only wish I'd known it a year ago. So what, then, Miss Tilney, will you do with this money?'

Pansy grinned. She would say it aloud. 'I'm going to university, sir. Not for a little while yet – I have to catch up with my studies first – but one day. I'm going to study the law.'

The look on his face was priceless. He pulled out a chair and sat down across from her, picked up a candlestick and rag, and started polishing. Pansy blinked. It was an exact re-enactment of that day in February, except that instead of a footman, her companion was the eldest son of the house. It was like a dream where everything goes wrong end up. 'I'm fascinated, Miss Tilney,' said Felix. 'I didn't even know women could do that. Please will you tell me everything and furnish me with a more interesting half hour than I'm likely to have for the rest of the day?'

Pansy obliged. He proved a gratifyingly admiring audience and somehow she found herself telling him about her recent experiments in the world of work as well as her plans for the future. She felt proud of the story it made. When she had finished, instead of leaving, he told her a story of his own, that he had recently travelled to Cumbria, where he made enquiries about local landscape painters and newly arrived apprentices.

'Oh, please tell me you did, sir,' she urged, guessing the outcome.

He grinned ruefully and held out bruised knuckles to show her. 'I found Bartek easily enough,' he said. 'I paid the fellow a visit and told him I had come to drag him back to London to marry Rowena. I had no such intention, of course, for nothing would make her unhappier but I wanted to enjoy watching his squirming and evasions after my long journey. They made fine entertainment, I assure you. Then I told him she wouldn't have him for all the tea in China and I gave him a good trouncing. The days of duelling pistols are gone but there was a savage satisfaction in avenging my sister's honour and I was always handy with my fists in school.'

Pansy smiled. So Felix was a bit fierce, behind his gentlemanly exterior.

'I did no lasting damage,' he added. 'Not physically, anyway. But I had a word in several ears around the town where he now lives. I made it known what kind of fellow he is. If it damages his prospects, so be it. I hope it helps any lovely young ladies in Cumbria who might fall for his charms. Though he may be a little less handsome with a broken nose.'

'Have you told Rowena?'

'Not yet. Perhaps I will. But it was gentleman's business. You are the only one I have told. I trust you to keep the secret, Miss Tilney.'

Pansy promised, then Felix realised that far longer than half an hour had passed. He leapt to his feet in a rush. 'It's the jubilee day. My wife requires me . . . Good luck with your studies, Miss Tilney. I'm so happy that the money will contribute to something important,' he added, hesitating at the doorway. 'But I'll be sad not to see you around the place when I come to visit. I should have liked to hear how you get along. There, the regret is mine, not yours. You'll be delighted to be shot of the place, I'm certain. Good luck, and thank you again.'

When he was gone, Pansy sat quietly for a moment. He was right that she'd be glad to leave Garrowgate Hall. But she too felt some regret that they'd never talk again. She had never enjoyed any conversation so much as she had this last . . . *hour and a half*! She could hardly believe the little clock in the corner; it had felt like ten minutes. He was so handsome and unpretentious and funny.

'Oh, no, Pansy,' she scolded herself aloud. 'Don't think like that even for one moment.' She had scoffed at John often enough for loving Rowena when he worked here. She wasn't about to go down the same path with Felix. *Married* Felix. What was it about this scullery and the spell of unreachable Blythes?

She got up hastily and went to find Mrs Clarendon, to warn her that she would be leaving the very first day that she could be spared. It was time to start her new life.

Sixty

Rowena

U ntil John withdrew his proposal, I, like everyone else in London, had looked forward to the diamond jubilee. It is *such* an occasion and everyone in the whole of London is talking about it, rich and poor alike. The dear queen's popularity waned during the 1870s and early 1880s – we women can so easily go from being adored to scorned, like a fashion for glass hat ornaments. But now everyone has forgotten that, and she is to be celebrated again as the incarnation of all that is great about Great Britain. Poor woman. I'm sure she'd rather just stay in bed and eat candies.

I know I would. The loss of John has stricken me like a fever, afflicting me with aching limbs, a painful head and a great crushing weariness of body and soul. From the moment I wake, a festive air slides in through my window, riding on the morning sunbeams, but I care nothing for this momentous day now that John is lost to me.

It is more than two weeks since I learned that I am an heiress and lost my fiancé in the process. I have not seen him since. I have written to him, you may be sure, but received only one reply, lengthy, professing both his undying love *and* his steadfast refusal to marry me; he would not 'hold me back'. I am furious and heartbroken in equal measure, both with

John for his stubborn pride and with life itself for its mischievous vagaries.

Without doubt the happiest days I have ever known occurred when I was penniless. That is a somewhat ironic admission for a spoiled rich girl to make. During the years of great wealth before that, I had luxuries aplenty but I was lacklustre and uninterested in my own life. Then everything got far, far worse for a while. But I found true friends and new parts of myself. My pleasures were fewer, but vivid, appreciated. Life became a richer tapestry when wrought to my own design. Now I am wealthy again and utterly, utterly miserable. There is a malign sense of humour somewhere at work! It is not the fortune itself that makes me unhappy – I have already thought of a dozen wonderful ways to use it. I simply struggle to feel joy in anything without John.

Hetty rattles her knuckles over my bedroom door. I mentioned last night that I did not think I could muster the spirits to go to the parade today. She was not happy. She believes I shall languish in bed all day if I'm left to my own devices – and I *would* like to. But I have made a promise to her and Olive and I shall honour it, even if all I want to do is curl up and weep.

'Good morning, Hetty,' I call in a bleary voice.

'You wouldn't know it from your tone of voice,' she replies but I hear her footsteps retreat.

We *had* planned to watch the queen's progress with John. When John broke our engagement, I'd assumed that Hetty would still wish to go with her brother, but she will not hear of it. She is every bit as angry with John as I am and refuses to see him until he 'comes to his senses'.

Then the question of what we should do arose, without John to chaperone us. For weeks now, the newspapers have teemed with lists of rooms to rent for the day, or even *views* to rent, with prices varying from two guineas to twenty pounds! I could afford the best, but by then there was simply nothing available. Hetty was surprisingly distraught. But Olive, of course, offered a solution. *She* has a first-class position in her father's office opposite St Paul's itself so Hetty and I shall join her there, along with her parents, Clover, Angeline and all the Westallens' staff. We shall be quite a party and Hetty is beside herself. Pansy is not going at all, since my parents refused to give their staff time off to celebrate. *Plus ça change!*

I should rise. I cannot make us late for the carriage Olive has promised to send. We've been advised to make our way into the city early since the crowds are expected to amass hours in advance of the ceremony. The queen herself will be in transit for three hours, if the papers are to be believed, winding her way around London so that her loyal subjects may catch a glimpse. The day is gorgeously sunny, as if the sun himself is doffing his crown to the earthly monarch for this one special day. But oh, I want no part of it. I should rise, but I stay in bed, heavy, lethargic, unhappy.

I am roused at last by a sudden great hammering at the door. It is so urgent that I sit up in a shock. Has there been a disaster? Has someone died? I hear Hetty creaking at speed down the stairs and I listen breathlessly, heart pounding. I hear voices and then the front door closing. Hetty's voice calls up to me: 'Rowena, you have a visitor.'

I leap out of bed, not knowing what to do with myself. I'm not dressed! I go to my door and open it a crack. 'Who is it, Hetty?' I call with trepidation. 'I'm not quite . . . presentable.'

Footsteps run up the stairs and there is John before me, awash with perspiration as he was the very first time I ever talked to him. 'Forgive me, Rowena,' he bursts out and for a moment I think he refers to the impropriety of coming to my room whilst I'm in my nightgown. But it seems he has a far bigger apology to make. He seizes both my hands and stares into my eyes. 'Forgive me, forgive me. I'm a blockhead. I cannot stop thinking about you. I've examined this question from every possible angle and I've realised . . . that you are not as you were, that money alone will not make you happy now and that I do us both the gravest disservice by continuing in obstinacy and pride. Please, Rowena, please say you forgive me.'

My heart turns over. I am speechless. I have thought of him all day every day since we parted and cannot quite trust that he is not a figment of my wishful thinking. 'Rowena?' he adds, faltering. Beyond him, hovering on the stairs, I see Hetty, staring at us. She will beat no tactful retreat; she is agog. I look at John again, his broad shoulders, his handsome face and imploring blue eyes. What does this mean? What is he asking me?

'That depends,' I manage to say.

'On what?' he pleads.

'On whether or not you will change your mind and marry me.'

He kisses me then, a dozen times, awash with relief, and laughs; I adore his ready laugh. 'The marrying was implied within the forgiveness,' he explains.

I can feel myself beaming, my first smile in two weeks. 'In that case yes, I forgive you,' I reply, 'and we may be thankful I am more sensible than you . . .'

'Oh, thank God. At last!' cries Hetty. 'Can you please both come down so that I can see you properly? Then, Rowena, you *must* get dressed! What on earth have you been doing for the last twenty minutes?'

'Wallowing in misery.' I grin. 'But that is at an end now.'

We all descend to the front room and Hetty takes first John, then me, by the shoulders. She gazes at our happy faces and kisses us each in turn.

'John, the state of you!' she exclaims as he pushes back damp hair from his forehead. 'Have you run all the way from Chelsea?'

'Yes.' John wipes his forehead and upper lip self-consciously. 'There was no cab to be had for love nor money on jubilee day. I'm sorry, Rowena, I didn't want to propose to you looking like this but I couldn't wait one more moment.'

'I know how that feels,' I remind him. 'And do you join us today after all, John?'

'Sadly I cannot. I promised to work today, when I was stuck on my course. It's too late to let the Prentisses down now. I must go, almost at once, but I had to see you, I had to tell you, I had to know . . .'

'Of course you did, my darling.' I put my arms around him and he cradles me. Oh, that feeling again, after far too long. 'We are as we should be now, truly? You will not change your mind again?'

'Never,' he vows.

'And we shall see you on Sunday as usual?'

'Even before, if I can arrange it.'

'Then all is well.'

'Go, if you can't stay, then' – Hetty gives him a little push towards the door – 'for Rowena will do nothing but stand and stare at you while you're here and she cannot join the Westallens dressed like Sleeping Beauty.'

John kisses me, a long, lingering kiss, and when he pulls away, I see that Hetty has made herself scarce at last. He lets himself out and I turn and float back up the stairs.

I am only just ready when Olive's carriage calls for us. Everything I see takes on a gilded glow because of my happiness. Everywhere there are smiling faces; even those who are dirty and ragged are glad of a reason to rejoice. And everywhere, everywhere there are flowers: flowers draping the bridges; purple flowers arranged in garlands forming the dates 1837 and 1897; red, yellow and white flowers arranged in the shape of imperial crowns, all along the route. In my haze of relief and joy, I am delighted by it all.

Near St Paul's, the carriage is obliged to set us down for it can go no further. The obelisks in Ludgate Circus are draped with cloth of purple and gold. There is bunting of blue, red and white. There are banners depicting elephants harnessed in purple and gold. I can absorb no more as we walk the rest of the way; battling through the crowds is like trying to walk through a river against the current. We are assailed by envious glances as we find the address Olive gave us and go inside. People have gathered in such numbers that most have no hope of seeing a single thing except the backs of other people's heads. Even so, they wait.

I have never been less interested in my appearance than I was of late so I simply wear my old sea-green gown and I retrieved my engagement ring from the drawer to which I had entrusted it; the gold band and cheerful diamond are all the adornment I need to feel special. Thankfully, even through my recent fog of gloom, I did realise that Hetty had nothing to wear in which she would feel comfortable meeting Captain and Mrs Westallen so I roused myself and took her shopping. We chose for her a wonderful lilac silk. The soft colour compliments her pale face and dark hair and I bought her new shoes, a bonnet, a reticule and gloves to match. Mrs Simon looks quite the lady as she ascends the stairs to her prime viewing spot for the event of the century!

Olive is delighted to see us and makes the introductions all around. I shake hands with her father and he is as gracious as Olive. Olive's mother scoops me briefly to her bosom. It takes Olive all of about two minutes to notice that my engagement ring is back in its place – perhaps my joyful face alerted her – and I am scooped once again. 'I couldn't be happier, my dear,' she says.

A table is spread with a white cloth and a lavish picnic boasting champagne and sweetmeats in addition to a more substantial luncheon. I have never seen Hetty's eyes, usually so narrowed and doubting, open so wide. At first she is diffident but Olive will not allow for anyone to feel less than at home in her presence and soon Hetty is quaffing champagne in a way that I wish John could see. I wish he were here beside me, but the loss of one day with him, even a special one like this, is not so very great now I know that we have all the days to come together.

Well in advance of the sovereign's arrival, batteries of artillery and squadrons of cavalry pour beneath our windows. And then at last the queen is there! If we couldn't see it, we would hear it, a rousing cheer that drums in our chests, even all the way up here, and rings on and on. The carriage door opens and a small figure in black silk steps down. Her carriage is drawn by eight cream horses in gold and leather harness who stand amidst the uproar with impressive calm. I'm glad I am nowhere near them and remember hairy Prince, the canal boat horse, for an alarming instant. Then I forget all that as I witness history being made.

Five hundred choristers, ranged on the steps of St Paul's, sing the 'Te Deum'. Bishops and archbishops aplenty preside. The service is carried out in the open air. We cannot hear it from up here so we lose interest after a while and fall to talking.

'It's all very well,' muses Olive. 'I do believe that celebration is good for the soul. And I think a little lavish spending now and then keeps money in its place, you know, so it knows it's not the only thing that matters. It can be very arrogant, can money. But do you know that there's a jubilee meal for the destitute of London? The Princess of Wales launched an appeal to raise the money – all well and good. Except it's priced at a shilling a head. And it's one day. What are they to do after that meal, when they are hungry again? Wouldn't you think a *little* less pomp, and another meal for the poor on some ordinary day would be a finer thing?'

'If the reports are to be believed, the dear queen has gold embroidery on her gown and diamonds in her cap,' sighs her mother, peering out of the window again.

'And banquets will be held for the visiting dignitaries,' adds Captain Westallen. 'Crowned heads and representatives from all around the world. *They* won't be fed on a shilling a head. It's not that Her Majesty shouldn't be honoured – and royally so – ha!' He pauses to chuckle. Thence Olive has inherited her love of puns. 'But there are forty thousand destitute in Clerkenwell alone. The distribution of the funds is unbalanced, is it not?'

'Yes. But we are not a moderate species, are we?' reflects Mrs Westallen. 'Nor are we temperate, nor, oftentimes, rational.'

That is certainly true, I muse, thinking how I threw everything away to run off with a man I hardly knew. Then I think of John pining for me all those long years, having happiness within his grasp, then almost throwing *that* away, all because of my fortune. Perhaps it's no wonder that we humans are blessed with good fortune so inconsistently, since we hardly seem to know what to do with it when it comes.

I lay my hand upon my belly. My little baby cannot be seen

yet for I'm still very slender. Even so, I want a better world for him or her, a beautiful world. Now the three of us can afford a happy and comfortable life, with treats and blessings and good company and plenty to eat and, of course, I want all those things. But I want others to have them too.

A long while later, after an unforgettable day, we start for home. We have to walk a fair way before we can find cabs to bear us north and then we are reluctant to part. There has been champagne and feasting and a spectacle and the day wears on, bright and dusty and splendid. Olive's cook, Mrs Brody, suggests a walk on the heath and Hetty brightens at the idea; she is not ready for the quiet comforts of home. The little girls are tired so their doting grandparents bear them home to allow Olive and the staff to continue their merriment. I laugh quietly at the thought of my parents ever doing such a thing. We set off towards Parliament Hill.

'It's my favourite spot,' Olive tells me. 'Won't it be a fine thing to see all of London from up there on this of all days?'

A great many people have evidently had the same idea and there are crowds here, as everywhere today. Picnics are spread out over every patch of grass. 'You can't move an inch without steppin' on a boiled egg,' grumbles Mrs Brody. We are all engrossed in watching our step, avoiding picnic rugs, outstretched legs and toddling children, and so we do not notice the group of people walking towards us until we have almost collided. In fact, I hear them before I see them – or rather I hear *one* of them. It is Verity. I would know her silvery giggle anywhere. I have heard it nearly every day of my life.

I look up and see that Olive has spotted them just a fraction of a second before. I can tell by the brief ripple of shock that passes across her face and the way she turns to me at once with a protective air. The servants keep walking, unaware that

anything is amiss, but Olive recognises the other party immediately and Hetty's arm is linked through mine so she is instantly
alert when I falter. There, before us, are my parents, my brother
Crispin and Verity. I know Felix had planned to escape from
all jubilee-related activities as soon as he could make a run for
it. Evidently he has succeeded. Three out of the four of them
are the last people I ever wanted to see again. Yet here we all
are, almost nose to nose.

We stop. They stop. It is like the Montagues meeting the
Capulets.

'Rowena!' My mother speaks first, her voice a mere wheeze,
as if some body blow has constricted her lungs.

'Let us continue,' says my father, but my mother cannot
move – at least, she does not. She continues to stare at me
aghast. I want to run. I want to turn on my heel and disappear
into the crowd and pretend I never saw them. I can feel my
body shrinking into itself; the memory of the last time I saw
them rings in my head like a hammer blow.

Now we know your true nature and we are sick to the
core . . . No lady at all.

I cannot bear to look at you. You're like a smut on the carpet.

You are not welcome at Garrowgate Hall and you never will
be.

'What ho, Ro,' Crispin offers with a brave attempt at
normality. I know he loves me for he sent me the sweetest
letter and there is delight in his eyes at the sight of me, yet
fear is all over his face as he glances at our parents.

'Hello, Crispin, dearest,' I reply.

'Well, well,' says Verity in her light drawl. 'I never thought
you'd have the gall to show your face in public on a day when
the world and his wife is at large. You clearly have no right
feeling, no compassion for your parents whatsoever.' She shakes

her pretty head, brown ringlets bouncing beneath a delectable peach-coloured bonnet ornamented with glass beads like dewdrops. They catch the light with a fairy-like twinkle that seems at odds with her hard expression.

For a moment I believe myself to be everything they think me: licentious, depraved, disgusting. *Disappointing*. I want to sink into the floor and vanish. But then my other arm is taken and it is Olive. I look into her face, then at Hetty's. They are waiting. They do not want to fight my battles for me but they are ready for whatever I need. I stare back at Verity and tilt my chin upwards. 'Hello, Verity,' I say. 'Mother, Father.'

'How dare you?' breathes my mother in that same laboured voice. 'How *dare* you talk to us as if there's nothing wrong, as if you've *done* nothing wrong, when you should be *ashamed* of yourself! How dare you walk around in public . . . *gallivanting* as if life is some merry endeavour?'

'I am still alive, Mother,' I answer. 'I cannot creep away and hide in a darkened corner for the rest of my days, much as you might wish me to.'

'You must see, Rowena, that you cannot stay here.' My father's voice is low and cold. 'The very sight of you must be repugnant to any right-thinking person. London society is closed to you now. Go abroad; I understand you now have the means to set yourself up very nicely on the continent. You may have quite a life there, for they are not so delicate of sensibility as the English. And perhaps it will satisfy your taste for the . . . exotic.'

Beside me I feel Olive and Hetty fidgeting like restive horses. I squeeze their arms to reign them in else they'll be off, and charging!

'Thank you, Father, but I have sufficient friends here who do *not* find me repugnant. It saddens me that you could not help me when I needed you most, that you do not wish to know me now. But those are your choices. I must make my own.'

'Indeed you must *not!*' vows Verity, narrowing her brown eyes. 'You are part of a family, Rowena, part of a society. You cannot simply strut around here as if your actions don't affect any of us. You must think of your parents and how it reflects on them. You must think of your brothers and pursue a discreet course! Otherwise you shall prove yourself very selfish.'

'Ah, my brothers.' I fix Verity with the coldest glare I can muster. 'You mean Felix, who considers me gristle in his throat, and a burr upon his skin? I have destroyed him, have I not?'

'*Yes!*' Verity cries. 'Yes, you have! My poor, dear husband whose heart has been *broken* by the dreadful shame of his sister.'

'Faddle!' Crispin bursts out.

'Are those his words or yours, Verity? It was you who turned me away that night when I'd been attacked by vagabonds, when I had no money and nowhere to go. It was you, not Felix! And you used to call us the best of friends! You should be ashamed.'

'I should *not*! I couldn't be associated with you – *my* reputation must be stainless too, you know. I have the whole Blythe family to think about, *and* the Crawfords. They depend on *me*, now.'

'Oh, for heaven's sake,' mutters Olive. 'You're not that important. No one really cares what you do.'

'Olive Westallen,' sneers Verity. 'With your unconventional life and your adopted ragamuffins and your plain face . . . you *would* take her side, just to be perverse!'

Olive merely raises her eyebrows and there is an uncomfortable pause in which Verity's words hang in the air, revealing her for the spoiled, petulant child in grown-ups' clothing that she really is. But I am not content to let her speak to my friend that way.

'*I* am ashamed, Verity,' I say. 'I'm ashamed that I ever giggled and gossiped with you about people far worthier than either of us. I'm ashamed that I took my lead from you in making unkind judgements about people we barely knew. I'm ashamed of how I *was*, but not of how I am now. I am here to stay, and if respectable people must faint and gossip over it, then let them.'

'That's your old dress!' says Mother, rousing from her trance. 'How did you get hold of that? I *knew* one of the maids had been helping you! Which one was it? I'll see them gone before morning.'

'None of the staff, Mother.' But there I hesitate. I don't know if Felix is ready yet for them to know of our friendship. I look at Verity's scrunched-up face and I don't want to make things worse for him than they already are.

My middle brother takes the dilemma from my hands. 'It was Felix,' Crispin announces calmly. 'He found Rowena and we've all written to her, all three of us. He went to see her and took her some things. You should have let her have her things. You should have helped her.' He nods decisively and steps forward to kiss me on the cheek. 'I'll call on you soon,' he tells me, then smiles at Olive and Hetty. 'A pleasure to see you both, ladies.' He tips his hat. 'Good day.' Then he turns on his heel and strides off over the heath.

When did Crispin become so grown-up? I fervently hope he is not walking away from his inheritance. But then, the loss of the Blythe fortune is not the worst thing that can happen to a person, as I well know, and he has plenty to recommend him besides wealth. He will find his way in life, just as he now deftly weaves his way between hampers and sprawling picnickers.

Verity looks thunderous, and I quail on Felix's behalf. My parents look nonplussed. Perhaps it's dawning on them that if they carry on as they are, they will soon be at odds with all four of their children and there will be no one left to inherit anything. Compelling though the scene is, in a horrible, morbid way, I see nothing to be gained by prolonging our part in it.

'Perhaps it is time to continue our walk,' I murmur and Olive nods.

'*High* time, I should say,' decrees Hetty in her customary tart tone.

'Good day, Blythes,' sings Olive, as we depart. 'Always a pleasure.' Only Olive could make me smile at a time like this.

The proliferation of people and outspread blankets does not make walking three abreast a viable proposition. We have to unlink our arms and walk separately for a while, picking our own way around the obstacles. But once we reach clearer ground we link up again and I understand, with a great, soaring sense of gratitude, that this is the way it will always be from now on.

Sixty-one

Olive

FOUR MONTHS LATER . . .

The twenty-second of June was, for everyone else, the queen's jubilee, but it has become fixed in *our* minds as the day John Hobbs came to his senses. And so, as surely as night follows day, the gathering mists and turning leaves of mid-October bring with them another event for us all to enjoy.

If anyone had told me, six months ago, that I would willingly attend the wedding of Rowena Blythe – nay, that I would *look forward* to it – and more than that, *that I would be her maid of honour* . . . I would have accused them of snaffling generous amounts of my mother's sherry. Yet such is life: unexpected, tricksy, confounding. It is also magnificent and generous and offers never-ending blessings if one can only remember to throw out one's fixed ideas and expectations.

Rivals for twenty-three years. A heath and a whole universe between us. And no love lost, ever. Yet now she is a person for whom I would walk through fire. When her baby comes, we shall raise our children together. And, witnessing her pregnancy, I am rather glad that my own route to motherhood was adoption.

Thankfully the dreadful weather of recent days has relented.

We have had such a week of rain that I almost despaired for the bride. The vistas were all of twinkling pavements, streaked windowpanes and gloomy rooms. Then yesterday the downpour ceased, as if the weather agreed to a grudging truce; it did not actually *rain*, but it glowered, brooded and seethed.

And this morning the sun came out. Only in fits and starts, but that merely adds to the splendour of the prospect. The trees around the little church blaze with autumn fire: orange, crimson and bronze. The grassy churchyard is by turns the most vivid shade of lime or a demure sort of green that would not be out of place on a billiards table. I inwardly cheer every time the sun bursts forth and sets the sensible grass alight with that decadent, eye-watering lime.

The church is small and characterful, built of grey stone, with a modest steeple and low, welcoming porch. 'Come in, come in. Mind your head,' it seems to say. It is not grand but it is welcoming.

It is Rowena Blythe's wedding but not as anyone ever imagined it. She was always to have been married to some society notable in St Michael's in Highgate, with its tall, narrow spire and soaring transepts. She would have worn approximately forty yards of white satin and carried a fountain of white lilies and Verity Crawford-Blythe would have paraded beside her in some priceless gown fit for a duchess. At the interminable ceremony there would have been about three thousand attendees. I would not have been among them.

Instead, Rowena is to become Mrs Hobbs. Only a dozen guests are present. I am to stand up beside the bride, wearing a gold-coloured gown that Rowena insisted upon – and I confess I do feel rather handsome in it. Hetty, in her lilac silk, will stand up beside her brother.

John's plan to marry as soon as possible because of the baby was thwarted when no church could accommodate them in time. Rowena and Hetty would not hear of a wedding in a register office. So it is an October ceremony, with a bride six months pregnant, in an unfashionable church a mile out of Hampstead. It is a wedding fit for the woman she has become, not for the girl that she was.

Rowena wears a gown of cream-coloured faille with chiffon overlay. The shape is simple and drapes gently over her noticeably rounded shape. Summer's glow still lingers in her face. She is, of course, impossibly beautiful, with red and white sweet peas woven into her flaxen mane. They mean delicate pleasures, she told me, blushing.

Her bouquet, naturally, is carefully chosen; she has made it herself. It is an autumn arrangement, each bloom representing part of the story that has brought her to this moment. There are blazing orange nasturtium for impetuous love – for without that sudden, ill-fated passion for Bartek, she would now be Mrs Herrangrove or similar and John would still be Henry, at Garrowgate Hall. Instead, he is to leave his job at Christmas. He will train as a teacher and dreams of working at a village school. There are white anemones, meaning *forsaken*, to remind Rowena that even from the worst devastation, happiness can arise. Purple freesias symbolise lasting friendship – I accept the compliment proudly – and pinks represent pure love. There is fragrant white stephanotis, meaning happiness in marriage, and finally, yellow gerbera daisies for cheer, since above all else this must be a cheerful day.

I persuaded her to explain it all to me not only because I am interminably curious but in an attempt to soothe her nerves. This day means everything to her. We wait in the small church porch, which smells cool and a little musty. The sky outside is violet and amber and black and lemon; the flowers smell fairy-sweet. Rowena drops her head to her bouquet and breathes in.

I peer inside the church. The air is hushed and scented and everyone is there. John is waiting even now at the altar. On Rowena's side of the church are her brothers, of course. Mrs Clarendon, the housekeeper, has come and there are two of the girls Rowena has tutored at the foundation. On John's side Hetty stands with her brother. Their cousin Wesley sits in the pews and so does Pansy. Nowadays, Pansy is working harder even than she did at the Blythes', but with purpose, direction and hope. John's employers, Mr and Mrs Prentiss, are also present.

Felix Blythe, who is to give his sister away, appears beside us. It is time. The organist strikes up and Rowena gives a little jump. I nod and she walks before me along the aisle and into a future of her own making. It is sure to be as colourful and exhilarating, as vivid and glorious, as an October day.

Author's Note

Most of the characters in *The Elopement* are completely fictional. In Olive's daring scheme for Pansy to work in the law, however, she introduces her to Eliza Orme, who really was the first woman to earn a law degree in England. Eliza really did write for *The Examiner* in favour of degrees for women at the University of London and four years later the university reversed its policy on this issue.

She didn't gain her final degree until 1888 (nine years before Pansy would have met her) but had been working in the profession since the early 1870s, devilling, as she explains in the story. Women were not allowed to qualify as a barrister or solicitor until 1919.

Cornelia Sorabji was another real person, and the first woman to study law at Oxford. She was also the first female graduate from Bombay University. She became the first female advocate in India but could not practise as a barrister until the law in India was changed in 1923.

I don't know if Eliza and Cornelia were really friends, as they are in my story, but they were both members of the Equity Club and Eliza was known to correspond with other female members of that club, so it's certainly possible. Both were from large, educated and well-connected families and both were

highly intelligent. I don't usually include real people in my
novels but how could I resist mentioning these two inspiring,
groundbreaking women?

Acknowledgements

The moment I'd finished writing *The Rose Garden*, I imme-diately started writing what has become *The Elopement*. The brief glimpses of we saw of Rowena in *The Rose Garden* had me convinced, like John Hobbs, that there was more to her than met the eye and she poured out of my pen (or keyboard) with unprecedented ease. She was very insistent in fact! Despite this, there were several interruptions to the process and it took a long time (by my standards) to complete the novel. My first massive thank you is to my wonderful agent Hayley Steed (and all at MMLA) for her patience and forbearance while I worked my way through a plethora of existing commitments to reach this point. She has been consistently amazing.

The aforementioned commitments have meant a long stretch of exhaustion for me and many life lessons learned! So huge thank yous to all those who supported me through it, under-standing, comforting, checking in and making me promise never to do it again. Especially abundant in this regard were Teresa Sherlock, Lucy Davies, Kathryn Davies, Marjorie Hawthorne and Patsy Rogers. Thank you – I love you all.

And Mum and Dad, of course. I remain so incredibly blessed to have parents who are so loving, kind and supportive and I am as grateful as ever.

A huge thank you to my wonderful publishers, Pan Macmillan, who have worked their publication magic once again. Thank you to my brilliant editor, Gillian Green, for her sensitive editing and fabulous concepts for presentation, and to the whole team, including Ellah Mwale, Rebecca Needes, Rosie Friis, Becky Lushey, Anna Shora, Mairead Loftus, Elena Battista and Kate Bullows. Thank you to Lorraine Green, once again, for being such a fantastic copy-editor and to Neil Lang for another stunning cover. Just. So. Beautiful!

Thanks to my gorgeous writing group in Wales: Rebecca John, Kate Glanville, Sian Collins and Betsan Bowen – our gatherings always feel like a really special thing. And also to my writer friends everywhere – you know who you are and how much I love our conversations, whether spoken or typed.

Thank you to my first readers for cheering me on from first draft stage and providing invaluable feedback: Mum, Gill Paul, Beverley Rodgers and Marjorie Hawthorne.

Thank you, Gill, for a second Hampstead plotwalk and fabulous lunch. Any excuse, right? And thank you to Peggy Vance, who I've never met but who kindly lent me *Hampstead and Highgate Through Time* by Robert Bard, which was an invaluable resource and great inspiration.

I first conceptualised the worlds of *The Rose Garden* and *The Elopement* as being centred around a fictional community, with neighbours and gossip and friends and everything that features in a real neighbourhood. I'm blessed beyond compare with my own neighbours – and thankfully they're nothing like many of the folk in *The Elopement*! Special thanks go to Peter and Kay, Mary and Mike, Tom, Darren, Daniela and Andrew, Kate and Alan, Luke and, of course, Trisha, John, Alfie and Derrick!

Thank you to Mother Earth for keeping me sane when I would otherwise not have been.

Bookshops are another invaluable refuge and I want to thank booksellers everywhere for their tireless work and enthusiasm for the stories that we all love. A special word of thanks, too, to three bookshops who always have a warm welcome for me and are wonderfully supportive: Victoria Bookshop in Haverfordwest, Cover to Cover in Mumbles and Waterstones in Swansea. I love visiting and so appreciate all you do.

And thank you as always to you, my readers, for choosing *The Elopement*. Whether you're a book-lover, reviewer, blogger or fellow author, you make all the hard work worthwhile.